The Last Kiss Goodbye

KAREN ROBARDS

The Last Kiss Goodbye

HODDER &
STOUGHTON

First published in the USA in 2013 by Ballantine Books
An imprint of The Random House Publishing Group
A division of Random House, Inc.
First published in Great Britain in 2014 by Hodder & Stoughton
An Hachette UK company

1

A CIP catalogue record for this title is available from the British Library

Hardback ISBN 978 1 444 78613 2
Trade Paperback ISBN 978 1 444 78612 5
Ebook ISBN 978 1 444 78614 9

Typeset in Plantin Light

Printed and bound by CPI Group (UK) Ltd, Croydon, CR0 4YY

Hodder & Stoughton policy is to use papers that are natural,
renewable and recyclable products and made from wood grown in
sustainable forests. The logging and manufacturing processes are
expected to conform to the environmental regulations of the
country of origin.

Hodder & Stoughton Ltd
338 Euston Road
London NW1 3BH

www.hodder.co.uk

The Last Kiss Goodbye *is dedicated to*
my wonderful editor, Linda Marrow.
It is also dedicated, as always, with love to
my three sons, Peter, Christopher, and Jack,
and to my husband, Doug.

ACKNOWLEDGMENTS

Writing is a lonely profession until it's not. That's when the fantastic team at my publishing house steps in and starts to work their magic. My thanks to Linda Marrow, Gina Centrello, Anne Speyer, Ania Markicwicz, and the entire team at Ballantine Books.

The Last Kiss Goodbye

CHAPTER ONE

The sight of the dead man stretched out on her couch stopped Dr. Charlotte Stone in her tracks.

Except for the flickering glow of the TV, the house was dark, but his big body sprawled across the pale natural linen upholstery was impossible to miss. Freezing in place just inside the threshold of her living room, Charlie fought desperately to get a grip. Lying on his back with his head resting on one of the couch's thickly padded arms, eyes closed and arms folded across his wide chest, he could almost have been asleep. But she knew better: he was beyond sleep now. The sudden tightness in her chest as she looked at him made it difficult to breathe. Her heart pounded. Her pulse raced.

She was swallowing hard, working on corralling her runaway emotions and whipping them into some kind of acceptable shape, when he opened his eyes and looked at her.

Even seen by TV light, those sky blue eyes of his were enough to make an unsuspecting woman go weak at the knees. Luckily, she had experienced their power before. Plus, she knew what he was, what he was capable of. But the sad fact was, she was a sucker for him anyway.

He smiled at her. It wasn't a particularly nice smile. Didn't matter: her stomach still fluttered.

Idiot.

"So how's that whole moving on thing working out for you, Doc?" he drawled.

The hint of acidity in Michael Garland's honey-dipped voice didn't stop the warm rush of—let's call it relief—that had started flooding her veins the second she'd laid eyes on him. She absolutely should not have been so glad to see him. In fact, she should not have been glad to see him at all. But where he and she were concerned, "should" had flown out the window a while back.

"Fine." Charlie's answer was as cool and untroubled as she *wasn't* feeling. Regaining her power of movement, she hit the wall switch that turned on the lamps on either side of the couch. Then she walked across the polished wood floor to the bleached oak coffee table, picked up the remote, and turned the TV off, ending the deafening blast of the sports channel he had been watching. Cranked to an almost painful loudness, the sound was what had brought Charlie rushing in from the porch a couple of moments before—and what had broken up the more than friendly good-night that she'd been exchanging at her front door with Tony Bartoli, the handsome FBI agent whom Garland thought she was moving on to. Garland had clearly seen her kissing Tony, and he just as clearly hadn't liked it. What his jibe meant was that he thought that she was moving on to Tony from *him*. Not that she and Garland had the kind of relationship that she could move on from, exactly, but—well, it was complicated.

The short version was, she was a psychiatrist who studied serial killers. Garland was a convicted serial killer, and, as an inmate at Wallens Ridge State Prison, where she was conducting her latest government-sponsored study, her former research subject. That association had ended with his death.

This was the part that bore repeating: Michael Garland was absolutely, positively, no-coming-back-from-it dead. As in, what she was looking at and talking to was his ghost.

See, she had the unfortunate ability to see ghosts. Oh, not all ghosts. Only the recently, violently departed, who, confused about what had happened to them, sometimes lingered for a short period on earth after their passing. Garland had been murdered eleven days before, shanked by one of his fellow inmates. Charlie had tried to save his life, to no avail. In classic no-good-deed-goes-unpunished style, his ghost had attached itself to her at the moment of his passing, to torment and harass (among other things) her until he should finally pass on to the Great Beyond.

Which, in typically irritating fashion, he was resisting.

Usually the ghosts she could see lingered for no more than a week. By that yardstick, Garland was already well past his sell-by date.

Which was one reason she had been so glad—strike that—so surprised to see him. She had last set eyes on him some four days before, when he had saved her life. Since then, she had been afraid—strike that, too—increasingly convinced that she would never see him again.

Much as she hated to admit it even to herself, the thought had made her heart bleed.

But here he was, all six-foot-three hunky inches of him. Thirty-six years old at the time of his death. Chippendales-worthy body in a snug white T-shirt and faded jeans. A thick mane of tawny hair that didn't quite reach his wide shoulders. Square jaw, broad cheekbones and forehead, straight nose and well-cut mouth. Absurdly tan and healthy-looking for a ghost—or a man who had spent the last four years of his life in federal prison, which he had done. Outrageously handsome. Certifiably dangerous. The proverbial bad penny.

Who could make her heart pound and her blood heat and her good sense fly out the window. He was the very last thing she needed—or wanted—in her life.

Dead or alive.

Not that she had any choice in the matter.

She could no more control his presence in her life than she could control the sun, the moon, and the stars. He had just shown up, and one day—probably sooner rather than later—he would disappear. The universe was in charge here, not her.

The thought steadied her.

"Where have you been?" If there was a snap in her tone, he had earned it, simply because he had somehow managed to make her care about the answer. Still, afraid her question might reveal how stupidly involved with him she had become, she would have taken it back if she could have.

"Missed me bad, hmm?" Garland swung his long legs off the couch and sat up. Under other circumstances, Charlie would have given a dirty look to the scuffed cowboy boots that he hadn't seemed to have any qualms about planting on her pristine couch. But ghost boots—she was pretty sure that they didn't leave marks.

Anyway, the smirk in the grin he directed at her was way more annoying than the boots on the linen, so she directed her dirty look right into his twinkling baby blues before turning on her heel and walking away.

"Nope." She hadn't missed him one bit, she told herself. She threw the reply over her shoulder as she reached the hall and headed toward the kitchen, past the old-fashioned staircase that led to the second floor. Standing up, he followed her. She was wearing nothing more exciting than a silky white sleeveless blouse and a pair of well-tailored black slacks with heels, a little dressier than her usual attire because Tony had been taking her out to dinner but nothing special. Still, she could feel Garland's eyes on her, and strongly suspected that he was watching her trim backside with appreciation as she walked. Casting a quick, suspicious glance over her shoulder, she tried to catch him at it, but he was (a) too quick, (b) too wily, or (c) just too damned lucky to get caught. As their eyes met, he grinned at her.

"Liar," he said.

She snorted, shaking her head in firm denial. Terrifying to think that having a ghost following her made her feel more fully alive than she had in days. Even more terrifying to realize that what she really wanted to do was turn around and walk right into his arms.

Which she couldn't do, because he had no more substance than air. And which she wouldn't do even if she could.

Because she truly wasn't that self-destructive. She didn't think.

Moonlight pouring through the kitchen windows—a tall, wide one that took up almost all the back wall behind the eating area, and a smaller one set into the top of the kitchen door—illuminated the white cabinets and stainless steel appliances and hardwood floor. She'd left the curtains in the front of the house closed, so no one could see in from the street. The kitchen blinds were raised all the way to the top of the windows, because there was no one living behind her to see in, and because she liked the view. As she stepped from the hall's gloom into the silvery light, Charlie saw her reflection in the big window's dark glass. Her chestnut brown hair hung in loose waves around her shoulders. Her fair skin was, as usual, pale, but her denim blue eyes looked kind of sultry because she had deliberately played them up with liner and shadow, which she almost never wore, and an extra coat or two of mascara. Her wide mouth looked full and soft, but more vulnerable than it should have, given that right after dinner she had freshly applied deep red (vampy) lipstick. That softly smudged look would be because, she realized belatedly, Tony had subsequently kissed all her lipstick off, so her lips were now both slightly swollen and bare. She was five-six, slender and fit at age thirty-two, and over the years a lot of guys had told her that she was beautiful. If she remained skeptical, it was because most of the time those same guys had been trying to talk her into the sack. Tonight, the makeup plus the three-inch heels made her look, um, sexier. Ordinarily she wore low-heeled, sensible shoes because the last thing she wanted to do was give off any kind of look-at-me-I'm-hot vibe. This almost daily exercise in discretion owed a lot to the fact that her usual work was carried out in a prison full of incarcerated men. Which was also why she customarily wore her hair up and minimal makeup. But tonight, for Tony, she'd made an effort. With, yes, the thought that she might allow their relationship to progress to the next level, as in, sleep with him. Because Tony was way handsome and because she really liked him and because she badly needed a normal, uncomplicated man-woman relationship in her life.

And because she'd feared—thought—that Garland was gone for good and she was determined to eradicate any lingering memories of him. Of *them*.

In the end, she hadn't been able to bring herself to invite Tony in.

She'd already been sending him on his way when the blasting of her should-have-been-silent TV had reached her ears and caused her heart to swell with hope and hurried things along. Sex with Tony, she had decided somewhere between dinner and her front door, was something that just wasn't going to happen. At least, not yet.

But Garland didn't have to know that.

In fact, she wasn't about to let Garland know that.

He was way too full of himself already.

Charlie suddenly realized that hers was the only reflection that she saw in the window, although Garland was right behind her. A lightning glance over her shoulder confirmed it: he was still there.

But to judge by what she could see in the window, she was alone. His reflection didn't show up. And that would be because, in the physical world in which she and every other living creature existed, he did not.

Only she could see him.

"Admit it, Doc: you were worried about me."

Charlie closed her eyes.

Worried about him. That vastly understated the case. Truth was, when he had not shown back up after materializing for just long enough to take the killing blow meant for her, she had been sick with fear over him. Afraid that he had been sucked up into Eternity, and that she would never see him again.

The pain that had accompanied that fear had shown her how very vulnerable she had become where he was concerned. Now that he was back, she was determined to better guard her clearly way-too-susceptible heart.

Falling in love with him was not an option. In life he'd been the baddest of bad men, the convicted murderer of seven women, sentenced to death for horrible, brutal crimes.

And as sexy and charming as he might be, he was the exact same person in death.

That's what she had to keep reminding herself of, even if some too-stupid-to-live part of her refused to accept it.

He claimed he was innocent. All the evidence said otherwise.

Even if, for the sake of argument, she allowed herself to believe in his innocence, believe that the exhaustive police investigation and all the evidence and the courts and the entire criminal justice system were plain wrong in his case, she still wasn't about to let herself go where she feared their association was headed.

She wasn't about to commit the ultimate folly of letting herself fall in love with him. No way, no how.

Bottom line was, he was dead, she was alive.

Whatever their relationship was or wasn't, the hard truth was, there was absolutely no future in it.

If she let herself forget that, she deserved every bit of heartbreak that would be hurtling her way.

So get over being so ridiculously glad to see him already.

Charlie opened her eyes. There she still was, looking at her own reflection in the kitchen window, with not so much as a glimmer to indicate that a gorgeous (dead) guy was standing right behind her.

"I was actually very comfortable with the idea that nature had finally taken its course with you." She spoke over her shoulder, admirably cool, as she crossed to the light switch beside the back door and flipped on the kitchen light. A round oak table with four slat-back chairs stood in the eating area in front of the window. Because she had been away, the table was piled high with mail. Beyond it, out the window, she could see the tall, nodding shadows of the sunflowers that grew in a patch along her back fence. Backlit by moonlight, they were striping the grass with shifting lines of black. Beyond that, a thickly wooded mountainside formed an impenetrable wall of darkness as it rose to meet the night sky.

This old-fashioned, two-story white clapboard farmhouse with its gingerbread trim and wide front porch was the first real home she had ever had, and she loved it. Located on a quiet street at the edge of Big Stone Gap, Virginia, a coal mining town deep in the heart of Appalachia that was still reeling from the recession, it provided her with a much-needed respite from the daily grimness of her work at the prison, which perched like a vulture at the top of the mountain, overlooking the town. Decorating and furnishing the house had been a project that she had enjoyed.

Until right this minute, when Garland's presence suddenly seemed to fill it to bursting, she had never recognized that with only her in it, the house had sometimes felt empty. No, strike that: lonely.

"Bullshit," he said without heat, and the inescapable fact that he'd hit the nail on the head there made her lips tighten. Ignoring him, she crossed to the table with the intention of checking out her mail. He stopped in the kitchen doorway and, folding his arms over his chest, propped a broad shoulder against the jamb. *"Thank you for saving my life, Michael."*

His mocking falsetto earned him a narrow-eyed glance. But truth was, he *had* saved her life, and she was grateful.

"Thank you." She turned her attention to the mail. Nothing like a fat stack of bills to provide a distraction.

"Michael," he prompted. She could feel his eyes on her.

Ostensibly busy flipping through the pile of envelopes, she said nothing. The last time she had called him Michael—well, she wasn't going there. She was going to forget that whole mind-blowingly sexy episode.

Yeah, right. Never gonna happen as long as you live.

Well, she was going to try.

"So, you shack up with FBI guy while I was gone?"

The question annoyed her. Actually, he annoyed her. Greatly.

In the process of tearing open an envelope, she flicked him a look. And lied. "Yes."

"Your nose just grew, Pinocchio."

"If you're not going to believe me, why ask?"

"Good question." He shrugged. "So why *aren't* you shacking up with FBI guy?"

"Because, believe it or not, I don't sleep with everything in pants," she snapped before she thought. As a slow smile spread across his face, she felt like biting her tongue. Because, of course, she had slept with Garland. Sort of. As in, ghost sex. Again, it was complicated.

But whether or not it had been, in the strictest sense, real or not, it had definitely been the hottest sex of her life.

And she was not going there. Not again. Not even in her thoughts.

"I do believe it." He crossed the kitchen to stand across the table from her. His big hands curled around a chair back. His steady gaze made her uncomfortable. She concentrated on the mail. "Thing is, I think I'm starting to know you pretty well. I think you're a one-man woman, Doc."

Her eyes snapped up to meet his. At what she saw for her there, she felt a wave of heat.

God, don't let it show.

"You might be right," she said with a false cordiality of which she was justifiably proud. "And if ever I find that man, I'll be sure to let you know."

His answering look made her foolish, reckless heart pick up its pace. Afraid of what he might read in her eyes, she let them drop to the square brown packing box that had been the next item of mail to come within reach of her hands. Damned tape—the box was swaddled in it. Clear and shiny, it was stubbornly resistant to all her attempts to breach it. Reaching for the small pair of scissors she kept along with items like pushpins and paper clips in a basket on the sideboard behind her, she cast another glance at him. She was just in time to watch him fade into translucence. Eyes widening, hand tightening convulsively around the scissors, she registered with a tingle of shock that she could absolutely see the rest of the kitchen through him. Even as she stared, he wavered, then started to solidify once more.

She was still struggling to wrap her mind around what she was seeing when he did it again.

"Might want to close your mouth, Doc. Damned if you don't look like you've seen a ghost."

That at least had the virtue of snapping her out of total immobility. Her lips met and firmed. Her eyes collided with his. "Funny."

He seemed to look at her more closely. Of course, it was hard to tell when he was once again as diaphanous as smoke. "So what's up?"

"You—you're flickering." Her mouth had gone dry. Wetting her lips, she tried to swallow.

He was returning to being almost—*almost*—solid-looking. *Oh, God.*

"Flickering?" He glanced down at himself. Seeming to notice nothing amiss—okay, he looked solid again, so why would he?—he lifted his eyebrows at her.

"Fading in and out. Like—like Tinker Bell at the end of *Peter Pan.* You know, the Disney movie. When Tink was dying, and the children had to clap to bring her back." The comparison made Charlie feel cold all over. She was so rattled that she was hardly making sense, she knew. Her eyes stayed glued to him: he'd started fading again as she spoke, and was now as insubstantial as a layer of chiffon, and rippling like one, too, if said chiffon had been caught in a breeze. It wasn't the first time she'd seen an apparition flicker, but it was definitely the first time that the sight had made her heart lurch and her blood drain toward her toes.

The other times—she'd been relieved. And she'd been relieved because the flickering was a sign that the ghost she was looking at would soon cease to be a problem to the living. And that would be because that flicker meant the apparition was minutes away from fading into nothingness, and she was comfortable in the knowledge that it was leaving this earthly plane and never coming back.

But now, with him, she felt her composure shattering into a million lacerating shards as she faced what that flickering probably meant: either he was getting to the stage where she wasn't going to be able to see him anymore, or he was being drawn permanently into the Hereafter. One way or the other, it didn't matter. If what she'd seen happen in the past was a prologue to the present, he was going.

It wouldn't be long before she was free of him. For good.

Which she had known all along was going to happen.

He was a ghost, and ghosts couldn't stay.

So why did that make her feel so utterly devastated?

"Must've missed that one," he replied drily.

Her eyes stayed fixed on him with a kind of horrified desperation. The glowing green numbers of the digital clock over the microwave were perfectly visible through his wide and muscular chest. She could read the time: 11:22.

"How—how do you feel?"

"To tell the truth, like I died about a week back."

"Would you stop joking?" Her tone was fierce. "I'm serious."

He shrugged. "Thing is, I had a hell of a fight getting back here this time. Way harder than I've ever had before. Them Spookville walls—they didn't want to let me out. If I hadn't been so worried about you, I don't think I could have made it through. Ever since I did, I've been feeling the damned place pulling at me, like it's doing its best to reel me back in. Right now, it's pulling pretty strong." His eyes narrowed at her. "You got a particular reason for asking?"

"Oh, God." Her chest felt tight. Drawing a breath required real work. "I think—it might be time. I think—you might be getting ready to leave."

His brows snapped together. "What? Hell, no. I'm not going any-where."

"I don't think you have a choice."

"So do something. Ju-ju me." His relatively unalarmed tone told her that he did not perceive the immediacy of the danger.

Charlie shook her head, speechless because he was now pulsing like a lightbulb getting ready to burn out and was clearly unaware of it. Something that felt like a giant fist closed around her heart. She gripped the scissors so hard the metal hurt her fingers.

She already knew how this story had to end. But she wasn't ready. There was so much still unresolved between them, so much to say . . .

"Please don't take him yet." The words were scarcely louder than a breath. Emerging of their own volition, they weren't addressed to him: she was speaking to the universe, to the vast, unknowable forces of Eternity, to God himself. Then, realizing what she had said—and what it revealed—she shifted her grip on the scissors and looked down and started cutting through the tape on the box. Savagely.

Anything to keep from watching him disappear.

Because there was nothing she could do to stop it. Because this was the way it had to be.

"Whoa, hold on there. What was that?" Even in this moment of what felt to Charlie like extremis, there was humor in his voice. "Sounded to me like that was you admitting you're not ready to see the last of me."

"Oh, go—soak your head." Her fingers stilled as she looked back at him. She'd been about to tell him to go to hell, before it had hit her like a baseball bat between the eyes that that was in all likelihood exactly where he was going.

"Quit fighting it." He was all but transparent now, as see-through as delicately colored cellophane, coming in and out of focus faster than she could blink. Grief and dread combined to turn her blood to ice. "Would it kill you to give up and admit that you're crazy about me?"

His eyes teased her. Her heart felt as if it would crack in half.

Okay, so she'd known this moment was coming. Known it from the beginning, from her first horrified realization that this scariest of ghosts had attached himself to her: the affliction was temporary.

At first, she'd reminded herself of that as a source of comfort.

Then she had simply tried not to think about it.

But now, she discovered, she couldn't bear the knowledge that he was actually about to be gone from her world.

That she would never see him again.

That he would be caught up in the horrible purple fog of the place he called Spookville, forever.

Or at least until he was dragged off to someplace even worse.

Abandoning the box, she put the scissors down on the table. Her movements were careful. Precise. Otherwise, she feared her hands would shake. Then, because her eyes were glued to him, she accidentally knocked the box over. All kinds of white packing peanuts came tumbling out, spilling across the table, onto the floor, everywhere.

She scarcely noticed. She didn't care.

He was barely there at all now, with no more substance than a heat shimmer. Her fists clenched so hard that her nails dug into her palms. It was all she could do to breathe. Her heart wept.

In consequence, her tone was angry. "You think this is a joke? Look at yourself *now*."

He looked down at himself. It was instantly plain that he saw what was happening. Charlie could feel the sudden tension emanating from him, a new and electric sense of urgency in the air.

His jaw was tight as he looked back at her. "You might want to get cracking with that ju-ju, Doc."

"There's nothing I can do." At his behest and against her better judgment, she'd already used every scrap of spirit lore she'd ever learned that might keep him grounded to earth. There wasn't anything left, or at least nothing that she knew. If running to him and throwing her arms around him would have done any good, she would have been racing around the table to his side, but she already knew it would be easier to try to hold on to mist. *This is how it has to be.* She knew that, accepted it. And still her next words were nothing she had ever imagined she would say to him: "Concentrate. Try to hang on."

"Ain't working." He was fading so fast now, she was afraid he'd be gone in the next instant. "Better start clapping, Doc."

She sucked in air. "Garland—"

He was gone. Just like that. Her stomach dropped to her toes. Her knees went weak.

"Shit." She could still hear him. "I don't make it back, don't worry about me. Charlie . . ."

The rest of what he said was indistinct.

"Michael!" Forget keeping her distance, keeping her cool. Despite what she knew was the absolute futility of it, she rushed around the table to where he had been standing anyway, reaching for him, plowing her hands through the now-empty air. Nothing. Not even the slightest hint of an electric tingle—the telltale sign of contact with an invisible spirit—to mark where he had been. Defeated, she gripped a chair back hard. God, what had she expected? The universe always reclaimed its own. She knew that, knew it had to happen, knew this was no more than the natural order of things, but still she felt as if her heart was being ripped out of her chest. She wanted to cry. She wanted to scream.

"There has to be a white light," she called urgently through the pain, because helping him navigate Eternity was the only thing she could do for him now. "Michael, do you hear? You have to look for the light."

She thought he said something typical like, "Fuck that," and then, "Charlie," with something else after, but she couldn't be sure: his voice was too faint.

"Michael!"

This time there was nothing. No response. No voice. No sign of him. She took a deep, shuddering breath. Her throat closed up. The pain she was experiencing was acute. *This is what grief feels like.* Then she realized, *No, this is what* heartbreak *feels like.*

Her eyes stung: it was from welling tears. Second time in the last eleven days that she, who never cried, had found herself doing just that. Both times had been over him.

Cursing herself for her idiocy, she dashed her knuckles across her eyes.

Bam! Bam! Bam!

A frantic pounding on the kitchen door tore Charlie's eyes away from the spot where he had last been, made her jump and gasp and shoot a startled glance toward the sound.

Pale and big-eyed and terrified-looking in the darkness, a woman's face peered in at her through the diamond-paned window in the top of the door.

"Help me," the woman screamed, pounding the door again. *"Please, you have to let me in!"*

CHAPTER TWO

In an instant Charlie saw that the woman was young, with long, dark hair, pale skin—and a scarlet river of blood running down the side of her face.

"Hurry!" the stranger cried, rattling the doorknob now even as she continued to pound on the door. "Please let me in! Please!"

Her eyes locked with Charlie's. They begged. Charlie knew that look—it was mortal fear. She recognized it instantly because she had experienced it more than once herself. She knew what it felt like, processed it viscerally, and her pulse leaped and her gut clenched in response. Thrusting her own pain aside, reacting automatically to this new emergency, to this fellow creature in such obvious distress, she dashed her knuckles across her burning eyes one more time and flew to open the door.

"Goddamn it, Charlie, no!" It wasn't a roar, although she could tell that was what it was meant to be. It had more the quality of an echo, faint in volume but furious in tone: Michael. Glancing frantically around for him at the same time as she yanked the door wide, she saw nothing of him.

"Michael?" His name was wrenched from her. A warm wind, thick with humidity, ruffled her hair. The scent of the mountain in late August—mossy and damp, laced with honeysuckle—filled her nostrils.

There was no answer from him. No sign.

The woman spilled headlong through the door—*"Thank you, oh, thank you!"*—instantly reclaiming Charlie's attention. Bursting past her into the house, moving so fast that her wet, muddy shoes slipped and skidded on the hardwood, she was breathing in great, gasping sobs. Outside, fat drops of rain were just starting to fall. The steady plop as they splattered on the stoop and the concrete pavers leading up to it made Charlie think of fast-approaching footsteps, and the tiny hairs on the back of her neck stood on end.

"He's got a gun! He's coming! He's going to kill me!" Choking out the warning over her shoulder, the woman stopped and bent double, then dropped to a crouch as if her knees had suddenly given out. Coughing and gagging, she huddled near the table while Charlie stood stupidly gaping at her while even more stupidly holding the door wide.

"Who?" Hand tightening convulsively on the doorknob, Charlie cast a frightened look outside, searching the darkness for a sign of anyone who might be giving chase. Although she could see nothing out of place, the soft summer's night with its starry sky had changed dramatically in the brief time since she had stood outside on her front porch saying good-night to Tony. A gathering storm had blown in, transforming the sky into something dark and menacing. The light from the kitchen spilled over the small back stoop, turning the quickening raindrops to a mercurial silver, but beyond that Charlie could see nothing.

"Shut the door! Lock it! Oh, my God, he's right behind me!"

Charlie's heart jumped. Her pulse leaped into overdrive. Already slamming the door as the girl's nerve-jangling screech reached its apex, Charlie shot a jittery glance at the shivering figure crouched on her floor.

The woman—a girl, really, no more than twenty, was Charlie's guess—was soaking wet, far wetter than the newly falling rain would account for. She was also muddy, with a swampy scent that spoke of stagnant rather than fresh water. Slender and pretty, she wore shorts that had once been white, a red T-shirt with some kind of logo on it, and sandals. Visibly shaking, breathing like she had run for miles, she streamed water and blood. Charlie registered all that in the blink of an eye. Then, with a last apprehensive glance out the window into the night—she saw nothing that shouldn't have been there, but the sense that someone *was* there was strong—she shot the deadbolt closed.

"*Who's* right behind you?" Skin crawling as the probable inadequacy of the door as a source of protection from a determined intruder occurred to her, Charlie rushed forward to crouch down herself and wrap a steadying arm around the girl's heaving back. The slender body felt wet, cold, frail. A puddle of muddy water swirled with blood was forming around her feet. At Charlie's touch, the girl threw up her head and looked at her. Cold drops of water flung from the long strands of her hair spattered Charlie's cheek. Even as she automatically swiped the droplets away, Charlie registered that the blood came from an ugly, inch-long gash in the girl's forehead. "You're hurt."

"It doesn't matter. Don't you understand? *He's going to kill me.*" The shrill, unsteady cry sent a cold chill running down Charlie's spine. Every nerve ending she possessed quivered in sympathetic reaction to the sheer terror that was impossible to mistake. Fear was suddenly as tangible in the air as the smell of swampy water. Beneath her sheltering arm, Charlie could feel the girl's tremors. Her eyes—they were golden brown—were huge and dark with fright. "He was—I can't believe I got away! He made us—he made me—" Her hysterical voice deteriorated into a series of shuddering gasps. Wild-eyed, she looked around the kitchen. "We've got to call the police. Quick, quick, quick! Before he gets here! He'll kill me! He's got a *gun*!"

"Damn it to hell, woman, do you have a fucking death wish? You think whoever's after her won't kill you, too?" That was Michael again, closer, louder, still sounding as if his voice should have been a furious roar although it wasn't: it had a muffled sound as though it was reaching her through some sort of interference. Charlie's heart lurched. Then she could see him: a shimmer a few feet away.

She tensed, instantly riveted on that shimmer. *Michael*—even though every cell in her body yearned toward him, she retained just enough presence of mind not to call out to him aloud.

"Where's your phone?" the girl cried.

"On the wall." Charlie gestured toward it as Michael started to solidify, and then for a second there she forgot about everything but him. About the girl, and any possible looming threat, and her own burgeoning sense of danger.

"In the kitchen?" The girl followed Charlie's gesture with her eyes, then pulled away from her, scrambling forward, pitching upright, wet shoes noisily slapping the floor as she stumbled past the foggy shape that was Michael toward the far end of the kitchen, where the slim, beige landline phone hung near the microwave. Charlie registered her progress distractedly. She couldn't help it: in that heartbeat of time, her focus was almost exclusively on Michael.

She could see his face. His features. His eyes.

He was scowling at her.

"Jesus Christ, what part of 'man with a gun' did you miss? Run! Get the hell out of here! Get away from her!"

Relief at his reappearance was tempered by a stabbing fear that it might be very brief. In all likelihood, this was just another flicker.

Her throat tightened. Her eyes locked with his.

"I can see you. Can you hold on?" Her voice was low and hoarse, the words meant only for him.

"Who the hell knows?" He was almost completely solid now. Striding toward her, he made an urgent gesture toward the hall. "Go! That way! Run! If she's got some guy after her trying to kill her, the last thing you want to do is get caught up in the middle of it."

"I can't." The urgency of the present reasserted itself like a thunderclap. Even for her own safety, she knew that abandoning her traumatized and endangered guest was beyond her, and knew, too, that the hard truth was that agonizing over him—over something she couldn't control—was useless. Even as her heart was being put through what felt like a meat grinder, she had to leave him to the mercy (or not) of the universe and deal with the reality of the emergency in her kitchen.

"What do you mean you"—this time his response actually started as a roar, only to fade as he grew fainter again—"can't?"

A knot formed in her chest. He was once again barely there.

"Michael. If you get sucked back in, you need to ask for forgiveness. You need to pray." The words were wrenched out of her even as she tore her eyes away from him, got a grip, and launched herself after the girl. She might not be able to stop what was happening to him, but maybe she could make a difference here, tonight, this minute, in the real world, for this endangered girl. And maybe, if he followed her advice, she could help him avoid the ultimate horror, after all. It might be the only thing she was able to do for him. Because the sad truth was, even if he did deserve eternal damnation, she couldn't bear to think of him suffering it.

Fool.

He snorted. "Kinda late for that. Damn it, what the hell are you *doing*?"

As she raced past him she saw that he was little more than a shimmer again now, and her heart sank.

"What I can." Instead of running into the hall as he'd clearly expected, she darted around the breakfast bar into the food preparation area, which was basically a narrow galley kitchen that looked across the open counter of the breakfast bar at the table and the back door beyond. The girl was there, in the process of snatching the phone from the kitchen wall. She threw a wide-eyed look over her shoulder at Charlie.

"Who are you *talking* to? Oh, no, are you *nuts*?" The girl squeezed closer to the wall as though to put as much distance between them as possible. Of course, the girl could neither see nor hear Michael. Looking at things from her point of view, having the person she was counting on for help conduct a frantic, one-sided conversation with an unseen entity must be unnerving. Charlie sympathized, but there were more urgent matters to deal with. Like where the girl's attacker was now.

"How close behind you is he?" Casting another lightning glance out the windows—nothing to see but a whole lot of dark, plus silvery streaks as rain ran down the glass—Charlie felt her stomach cramp.

"Close. I don't know. It was dark." As she gasped out the words, the girl looked at Charlie as if she was afraid of her now, too.

"I'm a doctor, okay? You can trust me." Usually, when she was where anyone could overhear, Charlie was way careful not to talk back to the spirits who afflicted her, but this moment—Michael—was the stress-induced exception. God, he was gone again! Looking desperately around, she wanted to scream his name but did not. Not only to keep from freaking the girl out, or to save herself from looking, um, nuts, but also because she knew that it would do absolutely no good. Taking a deep breath, she did her best to focus on the girl. "Who's chasing you? Is it your boyfriend, or—"

"*No.* You don't get it, do you? He's a *killer.*" The girl kept throwing quick, terrified glances at the door. "Oh, my God, is it 911 here?" Shaking visibly, breathing as if she might hyperventilate at any second, she was already frantically stabbing an unsteady finger at the number pad. With her inky black hair streaming water and blood pouring down the right quarter of her face, she looked like something out of a nightmare—or a horror movie. The mere sight of her was enough to send goose bumps racing over Charlie's skin—and convince her that whatever the details might prove to be, the girl definitely had been the victim of something horrific.

"Yes." Shooting more increasingly spooked glances out first the window in the door and then the big window behind the table—as dark as it was outside, with the light on in the kitchen anyone out there could see everything that was going on inside, she realized with a stab of dread. Then Charlie had an epiphany: there was a better way to get help fast. But first things first. Working hard to maintain the outward appearance of calm, she grabbed a handful of paper towels from the dispenser and thrust them at the girl.

"Press that against the cut on your forehead," she ordered. "Hold it firmly. *Do it.*"

That last was in response to the girl's hesitation, which manifested itself in a suspicious look from the paper towels to Charlie. As the girl did as she was told, Charlie left her to run for the cell phone in her purse, which she had dropped on the console table in the front hall when she'd rushed inside earlier. She knew from experience that here the response to 911 could sometimes be slow, and every instinct she possessed screamed at her that they needed help *now.*

"This chick ain't your problem," Michael growled from behind her.

Looking around, Charlie saw the shimmer that was him at the top of the hallway, and drew a ragged breath.

"Did you do it? Did you pray?" she demanded fiercely.

"Hell, no."

THE LAST KISS GOODBYE

"Where are you going? Don't leave me!" the girl shrieked after her. The echoing shrillness of it practically curled Charlie's hair.

"I'm not leaving you." Charlie snatched up her purse. "I'm coming right back." Then, at Michael, she snapped, "Pray, damn it," and bolted past him.

"Leave her," Michael said furiously. "Run the fuck upstairs and lock yourself in your bedroom. You hear me? This whole savior complex you got going on is gonna get you killed."

"Savior complex?" Charlie was outraged.

"Oh, yeah." The shimmer appeared in front of her, blocking her path.

"Go *away*," Charlie snapped before she thought. Fumbling around in her purse in an effort to find her phone, a process that was slightly hampered by the fact that she was running and glaring at him at the same time, she dodged around him because that seemed more appropriate than running right through him, which she easily could have done, and immediately took it back. "I mean, *stay*. Only out of the way."

"Damn it, Charlie—"

"Who are you *talking* to?" Sounding terrified, the girl hugged the phone to her ear. Holding the clump of rapidly reddening paper towels clamped to her forehead, she jiggled from foot to foot in nervous agitation as she watched Charlie dart toward her while conducting a running argument with something she couldn't see.

"Don't worry about it," Charlie snapped, her façade of composure on the verge of coming dangerously unglued. Sliding to a halt feet from the girl, Charlie found her phone at last and snatched it out of her purse.

"A cell phone? Hell, I thought you were rooting around in there for a gun." Michael was right behind her. "You do have a gun around here somewhere, right? Now would be the time to grab it."

Unable to reply, both because she didn't want to be caught supposedly talking to herself again and because, in actual fact, she didn't possess a gun at all and didn't want to listen to him bitch about it, Charlie ignored that. Instead she fumbled to call up her contact list and listened as the girl gasped into the landline, "I need the police! Now! A man's chasing me! He has a gun and he wants to kill me!"

Then, to Charlie, who had just hit the button to call her across-the-street neighbor Ken Ewell, the (armed) sheriff's deputy, she cried, "They need the address! What's the address?"

"A death wish *and* a savior complex." Despite the savagery of his tone, Michael's voice in her ear would have been welcome if what he was saying hadn't been so maddening. "Looks like the real question is, how many ways can you come up with to get yourself killed before somebody actually wins the prize?"

Shut up, Charlie almost snarled, but managed to swallow the words in time so that the girl wouldn't go totally ape. Heart racing, working hard to focus on the here and now and at the same time disregard the furious vibrations Michael was sending her way, she listened to the Ewells' phone beginning to ring in her ear as she answered the girl in a carefully controlled voice, "23 Laurel Way."

"Take it from me, babe, being dead ain't that fun."

A quick glare over her shoulder in the direction of that velvety drawl found Michael in heat vapor mode right behind her.

Her gut twisted as she realized one more time how tenuous his hold on this world was.

The girl repeated the address into the phone then moaned to the dispatcher, "Hurry! Oh, please, please, hurry!" while giving Charlie another mistrustful look. Taking a shuddering breath, she added to the dispatcher in a wobbly, barely there voice, "There are two other girls—they're up there—they're dead!"

"*What?*" Charlie and Michael exclaimed in suddenly riveted unison.

Instinctively shooting Michael a did-you-hear-that-too look, Charlie encountered nothing but barely there shimmer. Was he fainter than before? Oh, God, he definitely was. Panic made her feel cold all over. Remembering something he'd once said to her—about running water drawing him back from wherever he had been at that time—she hastily leaned over the sink and turned the faucet on full blast. Cold water gushed out, splashing into the sink, the *whoosh* of it adding just one more jarring note to the discordant background symphony of drumming rain and shuffling feet and gasping breaths, plus the rhythmic drone of a distant telephone ringing away in her ear.

"Good thinking," said Michael, and Charlie felt a rush of relief as the shimmer seemed to grow brighter and denser.

"There were three of us." The girl's eyes were wide and haunted. She was talking into the phone but looking at Charlie, and besides the rampant wariness that Charlie knew was absolutely aimed at her, there was such fear in the girl's expression that Charlie felt sweat start to dampen her palms. In response to something the dispatcher must have asked, the girl repeated her words, then added unsteadily, "I'm the only one left. He made me—he made us—"

Tears filled her eyes, and she broke off with a shaky indrawn breath that turned into a sob. She trembled so violently that Charlie could hear her teeth chattering. Beneath the streaks of blood, her skin had gone beyond paper white to almost gray. If the girl hadn't been wedged in the corner formed by the wall and the counter, Charlie thought that there was a good chance she would have collapsed.

"You're safe now." Charlie felt a fresh well of fellow feeling: this kind of terror she knew. *Safe* might not be exactly accurate, but it was close enough: as long as there was breath in Charlie's body, nobody was getting to that girl again. She would have put a comforting arm around her guest, but the girl shrank away from her—clearly, doctor or not, she wasn't coming across as all that reassuring, for which she knew she had Michael to thank—and with some chagrin Charlie let her arm drop. She was doing her best to project steady strength, to ignore the rushing adrenaline that caused her nerves to jump and her heart to jackhammer. But the situation—Michael, the girl, the possibility that some kind of murderous lunatic was right outside—was making it difficult. Way difficult. As she processed the possibility that whoever was out there had killed two other girls, she felt a wave of fear threaten. What she had first thought was likely a case of domestic violence was starting to sound like something even worse.

Something horrifyingly familiar.

"At least get the hell away from the windows." Michael's voice held a note of barely controlled ferocity that made her breath catch. He, too, was clearly afraid—for her. "Unless you like the idea of giving some loony tune the chance to put a bullet in your brain, that is."

Oh, God, he had a point. Darting another fearful look at the black blankness of the windows, Charlie touched the girl's arm, say-ing, "Probably we should try to get below the counter."

The girl jerked her arm away, and moved as far from Charlie as she could get, which wasn't very far.

"I don't know," she sobbed into the phone while fixing wary, tear-filled eyes on Charlie. "He was chasing me. Oh, I need them to *hurry.*"

"See, that's normal survival instinct. Teen-queen there spots trou-ble, at least she has the sense to try to get away from it," Michael said. Charlie's response was an aggravated thinning of her lips and a quick glare thrown his way. That's when Charlie realized that she could see him again. Although he was still a little foggy around the edges, she was getting enough detail to know that he was looking at the girl like she guessed he might have looked at a live bomb.

"We need to get down." As Charlie gestured at the windows then dropped into a crouch, the girl's eyes went even bigger than before. "He could shoot through the glass."

With one more terrified glance at the windows, the girl followed suit, letting her back slide down the wall, sinking down until she was folded in a soggy huddle with her chin almost touching her knees. A puddle was already forming around her as her eyes locked with Char-lie's. They were glassy with fright.

"I don't *know,*" she answered the operator. "They just need to get here. *Please.*"

"Look, I . . ." Charlie began, meaning to conclude with, *I'm on your side,* only to be interrupted by the sound of the Ewells' phone being picked up at last.

"Hello," Ken's wife, Debbie, said in her ear.

"It's Charlie Stone across the street." In the spirit of not wanting to further spook the girl, Charlie tried hard not to sound as panicky as she was starting to feel. "I need Ken over here right away. There's a girl in my kitchen, and she says"—explaining the whole thing was going to be too complicated and time-consuming, and anyway Char-lie still had no idea precisely what the whole thing was, so she cut to the chase—"there's a man with a gun after her. We need Ken *now.*"

"Cops going to get here any faster 'cause you're hanging out with The Black Dahlia here in the kitchen trying to get yourself killed? Run upstairs and lock yourself in your bedroom and stay put until the po-po show up." A solid-looking presence now, Michael planted himself between her and the girl. That was deliberate, Charlie knew, as was his aggressive stance. Whatever he was or wasn't, where she at least was concerned he seemed to have a marked protective streak. Of course, since she was all that was anchoring him to the world of the living that shouldn't come as a big surprise. "Damn it, Charlie, you're not doing her one bit of good by sitting here looking into her eyes. You've done your Mother Teresa thing: you let her in. Cops are com-ing. So leave her to it and *go*."

Shooting him a shut-up-or-die look, Charlie gave a quick, nega-tive shake of her head.

"How far away are they?" the girl moaned to the dispatcher.

"He's in bed asleep," Debbie objected. Of course, it was nearing midnight. In Big Stone Gap, that was late for decent folks.

"Can you *wake him up*?" Charlie did her best not to yell on that last part, with indifferent success. At the same time she watched Mi-chael disgustedly mime a gunshot to his own head with a thumb and forefinger. Charlie frowned. The frown was directed at Michael, of course, but the girl, whose eyes she had been holding until she had flicked that sharp *stop it* look up at Michael, shrank away. "I really, really need him. Like I said, there's a girl in my kitchen being chased by a *man with a gun*."

"Well, I guess." There was a sound that Charlie interpreted as Debbie laying the receiver down. Over the still-open line, she listened to her neighbor calling to her husband. Who as far as she could tell wasn't answering.

Damn it.

"I'm Jenna McDaniels," the girl said into the phone on a shud-dering intake of breath, in obvious answer to a question posed by the dispatcher. "I was kidnapped three days ago. The other girls are—uh, w-were—Laura Peters and Raylene Witt. There has to be somebody looking for us. Are the police even *close*?"

Jenna McDaniels? Even caught up in the aftermath of a night-mare as she had been, Charlie had heard of the University of Rich-mond sorority girl who had vanished from a college-sponsored event just as preparations for the fall rush were getting under way: reports of the disappearance had been all over TV. But Charlie didn't have the chance to do more than look at her with widening eyes, because a sound—a faint rattle from the direction of the back door—froze both her and Jenna in place. Suddenly as still as rabbits with a dog nearby, united by fear, they shot simultaneous panicky looks in the direction of the sound, to no avail: the solid base of the breakfast bar was in the way, preventing them from seeing anything beyond it. But for Charlie at least, there was no doubting what they had heard: the doorknob rattling. Her heart thudded in her chest. Goose bumps chased themselves over her skin. As she strained every sense she possessed in an effort to divine what was happening beyond that door, she tried to swallow, only to discover that her mouth had gone desert dry.

This can't be happening.

"He's here," Jenna gasped on a note of purest horror, her hand around the receiver tightening until her knuckles showed white. The wad of paper towels she had been holding to her forehead dropped, forgotten, as her hand fell. Oblivious to the blood that still oozed from the cut, she shot Charlie a petrified look.

Charlie knew exactly how she felt.

"That's it," Michael barked at Charlie as his big, semi-solid-looking body surged right through the breakfast bar in a preemptive rush toward the back door and whoever was on the other side of it. "Move your ass. Upstairs. *Now.*"

CHAPTER THREE

"Don't go outside. You might get sucked in. You need to stay close to the running water," Charlie called urgently after him as, galvanized by fear, she shot into motion herself. If he heard her, she couldn't tell: he had disappeared from view. Physically formidable in life, in death Michael could provide her with about as much in the way of actual protection as a whisper of air, although he didn't seem to remember that most of the time and there were indeed occasional moments when he solidified and was once again the badass he had formerly been. Not that those moments were anything that he could control, or she could count on, so she didn't. Thrusting her cell phone into her pants pocket, careful to stay hunched over so that she couldn't be seen through the windows, Charlie lunged across the kitchen toward the only possible source of a weapon in the house: the silverware drawer.

Pathetic? Oh, yeah. But she had no gun, no burglar alarm, no real defensive system set up in the house, because after what felt like a lifetime of living in fear she had been sick to death of it.

"Who are you talking to? There's nobody there," Jenna wailed. Then, into the phone as Charlie threw her a startled, self-conscious look because she hadn't even realized that she had been talking to

Michael out loud, Jenna added in a voice that shook: *"He's here. He's trying to get in the door. Tell the police to hurry. Please, please tell them to hurry."*

Trotting out her standard line that she was talking to herself seemed pointless under the circumstances, so Charlie didn't bother. Pulse racing, eyes fixed on what she could see of the windows—she could make out nothing beyond the darkness and the rain, which was falling heavily now, but she knew, *knew* that someone malignant was out there—Charlie snatched a steak knife from the silverware drawer. Then cautiously raising her head above the level of the counter, she did a lightning scan of the kitchen. Despite the fact that she was focused on the whereabouts of the man with the gun, the thought that instantly struck her was, *No sign of Michael.* The panicked realization curled through her mind, threading through the more immediate issue of getting to safety like a worm through soft wood. Was Michael outside, or had he been sucked back into Spookville? Not that it made any real difference. In either case, there was nothing she could do.

And right then, living through the next few minutes was paramount.

Gesturing to Jenna to head for the hall, acutely conscious that the bad guy might be right outside and even, possibly, able to hear them, Charlie whispered, "Our best bet is to lock ourselves in my bedroom until help gets here. Upstairs, second door on the right."

Jenna nodded jerkily. Breathing *"Hurry"* one more time into the phone, Jenna dropped the receiver. Staying low, she darted toward the hall with Charlie right behind her. Without the sheltering breakfast bar to conceal them, they had to be perfectly visible to whoever was outside as they flew across those last few yards. Charlie imagined that she could feel eyes—evil eyes—trained on them the entire way, and a cold chill snaked down her spine.

"I'm scared." Along with that charged whisper, Jenna threw a hunted look back at Charlie as they gained the dubious security of the shadowy hall and raced down it toward the stairs. Blood and tears mixed on Jenna's face: she looked ghastly in the dim light. Drops of water splattered the floor in her wake, making it dangerously slippery beneath Charlie's unaccustomedly high heels. She would have kicked them off if it had been possible, but it wasn't: the elegant sandals had ankle straps. *Do not fall down.*

"He's going to kill me, I know it. Oh, please don't let him get me again."

At the terror in Jenna's expression, Charlie felt cold sweat break out on her own brow. "I won't. I promise. Head up the stairs."

A sudden loud *thud* from the kitchen—Oh, God, was that the sound of the door being kicked in?—sent Charlie's heart leaping into her throat. *This has to be a nightmare.* Only it wasn't. Jenna looked back at her, horror-stricken.

"What was that? Did he just break in?" Her eyes were wild.

Shaking her head—a silent *I don't know*—while her blood ran cold, Charlie mouthed, *"Go."*

The police—Ken Ewell—help—would be there at any second. Charlie hoped. No, she prayed. But would they be in time? If he was already in the house—she couldn't finish the thought. Strain her ears though she might, she could hear nothing else from the kitchen over the clatter of her own and Jenna's harried footsteps and the harsh pant of their combined breathing.

That very stillness made her stomach cramp. She couldn't stop herself from looking over her shoulder.

Where is he?

Jenna was on the stairs, clambering up them as if she expected to be grabbed from behind at any second. It was a noisy, clumsy progress that no one who was inside the house could possibly miss hearing. Clenching her teeth in an effort to keep a lid on her own fear, Charlie grabbed the newel post, meaning to fly up the stairs in Jenna's wake. The sudden loud buzz of the doorbell caught her by surprise before she could so much as plant a foot on the steps. Both she and Jenna squeaked and jumped like terrified mice.

"Oh, no, oh, no!" Jenna gasped, shooting a look at the door as, halfway up the stairs, she nearly lost her footing.

The killer wouldn't ring the doorbell. That was the near certainty that struck Charlie like a lifeline even as an instant, reactive terror exploded along her nerve endings and, heart in throat, she whirled to face the door.

"Are you kidding me? Is that a fucking *steak knife* in your hand?"

Michael demanded furiously. Charlie was so glad to know that he hadn't yet been trapped forever in the Great Beyond she didn't even mind the attitude. Along with a surge of profound thankfulness, she felt instantly safer simply because he was there, no matter how stupid that might be. "Well, that would sure scare the hell outta *me.*"

I don't care how relieved you are to see him: don't answer. The adrenaline she'd been mainlining made her shiver. Michael must have seen because he swore.

"It's got to be the police." Her pounding heart and jumping nerves notwithstanding, that doorbell had to be good news, she was almost sure. Charlie threw the reassurance up the staircase at Jenna just as the girl gained the second floor and scrambled from view. Certain that she was right—praying that she was right—even while her ears acutely sought any sounds of an intruder rushing at her from the kitchen and her eyes were busy trying to detect some glimmer of Michael, Charlie leaped for the door.

Enough doubt about who might be on the other side of it remained to prompt her to take a few nerve-racking seconds to peer through the peephole—"*She's* hiding and *you're* opening the door? You don't see anything wrong with that?" was Michael's incensed take on it, in reply to which she was goaded into hissing, "Shut up, you, it's my neighbor"—before fumbling with the lock and throwing the door wide.

"Oh, Ken, thank goodness!" The scent of wet earth rushed past her into the house. Outside, it was as dark as a dungeon now, with pouring rain that sounded like a waterfall and fell in silvery sheets. Across the street, she could see, pale and wavery, lights on in the Ewells' house. Hurtling toward her—thank God!—she could hear sirens, although from the sound of them they were still some little distance away. Right in front of her stood Ken, foursquare and solid, squinting questioningly at her. He wasn't tall, maybe five-nine or so, and wasn't particularly imposing, either, but as a sworn officer of the law he was exactly what she needed. Bathed in the porch light's yellow glow, fully dressed down to a clear plastic rain poncho with a hood that he had pulled on over jeans and a dark-colored shirt, he was the most welcome thing she'd set eyes on since finding Michael on her couch earlier. A solid family man, father of two young boys, he was around her own age, as was Debbie, but his stocky build coupled with thinning brown hair made him look older. Not that Charlie particularly noticed, or cared, beyond what interested her most about him right at that moment: his gun. The weapon was in his hand, covered protectively by a fold of the poncho.

"Would you look at that, it's Paul Blart, Mall Cop," Michael marveled, and Charlie's lips tightened. "I know *I* feel all safer now."

Okay, so maybe the physical comparison was apt. But Ken was still an armed deputy, damn it, which beat a sarcastic ghost hands-down in this situation.

"So what—" Ken began, his blunt, not unattractive features contracting in a frown, but Charlie didn't let him finish. Grabbing his arm through the wet layer of plastic, she pulled him into the hall. She didn't even need a sideways glance to spot Michael: he was right beside her, having progressed from a shimmer to being semi-transparent. Solid enough so that she could see the frown on his face.

"A man with a gun. He was in the kitchen." Talking fast, she pointed the way to Ken. "At least, I think he was. It sounded like he kicked the door in. I don't know if he actually came inside, though. A girl—Jenna McDaniels, she disappeared three days ago from the University of Richmond, you've probably heard about it on the news—banged on my kitchen door about five minutes ago. I let her in. She was hurt and frightened and said that a man with a gun was chasing her and was going to kill her. And then the back doorknob rattled and there was a huge thud that I thought might have been him kicking in the door and he may or may not be in the house now."

In her rush to get the most pertinent facts out as quickly as possible, Charlie realized she was probably being less than clear. Ken didn't seem to be paying a whole lot of attention to what she was saying anyway. He frowned in the direction of the kitchen. Then his eyes swept the hallway, missing nothing except, of course, Michael. Finally he looked at Charlie.

"Where's the girl?"

Charlie was about to tell him when two police cars hove into view at the far end of the street, their bubble lights pulsing brightly through the darkness and the rain.

"Thank God." She touched his arm and pointed. Turning, he saw

them, too. "Now you'll have backup," Charlie added on a note of
relief, because she really hadn't liked the idea of sending her mild-
mannered neighbor into harm's way alone.

"You can stop worrying. The boogeyman's long gone." Michael
was looking out through the rain at the cops. "I couldn't get outside—
when I tried I got yanked into Spookville and had to work like hell to
get out again—but after I finally broke through I ended up back in
your kitchen. The door's open, but nobody's in there."

As Charlie absorbed the information, she felt some of the desperate energy leave her tense muscles. Thinking about what he must have
gone through to return to her, she felt her heart quiver. What she
wanted to say to him was, *I'm so glad you made it back*. But she
didn't, and not simply because they had an audience.

"You say you've got Jenna McDaniels?" As he spoke, Ken was
fishing for something in his pocket—his cell phone, she saw as he
managed to free it from both his pocket and the protective plastic in
which he was shrouded. He looked toward the kitchen again, but
made no move to head in that direction. Probably, Charlie thought,
he was more than happy to wait for the reinforcements. Hitting a button, Ken lifted the phone toward his ear.

"He wants to take credit for finding the girl before the real po-po
arrive," Michael said. "You might want to think about losing the
steak knife, by the way. Unless you've got some late supper plans I
don't know about."

"She's upstairs," Charlie answered Ken, ignoring Michael—she
would be damned if she was going to acknowledge him in front of
anyone else again by even so much as a dirty look cast his way. At the
same time, she unobtrusively sidled to her left and put the knife down
on the console table. Not that she was doing so because Michael had
suggested it. It was only, now that the danger was past, clutching it in
her fist made her feel—okay, let's face it—foolish. "She said she was
kidnapped three days ago. She said she was with two other girls, both
of whom are now dead." Shivering again, she glanced up the stairs
and caught a glimpse of Jenna lurking fearfully in the shadows at the
top.

"It's safe now," Charlie called to her. "The police are here."

Ken looked up at Jenna, who shrank back out of sight. "That the girl?"

"Yes."

"Hey, Sheriff, you know that girl who's been missing for the last three days? The one who's been all over TV? Jenna McDaniels? I got her," Ken said into the phone on a note of excitement. "Yeah, she's alive."

"Made his day," Michael said. "Bet he gets a big ole attaboy for this."

"She says there are two other girls besides her, who are dead," Ken continued. "Dr. Stone's house. Right across the street from me. You know, Charlotte Stone, works up at the Ridge? Yeah, that's her."

The police cars pulled up in front of Charlie's house. As the sirens were cut and the lights died, Charlie took a deep breath and said to Ken, "I'll be right back," then went up the stairs to find Jenna—and, not incidentally, do what she could to help Michael.

The thought of him going to hell for all eternity was more than she could live with. Whether he deserved it or not.

She might be fresh out of ju-ju, but she'd just remembered someone she could possibly turn to for advice. The sudden rush of excitement that the tiny glimmer of hope brought with it was eye-opening.

You're getting way too involved here.

"You even got a gun in the house?" Michael growled. He was right behind her again, a semi-solid phantom whose presence would have been absolutely driving her around the bend by this time if the thought of him vanishing forever hadn't been so shattering. Since she was halfway up the stairs, equally far away from both Jenna and Ken and presumably out of earshot of both, Charlie whispered a short, "No."

"A burglar alarm?"

"No. Hush."

Michael replied to that with a snort and a disgusted, "Why am I even surprised?"

It was only as she reached the top of the stairs that Charlie realized her knees felt wobbly. Probably because the adrenaline rush that was part and parcel of all the stress she'd just been through was starting to subside.

"Jenna?" The second floor was dark except for a night-light sifting through the open bedroom doors, but because Jenna was crying Charlie had no trouble spotting the girl, who was huddled in a little ball in a shadowy corner slightly to the right of the top of the stairs. Behind Charlie, Michael was now so see-through that a shaft of light passing through him glimmered off dust motes where he stood, and with a shiver of fear Charlie was once again reminded of the small amount of time she probably had to work with before he was irretrievably gone. But then Jenna made an inarticulate sound by way of reply, and Charlie forced herself to focus on her.

The living have to take precedence over the dead. With that firmly in mind, Charlie switched on the light in the upstairs hall. It wasn't particularly bright but the instant illumination still felt shocking under the circumstances, and Jenna sucked in a ragged breath.

"It's okay," Charlie said again. Wet and bedraggled, visibly shivering, the girl was huddled in a ball with her dripping hair spilling around her like a curtain and her arms wrapped around her knees. Although more sluggishly than before, blood still slid down the right side of her face, which was white and pinched and suddenly very young-looking. Her eyes were huge as she stared up at Charlie.

"Is he"—Jenna's voice cracked—"gone?"

"Yes." As she spoke, Charlie took the two steps required to reach the linen closet and extracted a washcloth and a large green-and-white-striped beach towel from it. "The man in the hall is a deputy, and two police cars pulled up out front as I came upstairs. You don't have to be afraid anymore. You're absolutely safe, I promise. It's over."

"Oh, my God." Jenna dropped her head onto her knees and began to cry again, in great wrenching wails that had Michael grimacing and looking uncomfortable and backing off. Shooting him a *stay out of this* look, Charlie shook the towel out, draped it around the girl's heaving shoulders, then hunkered down beside her.

This kind of pain she knew.

"Jenna. It's all right. Here, let me hold this to your cut." Clutching the towel around her now, Jenna glanced up at that. Charlie smoothed the cold, wet strands of her hair back from her face, tucking them behind her ear before pressing the folded washcloth to the still-bleeding wound. The cut was jagged and the edges gaped, showing the layer of white tissue beneath through the oozing blood. It would need stitches, probably about a dozen.

For a second Charlie found herself speculating about what kind of weapon could cause such a wound.

"Can you c-call my mother?" Jenna asked between sobs.

"Yes. Of course. Here, keep this pressed to your head and give me her number." As Jenna's hand replaced hers on the washcloth, Charlie fumbled to pull her phone out of her pocket.

Jenna gasped out a number. Charlie tapped it in.

"Hello?" A woman answered on the first ring. From the desperate sound of her voice Charlie guessed that she somehow knew that this call was about her daughter. Maybe she had a special cell phone number that only certain people, like Jenna, knew. Charlie had no idea, but hope and dread were there in equal measures in the woman's voice. Charlie's heart went out to her even as she struggled to keep her own voice steady and calm.

"This is Dr. Charlie Stone. I have good news: Jenna's safe. She's here with me right now."

The woman let out a broken cry that it was apparent Jenna heard, because she reached a shaking hand out for the phone. "Mama?"

Charlie passed the phone to her without another word.

"Mama, I'm okay," Jenna said into the phone, then in response to whatever her mother replied once more broke down into noisy tears.

"Here come the cops," Michael said. Charlie became aware of the sound of heavy feet on the stairs seconds before Ken and two uniformed police officers stepped into the hall.

"Jenna McDaniels?" one of the cops asked. Weeping into the phone as if she was never going to stop this side of general anesthesia, Jenna nodded wordlessly.

"We need an ambulance," Charlie said, and one of the cops replied, "Already on the way."

"My mother's coming," Jenna told Charlie, tears rolling unchecked down her cheeks as she passed Charlie's phone back to her. "Can you tell her where we are?"

Charlie took the phone and complied.

The EMTs arrived just as she was ending the conversation by promising to call Mrs. McDaniels if Jenna should be taken anywhere other than Lonesome Pine Hospital, which Charlie was virtually certain would be the case. As they converged on Jenna, Charlie relinquished her patient to them. For a moment, because of a sense of duty toward Jenna, she watched critically: they seemed very competent. Satisfied, she stood up and moved out of the way to let them work. A wave of profound relief washed over her as she realized that her part in this was ending, that the cops and appropriate-for-the-situation medical professionals would take it from here. She had played her small role in rescuing Jenna McDaniels from whatever hell she had been caught up in, and now that role was played out.

By this time her house was filled with cops, upstairs and down, and from what she could glean from various conversations more were on the way. She knew how investigations worked: they would take Jenna to the hospital, take Charlie's own statement, take lots of pictures of anything that needed taking pictures of in her house, maybe check the back door, which the intruder had forced open, for fingerprints and the yard for footprints. Then they would be gone, to focus their investigation where it needed to be focused, which was on finding out what had happened to Jenna and the other girls.

Charlie would be left alone to get back to her life.

Which right at the moment included a maddening, not-much-longer-for-this-earthly-plane ghost who was dangerously close to becoming way too important to her. Him she needed to deal with immediately, if, indeed, she planned to deal with him at all. The easy route would be to do nothing. To simply let him go. Allowing him to fade out of her life would be the absolute smartest choice she could possibly make.

And Charlie already knew that she was not going to be able to do it.

"And there you see it again, folks: we have one more unfortunate victim rescued from the jaws of death by our heroic doctor, Charlie Stone." Michael accompanied that infuriating remark by making a show of ironically clapping applause.

Forget how drained and shaky she was feeling: Michael's sardonic pseudo-announcement had the effect of stiffening her spine and heating her temper. Still translucent as smoke, he was standing near the door to her bedroom, out of the way of the hive of activity surrounding Jenna. Charlie shot him a narrow-eyed look and managed not to snap *You know what you can do with that, right?* in reply. Instead she murmured to the nearest cop, "I'm just going to go wash my hands," which were, in fact, smeared with blood, and which did, in fact, need to be washed. The cop nodded, clearly uninterested. Charlie walked (stalked?) past Michael into her bedroom. As she knew he would, he followed her in, moving past her into the room. Clicking on the light, Charlie shut—and locked—the door.

Then she turned on him.

CHAPTER FOUR

"What is your problem?" Charlie demanded in a furious whisper.

Michael had stopped near the foot of her bed. Her big brass bed was dressed in layers of spotless white bedclothes that, fortunately, had been changed and made up yesterday in anticipation of her homecoming by the maid who cleaned her house once a week. The bed that she had last been in, less than a week ago, with him. Having the hottest, most mind-blowing sex of her life.

After a single comprehensive glance, Charlie jerked her gaze from the bed to Michael. Luckily, she wasn't prone to blushing. Luckily, too, he didn't seem to have been struck by the same memory that still had the power to curl her toes. Shrugging his broad shoulders, crossing his arms over his chest, looking as big and bad in death as he ever had in life except for the fact that she could see right through him, he looked her up and down.

"It's not my problem you should be worried about," said Michael. "It's yours."

"I don't have a problem." As she spoke, she stalked across the room to the first of the two long windows that overlooked her backyard and the mountain beyond it. Looking to her right, she was able to see part of the street. At least half a dozen cop cars were parked where she could see them, which meant there were more that she couldn't see parked right in front of the house. An ambulance, siren screaming, was just turning the corner, heading her way. Although the police cars were all dark and only the ambulance's stroboscopic lights were still flashing, she could see the vehicles even through the darkness and rain, courtesy of the house and outdoor lights of every single dwelling within view: the sirens had clearly roused the neighborhood. Knowing the way the community worked, she had little doubt that the neighbors who were not at this moment actively converging on her house were peering out their windows. Given everything that had happened, she hated the idea that anyone, good guy or bad, could see in, which with the overhead light on was a given. Jerking the curtains closed, then stalking to the other window to close those, too, she said, "My only problem is you."

"Hah." He had turned to watch her. Stopping in front of the fireplace, which was between the windows—it was a lovely room, big and high-ceilinged, with white walls and dark hardwood floors and an ornate fireplace below a painting of a waterfall splashing down in a woody Blue Ridge Mountain glen, her own oasis of serenity—she glared at him. He continued: "You really don't see it, do you? You think I was kidding, downstairs? I wasn't. You've got a fucking death wish. You need a shrink, shrink."

"What I need," she said, goaded "is an exorcist. Who specializes in removing unwanted ghosts."

"Baby, if I was unwanted you wouldn't have turned the water on in your kitchen."

Charlie's lips firmed: he had her there. And the fact that she was still frightened silly by his see-through state—okay, truth was truth. Dead serial killer or not, he had become (stupidly, dangerously) important to her. Not that she meant to admit it.

And he was right about the shrink. She was exhibiting classic symptoms of what even she recognized as a real self-destructive streak. But when she thought of trying to describe her current dilemma to one of her esteemed, non-ghost-seeing colleagues, she went cold all over. Nobody would believe her. They'd think she was delusional, possibly schizophrenic or the victim of something organic such as temporal lobe seizures. Whatever, the word would spread that she was a couple of spark plugs short of an engine. Best case scenario, she would lose her credibility. Worst case, her job and her medical license.

He added: "You've got blood on your face, by the way."

Without another word, Charlie turned and headed for the en suite bathroom, pulling her phone from her pocket with angry resignation on the way. If there was a chance to save him from whatever Eternity had in store for him, which from every indication was shaping up more along the lines of fire and brimstone than Pearly Gates, she was going to go for it.

Michael followed her into the white-tiled bathroom with its big, claw-foot tub and separate shower and pedestal sink and water-saving toilet: old-fashioned in style but completely modern, because she'd had it redone. "That's the second time I've been scared enough about what was happening with you to fight my way out of Spookville when I didn't think there was any chance I was going to be able to get out ever again. Second time since I *died,* which hasn't been all that long. You following me here? Twice in less than a week that you've scared me shitless because you've been that close"—he held his thumb and forefinger about a quarter of an inch apart—"to getting yourself killed. That I know of. Like I said, you've got a death wish."

"I do not." Charlie's back stiffened with indignation even as she went ahead and pushed the button on her contact list that would place the call she knew she would never forgive herself if she didn't make. "What difference does it make to you anyway if I get killed? Looking at it from your point of view, I think I'd be thinking we could be two little angels—or whatever—together."

He snorted. Mouth twisting, he met her eyes as she glanced around at him. The expression in his was impossible to read. After a second he said, "You're not me, and you don't know shit about my point of view. What I've learned from being dead is, your life is something that has more value than you realize. You did your best to save mine; I'm doing my best to save yours."

"Quid pro quo, hmm?"

"Whatever them fancy Latin words mean, Doc."

"If you know they're Latin, I'm guessing you know what they mean." She'd already discovered that his laid-back southern exterior concealed a keen intelligence.

"Yeah, well, take them fancy words you just threw at me and add in the fact that if you bite the big one, I'm toast. You ready to sentence me to an eternity in whatever the hell—and *hell* sounds about right—I'm looking at after Spookville?"

No, she wasn't. And he knew it as well as she did, so she didn't even have to tell him so. Instead, she sighed. "I don't have a death wish, okay? That's ridiculous. Didn't you ever simply have a bad week?"

"A bad week? That's what you're calling it?" As they'd been talking, Charlie had put the phone on speaker, laid it down on the narrow glass ledge above the sink, and begun to wash her hands and face. He continued, "You're a scientist. Look at the facts: you spend your workdays penned up in a little room with serial killers. Oh, I know you like to think you're protected because you're in a prison, and there are armed guards around, and the prisoners are locked in and shackled six ways to Sunday, but you're not. You think I couldn't have grabbed you if I'd wanted to? All I would have had to do was fake like I was choking or something, and you know as well as you know your name that you would have come on around that desk that stood between us to try to save me, and I would have had you. You think I didn't work that out about five minutes after we started our first session? You think I'm the only one who's thinking of trying something like that? Wake up, buttercup. The men you're working with have been sentenced to death. They got nothing to lose. Every single one of them who isn't crazy enough to want to die is thinking about how to break out of there. What's the best way? I can't speak for everybody, but I can tell you one of the possibilities I was considering: take the pretty doc hostage and use her as a ticket to the outside."

"You were thinking about taking me hostage?" Charlie looked around, blinking, from rinsing her face to ask indignantly. One shoulder propping the door frame, he was standing in the open bathroom doorway, his tall, muscular body oversized enough to fill most of the available space. He might even have looked scary if she hadn't progressed way past being afraid of him—and if he hadn't been as see-through as delicately tinted glass.

More see-through than when he had followed her into the bathroom? She wasn't even going to let herself answer that. Just asking herself the question was enough to make her stomach twist.

Damn it.

"Hell, yes, I was thinking about taking you hostage. I was thinking about trying anything that might have saved my damned life." The soft sounds of the phone ringing on the other end as the call finally went through caught his attention and he squinted at the distraction. As Charlie reached for a towel, he added on a note of disbelief, "You calling somebody? Right now? Really?"

"Yes." She ran a brush through her hair. Her cosmetics were kept in a small plastic case on the glass shelf. Her bare face was way too pale and tired-looking, so, after giving him a quick glare simply because he was in a position to watch, she picked up her blush, opened it, and brushed a little of the pink powder on her cheeks.

He *was* watching, critically. "Who?"

"What are you, my keeper?" she asked as she progressed to slicking a rosy lip gloss over her mouth.

He looked impatient. "Damn it, Charlie, I probably don't have a lot of time left, and there's a point I'm trying to—"

He was interrupted by the sound of the phone call being picked up.

"That you, cherie?"

The cheerful voice booming through the phone prompted Charlie to answer, "Hey, Tam. Yes, it's me. Listen, I have a problem and you are the only one I can think of who might be able to help me with it."

"I'm all ears," Tam said.

Mindful that Michael's time could very well be measured in minutes rather than hours, Charlie got right down to it. "I have a ghost who's getting ready to leave this plane. He doesn't want to go, and I need him to stay—and to stay visible to me. I've tried everything I know to do to fix him to earth, but I don't know all that much about it and nothing I do know seems to be working. If you can help, I'd owe you big-time."

"You want to keep a ghost? Why?" Charlie already had been re-thinking the use of the speakerphone as Tam's incredulous voice came through loud and clear, but because time was at a premium and because she had needed to wash her face and hands and because she really hadn't wanted to appear among all the people converging on her house looking completely unkempt, she had made the choice to multitask and here was the result: an initially intent look on said ghost's face that was morphing into an irritating twinkle directed right into her eyes.

"Yes, I do. And never mind why." Giving Michael a sour look, Charlie snatched up her phone and turned the speaker function off. Feeling hope spreading inside her like kudzu as her friend talked, Charlie listened intently, had a whole multitude of second, third, and fourth thoughts, then said, "Thanks, Tam," as she finally accepted the inevitable and disconnected.

"Did I hear that right? You putting that savior complex of yours to work on trying to save me now?" The slow, mocking smile he gave her as she stuck the phone in her pocket, turned, and marched toward him would have infuriated her had it not been accompanied by an almost tender glint in his eyes. Rattled, she scowled at him.

"Shut up and move," she said, hating to find herself in the position of having to do something that she feared (a) was a terrible mistake and (b) revealed way too much about the muddled state of her heart where he was concerned. Unfortunately, the thought of the consequences should she fail to act was enough to keep her with the program. "So I made a call to a psychic friend and asked her how to keep you here. Don't go reading into it."

"I won't," he promised as he obligingly moved out of the bathroom doorway to let her pass, and she guessed that he wanted what he hoped she could do for him more than he wanted to tease her, at least for the moment. Still, that smart mouth of his was going to get him killed one day, she thought savagely before she remembered that, oops, that horse had already left the barn. "So does your friend *know* how to keep me here?"

"Her name's Tamsyn Green. And *maybe* she knows how to keep you here." Being careful to keep her voice low as muffled sounds from beyond the bedroom door reminded her of the activity in the hall, Charlie headed for her long, low mahogany dresser, where she kept a supply of jasmine candles in a drawer. The candles were a staple of her Miracle-Go kit, which was so named because the items in it were useful in dealing with the occasional ghost with evil intent that occasionally afflicted her. She'd already used a jasmine candle once in an attempt to banish Michael, with, as his continuing presence attested, less than stellar success. Now she would use one to do the exact opposite of what she had done to him the last time: instead of forcing him into the Hereafter, she would try to keep him in the Here on Earth.

"That word *maybe*? I'm not a fan." He was frowning, she saw with a quick glance at him.

"Tough. Maybe's the best I can do."

A sharp knock on the bedroom door made Charlie jump.

"Dr. Stone?" It was a man's voice, calling to her from the hall. She didn't recognize it.

"Shit," Michael said. "Take a number, buddy."

"I'll be with you in a minute." Charlie raised her voice in answer.

Michael made an impatient sound. "Forget about Snow White and the Seven Dwarfs out there. Let's get this thing done."

Charlie nodded: he had to be her first priority. Obviously tense now, Michael watched a little warily as she grabbed one of the smaller candles, fished out the cigarette lighter she kept on hand specifically to light them, should the need arise, from a delicate porcelain dish in the center of the dresser, and headed back toward the bathroom.

"So who's this Tamsyn Green?" He was following her.

"Your best hope for staying here," Charlie whispered sharply. Not that she thought anyone in the hall outside could actually hear her from the bathroom, which was where she was by then, but still. Her professional reputation wouldn't survive too many rumors that ran along the lines of *she talks to somebody who isn't there*. She could only hope that Jenna had sufficient traumatic memories to share with investigators to have forgotten about Charlie's seemingly one-sided chats with thin air. "She's from New Orleans. Her mother was some kind of voodoo priestess, apparently. I met her my freshman year of college, when I was still having trouble processing the whole I-see-dead-people thing. I went to this psychic fair, thinking maybe I'd find other people kind of going through the same thing, and she was one of the featured psychics. Since nobody was able to see the two or three spirits that I could see who were actually in the room, I had already more or less given up on getting any insight into what I was experiencing by the time I walked by Tam's table and she asked me why I didn't embrace what she called my gift and get over it. When she was able to describe the same spirits I could see, I knew she was legit. She's more than legit, actually: she's a full-spectrum psychic medium and clairvoyant who lives out in California now and makes her living giving readings for movie stars. She knows way more about this stuff than I ever want to or will." Mindful of the instructions Tam had given her, Charlie had been setting things up as she spoke.

Then she hesitated, looking at Michael.

"What?" he said.

"If I do this, you have to promise to abide by any rules I come up with," she said. "Chief of which is, do not be a pain in the ass."

"I promise," he said, way too promptly for her peace of mind.

She gave him a skeptical look.

The smile he gave her dazzled. "Cross my heart and hope to die."

Said the spider to the fly.

But she knew herself: charismatic psychopath or not, there was nothing else she could do.

"I mean it," she warned, and he laid his hand piously over his heart.

Fine. Get on with it.

Positioning the short, fat white candle on the edge of the sink, she dumped her toothbrush and toothpaste out in order to use the heavy, clear drinking glass they were kept in. With a couple of flicks of her thumb she got the lighter burning and, taking a deep breath, held the flame to the candle.

And tried to will away the nervous flutter in her stomach.

Please let this work.

"Whoa. Hold on a minute." Michael's expression was a study in alarm as the wick caught. Straightening to his full height, he shook his head at her. "We've been down this road before. You light that candle and I get vacuumed up by this big ole wind that spits me out right in the middle of Spookville. I don't think so. That hurt and—"

"Just trust me, will you please?" Charlie interrupted. The candle was burning strongly now, and the scent of jasmine was building.

Although she couldn't feel it, she could see the effect of the passage that was opening on Michael: his hair was beginning to ruffle, as if a breeze were blowing past him. Conscious of her quickening heart-beat, Charlie wet suddenly dry lips. Then she picked up the glass and waited.

Tam had warned her that timing was all.

If this doesn't work . . . She wasn't even going to let herself go there.

Michael was eyeing the candle uneasily. "Believe it or not, you I trust. This whole voodoo thing you're doing here? Not so much. Charlie—"

"You have any better ideas?"

"Goddamn it."

She took that as a *no*. His hair was really blowing now, and he seemed to be bracing himself against a force that she knew had to be substantial if he had to exert that much effort to resist it. The breeze had apparently turned into a strong wind, while on the other end she knew a steady suction was being created, although she couldn't feel a thing. Not that she was supposed to: only spirits were susceptible. The purpose of the burning candle was to open a portal to the Other Side while at the same time drawing the Light, that legendary white light that she thought of as the pathway to heaven, nearer, and from all indications at least the first part of it was happening. A vortex was being formed and it was growing stronger until, soon now, it would be strong enough to suck him up and whirl him away to where he was supposed to be. Even as she watched, the suction apparently in-creased. Michael instinctively tried to grab on to the door frame to resist its force, but of course that was useless: his hands went right through the wood. His widening eyes locked on hers as he was pulled, slowly and with a great deal of resistance, toward the candle.

"Charlie—" His voice was hoarse, with an unmistakable under-note of fear. To hear Michael sounding afraid—well, she didn't like it. "Can you hear it? The screaming?"

Oh, God. No, she couldn't hear a thing. But what he was hear-ing—in the purple twilight-y part of the Afterlife that he called Spookville there were, according to him, things called Hunters. They were called that because they hunted the screaming, terrified souls of recently deceased human beings who wound up there. Of which, if this didn't work, he would be one.

"It's okay. That just means it's working." *I think.* She didn't add that last out loud. Her throat had gone tight. Her heart knocked in her chest. If she didn't time this exactly right . . .

"Ahh!" His face contorted with pain as he was lifted off his feet and jerked toward her.

"Michael!" Heart in throat, Charlie snapped the glass down over the candle. As quick as that, the vortex dropped him like he was hot, as the suction pulling him in instantly ceased. Landing on his feet, he staggered, then dropped into a crouch inches away from her.

"Oh, my God," Charlie said, as, inside the glass, the flame flickered and went out.

"Jesus Christ." Michael flexed his shoulders as he looked at the still-smoking candle. "For the record, that hurt like a mother."

He had already solidified. Just like that: no more cellophane man. Did that mean it had worked? She thought it did. *Thank God.* Her racing heart started to slow. The tide of dread that had been building inside her began to ebb. Crouched at her feet, he now looked as vividly alive as she did. Probably more so, Charlie reflected with a touch of wryness, because she had never possessed his degree of magnetism—or good looks.

Okay. Deep breath.

"Don't be such a baby." Her tone was brisk because realizing how much the idea of him being in pain bothered her bothered her. Current crisis apparently averted, she had no intention of allowing herself to dwell on how frightened for him she had been—or to clue him in to it.

Bottom line remained: he might be here for the time being, but he was still dead—and still subject to the laws of the universe, which might decide to take him at any time. Whatever the (twisted?) relationship between them was, there was still absolutely no future in it. Not that she wanted a future that included him anyway.

But still, here they were.

What have I done? was the harrowing thought that occurred to her. It was almost immediately followed by its corollary: *Too late now.*

"Baby? Me?" Sounding mildly affronted, he looked up at her then. The shadow of pain still etched his eyes, and Charlie found the tightening of her stomach in response more than a little alarming.

Again she took refuge in flippancy. "No pain, no gain. The good news is, I think it worked."

"I sure hope so, 'cause I ain't doing that again. Next time you start ju-juing me, think you could go with something that doesn't feel like it's tearing me limb from limb?"

She smiled.

"Dr. Stone?" A brisk rapping on the bedroom door caused her to shift focus in a hurry. It sounded like the same male voice as before. "Could I please speak to you a minute? It's important."

She raised her voice. "I'll be right there."

Her eyes were already back on Michael before she had even finished speaking. She hated to so much as consider the possibility, but she discovered that she was terrified he was going to start fading out, or flickering, or something similar, again. If he did, she had no idea what she would do. That call to Tam had been the last card she had to play.

"Fuck." Michael slowly stood up, straightening to his full height, stretching and flexing and grimacing as if he actually had muscles and sinews and tendons that could actually hurt. "I feel like I got hit by a semi."

"You're dead," she reminded him in an astringent whisper. "You shouldn't be able to feel a thing."

"Like I think I may have told you before: you don't know shit about it."

For a moment they looked measuringly at each other. He was so close that she had to tilt her head back to meet his eyes. She could see the darkness in the sky blue depths, the tightness at the corners of his beautifully cut mouth, the tension in his square jaw. His hair, a sun-kissed dark blond that made her think of beaches and waves and sunny summer days, was tousled in the aftermath of the vortex. The fine texture of his skin, the slight stubble on his chin and jaw, the golden tan, all looked as real as her own slightly freckled, baby-smooth flesh. His broad shoulders and wide chest filled out the simple white cotton tee in a way that made her eyes want to linger. The brawny muscles of his arms, his flat abdomen and narrow hips and long, powerful legs, all proclaimed youth and strength and a healthy virility. Her breasts were millimeters from the muscled wall of his chest. If he had been alive, she would have been able to feel his body heat, feel the warmth of his breath on her face.

She would have been able to go up on tiptoe and kiss him.

For a second there, looking at the hard curve of his mouth, she wanted to so much that it made her dizzy.

But, she reminded herself savagely, *he is* not *alive. And if he were, he would still be locked up in that sad little six by eight cell in Wallens Ridge.*

And all you'd know about him is what you would know about any other death row prisoner who was your research subject.

She took a step back from him.

"Thank you, Charlie, for saving my life." She mimicked his mocking comment from earlier, then faltered as she remembered that it wasn't exactly his life that she had saved. "Or whatever."

"Thank you. For saving my whatever. Though I have to say, you're not looking any too happy about having snatched me off of the highway to hell."

"The thing is, I keep asking myself how evil you have to be to find yourself on the highway to hell to begin with."

The look he gave her was impossible to interpret. "I've got a question for you, buttercup: if you really think I'm so evil, then what the hell are you doing with me?"

His eyes bored into hers: she couldn't hold his gaze. With a small grimace she turned away from him, spotted the glass over the candle, and, glad for something to do, carefully lifted it off.

"Let's get this straight: I am *not* with you. At least, not on purpose." She replaced her toothbrush and toothpaste in the glass and carefully sat it back on the ledge above the sink. Then she placed the candle beside it. In case, she told herself, she ever needed to use it again. Although whether such a thing would work twice she had no idea. "Just because you happen to have barged into my life does not mean that I'm with you."

"I think it's the sex that means that." His voice was dry.

She threw him a quick, charged look.

"I—I—" Stuttering like that was idiotic. She was not the kind of woman who, when confronted with an awkward situation, stuttered. Her chin came up, and she turned to face him. "I'm not with you, okay? No way in hell am I *with* the ghost of a serial killer."

"I'll give you the ghost, but I'm no serial killer. Come on, Charlie, you know I didn't kill those women."

Surprised to find herself suddenly angry, she glared at him. "I do not know that."

"Yes, you do, if for no other reason than because I'm standing here telling you so."

A momentary lightness which she identified as hope fluttered inside her. "So I'm supposed to believe you in the face of all evidence?" Then she recalled said evidence and felt hope crash and burn. The case against him was overwhelming. Seven beautiful young women, brutally slashed to death. His DNA had been found on every victim and at every crime scene. Eyewitnesses had identified him. Security cameras had recorded him. He had no alibi for any of the crimes. The list went on and on. Even the fact that she was considering the possibility that he might be telling the truth concerned her. The stock-in-trade of a charismatic psychopath, which had been her diagnosis of him, was the ability to convince everyone around him that he was charming and likable and trustworthy. It was camouflage, similar to a chameleon's ability to change its coloring to match its surroundings. She *knew* that. *Unless I'm wrong. Unless the cops and the FBI and the judge and the jury and the evidence and the whole damned legal system is wrong.* Listening to that tiny voice of dissent inside her head, Charlie gritted her teeth. If her emotions started trumping her intellect, there would be no place left for her that was safe and true. "In your dreams."

His eyes hardened as they slid over her face. "You wouldn't believe me if I swore it on a stack of Bibles, would you? I know you: when it comes to everything except your damned ghosts, you believe in the infallibility of authority, of evidence, of the man. If some damned court says it's so then it must be. But here's the best part: I don't care what you think you believe, somewhere deep inside you know I didn't kill those women. You wouldn't be giving me the time of day otherwise, much less sleeping with me."

"I am not—" Charlie began hotly, about to deny that she was sleeping with him. The word was *slept,* as in past tense. Singular.

"You did," he interrupted ruthlessly. "Have a little faith in your instincts for a change."

A sharp knock on the bedroom door made Michael swear.

"Dr. Stone?" Same man. Same summons. It was all Charlie could do not to groan.

"I'm coming," Charlie called back, and, with a narrow-eyed look at Michael, started to suit the action to her words.

He didn't move.

"Do you mind?" If she sounded a little cranky, well, she had reason: *mess* did not begin to describe the situation she had gotten herself into with him. And reminding herself that none of it, not one teeny tiny bit (well, okay, except for maybe the sex part), was her fault didn't help at all. When he still didn't move in response to that very pointed hint, she edged around him, because walking right through him was beyond her for the moment. "*I* have better things to do than stand around and argue with you. Like go talk to the man who keeps banging on the fricking door."

"You're determined not to believe me, aren't you? Fine. If it gives you a thrill to imagine that you're fucking a murderous psychopath, so be it. Seems a little sick, but probably that's just me."

Which was infuriating on so many levels, Charlie didn't even know where to begin.

"You know what? I'm not talking to you anymore. I have a houseful of other problems to deal with."

"Before you give me the silent treatment, think you could explain what you did with the whole glass and candle thing? So I know what to expect if anything should come up." He was following her through the bedroom. Of course he was following her through the bedroom. After what she had done, for all she knew, he would be following her everywhere she went for the rest of her life. The only thing more horrifying than that thought was the one that he would not be. Who knew for how long the action she had taken would tether him to her? Days, weeks, years?

All she could be sure of was that he was here now. The future was up in the air.

In an effort to shake off the impossible-to-sort-out combination of anger and doubt and regret and relief that she was experiencing, her reply was coolly brisk.

"When you die, you're supposed to move on, you know. That's how it works. Sometimes spirits will stay for a few days, until they can accept that they're dead, but then they go on to where they're supposed to be. Since you weren't leaving voluntarily, a portal was opening to transport you to"—in his case, she didn't even want to try to put a name to his probable final destination—"the next place. That's why you were flickering. What lighting the candle did was go ahead and open the portal all the way, and then when the resulting vortex got strong enough to pull you in I slammed the portal shut again by dropping the glass over the candle before it could actually take you. Slamming the portal closed like that makes the vortex collapse. It can't open again, at least not in the same general area. In theory."

"In theory?"

"Tam said that's how it works. I've never done it myself, so I'm taking her word for it." Stopping at her closet, keeping her voice down because if she could hear the hubbub in the hall—which she could—then it was pretty obvious that she could be overheard, too, she shoved the folding, shutter-style doors apart.

"Close your eyes," she ordered.

"What?"

"Close your eyes." Her hands were already at her buttons as she looked around at him. "I need to change my blouse. I don't need you to watch."

"Oh, for God's sake." But when she glared at him, he obediently closed his eyes. Stripping off her damp and bloodstained shirt while casting him a suspicious glance—as far as she could tell his eyes were staying shut—she dropped the soiled garment into the laundry basket on the floor of her closet.

"Nice bra," he said. "Sexy."

It was, pale pink and lacy and low cut, carefully chosen along with a pair of matching panties because when she'd gotten dressed she had thought Tony might be seeing her in her undies later. That

hadn't happened, thanks in large part to the infuriating creature behind her. As she snatched a leaf green replacement blouse from its
hanger, the look she shot him should have fried his eyeballs. If his
eyes had been open to encounter it, that is. But they weren't, and—

She couldn't be sure they ever had been. In fact, she suspected
that they had stayed closed, that he was merely teasing her. For all his
faults, which were many and varied, he had never actually gone the
creepy Peeping Tom route on her. Which, given what he was, would
have been ridiculously easy.

"You're not funny," she said crossly, shrugging into her shirt. At
that he opened his eyes and grinned at her. And got a look at her bra
after all, between the parted edges of her shirt. "Hey, I didn't say you
could open your eyes yet."

Knock, knock.

"Dr. Stone?" It was the same man again, sounding as if he knew
she was standing right there on the other side of the door, a mere few
feet away from him. Damn it, had she forgotten to lower her voice on
that last exchange with Michael?

"Coming," she called back. Finishing up with her buttons, she
remembered something and gave Michael a quick, admonishing
frown as she whispered, "By the way, you need to stay close. Collaps-
ing a portal only works for a certain amount of space around it, apparently. Tam said, to be safe, we should consider that space about
fifty feet."

"Let me get this straight: now I have to stay within fifty feet of
you?" His slow grin made her want to throw something at him. She
knew how his mind worked: dirty thoughts abounded. "Works for
me."

"Yes, well, I'm not so sure it works for me. This is only temporary. Just until I can come up with something else," she warned in an
impatient whisper, and opened the door before he could reply.

"Dr. Stone." A bullet-headed bald guy in a police uniform greeted
her. Maybe five-eleven, fortyish, relatively fit-looking, he stood right
outside the door with his fist raised, obviously having been about to
knock again. If he was surprised that the door had opened so oppor-
tunely, he recovered fast. "I'm Detective Todd Sager." He held out his

hand. Stepping into the hall, Charlie shook it with a polite murmur. Sager continued, "If you could come downstairs with me, there's something I'd like you to take a look at."

"Sexy shoes, too," the curse she was afflicted with said. "Oh, right, you had a hot date with FBI guy tonight. I get it. Wow, Doc, you were pulling out all the stops. Things had played out different, right now you might have been wrapping up your evening right over there in your bed."

Since snapping *Shove it* was not an option, she didn't.

"Certainly," she answered Sager. Having slipped back into her professional persona with the ease of long habit, Charlie managed a tight nod, and in response to Sager's gesture preceded him toward the stairs. Her knees felt a little wobbly, and she had the beginnings of a killer headache: a reaction, no doubt, to the crisis-filled last half hour. A police photographer was busy taking pictures of the corner by the stairs where she had last seen Jenna. A record was being made of the wet spot on the floor where Jenna had crouched, plus the droplets of blood surrounding it. Charlie was busy processing the rise and fall of voices, the clicking of the camera and the rattle of metal and shuffle of footsteps, the swirl of activity around her and on the stairs and in the hall below when, just as she reached the top of the stairs, a woman's piercing scream stopped her in her tracks. A startled glance at Sager was all that it took to tell her that the scream causing the hair to rise on the back of her neck was unheard by him. No one else seemed to hear it, either. Looking down, she could see that Jenna, eyes closed, swathed in blankets, was lying on a stretcher in the hall below. Surrounded by paramedics in a hallway filled to overflowing with cops, she looked as if she was either asleep or unconscious. A square of white gauze covered the wound on her forehead. An IV drip had been inserted into her arm.

The scream was coming from a second dark-haired, wet, and bloody young woman. Flying across the hall toward the oblivious Jenna, the woman held a jagged rock in her upraised hand. Even as Charlie's heart jumped, even as she started to call out and alert Jenna, alert the people around her, stop the terrible thing that was obviously getting ready to happen, she realized that what she was seeing wasn't a living attacker at all, but a phantom.

A phantom who, even as Charlie watched, went through the motions of bashing Jenna's head in with the rock, slamming the jagged edge down into the pale forehead again and again and again. Without making a mark or disturbing so much as a hair on Jenna's head. Since it had no corporeal existence, the phantom rock passed right through the living would-be victim's flesh.

Even as the girl wielding it screamed over and over again, "You murdered me, you bitch! You murdered me!"

CHAPTER FIVE

Charlie's mind was spinning. What the phantom was saying—accusing Jenna of murdering her—was so off the wall that it couldn't possibly be true. Could it?

A low whistle from behind her told Charlie that Michael was witnessing the same thing. She almost turned to say something to him before she caught herself. As far as everyone else in the whole world was concerned, he—and the bloody, screaming phantom in the hallway below—was not there. If she wanted to retain any credibility at all, she could not let herself forget that.

"Now that's what you call a whole 'nother can of worms." Michael sounded more entertained than taken aback. Taken aback would be how *she* felt, Charlie realized.

"Dr. Stone? Is something wrong?" Sager asked. Since she had frozen at the top of the stairs, he had been forced to stop, too.

"No." Okay, she'd had lots of practice at keeping her cool in the presence of ghosts. She sounded perfectly normal, and was able to continue on down the stairs as if nothing out of the ordinary had occurred. The phantom girl had vanished, which helped. "Except for the fact that I've got a girl who apparently barely escaped being murdered in my house, of course."

"I hear you. Not the kind of thing that usually happens around here." Sager made a sound that almost could have been a grim chuckle. Charlie couldn't be sure, because right as he finished speaking the spine-tingling scream was repeated. It was all Charlie could do to control her impulse to fly to Jenna's aid as the phantom girl reappeared. Instead, she could do nothing more than watch as the phantom rushed across the hall toward Jenna, who still lay, eyes closed and unmoving, on the stretcher while the paramedics rigged up some kind of waterproof shield above her to protect her from the rain that was still falling outside, in apparent preparation for moving her to the waiting ambulance.

"How's she doing?" Charlie asked the closest paramedic with careful control as she stepped down into the hall. The paramedic, a young Asian woman in a blue uniform, looked around at her just as the phantom reached the side of the stretcher and brought the rock crashing down.

Charlie felt her pulse jump.

It can't hurt her, she reminded herself. Looking at Jenna's color-less face, Charlie tried turning the scenario she'd been picturing on its head and envisioning Jenna inflicting the hideous wounds that the phantom girl exhibited.

Her mind boggled.

"Her vital signs are stable. We've sedated her because of the degree of emotional upset she was experiencing. We'll know more once we get her to the hospital."

Had Jenna killed that girl? What was the alternative, a lying—or mistaken—ghost?

Grappling with the need to warn him to keep Jenna in custody until the investigation could determine the facts—and how could she do that, without revealing what she had seen?—Charlie looked at Sager. "Did she say anything? Did you get her statement?"

Sager shook his head. "We're waiting on the FBI for that. We've already been informed that they're on the way."

Of course the FBI would be involved in such a high-profile disappearance.

"You'll keep her in some kind of protective custody, won't you? Because whoever did this is still out there." Asking for a guard to be kept on Jenna was the best Charlie could do under the circumstances.

"She won't get out of our guys' sight," Sager promised.

"You murdered me, you bitch! You murdered me!" The shriek echoed off the walls. Charlie couldn't help it: what felt like a cold finger slid down her spine, and her notoriously sensitive stomach clenched.

I'll never get used to this.

Watching the rock slash through Jenna's forehead again, Charlie felt nausea building.

Oh, no.

"Hellfire, you been seeing this kind of thing your whole life?" Michael's question reminded her that, for what was practically the first time in her existence, someone else was seeing the same thing she was. It was unsettling, but kind of comforting, too.

I'm not alone in this anymore.

Since that thought was almost more disconcerting than the screaming phantom, Charlie was still trying to come to terms with it when the phantom girl suddenly looked her way. Their eyes met. Charlie felt the jolt of connection, and knew instantly that the girl could see her, which, with phantoms, wasn't always the case. Just like most people can't see ghosts, most ghosts can't see the living, but this traumatized spirit was clearly one of the exceptions—and she obviously knew that Charlie could see her as well.

"Look at me—I'm bleeding! There's so much blood! It hurts—oh, it hurts! She stabbed me! That bitch stabbed me! You have to help me—please!" The girl rushed toward Charlie, the rock still clutched in her hand. Her feet didn't touch the floor; her soaked, seal-black hair flew behind her. A gaping wound in her neck spouted a waterfall of bright crimson blood that gushed down the front of her body, staining her clothes, her legs, splashing around her feet. More blood ran down her face from a slash in her cheek, and there was another heavily bleeding gash in her upper arm. Like Jenna, she was dressed in shorts and a T-shirt, denim and pink respectively, both now saturated with blood, and she was wet and muddy and wild-eyed. Having learned already that (in every case she knew of, although it was possible there were exceptions) spirits couldn't harm the living, Charlie was horrified and filled with pity, but not afraid as a wave of freezing cold air engulfed her in advance of the spirit's arrival. Michael, however, hadn't been dead long enough to know the rules that covered ghosts on the ground, as she called them. Charlie realized that when he jumped in front of her, interposing his big body between her and the phantom before the girl could reach her. His intervention was effective: the phantom stopped dead, shifting her attention from Charlie to Michael.

"The bitch stabbed me!" she wailed again, lifting the hand that wasn't holding the rock to clutch at her bleeding throat. Blood instantly coated her hand, spurted through the spread fingers, and she pulled her hand back and looked at it in horror. Her eyes shot to Michael's face. "Oh, oh, I'm bleeding! What do I do?"

"It's over. You're dead. There's nothing to do," Michael said brutally, employing way less than the degree of tact Charlie would have used, if she had chosen to convey the same message. Hamstrung as she was by being surrounded by the living, however, Charlie couldn't say a word.

The girl screamed as if she was being stabbed again. Then she vanished.

Charlie couldn't help it. Gathering herself, moving on toward the kitchen, she shot Michael a condemning look.

"What? She needed to know," he said.

"If you wouldn't mind, I'd like to get this cleared up before the FBI gets here." Sager took her arm, discreetly urging her along toward the kitchen in an obvious indication that he thought her progress was too slow. Charlie nodded and picked up the pace, moving past the knot of people in her entryway with only a few blind nods to those of them she thought she might know: neighbors, she was pretty certain because of their civilian clothes, but she was so distracted by this sudden shocking revelation about Jenna that she couldn't concentrate enough to even start putting names and faces together. Plus, she had another pressing concern. She had taken only a few steps down the hall when the nausea that had been building inside her hit full bore. Swallowing, she pulled her arm free.

"Excuse me," she managed, before bolting into the small half bath beneath the stairs.

She barely had time to hit the light switch, lock the door, and stumble to the toilet before she vomited.

"Jesus H. Christ," Michael said.

He was in the bathroom with her, leaning against the locked door, Charlie saw as she straightened.

"Go away." Feeling weak but definitely better, Charlie glared at him as she flushed the toilet and went to the sink. Turning the cold water on full blast, she washed her hands and rinsed her mouth. The blush and gloss had been a waste of time; she looked as white as a sheet, she saw with disgust. "Do you have no understanding whatsoever of the concept of privacy?"

"I was worried about you." It was a small bathroom, and he took up way too much space in it.

For just a second or two, the idea that he had been worried about her made her feel all warm and fuzzy inside. And that annoyed her.

"Seeing ghosts makes me sick, remember?" she reminded him tartly. Although apparently she was now immune to him. Repeated exposure to the same stomach-churning stimuli obviously mitigated the effect. "And I don't *want* you worrying about me. I don't want you trying to protect me, either. I don't need you jumping between me and other ghosts."

He shrugged. "Get used to it. It's part of the deal."

"What deal?" She was drying her hands. "We don't have a deal. There is no deal."

He snorted, looked at her. "You need to find a new line of work."

"Wouldn't help. Ghosts are everywhere." Taking a deep breath, she turned toward the door. He was blocking her way.

"Screaming, bleeding murder victims aren't. They're kind of like psycho murderers: you don't go poking around in their business, you're probably not ever going to encounter one."

"Would you move?" She reached for the knob, prepared to thrust her hand right through him if she had to. She didn't have to: he stepped aside.

"It ain't healthy, what you do. Mentally or physically."

"Quit talking to me. We're not speaking, remember?" Opening the door, she stepped back into the hall. Detective Sager was waiting for her.

"You were the one who said you weren't speaking to me. I never said a thing about not speaking to you."

Charlie swallowed a growl.

"Are you all right, Dr. Stone?" Sager, frowning in concern, asked as she rejoined him. "You've been through quite an ordeal, I realize. The paramedics—"

Charlie shook her head. "I'm fine."

Behind her, Michael made a rude sound. "You got low standards for 'fine.' I'm just sayin'."

With Sager looking at her, she couldn't even shoot a glare Michael's way.

Taking a cleansing breath, she focused on her surroundings instead. A glance told her that Jenna was no longer in the entry hall. The paramedics had apparently taken her away. The population of cops had thinned out, too. Two stood on either side of the front door as if stationed there, but the rest had gone. The neighbors—had she actually seen some neighbors mixed in with the cops? If so, they were gone now, too. As Charlie continued on down the hall toward the kitchen, she wondered how the spirit of the murdered girl had found Jenna. If someone suffered a violent death, it wasn't uncommon for the shocked spirit to stick around, attaching to something or someone (as Michael had attached to her) that had been nearby at the moment the soul exited the body. But if the phantom had been attached to Jenna, it would have been with her from the first.

Where, then, had the spirit come from?

Charlie had no answer for that.

Her kitchen was full of cops. The partially open back door was being dusted for fingerprints. Tape blocked off a path from the door to the kitchen table. A police photographer was taking pictures while something was being sprayed on the wood floor inside that path: Luminol, to check for blood? Charlie couldn't be sure.

The sense of violation that she felt because the peaceful sanctuary that was her house had been invaded by horror was suddenly immense.

"Did he actually come inside?" she asked Sager over her shoulder. Michael was back there, too, looking grim, but Charlie didn't have any trouble ignoring him.

"Looks like it," Sager replied. "Unless you left your back door standing open. Because it was open when we got in here."

Charlie shook her head. A breeze blew in through the open door-way, carrying the smell of rain on it. She could see that the downpour had eased off, hear the gentler splatter of droplets hitting the ground. Beyond the spill of light from the kitchen, the night was black as pitch.

"You keep your curtains closed at night, you wouldn't have to worry about some whack job seeing in," Michael pointed out tren-chantly. Irritating as the remark might be, their thinking once again seemed to be on pretty much the same page. Charlie was already re-pressing a shiver at the idea that an armed killer might be up on the mountainside watching them through the windows at that very mo-ment.

Only maybe there wasn't an armed killer. Maybe Jenna was the killer. Maybe Jenna's frantic advent into her kitchen had been part of some elaborate cover-up and . . .

No way. Jenna's terror had been real. And *someone* had opened the back door.

Sager continued, "I want you to look at something on your kitchen table for me."

Charlie nodded.

" . . . called my wife . . ." Ken stood right inside the entrance to the kitchen talking earnestly to a cop, who was writing down what he said. His eyes tracked Charlie until she met them, when they slid away. "When I got here Dr. Stone let me in and . . ."

Charlie overheard those snippets as she walked past him. By then his arms were crossed over his chest, his head was down, and he seemed to be trying very hard not to look at her.

"Can you tell me if there's anything on the table there that wasn't on it before?" Sager asked.

Charlie looked at the table. There was the mail she'd been open-ing, the overturned box, the spill of foam peanuts—

And a white, business-sized envelope with a knife resting on top of it.

The knife was about five inches long, with a wooden handle, and looked old. The handle was damp, and the blade appeared clean and razor sharp. Just looking at it made Charlie feel cold all over.

"That settles it. Looks like Teen Queen was telling the truth." An involuntary glance his way told Charlie that Michael was looking at the same thing.

Although she couldn't say so, that was Charlie's conclusion, too. Because Jenna had never gotten out of her sight from the time she had entered the kitchen, and the door had been forced open, and the knife and envelope, which had definitely not been on the table when they had fled the kitchen together, were now there. Ergo, someone else had to have put them on her table—such as the man with the gun Jenna had insisted was chasing her.

It was a relief to definitively conclude that he was real. That whatever had prompted the phantom girl's accusation, Jenna's terror had not been faked.

"The knife—and the envelope," Charlie said to Sager. "They aren't mine. They weren't on the table."

"That's what I thought." Sager nodded with satisfaction. He waved a hand at the photographer, who was busy snapping pictures of the door. "Hey, Torres, you get a picture of that table?"

"Yeah. The whole thing, plus close-ups of everything on it."

"The knife and envelope?"

"Oh, yeah. At least a dozen."

"Okay." Sager looked at Charlie. She was close enough to the table now that she could see the wet splotch the knife had left on the envelope. She could see something else, too, that made her eyes widen. Her name was written on the envelope: Dr. Charlotte Stone. In what looked like black Sharpie, unsmudged despite the damp spot in the middle of it. The writing was large enough so that her name was easily readable. The script itself was delicate, flowing.

A shiver slid over her skin as she looked at it.

"Envelope's addressed to you. Would you mind opening it?" As Charlie nodded assent Sager added, "I'll need you to put on some gloves first."

Michael was frowning at the table. He cast a sharp look at Charlie. "You get that your name on that envelope means the sick bastard thinks he's got some kind of connection going on with *you*."

Charlie got it, all right. Her pulse picked up the pace as, briefly, she held Michael's gaze. Once again she was burningly conscious of the open curtains. The sudden sense of vulnerability she felt at the thought that whoever had left that envelope on the table might be watching through the window was only slightly mitigated by reminding herself that her house was full of cops.

"Dr. Stone." A cop handed Charlie a pair of latex gloves. As she pulled them on, another similarly gloved cop picked up the knife and dropped it in a plastic bag.

"Tag that for the FBI," Sager told him, then added to Charlie, "Be real careful with that, please. I'll get my butt handed to me if there's damage to the evidence."

Charlie nodded, and picked up the envelope. It wasn't sealed, she saw as she turned it over. Of course, whoever had left it had wanted her to open it.

Taking a deep breath, conscious of the weight of many eyes on her, she lifted the flap and pulled out the single sheet of paper that was inside.

On plain white typing paper, in black Sharpie, in the same flowing script that was on the envelope, were written the words:

You can't catch me.

Looking at them, Charlie felt her heart start to slam in her chest. Her breath caught. She looked up quickly, her eyes going instinctively to Michael, who like Sager was watching her with frowning attention.

"I know who did this." There was a sudden tightness in her chest. Then, remembering that to Sager and anyone else who was watching it would look like she was directing her words to thin air, she transferred her gaze from Michael to Sager.

"I know who did this," she repeated urgently.

CHAPTER SIX

"Who?" Michael and Sager demanded almost in unison, as every eye in the kitchen that hadn't already been watching her turned her way.

Charlie took a deep, steadying breath as all the pieces suddenly started fitting together in her mind. The truth was terrifying: this was a case she had recently consulted on and she recognized the killer's signature MO right off the bat. She felt her blood drain toward her toes as she faced it. "I'm almost positive that we're dealing with a serial killer. He's known as the Gingerbread Man."

"You know what, you need to rethink this whole serial killer gig you got going on," Michael said. "And I'm being completely serious here."

"The Gingerbread Man?" Sager frowned doubtfully at her.

"He's been operating up and down the East Coast for at least the last two years." Talking around the sudden tightness in her throat, Charlie directed her remarks to Sager and ignored the grim stare Michael was giving her. She took one last look at the piece of paper—the words *You can't catch me* leaped out at her like the taunt they were meant to be—then carefully refolded it, slid it back inside the envelope, and started to put the envelope on the table.

It took every bit of self-control she had to keep her hands steady.

"You can get another job," Michael told her. "Most shrinks write prescriptions for kids with ADHD. They talk fat cats off the ledge when the economy tanks. They listen to middle-aged women cry about their empty nests. They don't put their lives at risk every single day. That's crazy."

"Uh, would you mind dropping that in here?" The same cop who had bagged the knife held open another plastic bag to receive the letter. Doing her best to keep a clear head, Charlie obediently dropped it in. The idea that yet another serial killer had her in his sights was stirring up nightmare memories that she'd thought, hoped, and prayed she'd put to rest.

"Well, now, I never heard of anyone called that," Sager said. "A serial killer, you say. Here in town?"

"Yes. At least, tonight he was." Serial killers had always existed. They always would. That she had become enmeshed in their darkness was her bad luck. As she accepted the harsh truth of that, Charlie forgot all about her wobbly legs, the lingering remnants of nausea, the exhaustion that had been creeping over her, her very mixed emotions about what she had done with Michael. What she had been hoping to return to—her peaceful existence, her safe little house, the distance she had carefully crafted between herself and the serial killers she analyzed in hopes of learning what made them tick so that others of their ilk could be identified and stopped before they hurt anyone else—had just been blasted to hell. Once again, she was being plunged into the horror she had spent most of her life trying to avoid.

The Gingerbread Man had been in her house less than an hour before. What she wanted to do—turn back the clock, erase the last hour, go on like Jenna McDaniels had never come banging on her door—was impossible. That being the case, she had no choice but to deal. And dealing meant taking up the Gingerbread Man's challenge, doing her best to make sure that he got caught. If she did not succeed, he would kill again, and soon. Even if she turned her back on the challenge, left the investigation up to Sager and the FBI agents who were supposedly on the way, she still would not be able to simply go on with her life. A vicious, conscienceless serial killer had entered her house and left her a message. He knew who she was, where she lived, and what she did. He was interested in her. What were the chances that he would just forget all about her, go away and leave her alone if she refused to play? None. Zero. Zip.

She had always been good at grasping the reality of a situation, and as she recognized the reality of that she pushed the fear and dread that were her first reactions aside. They would do her no good at all. For whatever reason, this was the hand she had been dealt.

If she had no choice but to play, then she was damned well going to play to win.

You have to outthink him, she told herself, and squared her shoulders in preparation.

Okay. He had to have left trace evidence behind. For one thing, it was raining: there should be footprints in the muddy yard. Jenna had run to her house from somewhere presumably nearby. If investigators were very, very lucky, it would be the crime scene, where two bodies could possibly still be found. A fresh, intact crime scene.

Plus, in Jenna, they had a living witness. A living witness with the crime still vivid in her mind.

Maybe, this time, this particular monster had cut it too close. Maybe this was the mistake that would cause him to be caught. Maybe she could help put one more dangerous predator away where he could never hurt anyone again.

The thought strengthened her. It cleared her head, fired her determination.

I can do this.

The local PD and sheriff's department were great. She was sure the FBI agents who were coming, the ones who had been spearheading the search for Jenna, were competent. But they didn't have the expertise or experience necessary to even begin to handle a monster like this one.

Fortunately, she knew people who did. In fact, earlier that very night she had regretfully kissed one goodbye. If she was lucky, he might still be within reach.

"Heads up, folks. We're going to be turning out the lights for a minute to see if our spray illuminates any footprints on the floor," a technician called.

So apparently the chemical they'd been using wasn't Luminol, after all.

As the lights went out, as darkness descended, Charlie felt a shiver run down her spine. Ignoring it, *resolutely* ignoring it, she pulled her phone out of her pocket, called up her contact list, and hit the number she was looking for.

"You phoning somebody?" Having moved closer to her in the darkness, Sager eyed her glowing cell phone askance. Unable to help herself—being too close to a stranger in the darkness didn't feel comfortable now—Charlie took a step away from him even as she replied.

"This is something that local law enforcement, no matter how good they are, isn't equipped for," Charlie told him as the phone rang in her ear. "If you've got men outside searching for evidence or for those other two girls or the crime scene or whatever, they need to stop where they are. I—"

"Charlie?" The warmly masculine voice answering the phone was music to her ears. "What's up?"

"Tony," she greeted him with relief, then felt even more relief as the lights came back on.

"Fuck," Michael said. "That guy?"

"Dr. Stone, I don't think—" Sager sounded unhappy.

"Stop everything," Charlie interrupted Sager, pinning him with what she hoped was a commanding look. "Stop. Now."

"I would." On the other end of the phone, Tony was sounding amused. "But I'm really not doing much. Napping in a chair. Looks like I'm going to be spending the next few hours right here in Lonesome Pine Airport. Plane can't take off because of the storm."

"With all due respect, Dr. Stone," Sager said, "we have an investigation to conduct. Stopping it isn't an option."

"When's the last time your department handled any kind of murder investigation at all? How many years ago? This is a serial killer. The case needs to be overseen by experts in catching them," Charlie answered Sager fiercely, while at the same time, except for shooting him a dirty look, doing her best to ignore Michael, who had just finished telling her, "You know you've got a major screw loose, right?" To Tony, whom she considered the only one really worth talking to at the moment, Charlie responded, "Thank God for the storm. Have you ever heard of the Gingerbread Man?"

"Yeah, sure. He's on the Active List"—meaning the FBI's list of serial killers who were known to be active in the country at any given time—"but—"

"He's here." Simply saying it made her palms go damp. "He's been in my house. Tonight."

"What?" From the sound of his voice, Tony had sat bolt upright in his chair. He responded to a sudden burst of chatter on his end of the call with an impatient, "Quiet, you two. I need to hear this."

As he was obviously not talking to her, Charlie had to ask. "Who's there with you?"

"Kaminsky and Crane. Their plane didn't get out of here, either." In the background Charlie could hear the other members of the team— FBI Special Agents Lena Kaminsky and Buzz Crane—demanding to know what was up. They were quickly silenced, and Charlie imagined Tony, who was their boss, gesturing at them to be quiet.

Charlie gave Tony a quick, condensed version of events, finishing with "The trail's still fresh. We've got a real chance to catch this guy if you can get here fast. We—"

"We?" Michael erupted. He was giving her the kind of hard, intimidating, *you will bend to my will* look that she hoped she had just turned on Sager. Once upon a time, coming from the big, scary convict in the orange jumpsuit who she was pretty sure had lied to her about her inkblots, she might actually have found that look alarming. Now, though, she found herself battling the impulse to stick her tongue out at him. "If you mean you and him, there is no *we* in this, buttercup. Your boyfriend there's a federal agent who gets paid to lay his life on the line. You're a shrink. You get paid to listen to people talk. Damn it, Charlie, I'm going to say this one more time: messing with serial killers is stupid. It's fucking *dangerous*. Didn't anybody ever teach you that if you poke a sleeping bear enough times sooner or later it's going to wake up and eat you?"

Charlie shot Michael a narrow-eyed *mind your own business* look. Replying to him was, of course, out of the question.

So she continued talking to Tony instead.

"—have a survivor, we have an envelope with handwriting on it as well as other possible trace evidence, we have a knife that may or may not be a murder weapon, we have—"

"We're out the door," Tony interrupted her to say. "Thirty minutes, max."

That was exactly the response Charlie had hoped for. Tony and his team were as invested in the apprehension of serial killers as she was in the studying of them. She knew how good they were at their jobs because she had watched them work: on the very day that Michael had been killed, Tony and his team had come to her and asked for her help in finding the Boardwalk Killer, the serial killer who had murdered her best friend, Holly, and Holly's family when she and Holly were only seventeen. Charlie had been staying the night with Holly at the time, and had hidden from the killer and survived. When the Boardwalk Killer had resurfaced after fifteen years, she had been reluctant (okay, afraid) to get involved—but she had done it anyway. As a result, the Boardwalk Killer had been captured, and, not incidentally, Charlie had been freed of the secret terror she had lived with ever since she'd survived the attacker who had killed Holly: that the Boardwalk Killer would sooner or later come back and kill her, too. And in the process, she had been enormously impressed with Tony and his team.

Now there was another madman, more victims, fresh horror. Another serial killer who had turned his eyes toward her. Simply thinking about it made Charlie imagine that she could feel the darkness closing in. *Her* darkness, her own private one, the one that came from looking evil in the face and barely surviving. The darkness of her own mortal fear.

She could feel a tightening in her chest.

I don't know if I can go through this again.

Tony was saying, "Did you say the local police are there now? Could you let me speak to whoever's in charge?"

Stay in the moment. "That would be Detective Todd Sager."

Passing her phone to Sager, Charlie told him, "This is FBI Special Agent Tony Bartoli, from the Special Circumstances Division out of Quantico. They're an elite team whose sole purpose is to track and catch serial killers. They're on their way here right now."

"Well, hell, there goes the neighborhood," Michael said with disgust, leaning back against the breakfast bar and folding his arms over his chest. Charlie shot him an angry look. Serial killers were evil by definition, and no matter how much he proclaimed his innocence, Michael was a convicted serial killer. She ought to hate him. She ought to fear him. She definitely ought to have let him go to his just reward when she'd had the chance. *He* was one of *them*.

You know I'm innocent. Oh, God, she didn't. The sad truth almost certainly was, he had said the words she needed to hear, and she just wanted to believe.

"Oh, so now you're mad at *me*?" Michael said. "Nice."

"I don't think—" were the first words Sager said into the phone. Then he was silent, listening, finally nodding. "I'll pass the word." He looked at Charlie. "Special Agent Bartoli wants to speak to you," he said, and handed the phone back to her.

"Sit tight. We'll be with you shortly," Tony told her, while Sager barked at the other cops in the room, "Everybody, change of plan. We're going to wait until Special Agent Bartoli's team gets here to go forward." He pointed to two cops near the back door. "Get out there and tell those guys outside to hold up. If we've got a crime scene, the last thing we want to do is contaminate it."

"You want I should finish up with the door?" The technician who was dusting for fingerprints asked. Kneeling on the floor below him, another cop was measuring the distance from the edge of the door to an area of damage in the door's lower third that hadn't been there previously and that Charlie assumed was the result of something like a hard kick. Looking at it and realizing how ridiculously easy it had been for a killer to gain access to her house made her skin crawl. What had she been thinking, to imagine that she could live in a world where there was no need to keep a gun for protection, or to have a burglar alarm or something more than an ordinary, run-of-the-mill lock on her doors? When had wishful thinking become her modus operandi? "In this rain, I wouldn't want to wait."

Sager hesitated. Then he nodded. "Go ahead."

When this guy's caught, I'll be safe again. And there will be one less monster in the world.

That was the thought that steadied Charlie's nerves, calmed her down, helped her pull herself together. Mentally, she took a deep breath and stood tall.

I'm not a scared teenager anymore. I'm an expert on serial killers. So this time the Gingerbread Man has messed with the wrong expert.

"Did Jenna tell you where she had come from?" Charlie asked Sager as, Tony having disconnected, she slid her phone into her pocket again. If she didn't have her emotions totally under control yet, well, she was working on it. Under the circumstances, there was no shame in taking a few moments to adjust.

Sager shook his head. "No. At least, she wasn't real specific. She was crying too hard to get anything of much value out of her, but she did say she ran down the mountain. Since she wound up at your back door, I figure she must have come down Big Rock Trail. Muddy as it's bound to be, she must have left some tracks. I figure we can follow them back."

Charlie nodded. Big Rock Trail was the dirt path that she favored for her almost daily runs. Starting only a few yards beyond her back fence, it wound up through the thick piney woods of Smoke Mountain all the way to the top of the ridge. She would have worried about the downpour washing away any tracks Jenna might have left, except for the fact that at this time of year the canopy was so dense she couldn't imagine much rainfall got through. Sager was apparently aware of that, too.

"The screamer said Teen Queen killed her," said Michael. "You say the killer is somebody called the Gingerbread Man. Want to explain to me what's up with that?"

Charlie caught herself just as she was about to answer, and almost had to bite her tongue to hold the words back. The glare she gave him this time was downright threatening. Fortunately Sager was talking to the fingerprint technician who apparently—from the fact that he was closing the back door—had finished, as had the cop who had been measuring the damage on the door and was now on his feet writing something on a clipboard. Point was, Sager wasn't watching her; otherwise, no telling what he would have made of her fierce scowl at nothing.

"Ooo," Michael said. "There's that *you're really pissing me off now* look of yours. You were always giving me that one back at the Ridge. Turned me on then. Turns me on now."

Bite me, her eyes said, but having a one-sided argument, she was discovering, only actually worked for the side who could talk. She might be seething inside, but Charlie was proud of her own self-control: she fell back on the one weapon she had that she knew from experience actually kind of bugged him, and ignored him. Pointedly.

"So what can you tell me about this Gingerbread Man?" Sager asked her as two of the cops he'd been talking to headed across the kitchen for the hall, signaling to a couple of others who fell in behind them. In response to her look questioning this mini exodus, Sager said, "They're going to be putting together some equipment so we can head up the mountain." He added hastily, in response to what she could only assume was a change in her facial expression: "We won't actually go until Special Agent Bartoli's team gets here."

"Did I hear you say there's a serial killer in town?" Freed from the cop who'd been questioning him, Ken came over to join Sager. Both of them looked at Charlie expectantly. At the breakfast bar, Michael lifted his eyebrows at her. The silent message she took from that was: *So, see, I'm not talking. You want me to keep it up, you talk.*

"Fine. Um, yes." After that first snapped-out slip of the tongue, she was careful to moderate her tone and direct her reply to Ken and Sager rather than Michael: "The Gingerbread Man is fairly unique in the annals of serial killers in that he doesn't actually kill the majority of his victims himself. What he has done historically is kidnap three people at a time and force them to kill one another. He appears to try to match them in terms of gender, with a lesser correlation in age and body size, although there seems to be a degree of correlation with those factors, too. Sometimes the victims know one another, sometimes they don't. In both of the last two years, he has kidnapped three disparate groups of three people within a period of about a month. Then he goes dormant for another year. As far as I know, the group in which Jenna McDaniels was a part is the first group for this, the third year. There have been five survivors if you include Jenna Mc-Daniels tonight, which I do, and much of what we know we've learned from them. The survivors consistently tell us that they were put into some kind of confined area together, given weapons, and told they would all be killed unless they started killing one another. They were promised that the last one standing would be released alive provided that whoever survived had participated in the killing of at least one of the other victims. The Gingerbread Man appears to keep his promise, although it's difficult to tell because only two of the survivors have admitted to investigators that they actually killed anyone. But they were released by the Gingerbread Man, which indicates that they fulfilled the conditions he set for them."

"So if Teen Queen was let go because she was the winner in a cage fight to the death, why was she screaming her head off about a man with a gun who was chasing her?" Michael asked.

So much for him not talking. Well, she hadn't expected it to last. Charlie looked at him, put her nose in the air, and deliberately transferred her attention to Sager, who said slowly, as if her words were just starting to compute for him: "Are you saying that Jenna McDaniels herself might have killed those other two girls she was telling us about?"

Bingo, Charlie thought, but that was one more answer she couldn't give.

"If she did, it was because she had no choice," she ended up saying. Revealing what she knew through the phantom girl wasn't possible, so she couldn't definitively say yes. "In the environment in which the victims find themselves, it's strictly kill or be killed."

"Come on, Charlie, talk to me," Michael said impatiently. "You really think you're going to be able to treat me like a potted plant?"

Since she caught herself shooting him a dirty look in response, the inescapable answer was, obviously not. She gave up: because he'd asked a legitimate question as opposed to being annoying, she would try to answer. To all appearances, she hoped, she was simply providing additional information to Sager and Ken.

"The first two survivors were let go. The last two, not counting Jenna, were apparently chased by the Gingerbread Man after he released them. All three, and I'm including Jenna in this, reported that he was armed with a gun. All three reported that when he let them go, he told them to run, then came after them. They were sure he was going to kill them, too."

Ken said, "Since there are eyewitnesses, I'm assuming law enforcement has a description of—what did you call him, the Ginger-bread Man?—on file somewhere?"

"He wears a mask," Charlie answered. "We have eyewitness descriptions of that."

Michael said, "Don't serial killers usually have butch names like the Boardwalk Killer and the Bind, Torture, Kill Killer? I mean, when I was on trial the news channels were calling me the Southern Slasher, for cripe's sake. What is this guy, the sissy serial killer? Where'd anybody come up with a name like the Gingerbread Man?"

"It's from the nursery rhyme," Charlie answered, and immediately gave herself a mental smack—she would save the glare at Michael for a time when it wouldn't simply serve to underline the fact that as far as anyone watching was concerned she was conversing with thin air—and transferred her gaze to Sager and Ken. "The reason he's called the Gingerbread Man is from the nursery rhyme. You know, 'Run! Run! As fast as you can! You can't catch me, I'm the Gingerbread Man!' Because he told several of his surviving victims to run, and because four times that I am aware of he has sent or left a letter addressed to someone in authority or an expert he wants to match wits with, saying '*You can't catch me.*'" She finished a little lamely, "I just thought you'd want to know."

"Debbie reads that nursery rhyme to the kids." Ken sounded appalled.

Michael said, "So what you're telling me is that now the sick bastard wants to match wits with *you*?"

Charlie gave a truncated nod. The icy little prickle that snaked down her spine as she acknowledged the truth of that was something she couldn't do anything about.

Soldier through the fear. She had done it before. She could do it now. No, she *would* do it now.

Sager was saying, "Yeah, go ahead, I guarantee you we'll be doing the grunt work anyway" in a low voice to the fingerprint technician, who apparently wanted next to begin work on the table and chairs. While the technician nodded and turned away to start scooping up the foam peanuts, which he dropped into a plastic Ziploc bag, Charlie said, "It's like a game to him. A challenge. As soon as I saw the words *you can't catch me,* I knew who it was."

"This guy knows who you are, too." Michael's voice was flat. "And that ain't good."

A commotion from the front hall distracted all of them. Hoping it was Tony and crew, Charlie started forward, only to fall back with disappointment when three strangers walked into her kitchen. The tall, burly, gray-haired man in uniform she had seen before: Wise County Sheriff Hyram Peel. The two men in dark suits were, of course, FBI, although not the agents she was anxiously awaiting. Introducing themselves as Agents Greg Flynn and Dean Burger, they were part of the team that had been involved in what apparently had been a massive search for Jenna McDaniels. While other agents had gone to the hospital to secure her, they said, they had been detailed to talk to Charlie.

She was just beginning to tell them her part of what had happened when Michael exclaimed, "Damn, that's my watch."

Distracted from her recital of events, Charlie quit talking to frown at him. He had been leaning against the breakfast counter looking grim. Now he was standing upright, staring at the table as if there was something on it that was getting ready to leap at him. Automatically she followed his gaze to find that, now that the technician had finished scooping up the last of the foam peanuts—he was shaking them in a plastic bag with fingerprint powder—it was possible to see a man's matte silver watch still resting inside the overturned package she had received.

"I told those damned clowns that it wasn't my watch they found next to that dead woman." Michael's charged gaze shifted to Charlie. "Did they believe me? Hell, no. But look at that: there it is. That's my watch."

CHAPTER SEVEN

"Pick it up. Look at it." Because Michael was talking to her, because of the intensity of his tone, because of the emotion she could feel rolling off him, Charlie completely forgot about Agents Flynn and Burger. "It's got *Semper Fi* engraved on the back of the case. Go ahead, check it out. It's my damned watch."

Semper Fi, Charlie recalled, was the Marine Corps motto. She was familiar enough with his file to know that Michael had spent eight years as a marine.

"Uh, Dr. Stone, you were saying?" Flynn prompted.

Realizing that she had broken off in mid-sentence, Charlie dragged her eyes away from Michael and sought desperately to recall where she had stopped. Flynn was frowning at her. He was a stocky, muscular man of about forty, with short brown hair and average looks. There was impatience in his narrowed brown eyes.

"Jenna was obviously traumatized," Charlie picked up the thread, and with that launched back into her story.

Even with Flynn and Burger both looking at her, even as she talked, it was impossible for Charlie not to watch, out of the corner of her eye, as Michael moved over to the table. His big hands wrapping around a chair back, his powerful shoulders bunching so that the muscles strained against his shirt, he stared down at the watch. Of course, it was impossible for him to touch it, much less pick it up. His hands would pass right through.

"How in hell is that thing turning up now?" Michael looked and sounded angry, and more as if he was talking to himself than her. "All this fucking time, and it turns up *now*?"

"Thank you," Flynn said, and Charlie realized that she had stopped talking again. Fortunately it was in a place where Flynn could conclude that she had finished with what she had to say. He nodded toward the galley part of the kitchen, where Ken and Sheriff Peel were quietly conversing. Charlie noted in passing that the kitchen faucet was no longer running: someone had obviously turned it off. She was only glad that Michael no longer seemed to need whatever strengthening effect it had on him. "Is that Deputy Ewell? Didn't you say that he was the first person on the scene here?"

"Yes."

"Excuse us. We have a few questions for him." With a nod at her, Flynn and Burger headed toward Ken.

A quick glance around told Charlie that everybody was now busy doing something else. She moved over to the table and frowned at Michael questioningly.

"Look at it." He nodded at the watch. "Tell me if it doesn't say *Semper Fi* on the back of the case."

Although as far as she could tell none of the other roughly half-dozen people in the room were paying the least bit of attention to her, Charlie knew that all it would take would be for her to start talking aloud, supposedly to herself, for that to instantly change.

Picking up the watch—it was cool and heavy, with all kinds of fancy little dials on the face and an expandable wristband—she turned it so she could see the back of the watch face. Engraved on the smooth metal surface was the Marine Corps motto.

"*Semper Fi?*" There was tension in Michael's face.

Charlie nodded. His gaze returned to the watch.

"Goddamn it. Of course the thing would show up now, when it's too fucking late." He sounded almost savage.

Charlie picked up the box the watch had arrived in. Fortunately, cutting through the layers of tape that had been wrapped around it had left the return address intact. It read *Mariposa Police Department.*

Her fingers tightened on the box.

I wrote to them. Of course.

Tiny Mariposa, North Carolina, was where Michael first had been arrested, for the last of the seven murders with which he had subsequently been charged. As part of her research into the backgrounds of the men she was studying, Charlie had sent the department an official request for access to any materials/information/files they still had concerning him.

This was their reply. In addition to the watch, at the bottom of the box was a DVD, and tucked to the side was a tri-folded sheet of letter-sized paper.

Charlie pulled it out.

"What the hell *is* this?" Michael growled as she unfolded the single, typewritten sheet. The letter was brief and she read it quickly. "Some kind of cosmic joke?"

"Ma'am, I'm going to have to ask you not to touch anything on the table until I'm done here." This interruption by the fingerprint technician, who had been standing a little distance away while his gloved hands busily rifled through the now powder-coated foam peanuts, almost made Charlie jump. "Could you put that back, please?"

"I'm sorry." She managed a smile for him. Then, with Michael in mind, she added, "Um, I just got this material from the Mariposa Police Department and I needed to look at it. I wrote to them, you know, about a month ago, concerning a research subject I was studying." She put the letter down on the table, open and positioned for Michael to read. He flicked her a glance.

"Don't let go of that damned watch."

She barely managed not to nod. Mouth tight, he leaned forward to read the letter.

The technician said in an apologetic tone, "That box was out on the table, wasn't it? It's possible that the perp touched it. I need to test it for fingerprints."

"I understand."

Charlie set the box back down on the table. The watch she slipped onto her own wrist. She was fine-boned, with long, slender limbs, and the watch, sized for a big man's solid forearm, was way too large for her. The expandable metal band was not adjustable, so there was nothing to do but wear it as it was. As it slid up her arm, as she felt the weight of it and the glide of the cool metal against her skin, a prickle rippled along her nerve endings. It felt weird to have something real and solid that belonged to Michael touching her.

It was almost like having him touch her himself.

"Sorry," she told the technician again. He nodded. It was clear that he was waiting for her to step away from the table, but she wasn't ready to do that until she saw Michael's reaction to what he was reading.

Having read it herself, she already knew what the letter said:

Dear Dr. Stone,

In response to your inquiry about County Inmate #876091, Michael Alan Garland, I am sending you a copy of what we have retained in our files. In addition, I am enclosing our department's video records concerning him, as well as a man's wristwatch that was tagged with his name and was found during the course of our recent move. As far as I can tell, this is the only personal effect of his still in our custody. Because of misfiling by a clerical worker, it was inadvertently left out of the bag containing his personal effects that was passed on to the FBI some years ago. We apologize for any inconvenience this may have caused, and hope that you will now pass it on to whoever should have possession of it.

Thank you.

If you have any additional questions, please feel free to contact me.

Sincerely,
Betty Culver
Executive Assistant to the Chief
Mariposa County Police Department

"Son of a bitch," Michael said. Charlie didn't say anything, but he must have felt the weight of her eyes on him, or else she must have made some small sound. Because his head came up, and he looked at her then, his eyes blazing.

"They found a damned watch exactly like this next to the body of the last chick I'm supposed to have sliced to ribbons. It was broken, had her blood on it. They said it was mine, ripped from my wrist in the struggle. I told the stupid bastards it wasn't."

Charlie's heart lurched. What he was telling her was that this watch was evidence of his innocence. Weighed against all the evidence of his guilt, it was a small thing, but still—it was something tangible.

If he was telling the truth. If he wasn't somehow playing her.

Charismatic psychopaths had a genius for playing people, she knew. They were so good at it that it wasn't even embarrassing to the people who studied them when they, too, fell victim to their lies.

The Mariposa Police Department had identified the watch as belonging to Michael right there in the letter. Plus, he'd known that *Semper Fi* was engraved on its back.

How could he have manipulated something like that?

She didn't think he could have. She didn't see how it was possible.

How important a part a watch such as the one she was wearing had played in his case was something she would have to check into.

For now—it wasn't nearly enough to persuade her.

Sway her a little, maybe, but not persuade her.

Still, it was something.

"Fuck." The blaze in Michael's eyes had hardened and cooled. "What the hell difference does it make now, right? It's done."

Shaken by the glimpse she had just gotten into what lay beneath the tough guy exterior, Charlie felt as if the earth were shifting beneath her feet, as if she were no longer standing on solid ground. Before she could formulate a response, the sound of new arrivals, coupled a moment later with a familiar voice behind her, distracted her, causing her to glance around.

"I'm Special Agent Tony Bartoli. This is Special Agent Lena Kaminsky. Special Agent Buzz Crane."

Bringing a whiff of fresh air with him into a room that was now overwarm and smelled faintly metallic, from either the aerosol spray or the fingerprint powder, Tony was there, in her kitchen, at last. *Thank God.* Raindrops gleaming on his hair and the shoulders of his jacket, he was shaking hands, first with Sager and then with Sheriff Peel, Ken, and Agents Flynn and Burger, as he introduced himself, Kaminsky, and Crane. As apparently all of the law enforcement types in the house converged on the newcomers, the room felt suddenly small and crowded. Relief welled up inside her, and Charlie cast one more worried glance at Michael. Still tense with anger and whatever other clearly negative emotions he was experiencing, he looked at the new arrivals, too, with a less than welcoming expression. But at least the raw pain she thought she had glimpsed in his eyes was gone, and he seemed more or less his usual badass self. In any case, there was nothing she could do for him at the moment, Charlie concluded. That being the case, her focus had to be on what was most important: catching a serial killer.

With that firmly fixed in the forefront of her mind, she hurried toward Tony, Kaminsky, and Crane.

"Hey," Tony said when he saw her, taking the hand she held out for him to shake—anything more intimate, like, say, a quick hug or a kiss on the cheek, would be unprofessional, and anyway she wasn't a huggie/kissie kind of person—and giving her a slow smile in which the memory of the very sexy good-night kiss they had so recently shared lingered. His coffee brown eyes crinkled around the edges when he smiled, she noted in passing, and his long mouth stretched and quirked up at the corners to reveal even white teeth. He had black hair, cut short and brushed back, and a lean, mobile face that, while not as flat-out gorgeous as Michael's, was nonetheless handsome enough to merit a second look. At the moment he was faintly red-eyed, with more than a hint of five o'clock shadow darkening his jaw, which wasn't surprising considering that it was now well after one in the morning and he had been going since seven a.m. She knew that for sure because seven a.m. (yesterday now) was when the four of them had risen to meet for breakfast before going over some files for what she had thought would be the last time; later, they'd driven to the airport to catch the private plane that had brought her back to Big Stone Gap.

Tony was six-one, about a hundred eighty pounds, lean compared to Michael's ripped body but still nicely muscled. Anyway, all that leanness looked particularly good in the well-tailored dark suits that were the Bureau's de facto uniform. He was still wearing the one he'd taken her to dinner in, as a matter of fact. His white shirt still looked fresh. His red tie was snugly in place.

Michael was right, Charlie decided as she smiled back at Tony: she did have a serious screw loose. This was the guy who should be making her heart go pitter-pat. This was the guy whose arms she should be wanting to walk into, whose mouth she should be wanting to kiss, who she should be wanting to fall into bed with. This guy liked her, more than liked her, wanted to sleep with her, wanted to have a relationship. This decent, gainfully employed, law-abiding, honorable, kind, very handsome, and *alive* man had happily ever after written all over him.

He had been clasping her hand just a couple of beats too long. Still smiling at him, she gently disengaged.

"I'm glad you're here," she said, and his smile widened.

Charlie was suddenly burningly conscious of the weight of Michael's gaze.

Sliding a sideways glance his way, she encountered blue eyes gone stony gray, a hard mouth, a granite jawline. His expression—no, his whole body—radiated frustrated, barely controlled tension. He made her think of a wild animal, a big one, a predator, that had suddenly been made aware of its situation, aware that it was trapped hopelessly and forever in an impossible-to-escape cage.

Charlie's heart unexpectedly stuttered. Her mouth went dry. She felt as if she was falling, the sensation as unmistakable as if she'd stepped into an elevator and dead-dropped three floors. The feeling wasn't good, and it certainly wasn't welcome, but there it was.

How Michael felt mattered to her.

As epiphanies went, that one kind of blew.

Talk about smart women, foolish choices, she thought, mentally aiming a swift kick at her own posterior. Lately she was practically its poster child.

"Long time no see, Dr. Stone," Kaminsky greeted her. Twenty-nine-year-old Kaminsky was small and curvy, with shiny, chin-length black hair that turned under on the ends and an olive complexion.

Pretty in an exotic kind of way, she favored snug, above-the-knee skirt suits like the pale gray one she was currently wearing and, because she was only five-two and sensitive about it, sky-high stilettos. Since Charlie had last seen Kaminsky only a few hours before, when their plane had touched down at the Lonesome Pine Airport to drop Charlie off in Big Stone Gap, and Kaminsky and Crane had been left behind to take a commercial flight to their home base of Quantico while Tony had gone with Charlie to take her to what he had described to them as a "thank-you" dinner, Kaminsky's sarcasm was not really a surprise. "Bartoli says you've managed to attract *another* serial killer. How is that even possible?"

"The Gingerbread Man, no less," Crane added on a note of what almost sounded like glee. In the classic combination known to any woman who frequented bars or other places where men tended to hang out, he was, at thirty-two, the geek to Tony's hottie. Five-ten and slightly built, with black-framed glasses dominating a thin, sharp-featured face topped by a halo of short brown curls, he was more clumsy-puppy cute than handsome. His bright blue eyes were alive with interest as he looked at Charlie. "He's somebody we sure would like to catch. In a little more than two years he's taken out fourteen people."

"I think that as of tonight the number is probably sixteen," Charlie said. "Jenna McDaniels said there were two other girls with her and they are dead. She told me their names were Raylene—" She stopped, frowned. "Oh, God, I'm drawing a blank here. I can't remember that girl's last name."

"Raylene Witt and Laura Peters," Agent Flynn finished for her. "I just got a call from our agents at the hospital who've been talking to Ms. McDaniels. She gave us the names. That's who we're looking for now."

"Is Jenna's mother with her yet?" Whatever Jenna had or had not done, Charlie hated to think of her being alone. She knew what the girl was going through: the sense of being caught up in a nightmare, the ever-present fear, the grief. She knew, because she had lived it herself. "Do you know?"

"I don't." Flynn shook his head. "Next time I talk to our guys I'll check."

Charlie nodded thanks.

"The McDaniels girl has been all over the news the last couple days, but I haven't seen anything about the other two," Sager said. "I didn't even realize there were two more young women gone missing."

"I'm not sure the other two have even been reported," Flynn said. "We haven't found anything on them. At this point, we're not even one hundred percent certain that they exist, to tell you the truth, or if they do that they're victims. They may be Ms. McDaniels' hallucinations, for example. Or her lies. I don't necessarily think that's the case, but I've learned to keep an open mind."

"So has Ms. McDaniels given a statement?" Tony asked, and Flynn shook his head.

"We've got guys at the hospital waiting to take it as soon as she's up to talking to them. As of right now, though, it hasn't happened."

"Kaminsky, when there's a statement from Ms. McDaniels, I want you to get on it. Flynn, if you'd make sure Kaminsky gets a copy as soon as it's available, I'd appreciate it. Anything that can help us locate those two girls, we need to know as soon as possible. The rest can wait for tomorrow." Tony looked at the assembled group. "Right now, our top priority has to be to find those other girls. Until we have proof that they're dead or don't exist, we can't just assume it. For all we know, one or both of them could still be at this guy's mercy, or lying out in the rain somewhere dying."

There were nods of agreement all around. Charlie didn't mention that she already had been furnished with proof positive that at least one of the girls was real, but also dead. From the background check he had done on her when he had first wanted her to come work with his team in their race to find the Boardwalk Killer, Tony knew that she had what he called "some psychic ability." She had even admitted to him that sometimes she saw the spirits of the dead, and he had used information that she had gleaned from her ghostly encounters to help solve the previous case.

Not that he knew anything like the full extent of what she routinely experienced. And he certainly didn't know a thing about Michael. No one did, and however the whole mess worked out, no one was ever going to.

She had her career to think about. Her personal life, too.

No real worries there, though: even if she flat-out told everyone she met about Michael, about the things she saw, nobody was going to believe her. Oh, they might pretend to, they might even kinda, sorta, halfway buy into it like Tony sometimes seemed to, but in the end they couldn't know, not for certain, and what they would carry away with them when they thought about her was something on the order of "headcase." That she knew from painful experience.

"Even if they're up the mountain, finding them in the dark and rain isn't going to be easy. That trail back there has dozens of branches, and the girls might not even be on any kind of trail." Sager looked at Sheriff Peel. "You get ahold of Jerry Ferrell?"

"I did," Sheriff Peel said. "He's on the way, him and the dogs."

"If they're up there, Jerry and his dogs'll find them." Sager addressed that remark to Tony. "Ferrell has the best damned tracking dogs in the state. We've got equipment coming to help us recover any bodies we might find, too."

"Let's hope we don't need it, but it's best to be prepared in case we do." Tony looked at Charlie. "So while we wait, why don't you tell us what happened, from the beginning?"

Charlie once again recounted the whole story (judiciously edited to leave out the phantom girl and, of course, Michael) from the time Jenna had banged on her kitchen door. Tony and the other newcomers examined the dent in the back door, as well as the knife and the *You can't catch me* message the Gingerbread Man had left, and Tony had Crane make arrangements to have the latter two sent on to the FBI lab for analysis on an expedited basis. After that, everybody in the room talked logistics as they discussed (argued about) the best way to mount a search and rescue or retrieval operation up a muddy, treacherous mountainside in the middle of the night in the pouring rain.

Leaving them to it, Charlie ran upstairs to change into a tee, jeans, and sneakers for the trek up the mountain. That's where she was when the dogs came. Although their arrival was almost certainly announced by some other method downstairs, Charlie was clued in by the sudden onset of a dolorous howling right outside her house.

"Your boyfriend had a lick of sense, he wouldn't let you go with them," Michael said sourly. Since she had forbidden him to enter the bathroom, where she was changing, his voice came to her through the closed bathroom door.

"I have to go with them." Charlie discovered that she almost welcomed the heretofore annoying boyfriend reference because it meant that Michael was starting to get back to normal. The silent and brooding presence who had followed her upstairs had been slightly unnerving. She was still pulling her hair back into a low ponytail as she emerged from the bathroom to find him stretched full length on her bed. His head was planted on one of her lace-trimmed pillows, his arms were folded behind it, and his booted feet were crossed at the ankle and resting on her snowy white coverlet.

Ghost boots, Charlie reminded herself, and limited her response to a disapproving glance along the length of his powerful body. The thing was, she had decorated her house to suit the needs of a single, childless woman whose workaday life was generally spent within the dull gray walls of a prison. It was light, airy, and, yes, feminine, with delicate, expensive fabrics and lots of pale colors and white.

He was entirely too masculine for it.

His eyes followed her as she walked across the bedroom, toward the door. "That's just plain stupid. You know that? You're not a cop. You're not a tracker. You're not part of a search and rescue team. It's pitch black out there and it's raining and muddy and it's a damned mountain and there's a psycho killer on the loose who's made himself your new pen pal. What part of that makes it smart for you to go with them?"

"If you say something about me having a death wish again I'll murder you." She said it lightly, deliberately, hoping to provoke a smile in return. He hadn't smiled, not once, since setting eyes on the watch.

He still didn't smile, exactly, but the quick upward quirk of one side of his lips was a start. "Too late."

Finishing with her ponytail, Charlie paused at the foot of the bed to look at him. It was a queen-sized bed, and she had always thought that it was huge. Now, with his big body taking up one whole side, it looked surprisingly small. Her hands curled around the cool smooth brass of the footboard as she tried to make him understand. "The one thing I can bring to this investigation that nobody else can is that I can sometimes see the dead. If the second girl is dead, and her spirit is still hanging around up there somewhere, I might be able to talk to her. And she might be able to tell me something we can't get any other way. Something that will help us catch this monster."

"Catching this monster isn't your job."

"I have to help if I can."

"No, you don't. Not if helping puts you at risk. And it does."

So much for trying to get Michael to see things from her point of view. Although why she cared if he did she didn't know. He was the intrusion into *her* life. Intrusions did not get to call the shots. They didn't even get a vote.

Enough already.

"I'm going. End of discussion." She headed for the door.

"You think I don't know that?" There was disgust in his voice as he swung his feet to the floor, stood up, and came after her. She had opened the door and was stepping out into the hall when he added, "Nice ass in those jeans, by the way."

CHAPTER EIGHT

Thanks to Jerry Ferrell's hounds, it took the search party not quite an hour to locate the bodies. There were two of them, floating in a water-filled, abandoned mine shaft some three quarters of the way up the mountain, about a mile and a half off the path where Charlie ran every day. Fortunately, by the time they got there the rain had slowed to little more than intermittent sprinkles. But the cloud cover remained, obscuring the moon, making the night almost as black when they stepped out into the open area around the mine shaft as it had been under the thick canopy of trees. So black that, without flashlights, they wouldn't have been able to see the ground beneath their feet.

"That's something you hate to see," Sheriff Peel said as half a dozen klieg lights that had been hooked to a generator powered on at once, illuminating the site so that there was no longer any hope of a mistake. The pale objects that could be glimpsed just beneath the shining black surface of the water were not the white bellies of dead fish, or quartz-laced rocks, or any of the dozens of other faintly luminescent things that they could have been. They were the bare and swollen arms and legs of the corpses that drifted facedown in a lazy rotation of death.

The dead bodies of two girls in shorts and T-shirts, with long dark hair floating around them, looking like grotesque lily pads in some horrible inky pond.

The sight of the bodies made Charlie feel sick at heart. It made her want to weep.

Poor girls, went the refrain that kept running through her mind. She wondered if, when the sun had risen that morning, they had guessed this would be their last day alive.

"Life's a bitch," Michael said from behind her. "No point in getting all teary-eyed about it."

A little annoyed because she was absolutely sure that she was *not* getting (outwardly anyway) all teary-eyed about it, she was startled by his apparent ability to read her mind. Charlie shot him a killing glare.

A corner of his mouth quirked up in response. Having apparently recovered from his earlier bout of the dismals—at least, if he was still upset, she couldn't tell—he was standing right beside her, his big body protectively close. Although nothing short of torture would have gotten her to admit it, Charlie was glad he was there. The hiss of the wind moving through the towering trees that crowded close around the clearing, the ageless quality of the absolute darkness beyond the reach of the klieg lights, the swampy scent of the place, which she had smelled before on Jenna, were combining to slightly creep her out.

Given what he was, Michael was an unlikely antidote for a developing case of the heebie-jeebies, but for her he was.

"Everybody keep to the edge of the clearing. Nontechnical personnel, stay out of the way. Let's try to preserve this crime scene as much as possible so we can get a good look at it when the sun comes up." Tony called instructions from the side of the pit. Like the rest of the agents, he had traded his sport coat for an FBI windbreaker, and the big white letters made him easier to keep track of in the confusion than he otherwise would have been. Charlie watched as he turned to speak to a body retrieval crew in blue jumpsuits who were standing by, presumably until the photographers were finished taking pictures. Off to one side, a police department sketch artist was looking at the pit as she drew. Charlie assumed she was making a rough drawing of the bodies and their position in the crime scene. Two cops were setting tall tent stakes and stringing yellow crime scene tape from them around the edge of the clearing, leaving only a narrow pathway between it and the trees.

"Boss, I think I've found our point of egress," Crane yelled, and Tony turned away from the pit to head toward him. Crane was on an upward slope at the right side of the clearing; since he was beyond the reach of the klieg lights Charlie could only locate him by his voice and the round glow of his flashlight. A moment later all she could see of Tony, too, was his flashlight. Several other flashlights converged on the spot, but it was too dark for Charlie to identify any of the people holding them.

"Being dead doesn't have a whole lot of good points, but one of them is not having to worry about mosquitoes," Michael said. "Just so you know, there's one on your arm. I'd smack it for you, but that ain't happening."

Charlie had already slapped at a good half a dozen. After a hasty glance down, she slapped again.

"Damned mosquitoes," Sheriff Peel said. "Perfect breeding conditions for them, though. All this standing water, and then it's been hot as Hades."

The rain should have cooled things off. It hadn't. The day—typical for late August—had been baking hot, and even in these, the small hours of the morning, the humidity made the air feel almost too thick to breathe. There were two water-filled pits on the site, although as far as anyone could tell only one held bodies. Steam rose up from the surface of the water in both pits, from the piled shale and mossy rocks around the edge of the clearing, from the thick mulch beneath the huge pines and oaks and beeches, from the flat grassy area where Charlie (and Michael) stood with Sheriff Peel and Ken, who were at the bottom of the law enforcement food chain on this investigation and thus had nothing to do at this point, and Jerry Ferrell and his dogs, whose part was played out. The dogs, big, loose-limbed, floppy-eared bloodhounds, lay panting on the ground at Ferrell's feet. They cast occasional suspicious looks at Michael, whom Charlie was almost certain they could see, but having been ordered by their handler to lie down and be quiet that's what they did.

"You don't think I ought to be getting on home to Debbie and the kids, do you?" Ken asked the sheriff uneasily as he, too, slapped at a mosquito. "Half the time, she doesn't even lock the doors."

"I were you, I'd wait for the rest of us," Sheriff Peel said. "No telling if the guy who did this is still on the mountain. And starting tomorrow, you make sure Debbie locks them doors."

"If you've finished with your pictures, I'd like to start getting the bodies out of the water now," Frank Cramer, the medical examiner, called to the police photographers. He was an older guy to whom Charlie had been introduced shortly after he'd arrived on the scene.

Tony and Crane were once again back within the glare of the klieg lights, Charlie saw. Tony was standing next to the ME looking down into the pit with the bodies, while Crane was now videotaping everything, with the purpose, Charlie knew, of allowing the team to play the footage over and over again in an exhaustive search for clues. Even as she looked at him, Crane panned the camera over her and the men she was standing with, then moved on to the cops and firefighters and coroner's assistants and the rest of what seemed like a cast of thousands currently milling around on the sidelines. Charlie knew what he was doing: watch the watchers was one of Tony's maxims. Sometimes it yielded surprisingly fruitful results.

Because a lot of times a killer would show up at a crime scene to drink in the efforts of law enforcement to find him. This killer in particular was likely to still be somewhere in the vicinity, Charlie knew. He would take pleasure in observing everything that went on in the aftermath of what he had done.

It was part of the power trip he was on.

One of the hounds—Mabel, Charlie thought her name was; the other one was Max—picked up her head and stared intently at the far side of the pit. Charlie followed her gaze curiously. What she saw when she did had her drawing in a sharp breath.

"You okay?" Ken asked.

"Damned mosquitoes," Charlie echoed Sheriff Peel, and gave her arm another slap.

But mosquitoes weren't what had caused her reaction. On the other side of the pit, just beyond the bright circle cast by the klieg lights, a girl sat with her knees drawn up to her chin, her arms wrapped around her legs, and her head bent and resting on her knees. A girl with long, curly dark hair that spilled around her body to almost brush the flat shelf of rock she was sitting on. A girl with bare feet, and bare legs beneath mid-thigh-length shorts and slender bare arms emerging from a dark-colored T-shirt. A girl who looked to be soaking wet, with water streaming from her body.

A girl who hadn't been there the last time Charlie had glanced that way.

A dead girl. The spirit of one of the two girls whose bodies were still floating in the pit.

Charlie felt her heartbeat speed up.

She looked fixedly at the girl, saw her shoulders heave, and guessed that the spirit was crying.

Every muscle in Charlie's body tensed.

I hate this.

But finding out what she could from the newly deceased victims was the primary reason she had come. If she had only wanted to look over the crime scene, she could have waited until daylight. Or she could have looked at pictures. There had been no guarantee that the remaining girl's spirit would be here, of course, but if she was still anywhere on earth at all, the place where she had been killed was the most likely for her to be found.

And here she was.

For a moment there, the small victory almost made Charlie feel good. Then the tragedy of what she was seeing reasserted itself, and her throat tightened.

All I can do for her is help find who did this.

"Excuse me, I'm going to go have a word with Agent Kaminsky." Charlie chose that excuse because Kaminsky, heels and skirt suit ditched in favor of an FBI windbreaker along with black pants and sneakers, which she had retrieved from her luggage when she'd changed at Charlie's house before tackling the mountain, had just walked briskly past. Small as Kaminsky was in flat shoes, she still looked formidable with a shovel in her hands and not so much as a sideways glance to spare for anyone. Speculating on what Kaminsky might do with that shovel was a waste of effort, so Charlie gave up on it almost at once. Instead she followed in Kaminsky's wake without the least intention of catching up, skirting the dogs, dodging the fluid clusters of law enforcement types who were presumably engaged in one evidence-gathering activity or another, keeping to the shadowy edges of the clearing as she headed toward the crying girl.

"You see her, too, huh?" Michael was right behind her. His voice had a resigned quality to it. "I figured."

Where they were, the darkness was obscuring enough that a quick nod in reply wasn't going to work. Cops, deputies, FBI agents, rescue workers, coroner's assistants, technicians—the clearing was swarming with official types. A steady stream of foot traffic moved continuously around the periphery as people went where they needed to go while trying to follow Tony's directive to stay out of the crime scene as much as possible. But most of them were busy, doing their jobs, bustling from place to place. As far as she could tell, no one was paying any particular attention to her.

So she took a chance.

"I see her," Charlie admitted, keeping her voice low. "I'm going to try to talk to her."

"You know, I kind of guessed that when you started heading this way. Got your barf bag with you?"

That bit of sarcasm earned him a glower. "Shut up, okay? I'm talking to her, and that's the end of the discussion."

"Go for it. Knock yourself out."

"Stay out of it," Charlie warned, his blunt treatment of the other girl's spirit still fresh in her mind. Then she had a corollary thought: "Unless I need you."

"Try not to need me. Weeping women ain't exactly my thing."

"So get over it already. Weren't you the one who just said life's a bitch?"

"Then I guess it's a good thing I don't have to worry about it anymore, right?"

At that, Charlie made an exasperated sound under her breath and abandoned the conversation. Cool and heavy, his too-big watch had slid down her arm to lodge against her hand, and with exasperation she shoved it back up almost to her elbow, reflecting that of course any possession of his would be as annoying as he was. Then it hit her: *Maybe he really* isn't *a serial killer. Maybe he actually* is *innocent, and this watch is proof.* Before she could even start to get all excited about that, a cool sprinkle of water distracted her as she passed too close beneath an overhanging evergreen branch and dislodged a shower of droplets that ran down her neck, making her flinch. In front of her, the long shadows cast by the trees seemed to twist in upon themselves like crooked, arthritic fingers. The smell of the woods—pine and moss and wet earth—was strong enough to supplant what was now the background note of the swampy scent of the water in the pit. Snatches of conversation rose and fell around her, their individual threads more discernible than before. The steady hum of the generator, the clank of metal on rock as a boat hook attached to a chain was readied for the removal of the bodies, the rustle of bright blue body bags being laid out by the side of the pit, filled her ears. The dead girl now looked almost more vivid than the living people on the scene. Charlie's senses had heightened. It sometimes happened when she was in the close vicinity of the newly dead. She cast a quick, consuming look all around to try to make certain she wasn't being observed. As far as she could tell, no one was paying the least attention to her. Still, the sensation she had of being watched could have come from anywhere, or nowhere, like her imagination. It could be the Gingerbread Man, who might be somewhere keeping an eye on the kill site. But she saw no one looking in her direction, and at the moment that's all she had to go by. Concentrating on the spirit, who was only a few yards away now, Charlie did her best to block everything else out.

As she approached she could hear the girl crying. The sound tore at Charlie's heart.

"I'm here to help you," Charlie told her, positioning herself so that her back was turned to most of the people in the clearing as she stopped a few steps from the edge of the rock shelf the girl was sitting on. She ignored the sudden queasiness that attacked her stomach like clockwork. She had no intention of letting anyone—read Michael— know about it unless and until it got to the point where she couldn't hide it anymore. Until then, she would power through and hope for the best. Thanks to the klieg lights, it wasn't entirely dark where she stood, but the tangled shadows were thick enough to obscure a lot of detail. Another uneasy glance around found tiny pairs of glowing orbs shining among the trees: animal eyes, Charlie identified them even as she shivered. At least they accounted for the eerie feeling she had that she was being intently watched. Without looking up, the girl continued to sob pitifully. The sound made Charlie feel sick at heart. "Are you Laura? Or Raylene?"

The girl cried on as if she hadn't heard.

Michael made a rough sound under his breath. He was no longer behind Charlie. Instead, he had moved to her left and slightly in front of her, not blocking her view of the girl but clearly positioning himself to step in between them if the need should arise. Noticing that with impatience, Charlie made a mental note to give him, the first chance she got, a quick overview of the rules covering ghosts on the ground.

"Hell, somebody's beat her to death," Michael said. His face had tightened. His position allowed him to view the girl from a different angle, and it was apparent that what he was seeing was bad. Even as Charlie instinctively craned her neck to look, Michael shook his head at her. "You don't want to see this."

Charlie shot him a look. This whole Protective-R-Us thing he had going on was actually kind of cute, but it was also annoying and, given who and what he was, ridiculous.

"Believe me, I've seen worse." Her response was tart. Charlie then got an eyeful of what he was trying to keep her from seeing and immediately wished she hadn't.

The back of the girl's head was bashed in. Crushed like an egg. Dark clots of blood matted her hair to the wound. More blood made the strands around the wound clump together. Shattered remnants of her skull were embedded in gelatinous brain matter. Part of the brain itself hung out of the hole, looking like a slimy lump of congealed oatmeal, dripping blood mixed with a milky liquid Charlie could only surmise was brain fluid.

It was, in a word, gruesome.

Charlie's stomach, which had been fighting the good fight against nausea so that she had been registering only mild gastric distress, started to churn.

"Told you not to look," Michael said, and Charlie guessed that she must have blanched.

"Hello?" The girl looked up suddenly, hopefully, her eyes going straight to Michael. Blinking, she peered at him as if trying to get him into focus. The light hit the tears rolling down her face so that they made glistening tracks along her cheeks. She was a pretty girl, twenty-ish, small and slender, with big dark eyes currently welling with tears and delicate features framed by masses of wet black curls. As she blinked at Michael, her breath caught on a shuddering sob. From her expression it was clear that, if she hadn't been able to see him before, she could see him now. Her voice took on an urgent note. "Who are you? Do you know what's happened?"

She scrambled to her feet as she spoke: she was maybe five foot two. More tears spilled from her eyes. Taking first one and then another hesitant step toward Michael, as if she wasn't quite sure she was actually seeing him, she then whispered, "Oh, thank goodness!" and broke into a run. An instant later she threw herself against him, wrapping her arms around his waist as she started to cry again in earnest. Michael looked down at her with as much alarm as if he had just been grabbed by a ghost—and he wasn't one himself.

Well, the ins and outs of finding himself among the dead were new to him. He was still adjusting.

"Yo," he said, his eyes sliding Charlie's way. Sobbing loudly, the girl buried her face in the front of his white T-shirt and clung. His hard, handsome face turned grim as he looked down at her shattered head. Seeing how small the girl looked in comparison to him— the top of her head didn't even begin to reach his broad shoulders, and a whole lot of wide chest was visible on either side of her— Charlie registered again in passing how tall and muscular he truly was. Add his surfer God good looks to the mix and, in life, he must have had women hanging off him like Christmas tree ornaments. Except as part of appraising his qualities as a predator, it wasn't something she'd really thought about before, but . . . now she did. She also registered something else: a tiny niggle of—what? Aware-ness, that was it. Seeing Michael with a woman was new, and what she was feeling was simply herself becoming aware of the newness of it.

It was different, that was all. And that's why she was feeling the niggle.

"So do something already," he said, glancing at Charlie again.

"Don't talk to me. She doesn't know I'm here," Charlie instructed. "I want you to talk to *her*. Tell her you're here to help."

Lips tightening, he transferred his attention back to the weeping girl and gave her a couple of clumsy-looking pats on the back.

"Don't worry, I'm here to help," he said.

"Good job," Charlie encouraged him, and in return received a look that she roughly interpreted as meaning something on the order of *eat dirt*. The niggle that was her awareness of him with a woman in his arms subsided—he couldn't have looked more uncomfortable if a python were twining itself around him—and Charlie was glad to dismiss it as the nothing it had been. She would have found his obvious unease with his situation almost amusing if the girl's distress hadn't been so heartrending. "You're doing great."

"Please." The girl's voice trembled as she looked up at him. "I don't know where I am. I—I think I'm lost. Can you help me?"

It was obvious to Charlie that, as was the case with many new spirits, she had no idea she was dead. She also was no longer able to experience the world of the living. The girl could see only Michael. The people around her—Charlie, law enforcement, rescue workers, everyone on the scene—were invisible to her, as were the details of her surroundings. Why? Because she was dead and they were not: each existed in a different plane. Here in this moment, in this place, for this dead girl, only Michael existed.

"Don't come right out and tell her she's dead," Charlie said quickly to Michael as he looked like he was getting ready to do just that. She had a lively fear that he was about to be as forthright with this girl as he had been with the one in her house. "Ask her her name."

Michael sent Charlie another of those narrow-eyed *this sucks* flickers before looking down at the girl again.

"Everything's okay," he told her, rather gingerly putting an arm around her shoulders as, with both arms still wrapped around his waist, she looked beseechingly up into his face. Charlie had to admit that she was impressed by how reassuring he was actually being. "My name's Michael. What's your name?"

"L-Laura. Laura Peters." The girl looked wildly all around. "Where are we? What's happened?"

"Ask her what she remembers," Charlie instructed, and Michael did.

"Oh. Oh, oh." Laura's expression changed dramatically. Pushing away from him, looking all around, she suddenly started gasping. "I'm drowning. The water—the water's pouring in. I can't—they said kick your feet, and move your arms like this." She mimed trying to breaststroke. "They're trying to help me. But I'm sinking—" She started to cough violently. "I can't swim! I can't swim!"

"You don't have to be afraid. You're safe now," Michael told her. Shaking her head, Laura looked up at him with blind terror, then sank down on her haunches and covered her face with her hands as she burst into tears again. With a glinting look at Charlie, Michael crouched beside her.

"Ask her who tried to help her swim," Charlie directed.

"Laura. Can you tell me who tried to help you swim?" In contrast to his face, which could have been carved from stone, Michael's voice was soft and steady.

Her hands dropped away from her face. Her expression was agitated as she looked at him. "The other girls. They can swim. They tried to help me, but I can't. I can't swim! My head keeps going under and—" She broke off, gasping and gagging as if she was choking. "There's a man. I'm afraid of him. He's drowning us. He wants us to—he wants us to— The water's pouring in. Oh, no! Oh! Oh!"

"You're all right," Michael told her swiftly, and when she dropped her head and burst into tears again his arm went around her once more.

"Ask her about the man. Can she describe him?"

Encountering his gaze, Charlie was surprised at the anger in his eyes.

"Did you see the man, Laura? What did he look like?" Michael's tone as he shifted his attention back to the girl was, in contrast, very gentle.

Laura shivered violently. "Death. He looks like death. All in black—his face, it's white. Horrible white. Oh, no, *please*. He's going to kill me—*why?* I was in the bar and then . . ." Closing her eyes, she gave a piteous-sounding whimper.

"What bar?" Charlie prompted. Michael, face taut, repeated the question.

Laura's eyes were still closed. "Omar's. I didn't win. I—I left, and then—there was a van." She moaned, and Michael's arm tightened around her.

Charlie knew the signs. The spirit was growing increasingly distressed. They needed to get as much information out of her as they could as quickly as they could. Charlie prompted Michael: "What did the van look like? Color, make, model?"

He said, "What did the van look like, Laura? What color was it? Do you remember the make or model?"

"I don't know. I don't know! It was blue, I think. Or maybe gray. Old. It—it smelled bad. Like fish."

Charlie said, "Does she remember anything else about the van? Or the driver?"

Michael asked.

"I heard—a phone call. Ben. *I can't talk right now, Ben,* is what he said. I tried to scream but I couldn't. That's all I remember. Oh, won't you please help me? Please! I just want to go home! Can't you please take me home?" Laura started to sob again, while Michael shot Charlie a seething look and rubbed the girl's shoulder comfortingly.

"Ask her: where is Omar's?" Charlie said, but before he could, Laura shook free of Michael's arm and jumped to her feet, glancing behind her in shock as she clutched the sides of her head with both hands. "No! That hurts! Oh! Jen—Raylene—something hit me in the head! Stop! It hurts! It hurts!" By the end, she had whirled around to bat at an unseen assailant even as Michael, having straightened to his full height beside her, put his hands on her shoulders to try to calm her down.

"Laura . . ."

"No, no, no!" She looked at him with abject fear in her eyes. *"They're killing me."*

Her voice rose to a screech on that last. Then, abruptly, her face turned up toward the lightless night sky as if she heard or saw something there that Charlie at least could not. Laura's eyes widened. She shook from head to toe.

"Laura. It's okay." Michael's voice sounded strained.

"There's Kylie," Laura moaned. "And Sara. Oh, my God, where am I?"

CHAPTER NINE

In the next instant Laura dissolved into nothingness beneath Michael's hands.

"Holy fucking hell," Michael said.

"What?" Charlie demanded. It was obvious that Michael was seeing—had seen—something that she had not.

"Two little girls came down out of the fucking sky. Two little girls who were covered with blood."

"Laura must have known them. Something bad must have happened to them."

"Yeah, I gathered that." The look he turned on Charlie was grim. "Jesus Christ, don't you ever see any happy dead people? You know, old folks who were ready to go or somebody who was so sick death was a release? Somebody like that?"

"No." Charlie's response was flat. Her stomach continued to churn, but her senses were getting back to normal. The hypersensitivity was going, and that meant the spirit(s) were gone, too. Well, present company excepted. She fought to get the nausea under control.

I will not throw up.

"No wonder you're twisted," Michael said.

"Twisted?" Charlie began indignantly, only to jump sky-high as someone behind her asked, "What's twisted?"

Tony. Charlie recognized his voice even before Michael had finished with his sardonic, "Oh, yay, it's Dudley Do-Right," even before she had finished whirling around to confront the newcomer. The sight of Tony was instantly steadying: he looked so normal, so *real.* So totally nice and uncomplicated: a genuine good guy. Exactly what she needed in her life, in fact.

Instantly she vowed to try harder where he was concerned.

"Uh—what was done to these poor victims," she said. Luckily, thinking fast on her feet was something she was getting really good at. "It's twisted, is all."

"It is that," Tony agreed, while Michael said, "Just so you know, every time you tell a lie you stick out that pretty pink tongue of yours. Only a little bit, like you're getting ready to wet your lips. I caught on to it while you were still doing the starched-up-shrink thing back at the Ridge. It's sexy as all get-out, but it's a dead tell."

Charlie's reaction to that was to clamp her lips together. Realizing what she had done, she barely managed to not shoot the thorn in her side a dirty look. Instead, with what she considered commendable control, she ignored him in favor of saying to Tony: "So how's it going?"

Okay, the question was inane. It was the best she could do with Michael mock-sexily wetting his lips at her.

Tony appeared to notice nothing amiss. "We've got the bodies, which should give us time and cause of death. Including the knife that was left in your kitchen, we've got a variety of possible murder weapons. The rain's made everything else problematic. It's going to be hard to tell what we have that's usable until the sun comes up and everything dries out."

"Try telling him about Laura," Michael said. "Go on, I want to hear this."

It took effort, but Charlie managed to keep her expression neutral. Curling a hand around Tony's arm, which felt strong and firm through the slick windbreaker, she tugged, towing him with her as she walked determinedly away from the font of perpetual annoyance.

Mindful of the possibility that her stomach might disgrace her at any second, she headed for a relatively secluded section of the site, away from the klieg lights. But the increasing darkness made her skin crawl, and she was suddenly thankful for Tony's solid presence. Unlike Michael—who was, of course, dogging her every footstep—Tony could actually offer something in the way of physical protection. Plus, he had a gun.

Charlie said, "I—uh—actually have some information that might help the investigation."

Tony lifted his eyebrows at her. "Oh, yeah?"

"Laura Peters was at a bar called Omar's right before the Ginger-bread Man got hold of her. She was put into an old blue or gray van that smelled like fish. The man who took her spoke to someone named Ben on the phone." Even as Charlie recited the details that Laura had passed on to Michael, her stomach roiled. Taking a deep breath, she swallowed hard in an effort to make the sudden upsurge of nausea go away.

Michael said, "You left out the part where he looked like Skele-tor. You know, all in black with a white face."

Swallowing hard, Charlie stopped walking as she willed her stom-ach to settle. Tony stopped, too, to look down at her with a frown.

She said, "The man who took Laura Peters—the Gingerbread Man, unless he has an accomplice, which I don't think he does—was dressed all in black. His face appeared very white. Like death."

"There you go," Michael said. "That's what she said."

"How do you know all that?" Tony's eyes were intent on her face. Then they flickered, and he frowned. "You have one of your psychic experiences back there?"

"A psychic experience? Is that what he calls them?" Michael stopped on her other side.

"Yes," Charlie said to both of them. Defiantly.

Michael grimaced. "From what I've seen, what you go through is more like full-on *American Horror Story*. You planning on keeping Dudley around, you probably ought to tell him how bad it gets."

"Okay," Tony said at the same time. He had pulled out his cell phone, and was busy pecking at its virtual keyboard. She assumed he was making a note of what she had told him, or perhaps texting or e-mailing it, although whether or not there was cell service up here on the mountain was questionable. Finishing, he looked at her. "You sure of your information?"

Charlie nodded, smiling at Tony gratefully because dealing with him was just so damned easy. Then, since she really was feeling sick as a dog, she turned her back on both of them to head for a nearby rock, where she abruptly sat down.

"Here we go again," Michael said grimly. "For God's sake, put your head between your knees. You look like you're about ready to pass out."

Tony, having also followed her, stopped on her other side to say, "You've gone a little pale. Are you all right?"

Michael snorted. "A little pale? You're white as a fucking ghost—no, whiter, if the ones I've seen are anything to judge by. If you need to barf, do it. Maybe your boyfriend will start getting a clue."

It took a moment's worth of deep breathing before Charlie could say anything at all. When she did, she ignored the irate-looking ghost looming over her in favor of smiling at Tony, who stood a few feet away watching her with concern. "It's nothing. I . . . well, get a little nauseated sometimes when I have these psychic experiences. If I sit here for a minute, it'll pass."

Michael said, "That's right, babe. Sugarcoat it," while Tony said, "Take all the time you need."

Charlie fought for control, both of her stomach and her temper. She was starting to feel like a Ping-Pong ball bouncing between the two of them, which, given the state of her stomach, was not good. The look she wanted to direct at Michael would be a waste of a good glare—glaring at him didn't seem to abash him one iota—and might be misinterpreted by Tony. Likewise, snapping something on the order of *stick it where the sun don't shine* was subject to misinterpretation by the only other living human being within earshot, who was not its intended target. Glancing around in hopes of a distraction, Charlie spotted the body that was at that moment being dragged from the pit by a boat hook and then, when it was close enough, by two of the coroner's assistants, who grabbed it under the armpits with their gloved hands and hauled it, streaming water, up on the rocks.

Having so recently seen Laura Peters, she was able to identify this body as belonging to Raylene Witt: the phantom girl with the rock from her house.

Funnily enough, the sight of an actual corpse didn't make her sick. It was only the close proximity of spirits that did that. What seeing that poor, limp corpse did was fill her with sorrow. And grief. And a deep and corrosive fear.

What was it about her and violent death anyway? Was it drawn to her, in some sort of hideous karma? Secretly, almost shamefully, Charlie realized that what bothered her most about the spirits she saw was her near conviction that one day, she, too, would come to just such a horrible, violent end.

The prospect made her shiver.

"You okay?" Michael frowned down at her.

"Better?" Tony asked at almost the same time.

Clearly Michael at least had seen that unmistakable sign of her distress.

Get it together.

"Yes," she said firmly.

Out of the corner of her eye, she saw Raylene Witt's corpse being zipped into a body bag. This time she did not shiver.

Instead she focused on staying strong.

Deep breath.

"What I can't understand is how the Gingerbread Man managed to get all three of the victims up here," she said, and was proud of how coolly professional she sounded. Her stomach still churned, but she was determined not to give in to it—or to the abiding fear that she had discovered curling like a parasite deep in her psyche. "Even if he brought them one at a time, it's a long way up the mountain. I don't think he can have carried them, and if he made them walk—" She considered Laura's failure to relate anything about what was sure to have been a harrowing journey. "Well, I don't think he did that."

"He didn't walk 'em. Too hard to control them over that kind of distance," Michael said, which earned him a sharp glance as Charlie instantly wondered how he would know something like that. Clearly (and correctly) interpreting that look to mean that she was once again picturing him as the serial killer she'd actually begun harboring doubts that he was, his mouth twisted.

"I was a *marine,*" Michael said. "Sometimes we took prisoners."

Considering that, she decided it made sense. Anyway, if she remembered the details correctly, at least the last woman he was supposed to have murdered had been killed in her bed. No death march required.

Okay, then.

"As a matter of fact, we just located an old mining road that passes to within about a quarter of a mile south of here," Tony said. "I'm betting that's what he used to get the victims in place. The ME has a truck coming up it right now to transport the bodies back down, which is why I came looking for you: I think you ought to ride down with his team, then grab a few hours' sleep. I'm depending on your expertise to help us tomorrow. I'll send Kaminsky with you, of course."

Although she couldn't argue about the value of sleep, Charlie looked at him with a gathering frown. "I don't need Kaminsky to babysit me."

"Oh, yes, you do," Michael said. "Sugar Buns kicks butt and takes names. She also carries a gun."

That nickname for Kaminsky earned him a glinting look. *Sugar Buns* was demeaning and disrespectful, and she didn't like it. He knew how she felt about it, which was probably exactly why he had used it. In fact, the quick quirk of his lips with which he responded to her look confirmed it: Michael was being deliberately annoying again.

"Given that the perp knows who you are and is specifically reaching out to you, I feel it's best that you have protection." Clearly recognizing the resistance in her face, Tony smiled coaxingly at her as he spoke. She really did like the way his eyes crinkled when he smiled like that. Unlike the mocking glint in the sky blue eyes currently sliding over her face, the expression in Tony's eyes was actually kind of sweet. "Come on, Charlie, don't give me a hard time about this. You know as well as I do that you need protection. And I need to be able to do my job without worrying about you."

"So bring on Kaminsky," Charlie capitulated with a sigh. Physically, she was starting to feel exhausted as well as sick to her stomach, and the thought of going home held increasing appeal. "She's not going to be happy about it, though. And what about you? And Crane? Aren't you coming? You need sleep to function, too."

She had already offered, and they had already agreed, that he, Kaminsky, and Crane would be spending what was left of the night at her house.

"Crane and I will be down as soon as I'm sure everything that can be processed or preserved here is being processed or preserved," Tony said. "I'll crawl into bed sometime before dawn, I hope."

Michael folded his arms over his chest. "You get that he's weighing his chances of topping off his night by crawling into your bed, right? And just for the record, it ain't happening. Not while I have to stay within fifty feet of you. I'm not big on watching."

Charlie's lips tightened, and she battled the urge to flip Mr. Infuriating the bird.

"I hope so, too," she answered Tony, and smiled at him way more flirtatiously than she would have if the ghost from hell hadn't been watching her with hawk eyes.

Which promptly narrowed.

Tony, on the other hand, smiled back.

"I've got your house key." Tony patted his pocket where the key presumably was located. "So no worries. You feel up to moving yet?"

The truthful answer was no, but Charlie nodded gamely. Tony reached out to help her up. Only when she felt the warmth of his hand closing on hers did she realize that, despite the clammy heat of the night, she was bone cold.

Tony said, "Let's go give Kaminsky the good news," as he hauled her upright, then released her hand, only to slide his fingers supportively around her upper arm. Conscious of Michael's gaze on her arm where Tony was holding it, Charlie straightened her spine and lifted her chin. Silent message: her real, live relationships were none of Casper's business.

"You know she's not going to like it," Charlie said to Tony. As they headed toward Kaminsky, who was directing a technician to store something in what looked like a black plastic garbage bag, what Charlie saw out of the corner of her eye made her chest tighten: Laura was back, standing beside the pit, watching as her corpse was hauled from the water.

Crying as if her heart would break.

"Oh, hell," Michael said, and Charlie knew that he saw Laura, too.

There was only one thing to do. The problem was getting the chance to do it.

It was while Tony was briefing Kaminsky that Charlie had a chance to step a little away and whisper to Michael, "You need to go tell her to look for the light and, when she sees it, walk into it."

He knew that she was talking about Laura: both of them had been watching her—Charlie covertly—as the spirit had hovered over her corpse while it was examined, photographed, and then put into the body bag. Now Laura was sitting cross-legged beside the zipped blue plastic shroud, rocking back and forth as she watched the other body bag, the one holding the remains of Raylene Witt, being loaded onto a stretcher to be carried the short distance to the waiting truck.

"What? No," Michael said.

"I would do it, but she can't hear me. It would be cruel to leave her like this."

"It would be cruel to tell her to look for a white light when there damned well isn't one."

"Just because you haven't seen it doesn't mean that there isn't one."

"How about we let nature take its course here?"

"Are you really willing to simply abandon her?"

"Hell, yeah."

Charlie made an exasperated sound. "Michael—"

Tony came up behind her. "Everything's all set. Come on, I'll walk you to the truck."

Trying not to appear as ruffled as she was feeling, swallowing the rest of what she had been going to say to Michael with an effort, Charlie managed a slightly strained, "You don't have to do that," for Tony. He smiled at her, a quick, intimate smile that probably would have made her feel all toasty inside if she hadn't been so aggravated at the blue-eyed devil on her other side, and said, "I want to," and slid his hand around her elbow, where it rested, warm and strong and unmistakably possessive. Seeing that, Michael shot Charlie a hard-eyed look. An instant later, over Tony's shoulder, Charlie encountered Kaminsky's frosty stare.

Okay, well, there are clearly no fans of Tony and me as a couple in the vicinity.

"*Really* glad to be working with you again, Dr. Stone," Kaminsky said as they all started walking toward the far side of the clearing. Having no trouble recognizing sarcasm when she heard it, Charlie made a face.

"The pleasure's all mine," she replied with false cordiality. Then, because Kaminsky was looking so miffed, Charlie's smile turned genuine. It lasted until she glanced toward where Laura's spirit had been, only to find that the girl was on her feet and moving now, forlornly following the body bag that held her corpse as it was carried to the waiting stretcher.

Charlie's gaze flew to Michael. Face tight, he was watching the same thing. He must have felt the weight of Charlie's eyes on him, because he looked at her then.

Please, Charlie begged him silently. He knew what she was asking him: the knowledge was there in the tightening of his lips and the narrowing of his eyes. There was only a small window of time in which he could act. Since he had to stay in Charlie's close proximity, he just had until she—they—reached the edge of the clearing. Of course, she could delay things—by, say, throwing up, which she absolutely felt like doing—but not for long. Once they were gone, it might be days before she could get back to the clearing. And she hated the idea of leaving Laura's poor confused spirit up here all alone.

"It's not like something's going to happen to her. She's already dead," Michael groused. Then in response to whatever it was he could read in Charlie's face, his mouth twisted. "You want me to try that bad? Fine. I'll try."

CHAPTER TEN

"So why is *this* serial killer such a threat to you?" Kaminsky asked Charlie. Having been occupied with watching Michael as he approached Laura, Charlie jerked her gaze to Kaminsky. Taking a second to process what she had just been asked, she frowned at the other woman even as Tony ordered, "Play nice, Kaminsky." If Charlie hadn't known how much Kaminsky hated being pulled off an active investigation to babysit, as she called it, as well as how much she disapproved of Charlie and Tony's developing relationship, she might have been taken aback by the other woman's attitude. But she did know both those things, and so she chalked it up to Kaminsky being Kaminsky.

"He's not a threat to me," Charlie answered, slowing her step as her gaze slid back toward Michael. Where he was standing, the night was dark and shadowy, but she could see that Laura, whose awareness of her situation was obviously expanding because she had been able to see enough of what was going on in the real world to identify and follow her corpse, had her face buried in his chest again. He was patting her back a little awkwardly, and his tawny head was bent as he talked to her. Charlie could only surmise that as soon as the spirit had seen him she had thrown herself into his arms. Charlie was too far away to overhear any of their conversation, but she could hear the sounds of Laura's steady weeping.

Seeing Michael with the girl wrapped around him bothered her *again,* Charlie realized. And she realized something else, too—the unpleasant niggle she was experiencing had nothing to do with the fact that seeing Michael with a woman in his arms was *new.* It had everything to do with seeing Michael with a woman in his arms, period.

Not good.

"I'd say that having the Gingerbread Man break in to your house and send you a personal message means he's a threat to you," Tony said dryly, pulling Charlie's attention back to the conversation.

Forcing herself to focus, Charlie replied, "The last person he sent his *You can't catch me* message to is still alive, I know for certain, and so are the other three, I'm pretty sure. Now that I've had a chance to think about it, I don't feel I'm in any physical danger from him."

"I'm not prepared to chance it." Tony's voice held a note of finality. Kaminsky grimaced, but didn't argue. Charlie didn't, either. Still watching Michael and Laura out of the corner of her eye, Charlie saw Laura lift her head sharply and look into the darkness on the opposite side of the clearing, as if she heard or saw something there. When Michael appeared to follow her gaze, Charlie was positive that those two were seeing something that she could not.

The white light?

Then the thought occurred: if Michael was with Laura when Laura saw the white light, would he be able to see it, too? If so, could he not walk into it along with Laura? *Would* he walk into it along with Laura?

Charlie's heart beat faster. She wanted to call out to him—to suggest that, if he saw the light, he should grab the opportunity to go into it, too? or to beg him not to go into it even if he got the chance? she wasn't sure, and really didn't want to know—but she could not say a word, of course.

All she could do was watch and wait.

Kaminsky said to her, "What, do you have, like, this photographic memory of how all the serial killers at large right now operate? Because knowing how many others were sent the same message you got tonight, and whether or not those recipients are still alive, seems pretty specific."

Michael's arms dropped away from Laura. The spirit looked up at him once, then started walking slowly away.

Toward what? On pins and needles now, Charlie had no way of knowing.

"Dr. Stone?" Kaminsky's voice pulled Charlie back into the conversation. It took her a beat to recall what she had been asked.

"No, of course not." She took a breath. Whatever was happening with Laura, Michael was simply standing there watching. He was *not* going with her, and Charlie was a little bit ashamed to find herself fiercely glad about that. "I know a lot about this particular serial killer because last year I was asked to consult on an investigation involving him. I turned them down."

Charlie's step faltered as Laura disappeared: the spirit was there one minute and gone the next. Tony's hand tightened on her arm as if to steady her, and she immediately got a grip and resumed walking. *Michael's still here.*

"Who asked you to consult?" Tony wanted to know. Michael was heading back toward them, his long stride eating up the distance.

"Dr. David Myers. After the Gingerbread Man attacked a previous group of victims, he was sent one of the *You can't catch me* notes," Charlie answered. Michael reached her side, said, "Happy now?" to her in a way that told her he was not. Since the truthful answer was *yes*—both because Laura was gone and equally because he was still there—it was, she reflected, just as well that she couldn't reply. Without answering Michael by anything more than a quick flicker of her eyelashes in his direction, Charlie continued, "He's a professor at the University of South Carolina. He wrote the definitive textbook on criminal psychology. He's one of the most widely respected experts in the field."

A hooded look—because it was filled with guilty knowledge?— from Tony reminded her that he undoubtedly knew the rest of the story. And he knew the rest of the story because he had done a thorough background check on her before he'd approached her for help in the beginning. She hadn't liked it then, didn't like it now, but there it was.

"And, yes, Dr. Myers and I were once in a relationship," Charlie added tartly. The look she gave Tony was cold with rebuke. "Which is why he contacted me to consult when he was pulled into the Gingerbread Man case. He went over the facts with me, asked for my input. I gave him what insight I could, but beyond that I declined to get involved."

"Didn't want to work with an old boyfriend, hmm?" Kaminsky sent a snarky glance her way.

"Didn't want to work on an investigation with an active serial killer slaughtering real-time victims," Charlie retorted. "What I do is strictly research based. Or, at least, it was until your team came along."

"We appreciate your help," Tony broke in smoothly before Kaminsky could reply. "We got the Boardwalk Killer off the streets, and we'll get this guy, too, believe me."

The sound of metal clanking loudly ahead of them caused Charlie to jump a little: despite her brave words, and the indisputable fact that the other recipients of the Gingerbread Man's message hadn't been harmed, she was still scared. It was, she decided, something visceral inside her that had been awakened by the Boardwalk Killer years ago and would probably stick with her for as long as she lived. Not that anyone was ever going to know it. Glancing through the woods, she saw the truck, which looked like a modified ambulance. Pointing the opposite direction, its headlights cut through the darkness, revealing a stockade's worth of sturdy tree trunks and a rutted gravel road that disappeared into the night. Two blue-garbed assistants had just loaded the last of the bodies inside and appeared to be getting ready to close the back doors.

"Hold up," Tony called to them, urging Charlie to a faster pace. "You've got passengers."

"We weren't leaving without your agents," a cheery voice answered, and the ME walked into view from behind the other side of the truck. Apparently having seen so much death had not affected a naturally sunny disposition, because Frank Cramer—short, stout, white-haired, a former pediatrician who'd been coroner for the past twenty years—was positively jolly as he assisted Charlie and Kaminsky onto the front bench seat, beside the driver, while he and one of his assistants got into the back with the corpses. Jolting down the muddy mountain road to the accompaniment of the running series of jokes with which Dr. Cramer chose to entertain the company, Charlie forced her lips into a smile when appropriate and kept a wary eye on the back, in case Laura, who seemed to have a strong affinity for her corporeal body, should reappear. But she didn't, and except for Michael, who sat silently in the back with Dr. Cramer et al, the journey was thankfully spirit-free.

"So did she go to the light?" Charlie hissed impatiently at Michael the first chance she got. Along with Kaminsky, they had just walked through the front door of her house, having been dropped off curbside by the ME's truck. Since everything that needed to be processed in her house had been processed and it was not officially designated a crime scene, all the law enforcement types had gone. Likewise, there was no sign of Raylene Witt. But there were plenty of reminders of what had happened. Starting with only what Charlie could see, the floors were streaked with dried mud and there were dirty footprints on the stairs. As she had been leaving with Tony's team to go up the mountain, she had heard Sheriff Peel order a couple of his deputies to fix the back door so that it would close and lock. Hopefully that had been done, although for the moment Charlie had no way of knowing for sure; she was confined to the front hall. With a peremptory, "Wait here," Kaminsky had gone off, gun in hand, to do a quick search of the premises. Since Michael had stayed with Charlie, that meant the two of them were briefly alone in the hall.

Michael said, "Nope."

"What?" Charlie was aghast. "What happened?"

"Remember those two little girls I told you about? They came back, only this time they looked like they were wearing their Sunday-go-to-meeting clothes. No blood on 'em anywhere. They called to Laura, told her to come with them. She went."

That was so unexpected that Charlie was nonplussed. "But— what about the white light?"

"Like I keep telling you, buttercup: there is no white light."

"There is!" An instant reflection that she had never seen it tempered Charlie's indignation. "There has to be. Oh, my God, where do you suppose Laura went?"

He shrugged.

She glared at him.

"You got me to do what you wanted, it turned out wrong, and now you're blaming me," Michael said with disgust. "Women."

"No sign of the boogeyman, Dr. Stone." Kaminsky's voice dripped sarcasm as, holstering her gun, she rejoined them. Without her customary high heels, she was surprisingly small: the top of her head reached the middle of Charlie's nose. Napoleon Complex, Charlie knew, was a real issue for some height-challenged men. Kaminsky, she decided, must suffer from the female version.

Whatever, Charlie was not in the mood. "Can you give the snark a rest, please? You're stuck with me, I'm stuck with you, and the only thing to do is make the best of it." She walked past Kaminsky toward the stairs.

"I'm fine with that," Kaminsky said. "Just so long as we're clear that I am a highly trained federal agent and not your personal bodyguard."

With one hand on the newel post, Charlie stopped to skewer Kaminsky with a look. "And I am a highly educated expert who already helped your team catch one serial killer, and may very well help you catch a second. Which is why I'm worth protecting." For a moment they stared measuringly at each other, while Michael, clearly having found a fresh source of enjoyment, added his two cents with, "Catfight! You know I've got your back, babe, but I gotta warn you that nowadays that don't count for much."

Ignoring him except for a slight contraction of her eyebrows, Charlie said, "I'm going to bed," to Kaminsky, who had already been given the room across the hall from Charlie's and, search completed, was free to go to bed herself at any time. "If you need towels or anything, you know where the linen closet is."

Then she turned and walked on up the stairs.

By the time Charlie reached her bedroom, it was a quarter to five in the morning. Exhaustion was blunting the horrors of the night and even tempering the aggravation that she was feeling toward every other being (both dead and living) in her house. The fact that she was drooping with fatigue wasn't even her most pressing problem. As soon as she (and her shadow) was inside with the door closed, she made a beeline for the bathroom.

"You. The bathroom is off-limits," she told Michael over her shoulder. Then, shutting the door firmly behind her—locking it was a waste of time, considering that the creature she most wanted to keep out could walk right through it if he wanted to—she hurried to the medicine cabinet, shook two Pepto-Bismol tablets into her hand, and chewed desperately, hoping they would quell the nausea that the ride down the mountain had done little to ease. While she waited for the medicine to (hopefully) work she managed to brush her teeth and, after a single regretful glance at the waiting tub, take a quick shower that was steamy hot enough to chase away the terrible chill that still afflicted her. After that, she was so tired she felt boneless, but she was warmer and the nausea was better. Michael hadn't put in an appearance—actually, she had trusted him not to—and she felt comfortable enough that he wouldn't to drop her towel and rub lotion into her skin before pulling on her nightgown. Then she covered the flimsy, mid-thigh-length thing with her blue terry bathrobe, which she tied firmly at the waist, shook her hair out of the knot she'd twisted it into for the shower, and even ran a brush through it (vanity, thy name is woman) before heading back out into the bedroom.

Where she knew Michael would be waiting.

Having taken his watch off before she showered, she was carefully carrying it.

"So, you upchuck in there?" was how he greeted her.

"No, I did not," she answered, nettled that he knew so much about her, before she regrouped enough to remember the watch and hold it up for him to see. "Is there somebody I can send this to for you? Someone you'd like to give it to?"

Because after all the watch was no good to him now: he couldn't wear it, would never wear it again, and there might be someone to whom he'd like to leave a memento. The matter could have waited for morning, but she was addressing it now as a way of sliding past any awkwardness that might result from him hanging out in her bedroom while she went (alone) to bed. She'd known that having him tethered to her would come with its share of drawbacks, but the reality of it was proving downright unnerving: if she didn't find some way to change the terms of his continued earthly existence, he might very well be dogging every step she took for as long as she lived. Then she realized that he was shirtless, and that the soft glow of the bedside lamp was playing over a magnificent display of rippling muscles and tanned skin, and she forgot what she'd been thinking. Despite being so weary that her legs felt shaky, as her eyes slid over his powerful shoulders and wide, sculpted chest and as much of his sinewy abdomen as she could see above the low-slung waistband of his jeans, her heart sped up and she felt an electric tingle that started deep inside and shivered across every nerve ending she possessed. He was standing sideways to her, on the far side of the bed, holding his T-shirt out at arm's length in front of him as if he'd been examining it. The tattoo on his bulging biceps caught her eye: like the rest of him, it looked totally badass and she was embarrassed to realize that the sight of it excited her. With a quick, comprehensive glance, she took in the smooth planes of his shoulder blades and his long, strong back, his brawny arms and square-palmed, long-fingered hands and felt a rush of heat. The instant quickening of her body was immediately followed by a sense of profound helplessness. Like practically everything else where he was concerned, she had no control over her body's instinctive reaction to him. The one saving grace in the face of what she could only consider her really stupid weakness for him was that there wasn't any way she could act on it. He might look as solid and substantial as any living, breathing man, but he was not. She could fantasize about running her hands over all that hard-bodied splendor, about kissing that chiseled mouth, about falling into bed and having mind-blowing sex with him all she wanted to, and it still wasn't going to happen.

Which, she told herself sternly, was a good thing.

His eyes met hers across the not-as-wide-as-she-might-have-wished-it-was expanse of her spotless white bed. Charlie felt as if the temperature in the bedroom had suddenly warmed by about a hundred degrees.

"You wearing something pretty under that robe?"

He knew her affinity for beautiful, feminine lingerie. It resulted, Charlie was sure, from the no-nonsense, practically androgynous clothes she chose to wear professionally. The answer was yes: her simple summer nightgown was cream silk with lashings of lace, and it was, indeed, very pretty. Not that she had any intention whatsoever of telling him so.

"None of your business," she answered. "What's up with your shirt?"

He smiled slowly back at her. His eyes had gone all heavy-lidded and hot. "Thought I'd try turning you on."

Her eyes narrowed. Her lips firmed. His smile kicked it up a notch.

"It's wet, okay?" he said. "Unless you have access to a ghost Laundromat, I'm just going to have to wait and see if it dries."

The sizzle that was suddenly there in the air between them made her body throb. It made her burn. Instantly she started doing everything she could to shut that down. There was no point in even taking so much as the first step down the path this thing with him was heading.

Hot, mindless sex was *not* going to happen. What *was* going to happen was that they would have the conversation about the watch, and then she would get some much-needed sleep.

"I asked you who you'd like me to send your watch to," she persisted, resolutely ignoring the shivery little tendrils of wanting she could feel coursing around inside her.

His mouth twisted. "Don't waste your time." His eyes slid over her again, lingering on the deep vee of the robe she had belted around her waist, openly assessing the scrap of creamy lace visible in the opening. "For future reference, I like lace."

There was a huskiness to his voice that made butterflies take flight in her stomach. Against the hardwood floor, her toes curled.

Do not let him see you react.

"For future reference, I don't care."

"There you go with that pretty pink tongue of yours again."

She was *not* wetting her lips. She didn't think. It was all she could do not to glare at him, but that would be a dead tell—giveaway—that he was getting under her skin.

"So are you going to give me the name of your next of kin or not?" Charlie snapped, attempting to battle her body's shameless response by trying to call to mind what she knew about him. For one thing, at the time of his arrest he'd had a girlfriend. Charlie even remembered her name: Jasmine. She liked the idea that she remembered his girlfriend's name only slightly less than she liked the idea of sending his watch to her.

"I got no next of kin." He was looking her in the eye again now, instead of staring at her chest. The sad thing was, that didn't help what ailed her a bit. The steamy glint at the backs of those sky blue eyes had the unfortunate effect of making her go all gooey inside. "You're it, babe: you're the closest thing I've got to anybody who gives a damn about me. You keep it."

There was no self-pity in his face, no chagrin that she could see, no sadness or sorrow. He looked perfectly fine, his usual drop-dead sexy self in fact, but Charlie felt a pang in the region of her heart.

It was wrong that he had no one.

Something of what she was feeling must have shown on her face, because his gaze sharpened.

"Are you standing over there feeling sorry for me?" he demanded.

"No," she replied guiltily.

"Yes, you are. I can tell." Wadding up the T-shirt, he threw it into the elegantly upholstered armchair in the corner. "There goes that soft heart of yours again."

Charlie raised her chin. "You say that like having a soft heart is a bad thing."

"Believe me, most of the time it is. But that's why you get the watch, Doc: because you have a heart as soft and squishy as a big ole giant marshmallow. And because you—how was it you put that once?—oh, yeah: you *care* about me."

About to deny it, Charlie realized that she couldn't. And the fact that she couldn't scared her enough to make her cross. Enough to make her brows snap together and her arms fold over her chest.

"Go to hell," she said, not caring much at the moment if he actually did. He laughed.

"You gonna show me that pretty thing you're wearing?"

"No." She was still scowling at him. A yawn caught her by surprise, and she clapped a hand to her mouth a split second too late.

His expression changed to something she couldn't read.

"You're out on your feet," he said in a totally different tone than before. "Go on to bed."

She almost said no just to be contrary. But she really was exhausted, and the thought of climbing into bed and closing her eyes was all but irresistible.

Of course, before she did that, she was going to have to lose the robe.

Giving him a peep show was *not* on the evening's agenda.

She could tell from the hooded way he was watching her that he was waiting for it. Lips curving in secret triumph, she set his watch down on the bedside table, pulled back the covers, positioned her pillows—and turned off the lamp, which was on her side of the bed. When he said *"Shit,"* she smiled. With the room plunged into almost complete darkness, she took off her robe, crawled into bed, and curled up with her back to him.

Then she lay there sightlessly listening to the too-rapid beating of her heart, so conscious of him standing there on the other side of the bed looking down at her that she couldn't even close her eyes, that she had to remind herself to breathe. He didn't move, or make a sound, and she knew that the most he could possibly see of her was a shadow-enshrouded shape beneath the covers. But simply knowing that he was there made her supremely conscious of the cool slide of her silk nightgown against her skin, of the tautness of her nipples against the slight abrasion of the lace covering them, of the dampness between her legs. The body lotion she used was scented with lavender: she could smell it on her own skin.

"Just for the record"—his voice was low and thick enough to send a shiver down her spine—"I want to fuck you. Bad."

Her breath caught. Her hands fisted in the sheets. Her bones turned to water. Her body caught fire.

Oh, God, I want you to.

But she didn't say it. Wild horses couldn't have dragged those words out of her mouth.

What she did say, very firmly, was "Good-night."

Then she closed her eyes.

So aroused it felt as if flames were licking over every inch of her skin, she practically prayed for sleep.

CHAPTER ELEVEN

Of course she had bad dreams. Who wouldn't, under the circumstances? But when Charlie woke up in the morning, she couldn't remember them. All she remembered was crying out once, and hearing Michael say, "Don't worry, babe, I'm right here." Which had made her feel absurdly safe and protected, and so she had fallen back to sleep until sunlight filtering through the curtains—and her shrilling alarm—announced the arrival of another day.

Michael was nowhere to be found. That worried her. At least until she got downstairs, followed the smell of coffee to the kitchen, and discovered him with his back to the room, looking out through the big kitchen window while Crane hovered over the coffeemaker and Tony and Kaminsky sat at her breakfast bar discussing something that Charlie surmised had to do with the laptop that was open in front of Kaminsky. A sweeping glance told her that the back door was indeed, to all outward appearances anyway, repaired, and the mail was still piled as she had left it in the center of the table, which was probably why no one was using it. The gang was dressed in their usual FBI-agent suits, and Michael was once again wearing his T-shirt. Charlie presumed it had dried. Although how he had gotten down to the kitchen while still staying within the prescribed fifty-foot

limit mystified her, until it dawned on her that Michael could go
through the floor. As the ghost traveled, she calculated swiftly, her
bedroom was only about thirty feet away.

"Morning," Tony greeted her as she walked into the kitchen.
"Hope you don't mind us making ourselves at home."

"Not at all," she said, as Crane waved a spoon at her, Kaminsky
favored her with a sour look, and Michael turned to face her. He was
unsmiling, and the sunlight pouring in through the window spilled
over his tall, powerfully built body as if he were as solid as the house
itself. It picked up golden threads in his tawny hair and emphasized
the hard planes and sculpted angles of his face. If she hadn't known
for sure that what she was looking at was his ghost, she wouldn't
have believed it: that's how alive he looked. Even across the distance
separating them she could see the beautiful sky blue of his eyes. *God,
he's gorgeous,* was the thought that ricocheted through her idiot
brain, only to be squashed like an annoying little bug with the reality
slap of, *And dead.* She pulled her eyes away from him to concentrate
on the living, breathing good guy she was talking to. "Only I didn't
think I had any coffee in the house."

"You didn't." Tony smiled at her. Obviously not long out of the
shower, he was looking very handsome himself with his well-groomed
black hair brushed back from his face and his brown eyes crinkling at
her. "Crane ran to the store. Got some doughnuts, too."

For people who she knew were operating on only a few hours'
sleep, everybody looked good, Charlie thought. Bright-eyed and ready
to go. The men clean-shaven. Kaminsky in one of her snug skirt
suits—this one had pinstripes—and, God help her, her usual towering
heels. Knowing that they would be going after the Gingerbread Man
full bore, Charlie, too, had put on a work-appropriate outfit, consist-
ing of black flats, slim black pants, and a sleeveless peach silk blouse.
She had twisted her hair up in a loose knot in deference to the heat,
and when they left would take her black blazer with her, to be carried
until she needed to put it on.

She wore jewelry, too—small, tasteful silver hoops in her ears,
and Michael's big silver watch pushed halfway up her arm.

Leaving it behind on her nightstand just hadn't felt right. If what
he had told her was the truth, it was too important as evidence—and

clearly too important to him personally as well. Now, as Michael's eyes touched on the watch then rose to meet hers, she returned his gaze a tad defensively: *don't read anything into it.*

He smiled at her. She refused to even allow herself to speculate on the meaning behind that smile. But a shiver passed through her at the sheer seductive charm of it, and she realized with a thrill of alarm that she was in even bigger trouble where he was concerned than she had thought.

Do not fall in love with him.

She was horribly afraid that was like warning herself not to breathe.

"Coffee?" Crane asked her, and she nodded. Glancing at the clock over the microwave, Charlie saw that it was a couple of minutes after nine a.m. It was Saturday, which was a good thing because it meant that she didn't have to worry about going in to work, and already so bright with sunshine that simply looking out the window made Charlie want to wince.

It was hard to reconcile a world that looked as if it belonged in a happy Disney movie with the terrible things that she had seen last night.

Michael said, "You've got chickens in your backyard. And a big ole orange tabby looking like he's thinking about having McNuggets for breakfast."

"Oh, no." Charlie was already charging out the back door into what felt like a wall of steamy heat before it occurred to her that she had spoken aloud. Well, she would just have to hope that everyone thought she had seen the impending carnage through the window for herself. Mrs. Norman, the elderly widow who lived next door on one side, raised prize-winning Leghorn chickens of which she was fiercely proud; the Powells, a high school teacher, his K-Mart assistant manager wife, and their twelve-year-old daughter, Glory, who lived on Charlie's other side, adored Pumpkin, their cat. Unfortunately the cat and the chickens were the animal world equivalents of the Hatfields and the McCoys. Both warring parties frequently breached Charlie's fence, the chickens because of a partiality for her sunflowers and the cat because of a partiality for the chickens. Her backyard had become the battleground on which the two species waged their deadliest battles. So far, the toll was one badly mauled chicken and a frequently pecked bloody cat.

"Shoo!" Making the appropriate shooing motions with her hands, Charlie stomped toward the chickens. The big white birds were actually surprisingly aggressive, particularly toward Pumpkin, so the sides were not as unevenly matched as she had, upon moving into the house and discovering the ongoing war, at first supposed. At that moment the chickens were scratching around in the grass beneath the sunflowers, oblivious to Pumpkin, who crouched, tail twitching and eyes fixed on his putative prey, behind a nearby rock. "Go home, Pumpkin!"

Squawking, the chickens scattered at her approach, making for the fence and then launching themselves over it into their own yard with all the grace of boulders trying to fly.

Charlie turned back to see Pumpkin, his fun ruined, sitting up and eyeing her with an unblinking golden gaze. As if to allay her suspicions about his intentions, he lifted a paw and proceeded to wash his face.

"Yeah, right. I know what you were up to," Charlie told him. Scooping him into her arms, she turned to restore him to his own yard and found herself looking at the mountain behind her. Unnerving as it was to think about, last night a killer who had committed unspeakable crimes had been on that mountainside, peering into her windows through the foliage. The thickly wooded slope stretched upward against the background of cerulean sky until it was lost in a froth of low-hanging, misty white clouds. Despite the bright sunshine, the variegated green of the treetops struck her as dark and forbidding, and the entrance to the path where she always began her run to the ridge seemed filled with sinister shadows. Tamping down a shudder, Charlie reflected that it would be a long time before she ran that particular path again. Always before, she had thought of the mountain as a place of renewal, of peace and tranquillity.

Now just looking at it made her feel as if a clammy hand had gripped the back of her neck.

"Charlie?" At the sound of her name, uttered on a note of uncertainty, Charlie turned to see Melissa Powell waving at her from her own backyard on the other side of the fence. Since Charlie had lived there for only a few months, she was still getting to know her neighbors, most of whom had lived in the area all of their lives. They were a close-knit group who were friendly and welcoming but a little slow to fully accept a stranger. Having never had a settled existence, much less a hometown full of family and friends and neighbors, Charlie found their easy connection to one another enviable. It was something, she had decided when she had moved in, she would like to try to be a part of. A year or so previously, it had occurred to her that she didn't really know how to have friends. After her unstable childhood, and especially after the trauma of what had happened to Holly, she simply hadn't wanted or perhaps she'd been unable to form many lasting bonds. Cautiously, like a swimmer putting a toe into a pool she feared might be icy, she was working to remedy that now. Here in Big Stone Gap, she was trying small town life on for size. That kind of happy normalcy was something she badly wanted for herself, even though she wasn't quite sure if it was going to fit.

"Hi, Melissa." Pumpkin was wriggling in Charlie's arms now that he saw his owner, and Charlie carried him to the fence and handed him over. Probably no older than Charlie's own age, attractive rather than pretty, Melissa had short brown hair and a thin, boyish figure. Having apparently seen Charlie with Pumpkin from her kitchen, she had stepped outside in a knee-length, zip-up pink robe. Except for the length of her hair, which reached halfway down her back, Glory, who was standing on the back porch watching Charlie, too, looked exactly like her mother, while Brett, the husband and father, whom she could just glimpse inside the open back door, was a big guy, with a bluff laugh and a beer belly. Charlie smiled a little apologetically at Melissa. "He was after Mrs. Norman's chickens."

"Oh, dear." Melissa looked dismayed. Glancing down at the cat in her arms, she said, "No, Pumpkin. Bad kitty." Shaking her head at Charlie, she added, "We're trying to keep him in, but—" She shrugged, then gave Charlie an almost shamefaced look. "I heard—everybody's saying—I wouldn't pry, but with Glory, you know, I have to be so careful—did a *serial killer* murder two girls up on the mountain last night, and did a third one escape by running to your house?"

So Melissa hadn't been one of the neighbors who had flocked to her house in the aftermath—but still she knew what had happened.

Well, of course she did. That was part of the reality of small town life. It was part—Charlie thought—of what she wanted for her own life.

Charlie gave her neighbor the bare bones of the story in a few quick sentences. Eyes rounding in horror, Melissa listened, exclaimed, "Oh, my goodness, I'm never letting Glory out of my sight again," and "The police department needs to release a city-wide alert!"

"Did you hear or see anything unusual out here last night? Say, between 11:30 and midnight?" Charlie asked.

Melissa shook her head. "We were in bed by eleven. All of us." She made a little face. "Everybody says there were police cars and ambulances and all kinds of commotion going on, but we didn't hear that, either. We didn't know a thing in the world was wrong until Sally Bennett called me this morning."

"If you can think of anything, will you call and let me know?"

Melissa nodded. Then, with a quick "'Bye" and Pumpkin still clasped in her arms, she rounded up Glory and hurried inside her house, where Charlie had little doubt that she would soon be burning up the phone and Internet.

Suddenly conscious of the humidity wrapping around her like a blanket, sure she was already rosy with the heat, Charlie turned toward the house to discover Michael standing not ten feet away.

His eyes twinkled at her. "Anybody ever tell you you look cute chasing chickens?"

Her eyes swept him. "It's nice to see you with all your clothes on."

He grinned. "The shirt dried. That silky nightgown you were wearing last night? Real pretty."

She was not about to ask *How do you know?* But her face must have said it for her, because after a single comprehensive look at it his grin widened and he continued, "You kicked all the covers off. About the same time you started letting out panicky little cries like something was after you."

Remembering how comforting she had found his presence in the middle of the night, she scowled at him. "What did you do, spend the entire night hovering over me?"

"Nah, I spent most of it in Sugar Buns' bedroom. I just checked on you occasionally."

Now, that would have been infuriating if she had believed it. The thing was, she didn't. He might (or might not) be a charismatic psychopath/serial killer, but she'd already figured out that he wasn't a creep. Flicking him a look that said *Aren't you funny,* she walked on past him through the door into the blessedly cool air-conditioning. She was impatiently waiting on Michael to follow her so that she could close the door on the heat that billowed in behind her—she hadn't yet quite totally internalized the fact that he could walk right through a closed door anytime he wanted to—when Kaminsky, half turning on the bar stool to look at her, said, "So what did your gossipy neighbor have to say?"

"She wanted to know what had happened," Charlie replied, closing the door after Michael did, indeed, walk through it—and while she was still holding it open, too. "She'd heard things, and she wanted to check."

"We need to canvass the neighbors, see if they saw or heard anything," Tony said.

Skirting the table, Charlie headed for the breakfast bar. "I already asked Melissa. She said the entire family went to bed at eleven and they didn't know a thing about it until this morning, when a friend called and told her."

"I bet the whole town's running scared," Crane said. He looked at Charlie. "You want a cup of coffee?"

"Thanks." Charlie slid up onto the bar stool beside Tony, who smiled at her. "The horrible thing about it is, this wouldn't have happened here if I didn't live here."

"Tell me you're not gonna start feeling guilty about it." Michael leaned against the bar on her other side. Having his big body close enough to where she could have shifted an inch or so sideways and brushed him with her arm if she'd wanted to was vaguely unsettling. The thing was, every single bit of him from the faintest suggestion of stubble on his square jaw to the rock-hard abs inches from her elbow looked as real and solid as Tony did on her other side. It was difficult to keep her eyes off him, difficult to keep from letting his nearness kick her pulse rate up a notch. "The whole world ain't your problem, babe."

"It would have happened somewhere," Tony told her. "This

guy's a killer, and whether you're involved or he's pulling in some other expert he feels like challenging, he'll kill until we catch him. Simple as that."

"The locals shouldn't be in danger anyway. I've plotted out the location of the kill zones, which in this case are always the same as the disposal zones, and he never goes back to the same place," Kaminsky said. "Right now, as far as this unsub is concerned, this town is probably the safest place on the planet."

"Oh, yay, I'll tell my neighbors." Charlie's response was wry. "I'm sure that'll make up for everything."

Tony's eyes touched hers, dropped.

"Just so you know, from where I'm standing, right above that first button you've got done up on your blouse, I can see this really mouthwatering little bit of cleavage. What do you want to bet Dudley can see it, too?" Michael drawled.

Charlie couldn't help it. Even as she shot him a fierce *Stop talking to me* look, she laid a protective hand across the bottom of the vee formed by the open collar of her blouse. It was all she could do to keep from doing up another button, simply to make sure that there was no cleavage to be seen. But that, she knew, would provide Michael with way too much entertainment. And would be a dead giveaway to how easily he could get under her skin, too.

"After we go over some things, I'd like you to come with me to the hospital to talk to Jenna McDaniels," Tony said to Charlie, who (a little jerkily) nodded agreement. Very subtly (she hoped) she adjusted her position so that she was sitting straight enough that presumably neither of the men on either side of her could see down her shirt. Not that she had any evidence except Michael's suggestion that *Tony* had been looking. "Crane, when we're through here you and Kaminsky can get busy talking to the neighbors. Plus, we need to pull all the surveillance video from every ATM, every convenience store, every traffic cam in the area. If the police cruisers have video, pull that, too. Everything. We know this guy was here in town yesterday and last night. It's possible that he, or his vehicle, were caught on tape."

"Sure thing, boss," Crane said as he handed Charlie a cup of coffee. Charlie dosed it liberally with Sweet'N Low from the sugar bowl on the counter, pointed Crane to a cabinet when he bemoaned the lack of real sugar, declined a doughnut (despite Michael telling her, "Take it. You need to eat."), discreetly did up another blouse button when she judged that everyone (read Michael) was looking elsewhere, and allowed her attention to be directed to the laptop screen as Tony gestured at it and said, "Kaminsky, bring us up to speed, would you please?"

Kaminsky put down her coffee cup.

"First, there are seven separate groups of three victims each, for twenty-one known total victims of the Gingerbread Man." Kaminsky tapped the screen, which displayed what looked like a bulletin board with small photos grouped together by threes. "Of that number, there have been sixteen fatalities. Five survived the attacks, including Jenna McDaniels." She pointed to a line-up of five photos at the far side of the screen: the top one was of Jenna. "Three attacks occurred in each of the last two years and one attack—that would be Jenna McDaniels' group—has occurred so far this year. The time frame for all of them is August/September. If the Gingerbread Man stays true to pattern, the attack on the McDaniels' group is only the first this year. We can expect three more victims to be kidnapped approximately ten to fourteen days from now. The next kill date should be two weekends away, on either Friday or Saturday. That's the pattern."

"So we've got about ten days to find this guy before he starts up again," Crane said, and Kaminsky nodded. "Always supposing he stays true to the pattern."

"Any idea how he chooses his victims?" Tony took a bite of a doughnut. From the corner of her eye, Charlie saw that Michael was watching Tony almost broodingly, and frowned. Surely he wasn't looking like that because he thought the other man had been ogling her cleavage. After all, he had been doing the same thing. Then she had another thought: she was thinking of her pesky ghost strictly as Michael now. Calling him "Garland" no longer entered her head. And what that said about the changing state of their relationship she didn't even want to contemplate.

Kaminsky shook her head. "I've listed the victims' names, ages, genders, races, marital status, occupations, and hometowns, and any other known identifying characteristics. I can't find a pattern in the criteria he uses to select them—yet."

Charlie said, "If I'm remembering correctly"—she scanned the identifying information for each group to confirm it—"each group is roughly similar in composition. For example, the first group was made up of boys aged twelve, thirteen, and fourteen."

Kaminsky nodded. "That's right. Group Two was three fifteen-year-old girls. Group Three was teenage boys again—two fourteen-year-olds and a sixteen-year-old. Group Four was a departure in that two of the victims were adults and one was markedly dissimilar to the other two—two women in their forties and a fifteen-year-old boy. Group Five was a sixteen-year-old girl, a seventeen-year-old girl, and seventeen-year-old boy. Group Six was a fourteen-year-old boy, a fifteen-year-old boy, and an eighteen-year-old girl. Group Seven— well, that was the group last night. Raylene Witt and Laura Peters were both twenty-one. Jenna McDaniels is twenty."

"Who are the survivors?" Tony asked, polishing off his doughnut with a last, super-sized bite then wiping his fingers on a napkin. Michael was still watching him as he chewed and swallowed, Charlie saw. But when she took another sip of coffee, Michael's eyes, glinting with some emotion she still couldn't quite pinpoint, flickered to the cup she had just set down, where they lingered. It took a second, but then Charlie had an epiphany: she realized that Michael wasn't ticked off at Tony at all. He was envying them their breakfast.

Of course, he missed eating.

She hated the idea of that.

Michael must have felt her gaze on him, because he looked up then, saw her expression, and frowned at her.

"So what's up with the big sad eyes you're giving me?" he demanded suspiciously.

Charlie altered her expression in a hurry. *No idea what you're talking about,* was the first part of what she hoped her expression conveyed. The second, which she already knew he was about as likely to pay attention to as he was to suddenly sprout an angelic halo, was *Hush.* Then, as Kaminsky started talking, Charlie wrenched her gaze away.

"Ariane Spencer, fifteen at the time, from Group Two." Not quite touching the screen, Kaminsky pointed to what looked like a yearbook photo of a pretty blond teen. "Matthew Hayes, sixteen, from Group Three." The kid was wiry, with spiky black hair and a small silver ring piercing a nostril. "Andrew Russell, seventeen, from Group Five." This boy had very short brown hair and thick black glasses. "Saul Tunney, fifteen, from Group Six." He had a round, earnest-looking face and blond waves. "And, last but not least, Jenna McDaniels from Group Seven."

"So what we've got are sixteen teenagers ranging in age from fourteen to eighteen and five adult women, if you count Jenna McDaniels at twenty as an adult," Tony said.

"Did any of the victims know one another?" Having polished off his meal, Crane had come around the breakfast bar so he could look at the computer screen, too. Leaning toward it, he started to rest a hand on the counter. It passed right through Michael, who grimaced. Snatching his hand back, Crane straightened with a sharp *"Ah!"* and started rubbing his fingers.

"Counter shocked me," he said defensively in response to the surprised looks he got from the others. "Damned static electricity."

"Boo," Michael growled after him as Crane moved on down to stand on the other side of Kaminsky.

Involuntarily, Charlie smiled.

Michael was smiling, too, as he met her gaze. After a second his eyes darkened. Then they moved down to her lips.

"When you smile like that, all I want to do is kiss you," he told her. "Damned shame I can't. But I'm working on it."

He was trying to get a reaction out of her, Charlie told herself. She knew he took a great deal of pleasure from teasing her, rattling her composure, provoking her, turning her on. The only defense she had against him was to not respond. So she didn't. At least, not outwardly.

But there wasn't a thing in the world she could do about the instant mental image she had of his mouth covering hers. Just like there wasn't a thing in the world she could do about the way her body suffused with heat.

"I think some of them did know the others in their group." Looking away from Michael, who, having clearly seen something that interested him in her face, was now watching her like a cat at a mouse hole, Charlie concentrated on Crane instead as she picked up the thread of the (important, real-world) conversation. "Which ones and what the relationships were exactly I don't recall right off the top of my head."

"We need to find that out." As Tony spoke he looked at Kaminsky, who nodded.

"What strikes me is that all the males are kids. I'm betting that seventeen-year-old boy was undersized. This guy's afraid to tangle with a grown man. Which makes me think he's not a real big guy himself, and probably doesn't have any military or police background. No combat training or anything like that," Crane said.

Tony made a face. "I don't think we can rule out a military or police background on the basis of that. A grown man is harder for anyone to deal with than a woman or a child. And it may be that grown men aren't this guy's thing."

Crane shrugged. "Good point."

"Forget the damned victims. You're the key," Michael told Charlie. His face had hardened, and the look he gave her was suddenly grim. "You want to figure out who this guy is, figure out how he knows *you*."

CHAPTER TWELVE

Charlie cast a surprised look at Michael: she hadn't expected him to have tuned out the conversation, exactly—knowing him, that would have been expecting too much—but she equally hadn't realized that he had been following it to such an extent. Certainly she hadn't expected him to make such an astute observation. As soon as the words came out of his mouth, she realized that he was right.

"Faster this guy's caught, faster I quit having to worry about you getting yourself killed. And the faster Dudley there goes back to where he came from," Michael replied to the look she gave him.

Remembering in the nick of time that she had an audience, Charlie didn't respond to that by so much as the flicker of an eyelash. Instead, she looked at Tony as she repeated Michael's suggestion aloud. Only she expanded it to include figuring out how the Gingerbread Man knew all the experts to whom he had sent his message.

"That's a really good idea. Four's a much more manageable number to start an investigation with than twenty-one," Tony said thoughtfully. "Who're the experts?"

"Dr. David Myers, who as I told you last night wrote the definitive text on criminal psychology. Dr. Jeffrey Underwood, research geneticist and professor at Wake Forest School of Medicine. And Eric

Riva, a reporter who wrote a series of articles about the case for the *Charlotte Observer*. That would be the primary newspaper in Charlotte, North Carolina," Charlie said.

"And you," Kaminsky added, giving Charlie an inscrutable look. "Dr. Charlotte Stone, certified forensic psychiatrist, one of the top serial killer experts in the country."

"Who needs to find a new specialty," Michael said, while Charlie, ignoring him, said to Tony, "I think what we need to ask ourselves is how the Gingerbread Man came to know about each of the experts. For example, I don't think anybody outside of academia or the forensic psychiatric community has ever heard of *me*. So that should narrow the list of possible suspects right there."

"Are you kidding? You've been all over TV," Kaminsky shot Charlie an incredulous glance. "For a few days there, practically every news channel and talk show host in the country was covering the Boardwalk Killer case twenty-four seven. You included."

"The girl who lived," Michael told her on a satiric note. "Think about it: as a theme, it's classic."

Considering the source, this clear reference to Harry Potter came as a shock. Michael had told her before that there wasn't much to do in prison besides read and work out, but at the time they'd been talking about Shakespeare. Charlie decided that her mind had just officially been blown by the eclecticism of his literary choices.

"Prison library," Michael explained, clearly able to correctly interpret the look on her face. "If they had it, I read it."

"You *were* all over TV," Crane was saying to her when she forced her attention to return to the living. "Including CNN. Anybody in the whole world practically could know who you are and what you do."

Charlie hadn't realized. Or, rather, she hadn't let herself realize. Probably, she decided, because she hadn't wanted to know.

"I forgot about that." Okay, that sounded lame.

"You've been busy," Michael said excusingly.

"So let's consider the other three," Tony said. "How could this guy know them?" He looked at Charlie. "How did you know who they were?"

She said, "I knew their identities from looking over the case for Dr. Myers. I knew him, of course, and I had heard of Dr. Underwood, but I had never heard of Eric Riva before Dr. Myers sent me the case files."

"Eric Riva was the first person to receive the Gingerbread Man's *You can't catch me* message, right?" Tony asked. When Charlie nodded, he said, "Let's start with him." He looked at Kaminsky. "Find out how widely read those columns he wrote were. And how he came to write them in the first place."

Kaminsky nodded. "I'm on it."

"I would say the first group of victims is the most important, too," Charlie said slowly. "Something caused the Gingerbread Man to start with that group. I would posit that either he knew one of the victims in some way, or that he saw himself in one of the victims. Something traumatic may have happened to him at that age."

"Check them out, too," Tony directed, and Kaminsky nodded again.

Then, remembering Raylene Witt's appearance in her front hall—to be there, the spirit almost had to have been attached to someone or something nearby—Charlie added, "One more thing. We know the Gingerbread Man chased Jenna down the mountain. He—or a confederate, although I am almost one hundred percent certain we'll find he works alone—kicked open my back door and entered my kitchen to leave the note and the knife for me to find. He may very well have walked around to the front of the house after that, and may even have come inside with the rescuers. We should check for video or photos of the front of my house—maybe one of the neighbors whipped out his phone and took pictures of the ambulance crew, or of Jenna on the stretcher, for example. We should compare fingerprints from the front door and hall with fingerprints on the back door. Also, we should probably get as complete a list as we can of who was on the scene."

Tony looked at Kaminsky and Crane. "Got it covered, boss," Crane said.

"Anybody up for grisly details?" Kaminsky cast an inquiring glance around.

"No," Michael said. As Charlie glanced at him in some surprise it struck her that, for a supposed serial killer, he didn't seem to have a real high tolerance for gore. In her experience of him, every time he'd been exposed to it—take Laura Peters' bashed-in head, for example—he had seemed more bothered than she would have expected the typical serial killer to be, because serial killers have no ability to empathize with anyone. Had he been faking an empathetic response? Maybe, but she didn't think so: the reactions were too consistent. Then she remembered his descriptions of her inkblots: they had been gory enough. Of course, she had suspected at the time that he was messing with her, and even if he hadn't been, that had been before he was killed. Maybe death had changed that part of him. Maybe death had changed everything about him. Maybe, in death, he was not the same bad-to-the-bone person that he had been before.

"A heads-up, babe. You're staring at me with your eyes wide and your pretty lips parted. Now, me, I think it's because you're fantasizing about jumping my bones. But your friends might wonder." The slow half-smile Michael gave her then really might have sent Charlie's thoughts running along the lines of jumping his bones if his words hadn't been so annoying. He was doing it on purpose, of course, just as he had been annoying her on purpose ever since, as a shackled and jumpsuited convict, he had first shuffled into her office. Snapping her mouth shut and dragging her eyes away from him even as she did a lightning mental review of every interaction she'd ever had with him, alive or dead, she came to an inescapable conclusion: in every way that mattered, he hadn't changed a bit.

For him at least, death was no magic elixir washing away his sins. He was still whatever he had been before.

How bad a thing that was Charlie couldn't quite decide. But annoying was definitely still there in the mix. So, unfortunately, was sexy as hell.

"Snakes," she heard Kaminsky say, and the word jerked her attention back to the real world conversation like very few others could have done. "The bastard locked those three girls in Group Two in a roomful of poisonous snakes." Charlie wasn't a fan of snakes. Merely thinking about it made her shudder. From reading the files, she had a vivid mental image of what Kaminsky was talking about— how the Gingerbread Man had coerced the girls in that group into killing one another by dropping snakes on them from a grating high above—but she needed a second to refresh her memory on what had been done to the previous group, the description of which she had obviously missed: oh, yes, Group One, the young boys, had died of thirst. No one knew whether or not the Gingerbread Man had offered to let one live if the others were killed, because no one in that group had survived. "Group Three was forced to choose who would be shot with an arrow. Group Four was menaced with a propeller; Group Five was locked in a trash compacter; Group Six faced suffocation; and Group Seven, as we know, was threatened with drowning."

"Where are the survivors now?" Tony asked. Kaminsky hit a button, and a new screen popped up.

"Pretty much everywhere: I've got their addresses." Kaminsky indicated a map of the United States on which five blue dots glowed. Two of them, Charlie saw, were clear across the country. Well, she couldn't blame the victims for wanting to get as far away from what had happened as possible. In the aftermath of Holly's murder, she had experienced that impulse herself. Only she had been afraid that no matter how far away she ran, it wouldn't be far enough, which in the end had meant that she hadn't run very far away at all.

Instead, she'd tried hiding in plain sight. And look how well that had worked out: she'd almost gotten herself killed, and had ended up all over CNN.

Tony was looking at the map with his brow creased. "So where are the experts?"

Kaminsky hit a button again, and four green dots showed up on the same map. They were all within the tri-state area of North and South Carolina and Virginia, which put them much closer at hand.

"Kill grounds?" Tony asked next. Kaminsky tapped another button, and seven red dots showed up. They, too, were all within the same tri-state area. Four of the red dots nearly overlapped the green dots that represented the experts.

"It's clear that the kill sights were chosen with proximity to the experts in mind," Charlie pointed out.

"Were all the *You can't catch me* messages hand-delivered to the intended recipient?" Tony looked at Charlie, who shook her head to indicate she didn't know.

"The first one, to Eric Riva, was snail-mailed to him at the *Observer*," Kaminsky answered. "The other three were hand-delivered."

"Okay." Tony nodded. "Maybe somebody saw something.

Maybe there's a description. Do we know the locations where the victims were last seen alive?"

"Not all of them," Kaminsky answered apologetically. "Crane and I are working on it."

"I found out where Omar's is," Crane volunteered. "The bar where you said Laura Peters was last seen, remember? It's in Hampton, Virginia."

"That's about seventy miles from Richmond," Tony responded with a frown. "We have information that Laura Peters was grabbed from right outside that bar. What about Raylene Witt and Jenna Mc-Daniels? Do we know where he grabbed them?"

"Not yet," Kaminsky said. "But we will."

"Do we know why there wasn't more of an outcry over the disappearance of Laura Peters and Raylene Witt?" Charlie asked. "Or if they were even reported missing?"

"Laura was, by her mother yesterday morning," Michael said, surprising Charlie into looking at him again. "Google her name and a Facebook page listing her as missing comes up. Apparently the mother thought Laura was staying with her boyfriend. The boyfriend thought Laura had gone home to her mother. As for the other girl, I didn't get that far."

You were Googling? was the question that came rushing to the tip of Charlie's tongue, but she managed to swallow it just in time.

Michael's lips quirked. "I figured if I could learn to work the remote I could learn to work a computer. I spent part of last night playing with the one in the room across the hall from your bedroom. I'm getting pretty fair at it."

The room across the hall from her bedroom was the smallest of the three upstairs bedrooms, and Charlie had turned it into an office. She had a desk in there, along with a file cabinet and shelves of books. Her Mac Pro computer was on her desk, usually in sleep mode. Also in the room was a love seat that opened into a twin bed.

Last night, Crane had slept in there.

"You'll catch flies," Michael warned with a dawning smile.

Recollecting herself, Charlie pressed her lips together and dropped her gaze, which landed on her coffee cup. Automatically reaching for it, she remembered that Michael couldn't drink coffee, and stopped.

If you only do what he can do, you won't be doing much, she told herself severely. But then she thought, *By now, the coffee's probably cold.* So she didn't want to drink it anyway, and that had nothing to do with Michael at all. Having come to that conclusion, she glanced a little furtively around. If anyone else had replied to her question, she had missed the answer. With an effort, she tuned back in to the conversation.

"The kill methods require planning, and a fairly elaborate setup," Tony was saying. "He'd have to put some time into them. And some work, and some money. Which means he is either employed at something that pays fairly well, or he has access to money through family or some other means."

"The killings occur on weekends," Kaminsky pointed out. "That argues for someone who works, and works a fairly normal schedule, too."

Crane said, "But he grabs his victims several days earlier. And, while there is only one killing ground for each group, the groups are fairly far apart in terms of location. So we know he is able to travel, possibly through his job, and that he has someplace to keep his victims until he is ready to put his death scenario into motion."

"The physical description provided by the survivors is all over the map in terms of height and weight," Kaminsky said, "but we know he is male, and that he wears all black clothing and what is probably a mask over his face that makes it look unnaturally white and skeletal. And he drives, owns, or has access to an old blue or gray van."

"So who are we looking for?" Tony asked.

"I have no idea," Kaminsky said as Crane shrugged. Kaminsky glanced at Charlie. "Fortunately, our team now includes a highly educated expert to help us figure this out. Any insights you care to share, Dr. Stone?"

The look Charlie gave Kaminsky should have withered her. It didn't.

Transferring her gaze to Tony, Charlie said, "Like I said, the first group of victims needs to be checked out: something about them as a group, or one of them as an individual, has meaning for him. I feel fairly confident that at the time of the murders of that first group he was living or working within a twenty-mile or less radius of the kill site. Also, the method of coercion—how he terrified his victims into killing one another—is important. Why did he choose those methods? Were they particular fears of the victims, and, if so, how did he know about them? Are they fears of his, and if so, how did he come by them? Did he, perhaps, have an experience mirroring one of the scenarios? Or did a close family member? For example, did his father drown? Or was the Gingerbread Man himself, at a tender age, the victim of something involving a propeller, such as a lawn mower accident? Or—"

"Or maybe he's just plain evil," Michael interrupted. "No cause and effect, no traumatic childhood experience: just evil. That's where your soft heart's steering you wrong, buttercup: you want to think that people do bad things because bad things were done to them, and they're broken as a result, which means that they can be fixed. That *you* can fix them. I'm here to tell you that it ain't necessarily so, and that's the kind of thinking you want to be careful of because it can get you killed."

Charlie saw that for once he was being absolutely serious, and her brows contracted. A lightning-fast whisper of a question flickered through her mind—*Is he warning me about himself?*—before she noticed the gathering frowns on the faces of the three living beings she'd been talking to before Michael had butted in.

"Charlie?" Tony prompted. The look he was giving her was kind of weird, kind of questioning, and she realized that as far as Tony and Kaminsky and Crane were concerned she had totally spaced out in mid-spiel in front of them.

Damn it.

"Sorry, I had to stop for a moment to gather my thoughts," she said, as with her peripheral vision—because she was absolutely not looking his way again—she watched Michael smile with what she had no trouble identifying as sardonic enjoyment of her predicament. But she was *not* going to be distracted again, be that smile ever so maddening. Instead, she concentrated on Tony, and on getting out the rest of the facts about the killer that had been coalescing in her head.

"What we are dealing with here is a highly organized killer. He is almost certainly a white male, aged twenty-five to forty, intelligent, plans everything in advance, is a perfectionist with no tolerance for mistakes," she continued. "He sees himself as dominant, controlling, and powerful, so I would expect to find him in a job where he has quite a bit of authority. He is a sadist with a God complex. He enjoys having the power of life and death over his victims."

"If what that means is that he gets everything into place ahead of time, before he snatches the victims, then it's probable, even likely, that by now he already has the killing grounds for the next group of victims prepared, is that right?" Tony frowned thoughtfully, her brief lapse forgotten, she thought.

"Yes," Charlie replied. "He has almost certainly already prepared the killing ground for both groups of victims that remain to allow him to complete this year's ritual."

Tony slapped a palm down on the counter with satisfaction. "There you go. That gives us another possible way of finding him: find those killing grounds."

Charlie nodded. "They should be within a few miles of the next two experts he's planning to send a message to."

"Only we don't know who those experts are," Kaminsky objected.

"No." Charlie shook her head. "We don't."

"But you can make some guesses, right? Identify some possibilities?" Tony was looking at her intently. "That should help us narrow the places where we mount a search."

"Yes, I can," Charlie said. "But I have no way of knowing if I'll be accurate. With the first three groups, he didn't send a challenge to anyone at all that we know of. After that, he chose a reporter, a geneticist, a university professor, and a researcher. What the last three have in common is an interest in and a certain expertise in the workings of the mind of a violent criminal. But he could change his parameters for selecting the next individual he wants to involve in this case at any time."

"Understood." Tony's eyes met hers with a touch of humor. Charlie realized that she was probably sounding a little pedantic.

"The thing is, this is such an anomalous case," she explained. "I'm not sure how many of the rules apply."

"Understood," Tony said again, and slid off the bar stool. "If you're ready, I'd like to get going for that interview with Jenna McDaniels."

Charlie stood, too, and automatically began gathering mugs. "Give me a minute, and I'll be right with you."

"We've got this covered." Crane took the mugs away from her.

"Then let me get my purse," she said to Tony. As she left the kitchen, she heard him giving a brief recap to the others, prioritizing what they needed to do. With Michael trailing her—"I feel like a damned puppy on a leash," he muttered, which made her smile—she was back with her purse and jacket in no time. All traces of breakfast were cleared away. Kaminsky stood at the breakfast bar tucking her laptop into its case, Charlie saw as she reentered the kitchen. Crane sat on a bar stool beside Kaminsky fiddling with the controls on a video camera. Tony was over near the sink talking on his cell phone, and as he saw her held up a finger to indicate that he would just be one more minute. Charlie nodded at Tony, then headed for the kitchen table. There was something she needed to do.

"So, are you going to be working with us on this one all the way through?" Kaminsky asked her, her tone making it clear that she was hoping the answer was going to be *no*. Kaminsky was keeping her voice low, Charlie surmised, so as not to interfere with Tony's conversation. It sounded to Charlie as if he was giving a superior a brief overview as to where the team was and what it was doing, but Charlie didn't actually listen as she packed the DVD and letter that had come with Michael's watch safely into a zippered compartment of her purse, then moved the rest of the mail to the console table.

Besides those items, nothing was urgent; even the bills could wait a few days.

"Looks like it," Charlie replied, while Michael, having observed what she had tucked into her purse, said, "No point in wasting your time with that. What's done is done."

Last night's anguish was totally absent from his tone. It was cool, casual. Equally, there was no trace of emotion that she could perceive on his face.

Even if he really was that indifferent to what was on the DVD, she wasn't. And suddenly she was very sensitive to the cool weight of his watch on her arm.

Her eyes met his.

I owe it to you to check it out.

But, of course, she couldn't say it aloud.

"We're honored to have you, Dr. Stone," Crane told her, with a reproving look at Kaminsky. "You're a real asset to the team."

Charlie smiled at him. "Thank you. And call me Charlie, please."

"Charlie." Crane was stowing the camera away in a case full of miscellaneous equipment. "And why don't you go ahead and call me Buzz?"

His bright blue eyes gleamed at her from behind his glasses.

"Oh, please." Kaminsky rolled her eyes. "What are we, the Waltons? Let's try to keep it professional, people."

"Hey, *Lena,* guess what?" Crane's (no, Buzz's) voice was as low as Kaminsky's but that didn't blunt the edge on it. Knowing how Kaminsky felt about being addressed by her first name, Charlie almost winced: nothing good was likely to follow. "Nobody thinks being reasonably friendly with coworkers is unprofessional except you."

Kaminsky glared at him. "I don't notice you going around calling Bartoli *Tony.* Or would that be because you're only interested in getting *reasonably friendly* with Dr. Stone here?"

"Holy Mother of God, Lean Cuisine, you need to get a grip," Buzz snapped. He and Kaminsky were exchanging glares when Buzz let loose with an only partly masked yawn. For a moment Kaminsky stared at him in astonishment. Then, very softly, she began to laugh.

"Hours getting too long for you, *Buzz Cut?*" she jeered.

Buzz looked embarrassed. "I'm a little sleep deprived, okay?" He glanced at Charlie. "You might want to get your computer checked out. It kept turning on all by itself the whole time I was trying to sleep."

Michael chuckled. As Charlie made the connection—Michael had been on her computer in the room in which Buzz had been trying to sleep—her eyes widened with guilty knowledge. What Buzz or Kaminsky might have made of her expression she fortunately didn't have to find out, because Tony had finished his call and was coming toward them.

"If you two don't knock it off, I'm going to fire one of you." Tony gave both of his subordinates warning glances. Kaminsky, still looking mad, didn't reply, but Buzz muttered *"Sorry"* and Tony, with another hard look at Kaminsky, nodded.

"Ready?" he asked Charlie. Charlie nodded, and they headed toward the hall. He added, "I'd apologize for that little by-play, but you've seen it before."

"It's okay. I think they're kind of cute," Charlie replied.

Tony grinned. "For God's sake, don't let Kaminsky hear you say that. I really will have to fire her."

Charlie laughed. "Don't worry, I won't."

"Do you mind if we take your car?" Tony asked. "I'd like to leave the rental for Kaminsky and Crane."

"That's fine." She was fishing in her purse for her keys as they approached the front door. Tony reached around her to open it for her.

"You planning to drive?" Michael inquired as she produced them. "'Cause I can tell you right now that Dudley'd like to have the keys, but I'm betting he's going to be too politically correct to ask."

Charlie's fingers clenched around her keychain. Whether she'd been about to hand them over or not she had no idea, but now that he'd put the issue of gender equality into play she definitely would not. Lips compressing, she stepped out into the hot, brilliant sunlight, squinted a little, shaded her eyes with her hand, and shot Michael a blistering look as he appeared beside her.

"You'd want to drive, too, you—you man," she mouthed, piling a fair degree of venom on that last word. With Tony so close behind them, her voice wasn't even as loud as a whisper. But when Michael grinned, she was perfectly sure that he had understood.

"You're right, but the difference is that *I'm* not worried about being politically correct," he answered. "I'd just tell you to hand the keys over."

Unable to reply because Tony, clearly assuming that she had stopped to wait for him, was sliding a proprietary hand around her arm now as he joined her, Charlie gave Michael a fulminating look. It was wasted. He wasn't looking at her—or Tony. He was looking toward the street.

"Damn," he said in a totally different tone, and then as Charlie followed his gaze she found herself staring in horror at the tide of reporters rushing at them.

CHAPTER THIRTEEN

Ken Ewell and Howie Martin, another deputy sheriff whom Charlie knew vaguely, had been parked in their marked cruiser outside of her house since shortly after dawn. They were ordered there by Sheriff Peel when media types had first started arriving in town. (That would be shortly before dawn.) Their mission was to keep the press on the public streets and off private property (such as Charlie's yard and the yards of her neighbors), and to keep one of Big Stone Gap's residents (that would be Charlie) from being harassed as the eyes of the nation that had been following on TV the effort to find Jenna McDaniels now turned to where and how she had been found. Although for the last hour there had been satellite trucks and carloads of reporters parked out in front of Charlie's house, everything had been completely under control until Charlie herself stepped through her own front door.

Then all hell broke loose.

This Ken explained to Charlie in a breathless rush as he and his partner tried and failed to keep the press from completely surrounding her and Tony as they fought their way toward her garage, a detached, shedlike structure at the top of her driveway. By the time they reached it, Tony had his arm wrapped tight around Charlie's waist and she had her head bent against his shoulder to avoid the intrusive cameras.

"Dr. Stone, is it true that you rescued Jenna McDaniels?"

"What can you tell us about her ordeal, Dr. Stone?"

"Hey, Charlie, look this way!"

"Wait, aren't you the FBI agent who worked with Dr. Stone on the Boardwalk Killer case?"

"Yeah, you're right, it's Special Agent Anthony Bartoli! Is this another serial killer case, Agent Bartoli?"

The press yelled those and what felt like a hundred other questions at them until Charlie and Tony (and Michael) reached the relative safety of the garage. With Ken and Howie trying to clear reporters from in front of the garage door—she and Tony entered through the people-sized one on the side of the small building—Charlie forgot about asserting her equality and being politically correct and whose car it was anyway and all other possibly pertinent issues except expediency, and handed Tony the keys to her blue Camry.

Bottom line was, he had more practice driving through a horde of reporters than she did. Besides, she understood herself well enough to know that if somebody jumped in front of her bumper, she would hit the brakes. And she'd seen Tony drive a sufficient number of times to further know that he would not; she liked to think it was because he trusted whomever it was would get out of his way.

"That was a cluster fuck," Michael muttered as the Camry made it out of the garage, around Tony's rented dark blue Lincoln that was clogging up her driveway, and into the street, where it sped away from the media, all of whom had rushed to return to their vehicles to give chase. Ken and Howie had successfully blocked the pursuit by turning their car sideways in the street, but that wouldn't hold the reporters back long, Charlie knew. Still, it might give them enough time to get to the hospital unimpeded. "Good call letting Dudley drive, by the way."

The car was small, with lingering traces of new car smell (she'd bought it right before she had moved to Big Stone Gap, so it was only a few months old). It was as stiflingly hot as a blast furnace as the air-conditioning struggled to make a dent in the heat. Michael was in the backseat. Unwilling to do more than cast a quick glance around at him under the pretext of looking out the back window for chasing reporters, Charlie flipped down the passenger-side visor, which came equipped with a small mirror. Of course, she couldn't see him in it: she had forgotten. But it didn't matter: the image she'd gotten in that one glance was engraved indelibly on her mind. He was way too big for the cramped space. His legs were folded up in a way that would've been uncomfortable if he were alive, and his forearms rested on his knees. The disgusted expression on his face would have made her want to smile if she hadn't been battling off shivery little flutters of déjà vu. This degree of media interest was actually not as bad as the frenzy that had engulfed her when she had been the teenage survivor of the murder of Holly and her family. It was not as bad as what she had been through in the aftermath of the Boardwalk Killer's resurgence. But the memories it evoked— the terror, the helplessness, the sense of being both trapped and at bay—made her wonder, suddenly, if maybe Michael wasn't right. Maybe she should simply walk away from her work at Wallens Ridge, abandon her research, forget about her determination to find out the building blocks of a serial killer and how such monsters could be identified and stopped, and make a whole new life for herself in which serial killers were part of her past, not her present, and not her future.

The thought that it might be possible for her to do that briefly dazzled her.

But then she thought, No. *If I do that, if I walk away, all those horrible things that happened will have been for nothing. The deaths of Holly and her family, of the other victims, will be just that many more senseless killings. If what I am doing can save even one more life, then that's what I have to do.*

"You okay, babe?" Michael seemed to be able to read her thoughts with uncanny accuracy. She wasn't sure she liked that. No, she was sure: she didn't like it. Then she realized that, while she couldn't see him through the mirror, he could see her. He was reading her face, not her mind.

Frowning, she gave a barely there nod by way of a reply. And snapped the visor back up against the ceiling so that he could no longer see her eyes.

Hah!

"If you can give me directions, I won't have to stop and fiddle with the GPS," Tony told her, and, glad of the distraction, Charlie did. Past the church where Michael was buried—as far as she could tell, Michael didn't even give it a glance—and the Farmer's Market and Miner's Park, through the small downtown with its antique-style street lamps on every corner and Little Stone Mountain rising like a hulking, blue-gray sentinel above it, left at Traffic Light five (the lights were numbered one through eight), and finally into the hospital parking lot.

Unlike the town itself, which was light on traffic on Saturday mornings, the parking lot was crowded with vehicles. The hospital was a long, low structure of brick and white stucco with only sixty beds. There were at least that many cars in the parking lot. Charlie's eyes widened as she saw the crowd of reporters gathered in front of the entrance. Satellite trucks from stations as diverse as their local WAPK to CNN had set up shop on the sweltering blacktop.

"Oh, boy," Tony said, glancing at her. "I'm afraid there's nothing for it but to brave the gauntlet."

"Sneaking in the back isn't going to work, either: looks like they got the place surrounded," Michael added. Charlie could feel his eyes on her. "Look, you know you don't have to do this. Dudley and the gang have been catching serial killers just fine without you. You can hole up in a hotel or something until this is over. If you want to help them, you can do it over the phone."

She was tempted, of course she was, but only for a second. She gave a quick, negative shake of her head, and Michael said, "Fuck."

By the time they reached Jenna's room, Charlie was seriously wishing that there were another choice she could have made. Even after they fought their way through the reporters—the hospital's security guards had been supplemented by deputies and local cops to keep the media out of the building—there was still the hospital itself to deal with. The area around the emergency room in particular was thick with the phantoms of the recently, violently departed. Even with Michael playing bodyguard, two of them rushed her the moment they realized she could see them. She never did find out what they wanted, because Michael scared them off before they reached her, and with Tony at her side she had to continue on. To make things worse, she found that she was the object of a great deal of unwanted attention from the living, too. At first she couldn't understand all the sideways glances and nudges and not-quite-discreet-enough pointing fingers. Even though it seemed like almost everyone in the hospital recognized her and was interested enough to watch her for as long as she was in sight, that was, surely, only her own paranoia at work.

Or so she told herself.

But then, as she passed a half-filled waiting room and caught a glimpse of her own face on TV, she understood. It was starting up all over again. Just as Michael had said, she was the girl who had lived: a never-ending story, apparently, especially considering what she had grown up to become.

The knowledge made her feel cold all over.

Detective Sager was standing outside the door to Jenna's room, along with a second man—who Charlie assumed was another detective—and two uniformed cops.

"Since that initial interview last night, she's clammed up. We've been ordered to keep a guard on the door, but not to enter the room or let anyone else in—unless authorized by the parents. But only a few minutes ago we got a call telling us that you were on the way up and we should let you through," Sager informed Tony with barely concealed ire. "So I guess that makes you and Dr. Stone here special." His eyes slid over Charlie, and not in a friendly way.

Seeming to take no offense, Tony frowned at him. "Family has some clout, I take it?"

Sager grimaced. "Her father's a federal judge. He's in there now, along with her mother and somebody I think is the family lawyer. What I want to know is, why don't they want her to talk to us?"

Charlie was pretty confident she knew the answer.

"Teen Queen's feeling guilty," Michael said, echoing her own thoughts. Charlie knew he was remembering Raylene Witt's accusation just as she was. If Jenna had killed Raylene, and possibly Laura, too, she very well might not want anyone to know. Telling Jenna up front that having his victims kill one another was part of the Gingerbread Man's MO might or might not make her feel better about what she had done, but it would also taint any account that she gave of what had happened. When it came time for trial, defense lawyers would have a field day painting investigators as having led the witness. Tony had explained this on the way over, and Charlie knew it was true. She only hoped that Jenna knew what had happened was in no way her fault.

Tony shrugged. "Couldn't say." Then, with a nod at Sager and a brief knock, he opened the door for Charlie and followed her—and Michael—into the room.

It was a typical hospital room, small, cool from the air-conditioning, bright from the overhead light, and smelling of antiseptic.

"Special Agent Bartoli?" A tall, silver-haired man in a dark suit was the first to react to their presence. He stood on the opposite side of the hospital bed alongside another man, who was shorter, stockier, with thinning gray hair, in another dark suit. A well-dressed woman of around fifty was seated on the near side of the bed. She had short, expensively styled red hair, and as she looked sharply around at the new arrivals, Charlie saw that her features were remarkably similar to Jenna's: delicate, pretty, upscale. Jenna herself was in the bed, in a semi-sitting position which allowed her to see and be seen without obstruction. She was still pale, but aside from that and the bandage on her forehead there were no outward marks of her ordeal that Charlie could see. Her long, inky black hair hung in a single thick braid over one shoulder, and she wore a satiny pink bed jacket on top of her hospital gown. A blue hospital blanket covered her from the waist down. An IV was in her left arm, and her expression as she looked at the newcomers was both nervous and wary.

"Hello, Jenna," Charlie said softly as Tony and the silver-haired man, who introduced himself as Jenna's father, Judge Alton McDaniels, shook hands. For a moment Jenna's eyes locked with hers, and Charlie could see the horror lurking in that golden brown gaze. Jenna was going to see a lot of people who would talk to her about putting what had happened behind her, about moving on, about forgetting. Charlie knew the girl never would.

Jenna simply looked at her without replying.

"Who are you?" Jenna's mother asked sharply.

"I'm Dr. Stone. We talked on the phone last night, remember? Your daughter ran to my house for help." The woman's face wasn't exactly hostile, but it wasn't encouraging, either. However, it was

Jenna Charlie was interested in, Jenna she hoped to help. "I'm a psychiatrist. I'm working with Agent Bartoli"—she nodded at Tony,
who was talking to Jenna's father and the other man—"and his team
to help catch the man who did this."

"Why did the freak send me down to your house?" There was an
edge of suspicion in Jenna's voice. *The freak,* Charlie knew, was Jenna's way of referring to the Gingerbread Man.

"Did he specifically send you down to my house?" Even as Charlie asked the question, she knew the answer: of course he had. "How
did he do that?"

"He said that the only place in the world where he wouldn't kill
me was the big white house at the bottom of the path. He said if I
could make it there before he caught me, he'd let me live." The rising
emotion in Jenna's voice caught the men's attention.

"He wanted to get me involved," Charlie told her, at the same
time as Jenna's father said, "Jenna, are you all right?"

As Jenna nodded, the man looked at Charlie with narrowed eyes.
"And you are?"

His wife told him. Charlie allowed herself to be distracted by introductions, shaking hands with Judge McDaniels; his wife, Jill; and
Clark Andrews, their family attorney, in turn.

"Thank you for letting us talk to Jenna," Tony said when the last
of the introductions was finished.

"Only as long as she doesn't get upset." Jill McDaniels was holding her daughter's hand. Beneath the strain on her face she, too,
looked wary, and Charlie wondered exactly what Jenna had told her.

"We're going to do everything in our power to catch the person
who did this," Tony promised them all. He looked at Jenna, and his
voice gentled. "It would help us a lot if you could answer a few questions. We'll stop whenever you want."

After a moment's hesitation, Jenna nodded.

Tony asked, "Do you mind if I record this? So I don't have to try
to remember everything." Jenna looked at her father. Both parents
looked at the lawyer. He nodded.

"As long as you're prepared to turn it off if I tell you to," Clark
Andrews said.

Tony said, "Absolutely." Reaching into his pocket, he pulled out a small tape recorder and set it on the bed table alongside the glass of water and other miscellaneous objects that were already there. Pressing a button, he turned the machine on, and looked at Jenna again.

"Okay, here we go." Tony smiled at Jenna. Charlie found herself impressed by the air of calm reassurance he projected. "Can you tell me where you were and what you were doing when you were abducted?" Charlie knew that he wanted to get some concrete information under their belts as quickly as possible, in case the session had to be stopped.

Jenna took a breath. "In Hampton. On Pembroke Avenue, near the intersection with Mallory Street. We—my sorority—were having our run. You know, the No Excuse for Child Abuse 5k. I was handing out water at the three-mile mark. I gave out all my water, and everybody had passed, and then one of the golf carts came by and gave Skyler—the girl I was with, she was feeling sick—a ride to the finish line. They were going to come back for me, but it was getting dark, so I started walking on in by myself. There were other people from the race heading in, too, and I was kind of following them, so it didn't feel like I was really alone or anything. I remember the strap on my sandal came unfastened, and I sat down on a curb to fasten it, and everybody else was still walking and talking on up ahead. Then . . . I don't know, I . . . blacked out." Her mouth started to shake. "When I woke up I was in this—cage."

Tony asked: "While you were walking, did you see anyone suspicious? Anyone you now think could have been the man who grabbed you?"

Jenna shook her head. "No. Nobody unusual, nobody who stood out that I can remember. I only just—I heard a voice, okay? Then later, when . . ." Clamping her lips together, she swallowed.

"One of the doctors who examined her last night said that there are marks on her that are consistent with the use of a stun gun," Judge McDaniels told Tony. His face was rigid, and his eyes were alive with anger at what had been done to his daughter.

Tony nodded acknowledgment.

"You said you heard someone speak. Do you remember what he said, Jenna?" Tony's voice was incredibly gentle.

Jenna closed her eyes briefly. "Last thing I remember hearing before I blacked out was a man saying in this kind of weird voice, *'Hi, there.'* Like, behind me. I never saw who it was. Then, when I woke up in the cage, I started screaming. I screamed my head off. He—I couldn't see him. It was so dark. All I heard was this disembodied voice again. He told me that if I didn't shut up, he would cut my throat. I believed him. I shut up."

Even from where she was standing, Charlie could see the girl's shiver.

"Would you recognize the voice if you heard it again?" Tony asked.

"I—think so. Like I said, it was weird."

Tony's gaze was intent on the girl's face. "Where was the cage, Jenna?"

"In some sort of vehicle. A van, I think, or maybe one of those small camper trucks. The cage took up almost the whole back. It had sleeping bags. And—kind of a toilet." Jenna stopped, and took a deep breath. "There was food—packages of peanut butter crackers. And a two-liter of water. After the first day, we—we rationed it."

"We?" Tony questioned carefully. This was a sensitive area, Charlie knew.

"The other girls—and me."

"You were kept in the same cage?" Tony asked. "How many of you?"

"Three."

"Including you?"

Jenna nodded.

"Did you know the other girls previously?"

Jenna shook her head.

"Were the other girls put in the cage before or after you?"

"I don't know. I kind of kept passing out and waking up, but at some point I remember seeing them and realizing I wasn't alone. They were just—lying there, even when I was screaming, and later I figured out that they were passed out, too. Then we finally all woke up at about the same time."

Drugs? Charlie wondered. *Possibly a gas that was pumped into the back of the truck?* The autopsy on the two deceased victims, which if all was going according to schedule would be under way at that very moment, should tell them what substances the girls had been exposed to. Jenna's blood had certainly been drawn last night for testing, and the analysis might be able to tell them the same thing, although it was possible that whatever it was had already metabolized out of her system.

Tony asked, "Did you talk to the other girls?"

Jenna nodded again. "They were . . . nice. Whatever happened, we made a pact to stick together. When he came—we knew he would come—we were going to attack him. Raylene—Raylene . . ." Jenna's voice shook. "She was tough. She made a weapon out of this big metal comb she had in her hair, by bending over some of the teeth and holding it in her fist. Sort of like brass knuckles with spikes. She said she was going to go for his eyes. Only—she never got the chance."

Breathing hard, Jenna stopped.

"Oh, baby," her mother whispered, and Charlie could see how tightly their hands were clasped.

"Why didn't Raylene get the chance, Jenna?" Tony's voice was soft.

Jenna was lying back against her pillows now, looking at him out of eyes that were stark with remembered horror.

"We agreed to never sleep at the same time, that one of us would always stay awake to keep watch so that he couldn't sneak up on us. But—we must have all fallen asleep anyway. And . . . and when we woke up we were at the bottom of this well." She took a breath, glanced at her mother. "I was so scared."

"Jenna," Mrs. McDaniels said piteously.

"What happened then, Jenna?" Tony prompted.

"I won't have her getting upset," Mrs. McDaniels flashed at him.

"Jill, let her talk," Judge McDaniels told his wife.

Mrs. McDaniels cast her husband an angry look, then focused on her daughter. "Honey, do you feel like you want to go on?"

Jenna looked at her mother. They were holding hands so tightly now that Mrs. McDaniels' knuckles showed white. Jenna wet her lips. Then she nodded, and looked at Tony again.

"Last night—I can't believe it was just last night. Oh, my God." She paused, and swallowed. Then she went on. "Anyway, it was really dark. We could barely even see one another. At first we didn't know what was happening. We didn't know where we were, or anything. Only that we were in this moldy-smelling place that was wet. We got up and started feeling around, feeling the walls, to see if we could find a way out. Raylene's the one who said she thought it was a well, and I think she was right. It was really deep, with curved stone sides that were slimy and disgusting and impossible to get a grip on. Way up above we could see this little circle of night sky. There was nothing we could do, no way we could climb out or escape. We were screaming but it didn't help. It just echoed back at us, and nobody came. There was this rushing noise, and we looked up. Then water started pouring in on us, nasty cold water, like from this giant hose, gushing, and we tried to get away from it and we did, kind of, by hugging the edges of the well. But the water kept pouring in and getting deeper and deeper and Laura started crying and saying that she couldn't swim."

Jenna broke off. Her eyes closed.

"Everything's all right now. We've got you safe," Mrs. McDaniels told her daughter.

Taking a deep breath, Jenna nodded, then opened her eyes and looked at Tony. "That's when we saw him: when the water started getting up to our chests and Laura was freaking out and crying and we were trying to tell her how to swim. He leaned over the top of the well and shined a light down on us. At first I thought it was somebody come to help us and I was begging him to get us out of there. Then he must have slipped up with the light and I saw him. He was wearing a black hoodie or cloak or something with one of those Guy Fawkes masks, you know, all white with the creepy smile. And he said—and he said—"

When she broke off again, Tony waited a few seconds and then asked, "What did he say?"

Charlie could almost see the chill passing over Jenna's skin. The girl gave a long, shivery sigh, then squared her shoulders. She looked straight at Tony. "He said, 'Two of you are going to die here tonight. Maybe all three of you are. I'll let one of you live—*if* you kill the others. Kill the others, and I'll let the last one alive go home.'" Jenna's voice was cold and clear suddenly, as if she was repeating words that had burned themselves into her brain. Which those had, Charlie knew. She also knew that they would haunt Jenna for the rest of her life.

Charlie's heart ached for the girl.

"Then what happened?" Tony prompted.

"Then he threw a knife down into the water, and he said one of us should grab it and go after the others, but none of us would. He kept filling up the well. He'd fill it and leave us swimming in it for a while then let it drain, and each time he started to fill it up was worse than the last because he left the water in longer and we knew what was coming. Raylene and I could swim but it was awful and scary and the water was so cold and it kind of swirled around, which made it worse because there was a current that felt like it was trying to suck us down. We started realizing we couldn't do it forever. Laura kept trying but she really couldn't swim and she was getting tired and we were getting tired from trying to help her. After what I think was the fourth time, when most of the water had drained out again, and Laura, like, collapsed on the bottom, Raylene said, 'She's not going to make it,' and when I looked around she had picked up this rock. She was kind of sneaking across the bottom of the well toward Laura, and I looked at her and she said, 'She's going to drown anyway,' and then she hit Laura in the head with the rock. Laura started screaming, but Raylene kept hitting her and hitting her in the head with that rock and there was blood everywhere and her brains were coming out and then Laura just—she just curled up in the mud and died."

Jenna drew her knees to her sharply and covered her face with both hands. Charlie could see the shudders that wracked her.

"Baby." Eyes welling, Mrs. McDaniels rose from her chair.

Jenna's hands dropped. Tears spilled from her eyes. "Oh, Mama, that's when I—"

"Jenna," the lawyer interrupted. "That's enough for now. Agent Bartoli, please turn off the tape recorder."

CHAPTER FOURTEEN

Jenna started to sob. Mrs. McDaniels wrapped her daughter in a hug, which Jenna returned. The sight of mother and daughter so lovingly entwined made Charlie's throat tighten—her overly emotional reaction was, she knew, the result of her own mother issues, and nothing to do with the case. Tony turned off the tape recorder as requested, although as he punched the button he said, looking first at the lawyer and then at Judge McDaniels, "It would really help us to hear the rest of her story. We're all on the same team here."

When the lawyer shook his head and the judge answered with, "That's all my daughter has to say," Tony said, "Could I talk to you two for a minute in private?" and when they agreed the three men went into the hall.

Out of the corner of her eye, Charlie was aware of Michael moving protectively closer to her, and supposed that with Tony gone he felt he had to up his bodyguard-to-the-vulnerable-female game. But he didn't say anything. He just leaned against the wall near her, his arms crossed over his chest, a stalwart sentinel she knew she could count on to have her back. As her glance found him, and their eyes held for the briefest of seconds, she immediately felt calmer, more centered. She recognized the ridiculousness of it: how screwed up was her world when the ghost of Michael Garland served as a grounding presence? That's when Charlie remembered that he might be—*might be*—the exact same kind of monster as the one they were hunting.

A chill slid down her spine.

I have to know the truth. No matter what, she had to ascertain to her own satisfaction whether Michael was innocent or guilty. Not knowing would eventually tear her apart.

The door opened. Judge McDaniels poked his head into the room.

"Jill, could you come out here for a minute?"

"I'm not leaving her." Mrs. McDaniels was shaking her head even as she looked around at him. With her head on her mother's shoulder now, Jenna was crying in deep, shuddering gasps. Listening to her, Charlie remembered the fear and the pain, the shattering guilt, the desperation, she herself had felt all those years ago, and her heart broke for the girl.

"Mrs. McDaniels?" Charlie moved closer. "If you need to go talk to them, I'll stay here with Jenna. She won't be alone."

"It's important, Jill," Judge McDaniels insisted.

Jenna let go of her mother and wiped her eyes. "Mama, I'll be all right."

"Are you sure?"

Jenna nodded, and with a searching look at Charlie, Mrs. McDaniels joined the others in the hall.

"So is this some kind of trick to get me to spill my guts to you now that we're alone?" Jenna's eyes still brimmed with tears. Her voice was shaky in the aftermath of her sobs. It was also faintly hostile.

Charlie shook her head. "No, I promise. Anyway, I'm a doctor. All you have to do is claim doctor/patient privilege and I can't repeat anything you say to me."

She watched Jenna absorb that.

"Last night you kept talking to . . . some invisible person. What was up with that?"

Luckily, Charlie had already anticipated that Jenna might ask her that particular question.

"I don't like to talk about my beliefs, but I will tell you that when

I'm under a great deal of stress, as I was last night, I tend to pray out loud," she said with dignity.

"Oh."

Out of the corner of her eye Charlie saw Michael's wry smile. She saw Jenna digesting her words, saw the last of her hostility fade away. Jenna's eyes were red-rimmed and still wet with tears, and the occasional soblike breath still shook her. Charlie remembered way too vividly how it had felt to be in Jenna's shoes: terrifying, disorienting, soul-crunchingly lonely. As if her whole life had just been destroyed, and she had been left in a place she didn't recognize, in a place that didn't even feel as if it was real, with nobody who knew her, or that she knew. And she made a decision.

"Jenna," she said. "I know what you're going through. Fifteen years ago, I survived an attack by a serial killer, too."

The girl dashed away a tear that had started to slide down her cheek and stared at Charlie suspiciously. "What are you talking about?"

"When I was seventeen, my best friend and her whole family were murdered by a serial killer. I was in the house. I had a chance to save my friend, but I was too afraid that he would catch me and kill me, too. I—ran away and hid." Charlie hadn't expected the punched-in-the-gut feeling the confession would give her. She had to stop talking and breathe.

"Is that the truth?" Jenna demanded.

Get a grip, Charlie ordered herself fiercely, and nodded. Then she told Jenna about Holly.

By the time she was finished, she was sitting on the side of the bed and she and Jenna were holding hands.

"You'll experience survivor's guilt," Charlie told her. "There will be days when you wonder why you lived and the others died. You're going to feel depressed, and you're going to feel afraid, and you're going to feel angry. You may have nightmares. You may find yourself having flashbacks, or revisiting every little detail of what happened obsessively. You may lash out at the people who are trying to help you. All these things are normal reactions to the trauma you've been through. You'll never forget what happened, and you are never going to be the same person you were before it happened. There will always be a before and an after. But I'm here to tell you that you can get through this, you can get your life back, you can go on and be successful and be happy and fall in love and—"

Charlie broke off when the door opened and the McDanielses, Mr. Andrews, and Tony filed back into the room. As they gathered around the bed, Charlie squeezed Jenna's hand and relinquished her place to Jenna's mother.

"So are you going to tell me what the summit meeting was about?" Jenna looked from one parent to the other.

Her father cleared his throat. "After talking to Agent Bartoli, we think it's best if you tell him exactly what happened, exactly the way you told it to us."

Jenna sucked in air. She seemed to shrink, like a child caught doing something wrong. "Dad . . ."

"You can tell them, baby," Mrs. McDaniels said.

"I want you to start where you left off," Tony said. "What happened after Laura died, Jenna?"

Jenna met Charlie's eyes.

"It's all right, Jenna," Charlie said. "You can trust us."

Jenna nodded and closed her eyes. As she started to talk, with a nod at Judge McDaniels, Tony quietly turned the tape recorder back on.

"After Laura died, Raylene was kneeling there beside her holding that rock. The freak job at the top of the well yelled, 'Only one more, and you get to go home,' in, like, this gloating voice, and I knew he was talking to Raylene. I knew he meant she should kill me next."

Jenna broke off then, and wet her lips. Her eyes opened, and she looked at her mother, whose face was tight with love and anguish. As she continued, her voice was barely above a whisper. "So when she stood up, I grabbed the knife out of the mud and I stabbed her with it. I stabbed her and stabbed her and stabbed her until she was dead. Then the freak job yelled down, 'Congratulations, we've got a winner!' and he lowered a ladder into the well and I climbed out and he told me to run. And I did."

By that time she was utterly white and tears were sliding down her cheeks.

"You only did what you had to," Mrs. McDaniels sounded as if the words were wrenched out of her.

"All right, you've got enough," Judge McDaniels said abruptly to Tony, as his wife wrapped her arms around their daughter and Jenna burst into noisy sobs. Watching mother and daughter clinging together, Charlie had to turn away. The moment felt too private to witness.

"Thank you for your cooperation." Tony spoke to Judge McDaniels in a low voice as he scooped up his tape recorder and dropped it into his pocket. "We'll be in touch."

Charlie, meanwhile, pulled a business card from her wallet and scribbled her cell phone number on the back of it. By the time she and Tony had said their goodbyes to Judge McDaniels and Mr. Andrews, Jenna was once again leaning back on her pillows while her mother sat beside her clutching her hand. Jenna's breathing was still ragged, her eyes still gleamed with tears, but there was determination in the tilt of her chin and a new strength in the firm line of her mouth. Jenna, Charlie felt sure, would be all right. Holding the card up so that Jenna could see it, Charlie put it down on the bed table, within her reach.

"Call me if you want to talk," she told Jenna.

"Thanks." Jenna's voice was wobbly, but she managed the smallest of smiles.

"Yes, thank you, Dr. Stone," Mrs. McDaniels echoed over her shoulder, and Charlie nodded by way of a reply.

"You know what? You're a real nice person, Charlie Stone," Michael said in her ear as they were leaving the room. "And take it from me, that's a rare thing."

Charlie couldn't respond, because right at that moment Tony was exchanging a few quick words with Sager and the men with him, and with Special Agents Flynn and Burger, who had just shown up to relieve Sager and crew from door-guarding duty, and she was surrounded by the living. Then Tony took her arm and ushered her toward the freight elevator. He'd made arrangements for Kaminsky and Buzz to switch cars with them, leaving the rented Lincoln near the loading dock and driving off in Charlie's car. That worked like a charm—half the media types present were busy chasing Kaminsky and Buzz, and the other half, the half that held their positions, paid no attention to the Lincoln when Tony nosed it out of the parking lot. As they drove, she and Tony talked—for one thing, she asked, "What *was* the confab in the hall about?" and he told her that he had decided to tell the McDanielses and the lawyer about the Gingerbread Man's MO so they wouldn't be afraid Jenna would face legal problems if she confessed to killing Raylene. All the while Charlie was conscious of a warm little glow pulsing deep inside her. It served as a small but steady counterpoint to the cold wave of horror that the visit to Jenna had evoked, and it came, she knew, from Michael's words.

It wasn't so much what he had said, as how he had said it: there had been, she thought, genuine admiration in his tone. Approval and, yes, affection had been mixed in there somewhere, too.

His opinion of her meant something to her. Actually, it meant a whole lot.

The realization didn't exactly make her happy. Bottom line, though, was that it was a new fact of her life with which she was just going to have to deal.

She and Tony grabbed a quick lunch at the Mutual Drug Store and Cafeteria, which was so crowded with members of the Powell Valley High School football team who were having a meal after practice that they were able to eat undisturbed except for a few friendly waves. They talked shop throughout, although Tony did throw a couple of would-be-flirty comments her way. Given that Michael was lounging beside her listening to every word that was said, flirting with Tony was impossible, so she didn't follow through and that part of the conversation went nowhere. Which didn't exactly please her—a relationship with Tony was something that she really did want to explore—but under the circumstances what could she do? She did manage to consume her lunch without worrying too much about Michael, who was looking increasingly disgruntled as he listened to their conversation. But he did nothing more disruptive than make the odd annoying remark, which she, of course, ignored, and watch them eat.

Tony was paying the bill—Bureau expense account, he teased—when Charlie's cell phone buzzed. Having set her phone on vibrate, she'd been letting her calls go through to voice mail but this one, she saw, was from Tam.

Tam was different. Tam was important. Tam's call—and Charlie hated to think what that said about how her priorities were now ordered—might very well be about Michael. This call she needed to take.

Excusing herself to Tony, she headed for the ladies' room.

"You can wait out here," she told Michael at the door. A pair of elderly women walked out of the restroom at that moment. Michael glanced at them, then looked back at her.

"You see me arguing?" He settled his broad shoulders against the wall beside the door.

Charlie went inside and called Tam.

"Oh, cherie, I am in such a state!" Tam exclaimed without preliminaries when they connected. "Where are you?"

Charlie told her.

"You're safe? You're not in any kind of danger?"

Charlie looked around the small, blue-tiled restroom. The last stall was occupied by a woman and her little girl—Charlie knew, because she could hear them talking—but other than that she was alone.

"No. I'm fine."

"Well, you listen up: there's danger around you. Terrible danger. Ever since I talked to you, I've been getting visions of you being swallowed up in this giant gray cloud. It makes my blood run cold."

"What kind of danger?" Charlie tried not to let her voice change. She knew Tam: Tam was the real deal. If Tam said she was in danger, then Charlie was prepared to take her word for it.

"I don't know. It isn't clear. I just know it's close—closer than you think. For some reason you can't see it. It's like you're blind to it, or the wool is being pulled over your eyes or something." Tam's voice had an urgent undertone. "I wish I could be more specific, but I can't. Not yet anyway."

"Okay." Charlie felt as if a cold hand was gripping the back of her neck. She caught herself looking warily around the bathroom. It was no more than two sinks, three stalls. Wherever the danger to her lurked, she was pretty certain it wasn't in there. "Thanks for warning me."

"I'm focusing on you real intensely. I'll have a breakthrough soon." Tam was breathing hard; Charlie could hear it through the phone. "You be careful, you hear?"

The sound of the toilet flushing made Charlie jump. A moment later, the little girl and her mother emerged to head for the sink.

"I'll be careful." Charlie instinctively made sure her back was to the wall as she watched the mother and daughter at the sink. The knowledge that Michael was right outside was comforting. If she yelled, he would hear.

But then, given that he was as solid as mist, what good would that do?

"I'll call you, cherie, the moment I get more," Tam promised, and, as Charlie said, "Thanks," she disconnected.

Dropping her phone back in her purse, Charlie's first instinct was to run as fast as she could to first Michael and then Tony and tell them what Tam had said.

But as she considered it, the thought of telling Tony that her psychic friend had warned her she was in danger made her uncomfortable: how far on the nut-job side of the equation did she really want him to think she was? As for Michael, there was the solid-as-mist factor to consider. Plus he was already in overprotective mode, and did she truly want to risk having him start harping again on how she needed to find a new job?

As the mother and daughter left, Charlie washed her hands, splashed a little cool water on her face, then took a moment to brush her hair and smooth on lip gloss. All the while she was thinking the matter through.

She couldn't tell Tony. But Michael?

Charlie hadn't made up her mind when she exited the bathroom to find Michael, as she had expected, still stationed outside the door. Straightening to his full height as she approached him, he swept her with a sardonic look. Then his eyes narrowed on her face.

"So what's with you?" he asked.

Charlie's lips pursed. She walked down the short corridor toward the main dining room, where she knew Tony would be waiting for her. Michael fell in beside her.

"Something's up," he persisted. "In case you still don't get it, your face is as easy to read as a neon sign. You can either go ahead and tell me what happened in there, or we can play twenty questions until I get an answer. Your choice."

Charlie flicked him a look. Could he really read her that easily? The answer was: apparently so. Then she sighed and gave up. The truth was, she almost certainly had been going to tell him anyway. She badly needed to tell somebody, and Michael was the only one around who would not only believe her, but, because he'd had firsthand experience with Tam's gifts, appreciate the seriousness of the warning.

"Tam called." The corridor was deserted. Charlie stopped walking, turned to look at him.

He stopped, too. His eyebrows went up. "The voodoo priestess?" Then he frowned at her, as if it had occurred to him that he might have been the subject of the conversation. "What did she want?"

Charlie hesitated. While she'd been tangentially absorbing how tall and powerfully built and absolutely staggeringly good-looking he was, a horrible little niggle of a suspicion inserted itself into her brain. Once it was there, there was nothing she could do about it. It squirmed around taking on a life of its own. "She called to warn me. She said I'm in danger."

His eyes narrowed. His jaw tightened.

"What kind of danger?" he asked carefully.

She shook her head. "Tam didn't know. She simply said I should be careful. She said she saw me being swallowed up by a big gray cloud, and that that was bad."

Even as she said it, Charlie felt that creeping chill on the back of her neck again.

Michael swore. Then he said, "You take her seriously?"

Charlie nodded. "Yes. I do."

His face softened fractionally. "You don't have to look so worried, buttercup. I got your back. And from here on out, I'm not letting you out of my sight."

"Yes, but what if *you're* the danger Tam saw?" That was the niggling little thought that had been squirming around the edges of Charlie's mind, and now she'd come out with it. After all, it wasn't as if there was anything physical he could do to her even if the wool had been totally pulled over her eyes and he really was the psycho killer she had first thought him. She didn't think.

"Me?" He first looked surprised, then disgusted. "As in, you think you're in danger from *me*?"

The look Charlie gave him brimmed with all the latent mistrust she'd been arguing herself out of since he had died.

As he met her gaze his eyes cooled. Then they hardened. Then he gave her the smallest of mocking smiles. "If that's the case, then I guess I'd have to say that makes you shit out of luck."

Two more women appeared at the top of the corridor, clearly heading for the ladies' room, and Charlie started walking again. Michael stalked—that was the only word for it—at her side, and a glance at his face told her that he was seriously angry.

"You don't scare me, Casper," she hissed beneath a hand she lifted to ostensibly cover a yawn.

"Watch it, Doc," he said. "You're pissing me off. Lucky for you I don't have access to a ghost knife."

"*That* was out of line," she flared at him as they proceeded into the dining room, completely aware that they were no longer alone but hoping that amid the football team's rowdiness no one would notice her talking to empty space. "Tam said the wool was being pulled over my eyes. I'd be a fool not to be cautious."

"Oh, right, and that would be by me." His eyes glinted at her. "But you've figured out that you don't have to be afraid of me because I'm dead, right? It'd be different if I was still alive."

Before she could respond to that, Tony, spotting her, called her name, and she had to look away from Michael to smile at him.

———————

Two hours later, she, Tony, Buzz, and Kaminsky (plus a still obviously ticked off Michael) were on board the team's private plane on their way to Columbia, South Carolina, where David Myers lived. He had agreed to meet with them at four. After that, they would talk with local investigators, interview the surviving victim, who still lived in the area, and tour the kill site. Then they would fly on to Charlotte, North Carolina, where they would spend the night. In the morning they would interview Eric Riva, tour the Group Four kill site (there was no surviving victim in that group), then drive the eighty-three miles to Winston-Salem, where they would meet the final expert, Jeffrey Underwood, and visit the Group Five kill site. The Group Five survivor, then-seventeen-year-old Andrew Russell, had since moved to Seattle, Washington. It was agreed that the most time-efficient method of talking to him and other geographically distant survivors was via Skype.

On the plane, they all got busy doing their respective jobs, and for a while, except for the hum of the engine, quiet reigned. Charlie compiled a list of possible experts whom she guessed the Gingerbread Man might target next. By limiting herself to the general geographic area that seemed to be the killer's comfort zone, and doing her best to extrapolate what might draw the Gingerbread Man to a particular expert's résumé, she came up with a list of ten possibilities. It wasn't by any means comprehensive, as she told Tony when she presented it to him, nor did she have any idea if the Gingerbread Man would actually choose any one of the experts on the list. But as Tony said, it was a place to start, and he immediately alerted local FBI offices to keep a watch on the people she had named, and to start searching within a ten-mile radius of their locations for possible future kill sites.

There was no time to waste. None of them ever forgot for a minute that the clock was ticking. In approximately twelve more days, the Gingerbread Man would collect his newest victims, and the killing cycle would begin again.

"He would've needed some kind of equipment—an industrial-grade hose and pump, presumably—to siphon water from the secondary pit to the primary one," Tony said. By that time, they were all seated together in the cushy leather seats surrounding the small oval pop-up conference table in the middle of the plane. Kaminsky had her laptop on. The rest of them relied on their own notes or devices—or memories—to keep up. The day was beautiful if hot, the flight was smooth, and outside the window at Charlie's elbow the sky was endlessly blue above a layer of frothy white clouds.

"The secondary pit was fed by an underground stream, so it was always full," Kaminsky said. "Continual flooding was one of the reasons the site had been abandoned."

"Can we try to identify and trace the equipment?" Tony asked.

"On it," Buzz said, and pecked a note into his tablet. "It's probably a rental. If it is, this'll be a piece of cake."

"What we have here is a power seeker killer," Charlie said

thoughtfully. "There is no sexual component to the murders at all, and no gain motivation, either, as far as I can tell. But I think there is a purpose behind the killings other than the thrill he gets from acting as God to the victims. Of course, it might be something as simple as him getting a charge out of the challenge of coming up with and then acting out these death scenarios. Or it might be something else."

"The guy's a sick fuck." Michael was stretched out on the couch opposite the area where Charlie and the others were sitting. His blue eyes were impossible to read. His mouth had a hard look to it. "There you go, babe. End of story."

"We just got preliminary results back on the objects left in Dr. Stone's kitchen." Kaminsky was looking at her computer. "The knife was the weapon used to kill Raylene Witt. The only fingerprints on it belonged to Jenna McDaniels, which confirms her account of what happened. And the handwriting on the *You can't catch me* letter is consistent with Laura Peters'. Her fingerprints were all over the paper and envelope. There was no one else's."

"So the unsub made Laura Peters write the note," Tony said. "He's toying with us. He knew we'd be salivating at the idea that we had a sample of his handwriting. And I'm one hundred percent convinced that he left that knife because he wanted to make sure we knew that Jenna McDaniels killed Raylene Witt."

"Like I said, he's a sick fuck," Michael said. Charlie flicked him a glance—with one arm tucked behind his head he looked comfortable enough, although his broad shoulders were too wide for the narrow couch—then focused her attention on the others, who actually were trying to contribute something productive to the discussion.

"Omar's—the bar Laura Peters left right before she was abducted—is right around the corner from Pembroke Avenue, where Jenna McDaniels was picked up." Kaminsky was still peering at her computer screen.

"Which leaves us with the question: did he go there targeting them, or did he pick them at random?" Tony asked.

"There has to be a common denominator among the victims." Because she was basically thinking aloud, Charlie looked at Tony without really seeing him. "What makes him choose them? Laura

Peters couldn't swim, for instance, and he chose to subject that group to death by drowning. The question we need to ask is, did he *know* Laura Peters couldn't swim? And if so, how did he know it? And what about the others? Did he choose the death scenarios he placed them in according to their fears? If so, how did he know his victims, and what they were afraid of?"

"Raylene Witt was a manicurist at Hollywood Nails in Hampton. Maybe at some point she did the other girls' nails," Buzz offered.

Tony looked at him.

"I'll check it out," Buzz added hastily. Then he made a face. "She couldn't have done them on the day they disappeared, though, which was the only time Jenna McDaniels was in Hampton. Raylene had called in sick on Wednesday, which is the day she disappeared, and wasn't scheduled to work again until Saturday. Only, because she lived alone, no one knew she had disappeared."

"Maybe there's a twenty-four-hour clinic or pharmacy or something over there near that bar where Laura got nabbed and the street where Teen Queen got picked up. Maybe the screamer was over there because she was sick. Because it makes sense that they were all taken from the same area." Michael was frowning up at the ceiling rather than looking at Charlie. She knew that, she realized crossly, because *she* was looking at *him*. But his comments bore repeating, so she did.

"I'll check that out, too," Buzz said.

"You know what, I think I may have just found a common denominator for these last three victims." There was barely suppressed excitement in Kaminsky's voice. "They were all in terrible car accidents when they were young. Raylene Witt's mother was killed when a drunk driver hit the family car. Raylene was six years old. Her injuries were minor. Laura Peters was in a car crash when she was twelve. A friend's mother was driving a group of four girls to a birthday party. Kylie Waters and Sara Goldberg—who were both twelve, too—were killed." ("There you go," Michael said, his gaze shifting to Charlie. "Kylie and Sara." Remembering the two little girls who had come for Laura, Charlie thought, *Yes, that sounds right*. Those little girls, who were presumably her close friends at the time they were killed, would have come to take Laura to the light. Presumably.)

"Then there's Jenna McDaniels. At the age of sixteen, she was on her way to a dance when there was a rollover accident. The boy driving, Tommy Stafford, who I'm assuming was her date, was killed."

"Could be coincidence," Buzz cautioned.

"Ain't no such thing as coincidence," Michael said. He was looking at the ceiling again.

"All right, we want to check into first responders, hospital personnel, anybody who might have been on the scene of all three accidents," Tony said. "If that's a coincidence, it's a pretty big one."

"I'll get on it." Kaminsky typed something into her laptop.

The pilot's voice came over the intercom, telling them to prepare for landing. They were on the ground not long afterward.

"Oh, for God's sake, are you still pouting?" Charlie hissed at Michael, taking advantage of a semi-private moment as Tony talked to the flight crew, Kaminsky placed a phone call, and Buzz went to fetch the rental car. Michael was standing grim-faced and silent on the tarmac beside her.

"Pouting?" The look he slanted down at her was sharp with disbelief. "I don't pout."

"Oh, yeah? You could have fooled me."

Then Buzz pulled up in the rental car and any chance of further conversation, at least on her part, was gone.

"Just so you know, babe, fooling you ain't that hard," Michael said by way of a parting shot. Surrounded by the living again, Charlie couldn't do more than skewer him with a dirty look in reply.

A little more than forty-five minutes later, with Tony at the wheel of their rented SUV, they were on the University of South Carolina's campus driving down Sumter heading for their meeting with David Myers. Charlie cast a fond look at the Horseshoe, the quadrangle that was home to some of the campus' most historic buildings, admiring the huge oaks with their festoons of gray Spanish moss and the lush lawn where a handful of students lounged in the shade. Then they rounded a corner, and a moment later they were pulling into the parking lot of the very modern building that housed David Myers' office.

"So, you went to college here, huh?" Michael asked as they walked through the suffocating heat of the parking lot into the welcome chill of the building. "What, was this guy your college sweet-heart?"

Glad as she was that he seemed to have gotten over being mad at her, Charlie didn't care for the subject. Since it previously had been raised right after Michael had seen Laura go off with her two dead friends, and he hadn't commented at the time, Charlie had been hoping he'd been too wrapped up in what he had just witnessed to pay attention when she'd been admitting to a relationship with David Myers. Obviously, no such luck.

A firming of her lips was her only reply. Clearly he took that for the *yes* she really didn't want to give him, because interest sparked in his eyes.

When the door to David Myers' office opened in response to Tony's knock, Charlie thought she was prepared.

She should have known that she wasn't.

CHAPTER FIFTEEN

For a moment, for the briefest sliver of time as she found herself looking at David, Charlie was twenty-one again and achingly vulnerable.
She had an instant mental image of herself, slim in blue jeans with her
waist-length hair pulled back from her face by a barrette so that the
silky fall of it rippled down her back, as she had looked on the first
day of spring semester of her senior year in college. That was when
she'd come to work for Dr. David Myers as his research assistant. By
the end of that semester she had absolutely hero-worshipped him.

At least now she was mature enough to realize just how young
and foolish she had been. But still, as she came face-to-face with
David again, the memory was more embarrassing than she had expected it to be.

"Charlie!" He greeted her with apparent delight, smiling broadly
as his gaze swept her. "You look fantastic."

"Hello, David." Burningly conscious that she was the object of
the undivided attention of every other member of her group even if
none of them (except Michael) was blatant enough to be openly
watching her, she smiled her coolest, most professional smile and held
out her hand. When he shook hands with no more than the appropriate degree of friendliness, she found herself devoutly glad that he

seemed determined to keep things professional, too. "I'd like you to meet—"

"Holy hell, he wasn't a student when you were here anymore than I was," Michael said in her ear as she, trying her best to tune her bête noire out, performed the introductions. "What, were you boinking your professor?"

Actually, yes, she had been. Her psychology professor, to be exact. Only a few times, toward the end of the semester. And the last time they had set eyes on each other, when he had broken off their budding relationship because he was getting married to the woman he'd been engaged to, unbeknownst to her, all along, and then going to England to accept a fellowship at Oxford, she had told him she loved him and begged him to stay.

None of which she said out loud. That last part at least she never intended to share with anyone. Seen in the bright light of eleven years later, it was downright humiliating. Worse, it was stupid.

It was also one more example of her unerring instinct for choosing the absolutely wrong man.

His office was different than the one he'd had when she'd worked for him. Bigger. Not quite as messy. Of course, he was a full professor now, instead of a freshly minted, thirty-year-old Ph.D. in his first year as an assistant professor. Except for a well-trimmed mustache and goatee, he looked pretty much the same: a shade under six feet tall, with a slim build that showed no signs of softening around the edges and short coffee brown hair. A few gray hairs at his temples and some lines at the corners of his eyes and mouth that hadn't been there before were the only real indications of the passage of time. Even the Gamecocks tie and blue dress shirt he wore tucked into blue jeans could have been the same.

Charlie took comfort from the knowledge that she looked—and was—totally different from the academically accomplished but otherwise clueless girl that he had known.

"The Columbia Police Department took the letter the day after I got it," David answered Tony's question, which referred to the whereabouts of the *You can't catch me* message David had received. Tony sat in the chair across from David, who was ensconced behind his cluttered desk in what Charlie, in psychiatrist mode, recognized as his deliberate assumption of the power position. Charlie and Kaminsky sat on a tweedy love seat in front of the window. Buzz perched atop a small stool nearby. Michael leaned against the wall near Charlie. "I don't know if they still have it, or if they passed it on to the FBI. At first the detectives here thought they were dealing with just a bizarre double homicide. It was a couple of weeks before the connection to the previous murders was made and the FBI was called in. I spent quite a bit of time working with the detectives and the FBI to try to identify the killer"—he glanced at Charlie with the faintest of smiles— "and I even tried to enlist the help of the illustrious Dr. Stone here, whose work with serial killers I have followed with interest and admiration, but the fact is we made no appreciable headway. Of course, now that your elite team of serial killer hunters is on the job, presumably we can hope for better luck."

"Do you have any idea why you were chosen to receive that letter?" Tony asked.

David shook his head. "No, not really. I mean, I'm fairly certain it was because of my book. I'm the author of *Criminal Psychology: Understanding the Deviant Mind,* you know—it's the textbook of choice in most criminal psychology courses, so there's wide access to it."

"A fifteen-year-old boy survived the attack," Charlie said. "Had you ever met him before?"

"Saul Tunney." David turned his attention to her, and Charlie recognized that particularly intent gaze as the one he got when something truly interested him. "A remarkable young man. No, I'd never met him before, but we stay in fairly regular contact now. He's actually planning to matriculate here at USC when he graduates high school." He made a face at her. "I had to do quite a bit of talking to get him into regular counseling, but I did it. I've been acting as kind of a mentor to him. As horrible as what happened was, it doesn't seem to have done any permanent psychological damage to him."

"What about the two deceased victims?" Tony asked. "Had you ever met either of them?"

"No." David shook his head. "I'm sorry."

"Did you know Dr. Jeffrey Underwood or Eric Riva prior to receiving that letter?" Kaminsky asked.

"I knew *of* Dr. Underwood, of course." David glanced at Charlie. "I've been aware of his work for years, as I'm sure Charlie has. It's really very impressive." Charlie nodded in agreement. "I did not know him in any other capacity. And I had never heard of Eric Riva until I found out—weeks after I was dragged into the case—that he had been the first recipient of the killer's taunt."

"Do you have any idea why the Gingerbread Man chose a Charlotte newspaper reporter to send that first letter to?" Tony asked. "It doesn't seem to mesh with his selection of three widely heralded experts in the criminal psychology field as the recipients of the next three letters."

David's expression brightened. "Now, that I can tell you. We—the previous investigators and I—believe it was because Mr. Riva had written several newspaper stories about the ordeal suffered by the three boys in an earlier attack. I posited that the killer had read those articles, which I felt meant that at that time he had to be living somewhere within the readership area of the *Charlotte Observer.* I still think that."

Tony nodded. Remembering the file David had sent her to look at when he had asked her to consult and that she had sent back when she'd declined, Charlie said, "Could we get a copy of the file you put together on the case, do you think? As well as anything else you have that you think might help us."

"Yes, of course," David said. Then he smiled a little ruefully at Charlie. "Once the killer is caught, I'm hoping to turn my experiences with this into a book. So if you would treat everything in that file as confidential I would appreciate it."

"We will," Charlie promised, and Tony nodded agreement.

David summoned his newest research assistant—a pretty college senior who seemed just as eager to please David as Charlie, inwardly wincing, remembered she once had been—to make a copy of the file, and they all stood up to take their leave. David took advantage of the fact that the other three had moved ahead of them into the hall to pull Charlie aside and ask her quietly if she'd like to go out to dinner with him that night, "for old times' sake."

When foolish little girls grow a brain, was what Charlie thought, in the spirit of *when pigs fly.* What she said, with scarcely any acidity at all, was, "Don't you think your wife might object?"

"I'm divorced. Three years ago." He smiled at her. "That's one of the reasons I reached out to you when I got pulled into these murders. I've never forgotten you, you know. In fact, I've followed your career with great interest. And pride, I might add. After all, you were once my star pupil. I was hoping we could get reacquainted."

"We're leaving town tonight," Charlie said. Then she added, very gently, "And David—even if we weren't, I'm not interested."

She wouldn't have been human if that softly spoken rejection hadn't made her feel a little bit better. As far as her pride was concerned, it evened the scales to some small degree. But the other truth was that she would have refused even if there hadn't been a history between them that needed avenging. She no longer felt the slightest interest in him as a man: the girl who had thought that he was the greatest thing since sliced bread was long gone.

"Guy's a douche bag," Michael said as they joined the others in the hall and observed the adoring smile the research assistant gave David as she handed him the file she had copied for him. "One of these days you're going to have to tell me how you ended up hitting that."

The look Charlie shot him said *Not in this life*. And for the first time since lunch, he smiled.

Saul Tunney was waiting for them in his mother's home in Ballentine, a Columbia suburb. He was now sixteen, although he was still round-cheeked and faintly baby-faced, which Charlie thought he tried to counter by sporting a blond crew cut that looked almost defiantly masculine. At about five-eight and a hundred thirty pounds, his size wouldn't have posed much of an obstacle to someone bent on kidnapping him, especially since, a year ago when the crime had occurred, he'd presumably been even smaller. Having apparently told his story dozens of times, he related it to them in a few terse sentences. He had been snatched off a Columbia street after a baseball game. He'd found himself in a cage, and, later, a grain elevator with two other kids: Isaac Stein, fourteen, and Sofia Barrett, eighteen. If they wanted to know what had happened in the grain elevator, they could read the police reports: he was done talking about it. What it came down to was, in the end, he had lived, the other two had died.

No, he hadn't known them previously. No, he couldn't identify his attacker: he'd just caught a glimpse of the guy, who had worn black clothing and a white Halloween mask, with a Joker kind of grin. No, he had no idea why he had been targeted.

He did have two things of interest to tell them: he thought the attacker had used some kind of voice synthesizer to disguise his voice; and, four years previously, Saul had been out hunting with his uncle and cousin when his uncle had accidentally shot his cousin dead.

That last had been in response to Kaminsky's question about any other violent deaths he had witnessed in his life.

"I think that's the answer, it really might be our common denominator," Kaminsky said with barely suppressed excitement once the interview was over and they were on their way to meet with the local detectives and FBI agents who had worked the case, to see the Group Six kill site.

"Now all we need to do is uncover a violent death in the pasts of seventeen other victims, tie them all together, and figure out what it all means, and we'll have solved the case," Buzz said dryly.

"At least it's a place to look," Kaminsky snapped.

Their subsequent visit to the abandoned grain elevator that only Saul Tunney had escaped alive was, for Charlie at least, heartrending. At the time, the silo had been full of corn. Standing on the surface of the stored grain was much like standing on quicksand, one of the local agents who was walking them through what had happened explained. When none of the victims had done anything in response to his warning that he would kill them all unless they started killing one another, the Gingerbread Man had opened a floor hole, which was designed to speed the flow of grain from the silo to a loading chute. The girl, Sofia, had been swept away. Her body was found with grain clogging her throat, her nose, her eyes. It was, the detective said, a particularly hideous death. The boy, Isaac, had subsequently been killed by Saul Tunney. With a pickaxe, the kind that was sometimes used in grain elevators to break up hard clumps of grain. The silo had since been emptied of its contents, but traces of Isaac Stein's blood still stained the walls.

Looking at those rust-colored speckles, Charlie felt sick.

It wasn't until much later, when they were getting ready to land at the Charlotte airport, that Charlie finally realized what had been bothering her so much about this case. She'd been listening with only half an ear to the various discussions swirling around inside the plane while she mentally twisted the facts that they knew like the pieces of a puzzle in hopes of getting something to fit, when it clicked.

"I think," she said, looking at the others as if she was really seeing them for the first time in a while, "that he's killed before. Before these group murders began, I mean. This whole thing is too elaborate. He has to have worked up to it. This is his escalation. We need to start looking at unsolved single murders." She paused to let her thoughts settle. "We should probably begin in the same geographical area in which the first Gingerbread Man murders occurred. We should work backward from the date of those murders. He will have an MO, although it will be different from what he's doing now. There will be a pattern. There should be a series of single murders, because this— these death scenarios with multiple victims—represents a major escalation."

For a moment everyone simply looked at her.

"Makes sense," Michael said. He was lying on the couch again, and his eyes had been closed until he looked at her as he spoke. Charlie hadn't even realized that he had been paying attention.

"What kind of time frame are we talking about?" Tony asked.

Charlie shook her head. "If he is at the upper age limit for serial killers—and with this severe an escalation I'm guessing that he is— we're probably looking at the last twenty years."

Buzz whistled through his teeth. "What's the geographical area?"

Kaminsky consulted her laptop. "The first Gingerbread Man murders occurred right outside Clarksville, Virginia."

"Buggs Island Lake," Charlie said suddenly. She looked at Michael, started to say, *Remember, Laura said,* swallowed that, and quickly switched her gaze to Tony. By leaving off the first three words, the rest of the sentence was perfectly acceptable. "The van Jenna McDaniels and the other girls were put into smelled like fish, remember? Buggs Island Lake is this huge fishing destination. And part of it is near Clarksville, Virginia. We should check it out."

"That's in Mecklenburg County," Kaminsky said. "And how do we know the van smelled like fish?"

"We just do," Charlie said impatiently.

Kaminsky eyed her askance.

"Okay, we look for unsolved murders with a single MO in the vicinity of Clarksville, Virginia, and this lake," Tony summed up as the pilot announced they would be landing in Charlotte in five minutes. "Starting around the date of the Group One murders and going back twenty years."

"Got it," Buzz said, and Kaminsky added, "Not that this is going to be hard or anything."

"Look at it this way." Tony smiled tranquilly at the pair of them. "If it was easy, none of us would have a job."

It was full dark by the time they got to their hotel, which in late August meant that it was after ten p.m. Charlie was tired, wired, and a little on edge. They grabbed a quick dinner in the hotel restaurant—Charlie had salad and a bowl of soup—and then they went up to their rooms, which were in a block on the eleventh floor. They each had their own, with Tony on one side of Charlie and Kaminsky on the other. Crane's room was next to Kaminsky's. For security reasons (actually, Charlie knew it was for *her* security), Tony had requisitioned a local FBI agent to stand watch in the hallway all night.

She appreciated it. Now that it was night again, Tam's warning was crowding in on her. The thing was, she had never known Tam to be wrong.

"I've stayed here before," Tony said to Charlie as they walked along the hallway to their rooms. "They've got a great jogging track up on the roof. I'm going to go make use of it. Want to come?"

"Yes," Charlie said instantly. Running was what she did for relaxation, and tonight she badly needed to relax.

"You notice he's not inviting us," Buzz said to Kaminsky, only partly under his breath, as they passed Charlie.

"I noticed," Kaminsky agreed. They were moving on to their respective doors, while Tony had walked Charlie to hers and stopped.

"I heard that," Tony called after them good-naturedly. "And it's because you don't run. But you're welcome to come along if you want."

Declining, they both disappeared inside their rooms.

"I'll be back in ten," Tony told Charlie, who nodded. Then he waited until she was inside and closed the door.

Flipping the switch beside the door caused a lamp to come on, which allowed Charlie to see her surroundings. Decorated in soothing earth tones, the room was typical hotel: two queen beds with a night-stand holding said lamp between them, an armoire containing a TV and, on its lower level, a mini-fridge, an armchair with a floor lamp in the corner by the heavily curtained window, a bathroom, and, op-posite it, a closet. Having preceded her inside, Michael now stood in the middle of the room, giving her an unreadable look.

"What?" Charlie said.

"Not a thing," he answered. She didn't probe further. Instead she extracted her running clothes and her small cosmetics case from her suitcase and went into the bathroom to change. When she emerged a few minutes later, she was wearing silky black running shorts, a pale pink tee, and sneakers. Her hair was pulled back into a ponytail.

"Cute," was Michael's comment as his eyes swept her. "Dudley's going to think he hit the jackpot."

Charlie glared at him. She was carrying his watch—she didn't feel like having it slide around on her arm while she ran.

"Is there something you want to say about me going running with *Tony*?"

"Nope."

Walking over to the nightstand between the beds, she set the watch down by the phone. His eyes tracked her.

She gave him another inimical look. "Good. Then I'd appreciate it if you'd just let me enjoy my run in peace."

"Whatever you want, babe."

Then Tony was at the door and the three (!) of them were heading for the roof.

The track ran along the perimeter of it, which was thirty stories high and provided an excellent view of the glowing skyline of down-town Charlotte. In the middle was a swimming pool, lounge chairs, and a few fake palm trees all decked out in white Christmas lights. There were a couple of people in the pool. Otherwise, the roof was deserted. Almost as soon as Charlie started to run, she felt the tired-ness and tension and, yes, even the fear, start to ebb away. The warm summer breeze smelled faintly of chlorine. The black sky and full moon and twinkling stars overhead seemed almost close enough to touch. Street sounds drifted up from below. There was an occasional laugh or splash from the swimmers in the pool.

"I hate it that you're caught up in this, of course, but I have to admit I was glad to get the chance to work with you again," Tony said as they rounded the far side turn for the eighteenth time. They'd been talking about the case in a desultory way without coming up with anything new. A seasoned runner herself, Charlie appreciated the fact that they were at the four and a half mile point and he wasn't even breathing hard yet. She also appreciated how good his lean, fit body looked in his shorts and tee. It made a nice change from his FBI agent suits, and she thought for what must have been the thousandth time that she was a fool if she didn't at least give this budding attraction between them a chance.

Of course, the fact that she was afflicted with the ghost from hell was quite a deterrent. Especially given the fact that he was within easy earshot, keeping pace without the slightest difficulty. Not that she would describe what he was doing as running, exactly. She wasn't even sure his feet were touching the ground. But he was indisputably there, glancing at her from time to time with mockery in his eyes.

"I'm glad to have the chance to work with you again, too," Charlie replied. It was absolutely true. The seeds of a promising relationship were there, she thought: they simply needed nurturing.

Hard to do when she had a ghost on a leash.

This is my life, and I owe it to myself to make an effort.

"Oh, yeah? I got the impression, last night, that you were kind of in a hurry to get rid of me."

And that would have been because of a blaring TV and a blast of hope that said ghost had managed to stay earthbound rather than move on to his just rewards.

"It's only—I believe in taking things slow." That wasn't really a lie. At least, it had been part of the reason she'd sent Tony swiftly on his way. Okay, a really tiny part.

"You're not seeing anybody right now?" he persisted.

Charlie ignored the slash of a pair of sky blue eyes in her direction. "No, I'm not."

She'd definitely said it a little too firmly. Tony didn't seem to notice, though. In fact, he smiled. "Me either. So maybe we could take it slow together."

A sky blue eye roll. Which Charlie pretended she didn't even see.

"Maybe," she replied, and Tony laughed.

"You sound like you might be a little bit gun-shy."

"Just a little," Charlie agreed.

"Some bad relationships, huh?"

Charlie nodded. "A few."

He chuckled ruefully. "I hear you. I've had my fair share of those, too."

They reached the five-mile mark and pulled up. They were both breathing hard by this time, and Charlie at least was feeling one hundred percent better as they headed toward the elevators.

"How about we start with dinner again, the first chance we get?" Tony was smiling at her as the elevator doors opened and they stepped inside. Returning his smile, Charlie registered how handsome he was. With his dark, even-featured face and hard, athletic body, he would make any right-minded woman drool. *Plus, he's sweet and smart and I like him a lot,* she thought.

By turning her back on the six-foot-three-inch, sardonic-looking ghost who leaned, arms crossed, against the back wall of the elevator, Charlie was able to concentrate on the real, live man with whom she would truly like to begin a real, live relationship.

"I'd like that," she said. Tony's eyes moved over her face. Then, to her surprise, he slid a hand around the back of her neck, pulled her closer, bent his head, and kissed her.

There was nothing about the kiss that fell under the heading "taking it slow." Instead, there was tons of tongue action, tons of heat. Getting into the spirit of it, Charlie kissed him back, and thoroughly enjoyed the pleasant little tingle of excitement that chased around inside her.

The ping of the elevator announced that they had reached their floor, and Tony reluctantly let her go.

Charlie smiled at him. And to hell with her glowering ghost, who had straightened to his should-have-been-intimidating full height and had squared his impressively broad shoulders and was looking at Tony with violence in his eyes.

She didn't flick so much as a glance in his direction. The crux of it was, she had her life to live. And she refused to let *him* throw her off. He was an affliction with which she had been saddled. What she had with Tony—what she might be able to have, if she let herself, and put some effort into it—was real.

The borrowed FBI agent/security guard glanced at her and Tony as they emerged from the elevator. Tony lifted a hand in greeting as they passed him, then waited a beat before whispering to Charlie,"I don't suppose you'd want to stop by my room for a candy bar from the mini-fridge?"

Despite the semi-hopeful tone, it was so obviously said with no expectation of having her take him up on it that Charlie smiled.

"No," she said.

"Got it. We're taking it slow."

They had reached her room by that time. Tony waited while she unlocked the door and walked inside.

"See ya," he said, smiling at her, the memory of that kiss there in his eyes.

It had been a very nice kiss. One she wouldn't mind repeating.

She smiled back at him.

"Good-night," she said, and he nodded and turned away. Then she closed the door—right in the face of her pissed-looking ghost.

Of course, she should have remembered that unless he wanted it to, closing a door on Michael did absolutely no good at all.

CHAPTER SIXTEEN

He walked right through it.

The look he gave her when he did should have made her shiver. It should have made her quake in her sneakers. He was in full badass mode, all hard-eyed and hard-jawed and radiating barely suppressed hostility. Add an orange jumpsuit and some chains, and he would have been every bit as scary as the death row convict she'd first met.

Only he was Michael to her now, and whatever he had or had not done in the past, and however menacing he might look in the present, he and she were way past the point where he could actually scare her. Tam's warning about having the wool pulled over her eyes notwithstanding, she was now as sure as it was possible to be that the threat Tam had been warning her against didn't emanate from Michael.

In fact, Charlie realized, she was absolutely convinced that he would never hurt her, even if he could. At least not physically.

In other ways? Well, that was a different matter.

He stopped just inside the door. With the next item on her agenda being a shower, she had moved no farther than the bathroom doorway. As he came through she turned to face him, so that they now stood way too close to each other in the narrow space that marked the entrance to the room.

She didn't like being reminded of how tall he was, of how much bigger he was than she. She didn't like having to look so far up to meet his gaze.

Her first impulse was to take a couple of steps back, so she wouldn't have to tilt her head so far. Then she thought, *To hell with that,* and stood her ground.

Chin up, arms folded, challenge in her eyes, Charlie waited for him to fire the first (verbal) shot. He didn't say a thing. Instead he simply looked at her.

With grim eyes and a tight mouth.

"I can do whatever I want. I don't need your permission," she snapped. And knew as soon as she said it that she should have kept her mouth shut and gone into the bathroom without a word. But she hadn't been able to do it. Something about the way he was looking at her made her feel guilty, like she needed to defend herself.

Which was complete baloney.

He still said nothing.

She narrowed her eyes at him. "Just so you know, I'm going to be dating Tony for the foreseeable future."

Still nothing.

"Damn it, you and I are not a couple. If I didn't have this horrible cosmic curse, I wouldn't even be able to see you. You wouldn't be here. Because, you know, you're *dead.*"

"He turn you on?" Michael's voice was perfectly even. Without that gravelly undertone, from his voice alone she wouldn't have even suspected he was mad.

"Yes," she answered defiantly.

"If he turned you on, you'd be sleeping with him already."

"What, did you miss that part of Tony's and my *private* conversation? We're taking it slow."

"Oh, is that it?" He smiled. She knew what that mocking smile meant, and it sent fury sizzling through her veins.

"Okay, so maybe I didn't take it slow with you. Big deal. Bad decision. Anyway, I'm not even sure that the sex we had was real."

His smile got nastier. "Oh, it was real, Doc. Every little thing about it was real. You were on my side of the barrier that night. Remember how my shirt got wet when Laura leaned against me? That's because she and I are both as solid over here as you are right now over there. Remember me taking that knife in my back for you? That happened because I was able to cross the barrier for a second and be solid on the same side of the barrier as you. So yeah, when I fucked you, when you made that bad decision, you and I were both solid and on the same side of the barrier and it was real. And it was a big deal. Remember how many times you came? I do."

Lucky for her she wasn't prone to blushing, because, yes, she (unwillingly) remembered that, too. She also noticed something: he had called her Doc, which he rarely did now. Only, she deduced as she thought back, when he was seriously bent out of shape with her.

He added: "You really think Dudley can make you come like that?"

"Yes," she lied, caught herself as she was about to wet her lips, and clamped them together. His eyes were on her telltale mouth and some of the grimness had left them as she put an end to the (useless, infuriating) conversation by saying, "I'm going to take a shower."

Turning on her heel, she walked into the bathroom and closed the door. Gently. When what she actually wanted to do was slam it.

He stayed on his side. Not that she'd expected him to come barging in after her, but she was relieved when he didn't.

Too bad she had forgotten to bring her nightclothes into the bathroom with her. When she got out of the shower, she wrapped herself in a towel and studied her reflection in the mirror for a moment, less than pleased at what looked back at her. Then, because she knew he was out there, because sharing a room and a life and a sizzling, unwanted attraction with a man (?) meant that she actually cared what she looked like when she was around him no matter how much she might want to pretend to herself (and him) that she didn't, she muttered a curse under her breath and whipped the towel off her head and blew her hair dry until it curved soft and smooth around her shoulders. She rubbed lotion into her thirsty skin. She brushed her teeth, and even applied cherry Chapstick because she wanted her lips to be smooth in the morning (and, yes, all right, to give them a little flattering color). After that, after there was nothing left for her to do that wouldn't look too obvious, she discovered that she had the option of putting on her sweaty workout clothes again or of walking into the bedroom wrapped in a towel to retrieve her nightgown and robe from her suitcase.

For a moment she hesitated. Then she thought, *Screw it.*

When she walked into the bedroom, it was to find Michael stretched out fully dressed on the bed closest to the window. He appeared lost in thought, and whatever they were he didn't seem to be enjoying them particularly: he was frowning, and his mouth was tight. His eyes flicked her way, widened. She had on a white hotel towel, standard issue, and it was wrapped around her in perfectly adequate fashion, covering her from approximately the armpits to the tops of her thighs. He would have seen more of her if she'd been wearing a bathing suit. Still, there was something about slim, tanned legs and a hint of cleavage and bare shoulders and arms emerging from a towel that made her feel ridiculously self-conscious. His eyes stayed glued to her, and his frown smoothed away. She didn't say a word. Instead she walked (as opposed to stomped) to her suitcase, which was on the little folding suitcase stand at the foot of her bed, opened it, and started digging down for her PJs.

She couldn't help it if she could see him perfectly well even if she wasn't deliberately looking at him. She couldn't help it if the damned man (?) was drop-dead sexy enough to make thoughts of doing him almost impossible to keep from popping into her mind at odd moments (like now). She couldn't help it if said thoughts made her body tighten and burn.

But she could get mad at him all over again.

The merest suggestion of a smile touched his mouth. "You want to make nice with me, you could try dropping the towel."

She shot him a withering look. "In your dreams."

His smile widened. But she didn't care, because she'd found what she was looking for. Turning her back on him, she retraced her steps to the bathroom. She could feel his eyes on her every step of the way.

It was unfortunate that her favorite blue bathrobe had been too bulky to fit in her suitcase. Because the silky pale peach one that matched her silky pale peach nightie was a lot slinkier than she had realized when she packed it. It had long sleeves instead of the nightie's spaghetti straps, and it ended at mid-thigh instead of at the tops of her thighs like the nightie did, but the shimmery silk was thin, and clung because she was still faintly damp, and when she tied its silk ribbon of a belt around her waist it left way too little to the imagination.

When she'd been packing her PJs, she hadn't yet totally gotten her head around the concept that the ghost from hell was going to be seeing her in them on a nightly basis.

Reality bites.

Her only option was to wrap a towel around herself over the robe, and that was too ridiculous even to think about.

She thought *Screw it* again, and walked out into the bedroom.

Michael's eyes slid over her. As she headed around the end of *her* bed—i.e., the one he wasn't on—she watched them go dark and hot, and to her annoyance felt herself going all dark and hot inside, too.

The good news, she told herself savagely as she started to pull the covers back prior to climbing into bed, was that no matter how worked up either one of them got, sex wasn't going to happen.

"Okay, you're killing me here." His voice was husky. His eyes hadn't left her since she'd walked out of the bathroom. It occurred to her as she saw the look on his face that when she'd turned her back to him and leaned over the bed to free the far side of the covers, then tossed the decorative pillows to the floor, maybe he'd gotten more of a view than she'd meant to give him.

The possibility made her cross. "So close your eyes."

"Feeling a little bitchy, babe? I've noticed before that kissing Dudley has that effect on you."

"Ever think it might be *you* who has that effect on me?"

"Nah. We both know what kind of effect I have on you. You ever have phone sex?"

That was so unexpected she shot him a suspicious look. "No."

He had turned on his side and was watching her with his head propped on a hand. "That's where I tell you all the dirty things I want to do to you and you tell me all the dirty things you want to do to me and we both get off without either one of us laying a hand on the other," he explained helpfully.

She might not have had it, but she knew what it was. At the erotic images that flooded her mind in the wake of his words, her knees went weak.

"Not happening, Casper."

She climbed into bed, and pulled the covers up to her chin, and turned off the light.

His voice came out of the dark. "Sleeping in your robe tonight?"

Damn it, she'd forgotten to take it off. There was just enough light filtering in around the edges of the curtains to allow her to see the big, dark shape of him. Which meant that he could probably see her, too. Which meant that she was going to be taking her robe off under the covers, and dropping it discreetly off the far side of the bed.

Which she did.

"Dudley doesn't turn you on."

Punching a pillow into submission, she turned onto her side with her back to him and laid her head on it. "How would you know?"

"I know what you look like when you're turned on. And you don't look like that when you're kissing him."

"I'm not having this conversation with you. In fact, I'm not having any conversation with you. I'm going to sleep."

"If he doesn't turn you on when you're kissing him, he's not going to turn you on in bed."

She rolled so that she was facing him. "Damn it, Michael—"

"You don't want to have a relationship with a guy who doesn't get you hot."

"Are *you* giving *me* relationship advice?"

"If that's what you want to call it. Bottom line is, you deserve a guy who gets you hot, babe."

"I'm not talking to you anymore. Good-night." She closed her eyes.

"You like sex, Charlie. You know you do. You don't want to shortchange yourself in that department."

Actually, most of the sex she'd had could be classified as luke-warm rather than hot. If she had to come up with an adjective to describe it, it would be *fine*. *The sex was fine* would cover almost every relationship she'd ever had.

It didn't cover sex with Michael, though. In fact, it was about the last description she would use to cover sex with him.

Sex with Michael was not fine. It was—oh, no, she wasn't going there. Not even in her thoughts.

But her body went there anyway. She could feel its hungry tightening, feel her blood starting to steam.

"There's more to a relationship than sex," she growled.

He laughed. "You keep telling yourself that, babe."

Her eyes popped open of their own accord.

"Mutual interests. Mutual respect. Common goals. A shared life plan." She enumerated the building blocks of a good adult relationship.

"If I could come over there and put my mouth on your breast and my hand between your legs, I guarantee you wouldn't give a damn about any of that."

As her breath caught and her pulse rate surged and her bones liquefied, she sat straight up in bed and glared at him through the darkness. "Stop. I mean it."

"What? We're having a discussion. You know, you make your point, I make mine."

"I don't want to talk to you."

"I can think of lots of things I'd rather be doing to you, too—like, oh, I don't know, getting you naked and pushing up inside you and making you come for me."

Caught by surprise by an undulating wave of desire that was hot enough to make her press her thighs together and squirm a little, Charlie fought to keep her breathing under control so her tormentor wouldn't have a clue.

"Listen, you jackass, if you don't shut up I'll—" Since she couldn't think of anything that he might reasonably believe she would do to threaten him with, she broke off until something occurred to her. "Go knock on Kaminsky's door and tell her the air-conditioning's not working in my room and ask to sleep in her spare bed."

She could sense rather than see his smile. "And there you go: you just proved my point. You're not threatening to run to Dudley, because you're half afraid I'll do something that'll make you have to follow through, and you won't do it. And you won't do it because you don't want to make him think you want to sleep with him, because you don't, and that would be because he doesn't turn you on all that much. If he did, you'd already be over there in bed with him."

"That is a total crock."

"Anyway, even if you did run to Sugar Buns for protection, I'd come with you. Remember that short leash you've got me on? The only difference would be that with Sugar Buns there you wouldn't be able to answer back when I said dirty things to you."

"You know what? I don't have to listen to this. I'm going to sleep." She flopped back down and turned her back to him again.

"You wearing any panties under that nightgown?"

Charlie practically ground her teeth, but she didn't reply.

"Nah, I already know you're not. Tell the truth, babe: did you bend over that bed on purpose, to drive me crazy with a glimpse of your sweet—"

"Enough!" Charlie catapulted into a sitting position again and practically shot napalm at him with her eyes. "You want to talk? Is that it? Fine, I'm in. Why don't you tell me about"—it took her a second, but then she had a topic that she felt was pretty much a sure bet to redirect his thoughts—"your watch?"

There was a moment's silence. "What about it?"

Hah. She had him. She could hear the difference in his tone. "Where'd you get it? Was it a gift? What's with the engraving on the back? That kind of thing." She said it very much in the spirit of taking the battle to the enemy.

He rolled over onto his back. She could see his hard profile, see the firm musculature of his chest and the flat plane of his abdomen and the bulge in his jeans and the powerful length of his legs, all in outline against the curtains. *God, I want him.* The thought came out of nowhere, and she was helpless against it. If he'd been alive, if he'd been a man instead of a ghost, she knew as well as she knew anything that she wouldn't have been able to stop herself from crawling into bed with him and wrapping herself around him and letting him do anything he wanted to her while she sated herself with that hard body. But since he was a ghost, since doing what she was dying to do wasn't possible (which was, she told herself, a good thing), she firmly ignored the hot, insistent throbbing deep inside her body and the too rapid beating of her heart and every other physical manifestation of her inner-slut-where-he-was-concerned. Instead, she was going to take advantage of this opportunity to try to get some answers from him. Even if she still wasn't a hundred percent sure whether she could believe what he told her or not.

"Some buddies gave it to me," he said.

"What kind of buddies?"

"Marine buddies. Look, I don't feel like talking about my watch right now. What the hell difference does it make at this point anyway?"

"Oh, so we can talk about what you want but not about what I want? Is that it?" Crawling to the end of her bed, Charlie retrieved her laptop from its compartment in the top of her suitcase and clambered back up to the head of her bed with it. "So how about we don't talk at all, then?"

"What are you doing?" he asked as she pulled pillows into position, propped herself up against them, opened her laptop case, and turned her computer on. The soft glow of the screen allowed her to see that he was giving her a narrow-eyed look.

"I was sleepy, but now I'm not. So I'm checking something out." She clicked through to the file she was interested in.

"What?"

"None of your business." It was Michael's file, the digitalized combination of the boxes of papers and the Internet records and the medical and psychological assessments and everything else with his name on it that had been sent to Wallens Ridge when he had been acquired by her as a research subject. She'd had everything scanned and uploaded and cataloged into a master file which was kept on her office computer, and which had also been downloaded to her laptop for convenience, just as she had done with the files of all of her research subjects. Everything that was officially known about each of their lives, and their crimes, was in there somewhere.

Charlie located the section she was interested in, and started scrolling through the images.

"That's my damned file." Michael had rolled to his feet and was now looming over her as he frowned down at the screen.

"You're right, it is."

As the page she sought came up, Charlie sucked in her breath: three photographs recording a silver man's watch, its wristband twisted and broken, the glass covering its face shattered, with a terrifying brown staining that she knew was dried blood darkening the cracks and crevices. Taken from different angles against a white background, the photographs were labeled State's Exhibit 27A.

Reaching out, Charlie turned on the bedside lamp and picked up from the nightstand the man's watch she had worn all day. Then she held it up beside the screen, comparing the object to the images. As far as she could tell, the two watches were identical.

The pictures on the screen did not show the back of the face of the broken watch, where the words *Semper Fi* had been engraved on the watch in her hand.

"Checking out my story?" There was an element of careful control to Michael's voice. She glanced up at him, too engrossed in what she was doing to register the look in his eyes.

"The watches appear to be identical." Her tone made it a concession. She once again mentally checked off every similarity she could find: brand, features, size. "Of course, any engraving on the back of the face on this watch"—she tapped the screen—"is concealed by the angle of the pictures."

"There's no engraving on the back of that watch. I got a real good look at it at my trial. Like I told the stupid motherfuckers then, and like I'm telling you now, it ain't mine."

"Citizen men's 860 stainless steel watch, found beside the body of victim number seven, Candace Hartnell," Charlie read aloud. She had shifted into researcher mode. Her earlier tiredness—and arousal—was forgotten as she concentrated on the file. At the bottom of the page was a blue, underlined cross-reference number.

As she clicked on it, Michael settled himself beside her on the bed.

A moment later a video file labeled State's Exhibit 27B came up on the screen. She clicked on the play arrow. For a second the screen went black.

Then Charlie found herself looking at a grainy picture of Michael smiling a slow and seductive smile at a pretty dark-haired woman in a bar.

CHAPTER SEVENTEEN

It could have been any bar: dark gleaming wood, a long mirror fronted by a jumble of bottles and glasses, a heavyset bartender filling a mug with beer from a tap. Busy, with every bar stool occupied and more patrons crowding up to the counter. Dimly lit. Blue-collar and rowdy.

Charlie found herself absolutely mesmerized by what she was watching. There was no sound, only poor-quality footage taken from a security camera above the bar. Other patrons were visible, but Charlie had no interest in them. Her attention was all on the extraordinarily handsome blond guy as he laughed and chatted and bought drinks for pretty, twenty-five-year-old Candace Hartnell, whom Charlie recognized from the photos in Michael's file. She was obviously in the process of being swept off her feet. He was knocking back drinks himself at a rate that told her he was feeling no pain, and chasing the booze with an occasional handful of peanuts scooped up from the dish on the crowded counter. Watching the way Candace looked at him, the way she smiled, the way she first laid her hand over his and then playfully trailed her fingers down his muscular arm, Charlie saw with no surprise that the interest was at least as high on her part as it was on his. Finally, when he put his hand somewhere out of range of the camera, which Charlie thought from the angle of both their bodies must be her thigh, and in response she leaned toward him to whisper in his ear, Charlie could tell she was ready to leave with him whenever he wanted. The footage practically crackled with heat, but it was Michael who captured her attention. This younger, happier, deliberately charming version of him made her breath catch and her heart ache a little.

At least, until she recollected that the young woman he was using his devastating good looks to seduce so successfully would be dead before morning, her nude body found horribly slashed and mutilated in the tangled sheets of her own blood-soaked bed.

Once she remembered that, it was almost like watching a python toy with a mouse. Gritting her teeth, Charlie pushed emotion as far away as she could, and set herself to looking for details: Michael was dressed exactly as he was right now, white tee and jeans, and—she was willing to bet, although she couldn't see his feet—boots. The same outfit he was presently wearing, she was almost sure. On his wrist, plain to see and absolutely unmistakable in the context of what she now knew, was his watch. She looked at it closely. It appeared identical to both the intact one she was holding, and the broken one in the photos.

As she watched, video Michael rolled to his feet, snagging Candace with an arm around her waist and pulling her up with him. Laughing, she leaned into him while he nuzzled her neck. Then, close as a stamp to an envelope, she walked out of the frame with him. He seemed slightly unsteady on his feet. She was clingy and had both arms around his waist.

Candace Hartnell was slashed to death later that night. Early the following morning, Michael Garland was arrested and subsequently charged with the crime. Shortly thereafter he was linked with six previous knife murders of young women. The night she was watching had been the last night of freedom in his life: the five subsequent years had been spent in an assortment of jails and prisons. Charlie knew all that, knew, too, the overwhelming nature of the evidence pointing to his guilt that had been presented at his trial. The video she'd just watched, for example, was damning. It even showed him wearing the watch that had been found tangled in the covers with Candace Hartnell's dead body: State Exhibit 27A.

Only Charlie was holding an identical watch in her hand. One, moreover, that had been identified as belonging to Michael by the Mariposa Police Department, which had arrested him hours after Candace Hartnell's murder and had presumably taken it from him then as intake material. Michael had correctly described the engraving on the back to her before he'd ever gotten a look at it. It was sized to fit his larger than average wrist, and he insisted that it, and not the one in the pictures, was his.

That, to Charlie, raised at least a flicker of reasonable doubt as to his guilt.

Clicking off the video, she glanced his way. He was lying on his back beside her now, his head on a pillow, his hands laced behind his head. Instead of watching the video, he'd been staring up at the ceiling. As if he felt her eyes on him, he looked at her.

"After that, I took her back to her house and went psycho on her. Raped her. Cut her to ribbons with my handy-dandy hunting knife that I subsequently got rid of where no one could find it. Only I was too damned dumb not to get myself arrested, so I got nailed for her murder and six other murders besides. Does that answer the question you're getting ready to ask me?" His tone was *almost* casual. His eyes were savage.

Charlie sighed. She'd read those details in his file when he'd first become a subject of her study and, up until less than a week ago, had seen no reason to question them. Now she discovered that she was ready to consider other possibilities.

"You want to tell me what really happened?"

"What, you don't believe I went psycho and killed that girl? That's the conclusion a jury of my peers reached. They were so damned sure of it I got sentenced to death."

Tired of holding his watch, she slid it onto her arm. His eyes tracked the gesture, narrowed.

"I want to hear the truth, whatever it is," she said.

His lips compressed. "Does it matter? At this point, what the hell does it change? Unless you've got some cure for dead I don't know about."

"Michael. Please. Tell me what happened."

The look he gave her glittered with anger and frustration and a whole host of other emotions Charlie didn't even try to analyze.

"You want the truth? Here it is: I had a few drinks, I picked up a girl in a bar, I went home with her, we got it on. No rape involved. Hell, I never raped a woman in my life. When I woke up, it was about four in the morning. She was asleep—not dead, no blood, not a hair on her head harmed; in fact, last time she had anything to say she gave me to understand that she was feeling pretty good. I wasn't in any mood for the whole morning after thing so I put my clothes on and left. No, I didn't wake her up to say goodbye. Hell, at that point I couldn't even remember her name. But she was *alive*. So I'm driving home, and I guess I was speeding or something because I got pulled over by this damned little pissant of a cop. He arrested me on suspicion of drunk driving—no Breathalyzer or anything, but he said I flunked his damned field sobriety test, which I didn't. I guess he could smell the booze on me. So he takes me in and they lock me up, and while I'm asleep in their damned cell somebody comes across Candace—I found out her name pretty quick—sliced to pieces in her bed." He grimaced. "After that, things went downhill on a greased slide."

Charlie was remembering the evidence. "They found your DNA all over her, and her DNA all over you, which I guess makes sense if you'd just slept with her. There were dozens of eyewitnesses to you leaving the bar with her, as well as that video footage. Your watch—a watch that appeared identical to yours—was found in bed with her dead body, looking like it was ripped off your arm and broken as she fought for her life. According to all the evidence, you were the last person to see her alive. Plus, if I recall, she had your skin under her fingernails and you had scratches on your body."

"The scratches were on my back! She was wild as hell, and when we were having sex, she scratched my damned back! That's the kind of thing the prosecutors did: they twisted everything to make it sound like I was guilty. But I didn't kill her. Why the hell would I kill her?"

At something he must have seen in Charlie's face, his brows snapped together. "Oh, that's right: I'm a murderous psychopath. Who needs a reason?"

"Serial killers are compelled to kill," Charlie explained with automatic precision. "The compulsion is their reason."

The look he gave her was grim. "Like I said, she was alive when I left her."

Charlie clicked back through the file for the information she wanted. "Her body was found at eight a.m. by her sister. Time of death was estimated at three to four hours previous to that." She frowned. "That means she was killed between four and five a.m."

"Like I said, I woke up around four and left her house—with her alive in it—as soon as I got my clothes on. Probably around 4:10."

She was scrolling through his file. "You were logged in to the jail at 5:30 a.m."

He made an impatient sound. "That dick of a cop kept me on the side of the road for a good hour."

"If you left Candace Hartnell alive at 4:10, that means somebody else had to have entered her house and killed her within the next fifty minutes." It might be unlikely, but it wasn't impossible, Charlie decided.

"Yeah, I worked that out." His voice was dry.

Having run through the pages of photos of the evidence and not found what she sought, Charlie frowned. "What about the clothes you were wearing? I don't see them here, but they should have been introduced as evidence. The crime scene was apparently extremely bloody. You should have been covered in blood."

"You'd think, wouldn't you?" he said with disgust. "These are the clothes I was wearing—at least, the ghost version. Last civilian clothes I ever wore, except for a suit the lawyers scared up for my trial. They weren't any more covered with blood when I got arrested than they are right now. The prosecution claimed it was because I killed her while nude, then showered, then dressed."

Charlie considered: if there was no blood on his clothes, then the prosecution's theory was the only one that fit. "You were convicted of killing six other women over the two and a half years previous to Candace Hartnell's murder. How many of *them* did you sleep with?"

He snorted derisively. "None. Not one. Never even laid eyes on any of them. I swear to God. Yeah, I know they said my DNA was all over them and all that shit, but that's not possible. Either one of those testing labs fucked up big-time, or somebody framed me. Why? How the hell do I know? Maybe some asshole cop or FBI agent wanted to clear up some old cases and I was the best option they had for sticking 'em on somebody. Or maybe somebody didn't like me. Like I said, I don't know."

Charlie watched him carefully. "Every single murder was within a four-hour drive of where you lived."

"I don't know what to tell you."

"The murders started right after you got out of the Marine Corps, and continued over the entire period between then and your arrest. And you didn't have an alibi for any of the nights those women were killed."

He sighed. "I did have an alibi for some of them. I was living with a girlfriend for something like the last six months before Candace Hartnell was killed. We broke up the day before I hit that bar and the shit hit the fan. On the nights of two of the other murders I know for sure I was asleep in bed with Jasmine. Hell, I'd just opened my garage and I was trying to get that business going. I was working maybe eighty hours a week and I was tired—too tired to run around slicing up women in the middle of the night. Only the damned cops messed with Jasmine until they got her to agree it was possible that I snuck out of bed while she was asleep, killed those women, then got back into bed before she woke up in the morning. Which was total shit. But she was pissed at me anyway because of the breakup, and then they scared her to death of me. They kept telling her, 'You've been sleeping with a serial killer. Do you know how lucky you are to be alive?' That kind of crap."

Charlie glanced back at the file. "So why'd you and Jasmine break up?"

"Not because she was afraid of me. Nothing like that. She wanted to get married, and I didn't. Hell, I didn't even mean to start living with her. She just sort of moved herself in."

Charlie looked at him again. And realized only as she did so that she had been deliberately *not* looking at him as he talked about his girlfriend. She hated to admit it even to herself, but ever since she and he had started getting, uh, better acquainted, she'd been mentally poking around the fact that he'd had a girlfriend at the time of his arrest. The question that had burned unacknowledged in the back of her mind was, had he loved her?

From the tone of what he'd said, the answer was no, he hadn't.

Not that it makes any difference, Charlie told herself hurriedly.

"You got no call to be jealous of Jasmine, babe."

His words were so on the money that they almost made Charlie jump.

"What?" Her eyes flared at him indignantly. "I am *not* jealous of your girlfriend. You've got to be kidding me."

The hardness that had been hovering around his eyes and mouth relaxed as he gave her a slow, teasing grin.

"*Ex*-girlfriend. And I told you I could read your face like a neon sign."

"You are the most conceited—" She broke off, flustered, hoping he couldn't tell. The more she protested, the more convinced he would be that he was right, she knew. So she shot him a withering glance, and went for the best distraction she could think of: the DVD that the Mariposa PD had sent along with the (his?) watch. She had transferred it from her purse to her laptop case when she'd been packing for this trip, and now, with Michael beside her so that she could gauge his reaction to whatever was on there, was the moment to watch it. Whether or not Michael was a serial killer was something she needed to have settled in her own mind before this . . . this *connection* that seemed to be growing between them went any further. Most of the time, whether he was being charming or annoying or overprotective or sexy as hell, she didn't think about what he had done, and that, she decided, was due to the sheer force of his personality. But when she did, when she actually allowed herself to remember the seven women he had been convicted of slaughtering, the chill of fear and revulsion that went through her was enough to stop her in her tracks, enough to make her think she needed to get out of the way and let divine justice take its course where he was concerned.

"What's that?" he asked as she inserted the DVD into her laptop.

She told him. Neither one of them said anything as the screen sprang to life. The first shot was an identifying one: date and time, which placed the footage as running from 9:31 to 9:35 a.m. on the morning after Michael had left the bar with Candace Hartnell.

Then the camera was focused on Michael—the same younger, video Michael from the bar security tape. He was now seated in a small, gray police interrogation room, dressed exactly as he had been the previous night, exactly as he was right at that moment on the bed beside her, as a matter of fact. Only the smiling seducer of the bar footage was replaced by a still to-die-for hot, but now obviously angry, man with bloodshot eyes and a night's worth of stubble. Each wrist was cuffed to an arm of the straight-backed metal chair on one side of a small metal table, and almost the first thing Charlie noticed was that the watch he'd been wearing the night before was missing.

Which didn't mean anything, she reminded herself as her pulse quickened a little in response. Whether the watch had been taken from him at the jail or whether he had left it behind at the crime scene, by this time it would have been missing in either case.

"So what did Candace do to piss you off?" The blue-uniformed cop on the opposite side of the table was leaning forward in his chair, his forearms resting on the smooth metal surface as he stared at Michael. The angle of the camera, which was positioned to capture the person being interrogated, recorded the cop's beefy back, and the left side of a florid face beneath a close-cropped cap of reddish hair.

"What? Who the hell is Candace?" Glaring, Michael rattled his cuffs against the metal arm rails. "Look, I got things to do. How about you tell me how much the fine is and let me pay it and I'll be on my way."

"The lady you were with last night." Ignoring the last part of Michael's speech, the cop looked at him intently. "We both know what women can be like. She must have pissed you off pretty good. What'd she do?"

Michael's eyes narrowed. "I don't know what the hell you're talking about."

"Oh, come on, now, Mr. Garland. We both know you do. Why don't you just tell me what happened? Whatever the reason was, if you tell me about it now, I guarantee things'll go a lot easier for you."

A commotion in the hall caused both men to glance in the direction of the open door. A split second later, a woman burst through it, crying, "Michael! Oh, my God, Michael, what did you do?"

The woman was in maybe her mid-twenties, with a pretty, sulky-looking face enhanced by lots of mascara and bold scarlet lips, a riot of long black hair, and a va-va-voom figure in tiny shorts and a low-cut tank top.

"Jasmine!" Michael sat straight up as she flew toward him, her high-heeled sandals clattering on the industrial gray floor. Before she could reach him, the cop behind the table leaped to his feet and interposed himself between her and Michael, and another cop barreled through the door to catch her by the arm.

"Sorry about that! She got away from me—" the second cop said to the first as, drowning out the rest of what he had to say, Jasmine screamed at Michael, "You fucked another woman? We're broken up one day and already you're out fucking another woman? You . . ." The string of expletives she let loose with made the florid-faced cop whose chest she had run into, and who was at that moment backing her toward the door while the other cop pulled her in that direction with a hand on her arm and another on her waist, wince.

Charlie couldn't see Michael—the cops and the woman blocked the camera's view of him—but in the background she could hear him growl, "Jesus H. Christ, what the hell did you bring *her* here for?"

"Miss Lipsitz! You can't talk to him!" said the cop, urgently pulling Jasmine out the door.

Jasmine strained to get away. Every bit of her focus was on Michael. "You fucked her and then you killed her! That's what they're saying! Some bitch you picked up in a bar! Is it true?"

Although the camera's view of him was still blocked by the beefy cop who was shoving Jasmine out the door, Michael could be heard saying, "What the hell?"

Jasmine was once again screaming expletives as she was forced into the hallway and the door was shut on her.

The camera had an unimpeded view of Michael then. He was staring at the beefy cop, who'd turned back to look at him.

"That girl I was with last night . . . she's dead?" Michael asked slowly.

The cop didn't say anything. But even Charlie, watching grainy footage on a laptop, could read the answer in his body language: *yes.*

"I want a lawyer," Michael said. And that was it. The footage ended, and the screen went blank.

"Like I said, after that it went downhill fast," real, live (well, dead) Michael said. Charlie looked at him without really seeing him: she was too preoccupied with analyzing what she had just viewed. The news that Candace Hartnell was dead had definitely seemed to come as a surprise to him. Could he have been acting? Her best judgment said *no,* but she realized that she couldn't be sure. The psychology of serial killers was complex enough to preclude her being able to count on the veracity of his reaction, and her connection to him was too personal to allow her to count on her own reading of it.

"So that was Jasmine," she mused, and only realized that she'd said it aloud when Michael grinned at her. Immediately she wanted to bite her tongue.

"She was cute," he said. "And even fun for a while. Not the brightest, but then, I didn't keep her around to perform brain surgery on me."

"I bet." Charlie couldn't help it. That bit of sarcasm simply came out.

His grin widened. "Like I said, you got no reason to be jealous of Jasmine, babe."

Charlie gave him a look, decided she wasn't going there, and concentrated again on the evidence: the watch was the key.

She said as much, then added, "If that watch they found at the crime scene wasn't yours, and if that could be proved because it didn't have the engraving on the back that yours did, wasn't there anybody who could testify that it *wasn't* your watch because *your* watch had *Semper Fi* on the back of it?"

His eyes returned to the ceiling. "Everybody who could testify to that is dead."

"Everybody?"

"Yup."

Clearly, Charlie saw, she was touching on what was, for him, a sensitive area. Or else he was smart enough—and he *was* smart enough—to know that he could get around her by pretending it was a sensitive area. That she was so *softhearted* she wouldn't probe further if she thought the questions she was asking caused him pain.

Yeah, to hell with that.

"You want to elucidate on that a little?" she asked.

He smiled faintly as his gaze slanted her way. "You trying to confuse me with that big word?"

That didn't fly, either. "Michael."

The smile vanished. "The watch was given to me by members of my unit, who were killed in Afghanistan, all right? They're the only ones who knew what was engraved on it."

From the sudden tension in his jaw, she could tell he didn't want to talk about it. And, damn it, she discovered that she *was* too softhearted to push him to a place that was obviously (unless he was very, very good at faking it, which was possible) hurtful to him.

Kicking herself for her own lack of toughness, she moved on to something else that had occurred to her. But now that it had, it loomed large as a mountain right smack in the middle of the winding road she was traveling on the way to maybe actually believing him.

Her eyes skewered him. Her tone sharpened until it teetered on the edge of being accusing. "So tell me this: if you didn't kill those women, then how did you wind up in Spookville when you died?"

His expression turned grim. "Babe, I never said I didn't deserve to be where I was. What I said was, I didn't kill those women."

Charlie frowned at him. "So what in the world did you do to deserve Spookville?"

He shook his head at her. "I'm done talking about what I did or didn't do. The only reason I even told you any of this is because it pisses me off when every now and then you start looking at me like you think I'm Jack the Ripper. What it comes down to at this point is, either you believe me or you don't. Your call."

He sat up, and she was surprised at how physically close that brought him. As big as he was, he took up way more than his fair share of space on the bed, and her field of vision was suddenly full of his broad shoulders and wide chest. Their arms almost brushed, and she could see the muscles flexing in his, and in his torso beneath his shirt. They were both sitting on top of the covers, but she had her legs tucked beneath her and her laptop in her lap while his long legs in their jeans and boots stretched out almost to the end of the bed. He looked as solid and alive as it was possible for a man to look. Charlie was conscious of her idiot heart speeding up again just from his proximity.

"So?" he said, and she knew what he was asking.

She had to look up to meet his eyes. As she did, they darkened, and his mouth firmed. Searching his hard, handsome face, she realized that she had to consider the possibility that her original diagnosis of him might have been influenced by the fact that she had known he was a convicted serial killer. If she turned the thing on its head, if at the time of diagnosis she had been introduced to him as a normal, law-abiding citizen, would she have concluded that he was a charismatic psychopath capable of the ultimate in horrific violence?

Or would she simply have seen a gorgeous guy with a charming smile?

At this point, it was impossible to know.

"Okay, I believe you," she told him.

His eyes slid over her face. One side of his mouth quirked up in a wry half-smile. "With reservations, huh?"

He'd said he could read her face like a neon sign: here was more proof of it. She was still mentally sorting through the factors for and against his version of what had happened with Candace Hartnell.

"I haven't seen any overwhelming evidence that you're innocent," she told him honestly. "On the other hand, I've seen enough to make me think you could be."

"Your faith in me is staggering, babe." The dryness in his voice made her smile a little.

"What we need to do is find somebody who is willing to testify that this watch"—her voice was brisk with determination as she touched the watch on her arm—"is yours. Somebody who knows about the engraving on the back."

He smiled at her, a slow and ultimately dazzling smile that made her breath catch and her toes curl. Nobody, but nobody, looked like Michael when he smiled like that.

"There goes that savior complex of yours kicking into gear again," he said. "We don't need to do shit. There's no point in it. I'm dead, remember? Whether I'm innocent or not doesn't matter a damn anymore to anybody but you."

"But . . ." Knowing that he was right defeated her.

"You got to go with your gut here, babe. What's it gonna be?"

Looking into those sky blue eyes, Charlie silently acknowledged that for quite some time she had been having trouble picturing him as a merciless slaughterer of young women. It just didn't fit with the man she was getting to know, she felt, pretty well.

But there was no way to be sure. All she could do was go with—not so much her gut, she realized, as her heart.

Her stupid, soft, and way-too-vulnerable heart.

"I thought so," he said with satisfaction, and she knew he had once again successfully read on her face what she was thinking.

"Fine," she told him. "I believe you."

"You could sound happier about it."

"I probably could." If her response was tart, it was because she was disgusted with herself for being such a sucker where he was concerned. No good could come of it. She knew that, and was a sucker for him anyway.

As he watched her face his eyes darkened. Then his head bent, and she felt a shivery little thrill of anticipation when she realized that he was going to kiss her.

Despite all the reasons why she shouldn't, she closed her eyes and tilted her lips up to meet his. Meanwhile, her heart pounded and her pulse raced and her stomach fluttered like a thousand butterflies were taking wing in it.

Then her lips got hit with the slightest of electric tingles and he said *"Fuck"* and her eyes flew open.

To find his gorgeous blue eyes mere inches away, blazing down into hers.

In a flash she realized what had happened: for a moment there, they had both forgotten that he was nothing more than a spirit with no physical substance whatsoever. He'd bent his head to kiss her like he'd thought he actually could, and she'd lifted her mouth to his like it was really going to happen.

"Yeah," he said in grim acknowledgment of reality, and got off the bed. He was already on the move when he told her over his shoulder, "I'm going for a walk."

"You can't," she began in instant warning, reminding him that they were tethered.

"I won't forget that I'm on a fifty-foot leash. If nothing else, I'll probably pace back and forth in front of your door. You should go to sleep." His eyes slid over her, and then a quick, wry smile touched his mouth. "You look sexy as hell in that pretty nightgown, by the way. Not being able to do a thing about it is driving me out of my mind."

That was when she realized that ever since she'd clicked on the bedside lamp he'd gotten an up-close and personal view of her slinky little gown with its loose, cleavage-baring neckline that gave the impression of being barely held up by satiny spaghetti straps. A quick glance down at herself confirmed it: the shimmery peach slip clung to her full breasts and lay whisper close to her narrow waist and flat stomach, leaving little to the imagination before, lower down, her laptop obstructed his view of her slender legs. Her nipples stood up in taut supplication beneath the thin silk. He had to know, as she did, that they were like that because of him.

"I want you like hell," he said, his tone making it almost a throwaway line.

Then he strode out of view.

Charlie just sat there looking after him. Her lips still tingled in anticipation of that thwarted kiss. Her heart still pounded. Her pulse still raced. Deep inside, her body pulsed and burned. But even though she was now almost entirely convinced of his innocence, the hard truth was that the potent attraction that sizzled between them was still as impossible as it had ever been. If he was innocent—and she realized that on some deep, cellular level she had felt he was almost since he had died—that was terrifying in a whole new way. Because it meant there was now nothing to stop her from falling absolutely head over heels in love with him. Except for the fact that the only way falling in love with Michael could end was with her own heartbreak.

Because he was still dead, and there was still no future in it.

It took Charlie a long time to fall asleep.

CHAPTER EIGHTEEN

The next few days were grueling. Michael seemed preoccupied, and Charlie was glad that he didn't have a whole lot to say. Tony was sweet to her, but there was no time even to work in a run and they were rarely alone. The pace of the investigation was such that they were simply too busy to pursue a personal relationship further at that point, for which she was both glad and sorry. Glad because Michael— get real, her feelings for Michael—presented a definite obstacle, although she told herself fiercely that she was a fool to let that happen. Sorry since she really *did* want to pursue a personal relationship with Tony, because he was exactly the kind of guy she could see herself having a long-standing, mutually loving and supportive relationship with. Kaminsky and Buzz were their usual bickering selves, but nobody had time for much conversation that wasn't directly related to the case. As the hours flew by without anything turning up in the way of solid leads, frustration threatened to set in. All of them were too aware of the ticking clock. Like the others, Charlie couldn't rid herself of the tension-producing certainty that if they didn't succeed in discovering the identity of the Gingerbread Man soon, more innocent victims were going to die. That was enough to keep her pushing doggedly ahead.

Eric Riva was the first known recipient of the Gingerbread Man's *You can't catch me* letter. When they stopped by to interview him at his office at the *Charlotte Observer* he was glad to walk them through the circumstances surrounding the series of articles he had written on the Group Three (crossbow) murders two years previously. They had been published before he was contacted by the Gingerbread Man (which had happened in conjunction with the Group Four—propeller—murders) and before anyone had even realized that the killings were the work of a serial killer. Riva's focus in the articles had been on the three victims, and included detailed accounts of each of their lives before the crime, and, in the aftermath, the effect the crime had had on the murdered boys' families, as well as the survivor and his family. The articles, which Charlie and the others had read before meeting with Riva, packed a real emotional punch. Riva agreed with them that the articles were probably what had prompted the Gingerbread Man to send him the letter in the first place. Riva'd had unusual access to inside information on the victims because one of them, fourteen-year-old Brad Carson, had been the son of a former girl-friend. The articles detailed the murders, in which three boys had been forced to vote on which of them would be the first one to die, in terrifying detail. The boy chosen had been killed by an arrow shot from a crossbow from outside the enclosure in which they had been imprisoned, presumably by the Gingerbread Man himself. After that, the two remaining boys had been given the choice of firing crossbows at each other until one of them was dead, or of both being killed. There had been a survivor in that group—sixteen-year-old Matt Hayes—but he no longer lived in the area. Immediately after the kill-ings, he had been charged with the murders of the two other boys, because at the time the authorities hadn't believed his story of a white-masked, grinning sadist who had forced him to kill. It had taken al-most a year, and the commission of the Group Four murders along with the Gingerbread Man's taunting letter to Riva, for authorities to believe that Matt had been telling the truth about what had hap-pened, and to come to the conclusion that he should not, after all, be held responsible for the deaths of the other two boys. When Matt was finally exonerated, his parents took him and his three siblings and moved out of state. For which Charlie didn't blame them a bit.

When the team reached Matt on the phone, he declined to talk to them. His mother told Tony, who had placed the call, that he had worked hard to put the horror behind him, and to please not contact them again.

Charlie didn't blame them for that, either.

"Kelly—Brad's mother—was totally devastated by the murder of her son. She gave me access to everything she knew about the case. Plus I did a lot of research," Riva told them. Thirty-nine years old, of average height, with the kind of overmuscled build that told Charlie he spent a great deal of time lifting weights, he perched on a corner of the table in the newspaper's glass-walled conference room. His brown hair was thinning and worn overlong to compensate, his khakis were rumpled, and the knot on his tie hung a couple of inches below the unbuttoned collar of his shirt, making him, in Charlie's view, look like the quintessential reporter. "It was bad enough when she thought he had been killed by another teenage boy, but it was absolutely terrible for her to realize that he had been the victim of a serial killer. What made it worse was when she found out the same killer had struck in similar fashion at least twice before, and no one had known anything about it. She felt that if there had been any publicity about the previous killings, she would have kept Brad closer to home and he wouldn't have been taken and subsequently killed."

"Did Kelly Carson approach you about writing the articles?" Tony asked. Unlike the rest of them, who sat around the table, he stood in front of the long windows that provided a panoramic view of Charlotte's downtown. Tall and clean-shaven, he looked every inch the FBI agent in his dark suit and tie. The sun pouring through the window made his black hair gleam. Michael stood close by, a shoulder propping one of the struts between the windows, arms crossed over his chest, looking big and tough and gorgeous, a tawny-maned Sun God. Charlie couldn't help the thought that popped into her head as she looked at the pair of them: handsome and handsomer.

Then she determinedly refocused on the case.

"Kelly DeMaris," Riva corrected. "Brad's father died, and she remarried. She turned to me as a friend when Brad was killed. It was my idea to write the articles, so people would know that a monster was at large in our community."

"How and when did Brad's father die?" Kaminsky's eyes had sharpened with interest. Like Tony, she and Buzz were in their FBI suits, but Kaminsky's hair was still faintly damp from her shower and was slicked back from her face and tucked behind her ears. She'd slept through her alarm, she told the three of them with a glower when she joined them in the hall at the appointed time, and hadn't had time to blow-dry her hair. Since then, she'd been snappish, and Charlie, and the others, too, had done their best not to provoke her.

"He was killed in a small plane crash when Brad was nine," Riva said. "Brad and Kelly were with him and were injured, but they recovered."

"Where did the crash happen?" Kaminsky asked with an uptick of excitement as she typed something into her laptop, no doubt noting one more victim who had witnessed the violent death of someone close. The list was far from complete, but it was shaping up to be one of the best—or at least most tantalizing—leads they had.

Riva frowned. "In Indiana somewhere, I think. Why?"

Kaminsky made a face. "No reason."

See, that was the problem with this particular lead: it encompassed too much. The number of first responders, emergency room personnel, doctors, nurses, chaplains, etc., involved was just too large, and the geographic areas of the deaths were too diverse. In trying to track down exactly who had been present at each of these possibly case-related death scenes, they had found it was almost impossible to be as precise as they needed to be to draw any meaningful conclusions. The medical personnel could be identified with a fair degree of accuracy from the patient charts, but it was much harder to pin support staff to the same time and place as a particular patient. Plus they felt there was a very good chance that a number of unaccounted for people were in and about the accident sites, emergency rooms, and other venues where these patients had been cared for. And if compiling a list for each individual site was difficult, cross-referencing with other sites, which they needed to do to find any individual who might have been present at multiple deaths, was so inaccurate as to be practically worthless.

In other words, the lead was promising, but as far as useful results were concerned, they had zilch.

"Did the boys know one another prior to the murders?" Charlie asked. There had to be a common denominator: she was certain of it. They just hadn't found it yet.

"They weren't close friends, but they were acquainted," Riva replied. "They were all from Mooresville—it's a pretty small town— and they had all played in the same baseball league."

Charlie could see Kaminsky typing something into her computer, and guessed she was reminding herself to look into the other victims' sport team affiliations. After all, Jenna had been participating in a run when the Gingerbread Man had grabbed her. Perhaps they could turn up a similar link with the others. Because there had to be *something*.

"We have them, thanks," Tony replied to Riva's offer to get them copies of the articles under discussion. "What we'd like are copies of the notes you used in writing the articles, if you'd let us have them."

Riva agreed readily, but when Charlie saw the hundreds of pages of his photocopied notes, some of them of handwritten originals, that a staffer handed over a short time later, she felt her expectations plummet. Going through so much material as thoroughly as it needed to be gone through would clearly take a lot of time, and time was in increasingly short supply. What it came down to now was a matter of prioritizing what was most likely to yield results.

"When Kelly came to me, after Brad's death, I started trying to help her find out who did this," Riva said. "Then, when that next batch of kids was killed, when I got that letter from the bastard who did it, I did everything I could to track him down. I'm still working on it. I've consulted with the local cops and the FBI agents who were working this case before you guys were brought in. I've run down a thousand possible leads, and explored so many theories that I can't even remember most of them. And I don't think I've come anywhere near identifying him. I hope you have better luck."

"We will," Tony promised grimly. Charlie felt heartened by his confidence.

After that, they met with the local police and FBI agents, toured the Group Four (propeller) kill site, then drove to Winston-Salem and the Wake Forest campus. Charlie had long been familiar with the work of Dr. Jeffrey Underwood, who had a made a career out of studying the genetic makeup of violent killers and, most recently, serial killers. They met him at the medical school, where he was a distinguished professor.

"It's a pleasure to meet you, Dr. Stone. I'm a big fan of your work," was how Dr. Underwood greeted them when they joined him in his lab, where half a dozen graduate students labored diligently over implements ranging from microscopes to computers. Smiling at him, flattered at his words, Charlie returned the compliment. After shaking hands with her, and making a few remarks on her latest research paper, which had been published two months previously in *The American Journal of Psychiatry,* he turned his attention to Tony, Buzz, and Kaminsky.

"I have no idea who could be behind these atrocities," he said in response to Tony's question. Balding and bespectacled, distinguished in his white lab coat, he looked older than his forty years. He was a tall, thin man with a restless air who stood shifting from foot to foot, watching his assistants with eagle eyes even as he answered questions, and rapping out the occasional instruction or rebuke to his underlings as he felt the need.

"How was the letter from the Gingerbread Man delivered to you?" Tony asked.

"It was slipped under the door to my office," Dr. Underwood said. "I came in one morning, and there it was. Needless to say, I immediately contacted the police."

Tony looked at Kaminsky.

"We already have a copy of it," she answered, correctly interpreting his unspoken question. "Like the others, it was written by one of the victims, Liza Gill, under what we are sure was some sort of coercion. That was the group killed in the trash compacter, if you remember."

"Are there security cameras in the building?" Buzz didn't look particularly hopeful. Because even if there were, by this time the footage would have been about a year old, which meant that unless it had been deliberately preserved, it almost certainly no longer existed.

"There are," Dr. Underwood replied, "but I understand that nothing usable was found. By the time police thought to check, the images had been taped over. I think the cameras are set to do that every seventy-two hours."

That came as a slight disappointment, but no surprise. As they went through their litany of questions, Dr. Underwood answered readily, but he had very little new to tell them.

Still, Charlie found much of what he had to say fascinating, but that was because he kept getting away from Tony's questions to explain to her where he was going with his research.

"Right now we're doing DNA tests on a number of samples of genetic material to see if the CHRNA7 gene, which is often missing in schizophrenics, is also missing in serial killers," he told Charlie. "I'm hoping to get funding to do a large scale study on the subject, which includes mass killers as well, such as the Colorado movie theater shooter."

"Do you feel that mass murderers and serial killers will be found to have the same mutation?" Charlie asked, immediately interested. It wasn't often she had the opportunity to talk shop with someone whose area of expertise so closely paralleled her own.

Dr. Underwood nodded. "I think so."

"I'm not convinced that we'll ever find one single component that creates a serial killer," Charlie said, totally drawn into the discussion. "It may be that a number of factors have to be present. Genetics may certainly play a role, but I am leaning toward the theory that environmental factors may be as important."

"Perhaps we could collaborate on a paper at some point," Dr. Underwood suggested. "I'd be very interested in incorporating the work you're doing into my research."

"I'm open to that," Charlie agreed. A stray glance that happened to encompass the faces of Tony, Buzz, and Kaminsky reminded her that, involving though the discussion was, it wasn't their reason for visiting Dr. Underwood. Michael was smiling faintly as he watched her. As she met his eyes she thought that what she saw might be pride in them . . . for her. Silly as it undoubtedly was to let the thought that he was proud of her affect her, she felt the beginnings of a tiny little glow. It occurred to her that having someone show pride in her was a rare thing in her life: she didn't come from that kind of background. Funny (sad?) that it took her impossible bête noire to open her eyes to the fact that she had wanted that.

"I only have one more question for you, Dr. Underwood," Tony said. "We know that the Gingerbread Man is going to strike again, and soon. Do you have any suggestions as to which experts working in fields similar to yours and Dr. Stone's he might be planning to send his next letter to? Whoever it is will be within the three-state area of North Carolina, South Carolina, and Virginia."

Dr. Underwood thought for a moment, then named two researchers who were on the list of a dozen names that Charlie had already compiled. In response to the same question, David Myers had also given them a couple of different names that were already on Charlie's list, so the information was not particularly helpful.

"You kicked ass in there, babe," Michael told her as they left. Having forgotten herself so far as to glance at him in response, she caught the look in his eyes and knew that she hadn't been mistaken: he *was* proud of her. She couldn't help it: she smiled at him. Sometimes, having Michael in her life actually felt good. And she meant good in a way that had nothing to do with sexual attraction.

"At least we've got a sort of consensus about the probable next experts he'll contact," Buzz said gloomily when they were in the air again, en route to Hampton, Virginia. That was the town from which Jenna, Laura, and Raylene had been kidnapped, and the team hoped to find something there that linked the three girls. They were armed with fresh details of how Jenna had spent the hours before she was kidnapped, gleaned from another interview with her via Skype, into which her mother, hovering anxiously in the background, had continuously interpolated comments. They had also acquired comparatively fuzzier details about how Laura and Raylene had spent that day, which they compiled from interviews with family, friends, and the team's own reconstruction of events. Once the plane landed, they would be back to beating the investigative bushes in hopes that something substantive would turn up.

"We've got local teams conducting round-the-clock surveillance on the experts on your list, including their offices and residences," Tony said to Charlie. Like the rest of them, he was seated around the airplane's pop-up table. Since they were doing so much traveling, the sleek Gulfstream V had become their de facto War Room. "If the unsub delivers a letter to one of them, we should have him."

"The problem with that is, by the time he drops it off, he'll have already kidnapped and probably killed his next victims," Kaminsky pointed out.

"And it's possible that he won't personally drop off the letter," Buzz said. "He could mail it, like he did to Riva. Or convey it to the intended recipient in any number of ways."

"Or the list could be wrong," Charlie reminded them. "We wouldn't have put Eric Riva on it, for example."

"At least it's a starting point," Tony said. "If he's casing the expert ahead of time, surveillance should pick up on it. We've got helicopters and ground personnel looking for possible kill sites in the vicinity of the names on the list. If he shows up at any of them, we've got him."

"Here are the key points to keep in mind." Kaminsky had set up what amounted to a PowerPoint presentation for their delectation. They'd already gone over several facets of the investigation, but the discussion had for the last few minutes gotten diverted. Now she called their attention back to the slides she was projecting on a pull-down screen above the couch where Michael lay. Since Charlie was the only one who could see him, she was the only one who found his presence there distracting. To all appearances, he was napping, although, of course, he didn't nap.

"We know that the unsub is a white male between the ages of approximately twenty-five and forty. We know that he possesses or has access to a blue or gray van with an interior that may or may not (because it might not be permanent) be outfitted with a cage and that smells like fish. We know he spoke on the telephone to someone he called Ben. We know a stun gun was used to initially subdue at least some of the victims, and that later a sedating gas was used to keep at least some of them either semi- or unconscious. Blood work on the last three victims identified that gas as nitrous oxide, so the unsub will have access to it. We know that the murder scenarios he plans are unusually complex, and require significant prior preparation. We know that he somehow knows or knows of Eric Riva, Dr. David Myers, Dr. Jeffrey Underwood, and our own Dr. Stone. We know that all of the sites of the murders and kidnappings are no more than a seven-hour drive apart, which means he lives or is staying within

that area, at least during the time the murders are being carried out."
Kaminsky flipped to the next display, which was a bulleted list of
names. "We know that these victims witnessed or were present at the
violent death of someone close to them before they were involved in
this case. That's more than half. A large enough percentage to be sta-
tistically significant. In the case of the victims where we have not
confirmed close exposure to a violent death, it's because the information isn't available, not necessarily because it didn't happen. Which
means the incidence rate is likely to rise. So I think we can assume
that close exposure to violent death in victims is important. Also important is how the unsub knows of the violent death in the victim's
past. We need to determine how he has access to that information."

"Any insight into that?" Tony looked at all three of them in turn.

"Checking the medical personnel and hospitals involved," Buzz
said. "So far nothing's jumping out."

"I think we're going to find that our unsub was exposed to a
similar violent death at a young age," Charlie said. "So that gives us
one more marker to look for. It's possible his exposure will correlate
to the ages of the first victims, which was between twelve and fourteen."

"How about checking obits for past accidental or violent deaths
for something like ten years before those first murders?" Michael suggested without opening his eyes. "There can't be that many newspa-
pers in North and South Carolina and Virginia. And they all keep
archives."

Charlie almost said, *Good idea*. Catching herself in time, she instead repeated his suggestion.

Tony looked at Buzz.

"On it, boss," Buzz said.

"What about trying to find out where he gets his nitrous oxide?"
Tony asked.

Buzz shook his head. "You'd be surprised how many uses for nitrous oxide there are: dentists use it, race car drivers use it in their
engines, it's used in cooking and in aerosol products like whipped
cream, it's also used illegally, as in, teenagers inhaling it. All that
makes it fairly easy to come by."

"Suppliers?" Tony asked.

"Not that many, but the distribution is so widespread that it's taking some time to check," Buzz replied. "We're talking about going through thousands of individual bills of sale. Then there's the secondary market."

"Keep on it," Tony said.

Buzz nodded.

"People." Kaminsky's voice drew their attention back to her presentation. The screen changed again to show pictures of the five survivors, with a bullet list beneath each. Certain items were highlighted in red. Indicating it, Kaminsky continued, "We've talked to all the survivors now—well, Matt Hayes wouldn't talk to us, but all the other survivors—and their accounts are consistent: they were kidnapped, drugged, forced to kill, released, and ordered to run for their lives as the sole survivor. They describe the unsub as wearing all black with a white, grinning mask. Estimates of height and weight vary significantly. At least two thought he was disguising his voice with some sort of digital device."

"Does that mean the unsub knows the victims, do you think?" Buzz asked.

Tony shook his head. "It might just mean that he doesn't want the survivors to be able to identify his voice later."

Buzz nodded. Charlie concurred: that made sense.

"What about unsolved single murders in the Buggs Island Lake area around the time and previous to the first Gingerbread Man attack?" Charlie asked.

"Going back ten years from that date, there are two unsolved murders, neither of which seem to fit our criteria. One was thought to have resulted from a bar fight and one appeared to be a professional hit," Kaminsky said. "But there are a number of accidental deaths that might be something more. I'm still working on it."

"So what've we got?" Tony asked.

Kaminsky made a disgusted sound. "Not as much as you'd hope. Our best lead is a violent death in the victims' pasts. Like Dr. Stone said, we're looking for a common denominator, and that's the closest thing we have."

"Okay," Tony said as the pilot came over the intercom and advised them they were getting ready to land. "Let's keep digging. We'll figure it out."

Charlie was stepping down onto the blisteringly hot tarmac when it hit her. Her mouth fell open. Michael, beside her, saw the expression on her face and said sharply, "What?"

"Holly," she answered before she thought, and then as the others looked at her she pulled herself together and refocused on them. "I was exposed to a violent death at a young age, too. You remember, my friend Holly Palmer."

Who had died at the hands of the Boardwalk Killer, while Charlie had survived.

"Holy cow," Buzz said.

"That's a link." Kaminsky sounded excited.

"Check the other experts. See if Riva, Myers, or Underwood had exposure to a violent death in their pasts." Tony looked at Kaminsky. "Maybe that's how he selects the experts."

"If so, then finding the next expert just got a lot easier." Buzz sounded almost as excited as Kaminsky.

"And the next kill site. Because it will be within close proximity to the next expert," Kaminsky chimed in. She looked at Buzz. "You take the list of experts he's likely to target, and I'll take Riva, Myers, and Underwood. Let's see if this pans out."

Charlie missed Buzz's reply to that, because at that moment her cell phone went off. Glancing at it, she saw that the caller was Tam. Her heart sped up. This call was not likely to be anything good.

"Excuse me a minute: I need to take this," she said. Then she walked a few yards away from them for privacy's sake while staying within the shadow of the plane, and within their view.

"Hey, Tam," she said into the phone.

"Cherie," Tam greeted her. "Oh, cherie, I have something I need to tell you. First, are you someplace safe?"

Tam's tone made Charlie feel cold all over. A quick glance around found Tony and Kaminsky talking to each other and, hopefully, paying no attention to her, while Buzz was walking away from them, presumably going for the car. Michael was beside her, looking down at her with a frown. She was, she realized, glad he was there. He had somehow become a bulwark in her life.

"Yes," she said, while Michael drawled, "If that's the voodoo priestess, ask her if she knows a way to make this damned leash I'm on a little longer."

But Charlie didn't have a chance to ask Tam anything, because the other woman burst out, "I know where the danger comes from. It's water. You are in terrible danger around dark water."

CHAPTER NINETEEN

"You're getting Dudley all worked up, you know." Michael walked through the closed bathroom door, then stopped to watch her with hard eyes as she smoothed on fresh lipstick. Charlie flicked a look his way.

"What part of *the bathroom is off-limits* did you not understand?" she asked tartly.

His lip curled. She took that to mean, *it's only off-limits if I want it to be,* and frowned at him.

The bathroom they were in was a small, elegantly appointed ladies' room right off the Marriott's patio, where she, Tony, Kaminsky, and Buzz had not so long ago finished having a late, badly needed dinner. A little while earlier Kaminsky and Buzz had gone upstairs, where the team had four adjacent rooms on the twentieth floor, while Charlie, at Tony's invitation, had chosen to stay on for coffee and dessert. He'd ordered key lime pie and she'd ordered mango sherbet, which they'd eaten. They had been waiting for the server to bring the check when she had excused herself to go freshen up. Since the door to the ladies' room was visible from where they sat, neither of them had seen any need for him to escort her. The restroom contained a single stall, divided from the sink area by a partition, and once inside

Charlie had locked the door. Nobody was getting to her in there—except, of course, for Michael.

He'd been bent out of shape ever since Tam's phone call. He wanted her to tell Tony about Tam's calls, about the danger Tam said she was in. He wanted her to leave the investigation and go hole up somewhere until the Gingerbread Man was caught. He wanted her to abandon her entire career and find an alternative use for her medical degree that did not involve serial killers.

And he wanted her not to get involved with Tony. That one he hadn't said in so many words, but she didn't have any trouble interpreting the increasingly grim set to his mouth, or the antagonistic glint in his eyes, as she and Tony had talked more and more exclusively to each other over dinner, while Kaminsky and Buzz did the same. Then, when the others had been leaving and Tony had asked her if she wanted to stay on for coffee and dessert, and she had agreed without so much as a glance thrown at the frowning ghost sprawled in a chair across the table from her, Michael had started to radiate hostility like rays from the sun.

She'd felt that hostility all but scorching her as over dessert she and Tony had completely abandoned shop talk and he'd told her self-deprecating stories about his days as a college football player that made her laugh. Then when she had excused herself to go to the restroom and Michael had (of course) followed her, her back had practically blistered from the heat.

"The bathroom is off-limits," she had warned Michael out of the side of her mouth as she reached the ladies' room door, in an effort to avoid the discussion (fight) she had a pretty good idea was coming.

So much for that. At least he'd had the decency to wait until (she assumed) he'd heard the buzzing of the air dryer that had told him she was drying her hands.

The dress wasn't helping.

The thing was, she was wearing one. It was a sundress, a beautiful deep red print, with a thin strap over each shoulder and smocking that kept it snug to the waist and a floaty, tea-length skirt. She'd bought it in the hotel's upscale gift shop, when the four (five) of them had come in from walking Hampton's sidewalks as, straight off the plane, they had followed the route Jenna said she'd taken before being

grabbed. Evening had fallen as they went inside each of the establish-
ments Jenna would have passed, and examined the spot where the
abduction had occurred, but the temperature stayed in the nineties,
and the humidity was thick. By the time they returned to the car and
drove to the hotel, besides being cross from listening to Michael without being able to answer back, Charlie had been hot and sweaty and
heartily regretting the way she was dressed. Her sleeveless silk blouse
had been clinging unpleasantly to her skin and her lightweight slacks
felt like they were heavy wool and plastered to her legs. No surprise:
she'd packed work clothes, but what she had failed to consider was
that her work clothes had been chosen with an indoor, air-conditioned
office in mind. They weren't suitable for being outdoors in so much
heat and humidity.

So when she had seen the pretty, lightweight summer ensembles
in the hotel gift shop, she'd left the men to check in and, with Kaminsky following on her heels, headed for the clothes. If anything, Kaminsky in her fitted suit was even more inappropriately dressed for
what they'd just been doing and were planning on continuing to do
the next day than Charlie was. They had a brief meeting of the (female) minds and Kaminsky, too, had indulged in some shopping.

The result was that Kaminsky had worn a sleek, knee-length (she
told Charlie with a wry twist of her mouth that she couldn't go longer
because of her height) black linen shift with a nifty little short-sleeved
bolero to hide her shoulder holster, plus her own stilettos, which she
refused to forsake, while Charlie had worn the sundress, and a pair of
embellished sandals with delicate kitten heels that she'd purchased to
go with the dress.

Having of necessity followed her into the gift shop, Michael in
typical male fashion had displayed little interest as she had riffled
through the clothing. So when she'd emerged from the bathroom of
her hotel room to find him draped over one of the two wing chairs on
the other side of the single king bed, desultorily watching TV, the
night sky black behind him through the opened curtains and the room
itself softly lit by the floor lamp between the chairs, his eyes had widened in surprise as he glanced her way.

"You look beautiful," he said. Fresh from her shower, with her
hair twisted into a cool updo that left a few tendrils loose to curl

around her face and neck, and her makeup subtle but there (it had all but melted away earlier), she felt so much better that she smiled at him, which, because she'd been hot and cross and tired of him telling her what she needed to do, she hadn't done for a while.

"Thank you," she said.

He stood up and came toward her, his gaze sliding over her before lingering on her nearly bare shoulders. "All this for Dudley?"

Her brows twitched together. "All this because the dining room closed at nine, so we'll be eating outside by the pool, and it's hot out there." She reached for his watch, which she'd left beside her purse on the console table that ran along the wall opposite the beds, and slid it onto her arm. Then she picked up her purse and turned to head for the door.

"Listen to what you just said: you'll be eating outside by the pool. You know it's night, right? That makes the pool dark water. For that matter, this hotel's on the beach. The ocean is right there. More dark water."

Already having had the same thought and conquered it, and aggravated at having all that latent fear stirred up again, she turned around to glare at him. "If I stay in the room and run a bath, and turn the light out in the bathroom, the tub will be full of dark water, too."

His lips thinned. "The difference is, there's not likely to be a serial killer who knows your name in the bathroom with you."

"No, he'll be right outside the door," she retorted.

"Oh, ha-ha." From his expression, he clearly didn't find that amusing. "Your friend the voodoo priestess says you're in danger. You say the voodoo priestess is generally right on. How stupid is it to stay here in harm's way when it would be the easiest thing in the world to stay in your room tonight, hop a plane tomorrow, and fly somewhere safe?"

Charlie sighed. "That's the problem, don't you see? There isn't anywhere safe. I'm as liable to be running into danger as I am to be running away from it. Tam says I'm in danger near dark water. If you think about it, there's dark water everywhere. For my money, the reason I'm in danger near dark water is almost certainly because there's a serial killer out there who knows my name. Therefore, the way to make me safe is to catch the serial killer. And at a guess, I'd say I'm safer surrounded by three armed FBI agents than I would be on my own."

Their eyes met. *You'd be with me,* his said, and hers replied, *You can't protect me,* and his narrowed and his mouth tightened in angry acknowledgment.

"You're scaring me to death here, all right?" His words were abrupt. His face was tight. "At least tell Dudley about what the damned woman said so he's on his guard, would you please?"

"Fine," she snapped, annoyed at herself because it touched her that he would disregard the rivalry she knew he felt with Tony to try to make sure she was protected. "I'm scared, too, you know. I'm always scared, all the time. I live with this constant, low-grade fear and have since my friend was killed and I found out what kind of evil exists in the world. What Tam said simply cranked it up a couple of notches. But what I've learned over the years is that the only thing to do when you're scared is stay cool and keep moving ahead."

Even as the words left her mouth, Charlie realized it was the first time in her adult life that she had ever admitted to anyone that she was afraid. Fear had been her constant companion for as long as she could remember; she had learned to hide it, to deny it, to hold her head high in the face of it and carry on.

But she had never admitted to it out loud until right now—to him.

Her ghost.

And what did that say about the state of her heart where he was concerned?

"Charlie." His eyes darkened and slid to her mouth, and she knew he wanted to kiss her. And she knew that if there had been any way, any possible way to make that happen, she would have walked straight into his arms and slid her own around his neck and kissed him until kissing wasn't enough. And then she would have gone to bed with him.

Because that's what she was burning to do.

Just thinking about it made her go all soft and shivery inside.

Her face must have given her away, because his eyes blazed at her. Suddenly passion beat in the air between them, as tangible as the pounding of her heart.

A knock at the door broke the spell.

"That'll be Tony," she said, and saw his eyes flare.

She was still aching for Michael when she turned and opened the door to find Tony standing there.

"Why, Dr. Stone," Tony greeted her on a note of surprised pleasure, doing an exaggerated double-take as she stepped out into the bright light of the hallway and he took in her dress. He wasn't his usual FBI agent-correct self, either, having lost the coat and tie and rolled the sleeves of his white dress shirt up to his elbows. The tail end of his shirt was out, too, and she presumed that was to hide his gun.

"Why, Special Agent Bartoli," she echoed on the same note, giving him a copy of the exaggerated once-over he had given her, and he laughed and caught her hand and brought it to his mouth and kissed it. The brush of his lips on her skin was warm and pleasant, and the casual grace of the gesture made her heart hurt a little.

Because it served to underline the fact that she was never going to have that with the man (?) she really wanted. The simple pleasures of casual physical contact were never going to happen between her and Michael.

But, she decided as she smiled at Tony and he tucked his hand around her arm—it felt warm and strongly masculine against her skin, and she was suddenly acutely conscious of it—and they started walking side by side toward the elevator where Kaminsky in her new dress and Buzz in rolled-up shirtsleeves were waiting, she wasn't going to let her heart get broken. Having it break over a dead man would be stupid. Because it wouldn't change a thing: he would still be unavailable for the life she wanted—he would still be dead.

There was a phrase from a song her mother used to listen to: *love the one you're with.*

She liked Tony a whole lot. She found him attractive, sexy. His kisses turned her on.

Tony she could kiss. Tony she could have sex with. Tony she could even, eventually, if things worked out, make a life with.

Stupid she wasn't. She knew enough to choose the possible over the impossible.

So that's what she made up her mind to do.

They joined Kaminsky and Buzz at the elevators just in time for

Charlie to overhear Kaminsky saying to Buzz, "So where'd you go last night?" to which Buzz replied with a startled, "What?" while Kaminsky pinned him with a censorious look and answered, "I was in the room next door, remember? I heard you go out," before they both shut up as Charlie and Tony reached them. Charlie had the fleeting thought that Kaminsky's oversleeping that morning was thus explained: she'd obviously stayed awake listening for Buzz to return from wherever he'd gone. Which meant that the situation between them was getting interesting. Charlie realized that she hadn't been paying much attention to them, which wasn't surprising: she had her own (way complicated) situation going on, after all.

The elevator came, and the four (five) of them piled in.

When they emerged on the ground floor to head across the cavernous, marble-floored lobby and through the big glass doors into the covered outdoor walkway beyond, it was full night. A ruffle of strategically placed potted palm trees blocked the patio from view. Soft romantic music filled the air, along with the sounds of conversation and laughter from their fellow late diners. The moon was a tipsy crescent high in the sky and thousands of stars twinkled like tiny rhinestones set into midnight velvet. A few steps down took them to the wide patio with its wrought-iron tables and chairs. It was enclosed on two sides by smaller buildings connected to the hotel, but the front was open. The surrounding landscaping was lush and fragrant, and the flickering lights from dozens of jewel-toned hurricane lanterns glowing on the tables and on tall, willowy stands around the perimeter added a magical beauty. It was still hot outside, but the humidity was made bearable by a slight, salt-scented breeze blowing in off the ocean. In the distance, across a stretch of pale, barely seen beach, Charlie glimpsed the roll of whitecaps on the gleaming black water. Much closer at hand, down a path that led from the patio to the beach, the hotel's grottolike pool still accommodated a few die-hard swimmers. Dark water, Charlie thought, and felt a cold finger of fear slide down her spine. Her step faltered for a second—but really, what was there to do, run back to her room and stay there until Tam gave her the all clear? Saying, "At least stay away from the damned water" in a goaded tone, Michael moved in close beside her, placing his big body between her and the pool and the sea, but it was Tony's hand that slid around her arm again. It was Tony's touch she felt, Tony who was solid and warm and as physically present as she was. Refusing to even glance at Michael, Charlie deliberately leaned into Tony a little, just enough so that their bodies brushed, and looked up at him and smiled.

Over dinner, Charlie concentrated on the man she could have, and pretended the one she couldn't have wasn't there. Because in a world that didn't absolutely suck, he wouldn't have been, and she could have fallen in love with Tony without any damned infernal interference.

Which was why, when Michael joined her in the restroom, she was braced for him to be ticked off at her. And she already knew that, his anger notwithstanding, she was going to hold to the course she had chosen, and not back down.

She was choosing Tony, and Michael was simply going to have to live (or not) with that.

So now Michael was in the bathroom scowling at her. "You got him thinking he's going to get lucky tonight."

Finishing with her lipstick, giving herself a final check in the mirror, Charlie turned to face him. No point in beating around the bush. The thing about it was, with Michael attached to her like a tail to a kite there was no way he wasn't going to know. Not only about Tony, but about everything she ever did in her life from that point on until either she died or he disappeared. The knowledge was unsettling. No, terrifying. But all she could do was find a way to deal with it—him—on terms she could live with.

"Maybe he is." She gave him a level look. "I'm thinking about it."

"What?" To say Michael looked astounded was an understatement.

"At some point, if my relationship with Tony continues, we're going to have sex. I'm thinking about making it tonight."

Astounded gave way to flabbergasted, which was replaced almost instantly by plain mad.

"The hell you are."

"You don't have anything to say about it. I'm telling you as a courtesy, so you can stay out of the way. In other words, if I go into a hotel room with Tony, you stay outside, got it?"

"In your fucking dreams."

"I thought watching wasn't your thing."

"Baby, I'm telling you up front that if you go into a hotel room with Dudley with the intention of having sex with him, that's going to turn into the most haunted hotel room you've ever been in in your life."

Her brows snapped together. "Guess what, Casper: since I'm the only one who can see or hear you, if I simply shut my eyes and tune you out there's nothing you can do."

"Try me."

"Oh, I'm going to. I get to have a life."

His eyes narrowed at her. "You got turned on, didn't you? In the bedroom earlier. I turned you on, and now you're wanting to get your rocks off with Dudley. Just so we're clear, that ain't going to work for me."

"You're disgusting," Charlie hissed at him, her cheeks flaming. She started walking toward him, because she wasn't wasting any more breath arguing, and he was blocking the door.

"It's the truth and you know it. I'm the guy you want to fuck, not him."

"Get out of my way."

He folded his arms over his chest. "Uh-uh."

Her blood boiled. What he seemed to forget was that she could walk right through him, which was what she did, and the electric tingle be damned. Yanking open the door, she realized a couple of long strides beyond it that she was stalking instead of walking, and moderated her gait. By the time she reached the table, she was able to smile at Tony, who was signing the check and handing it back to the waiter, as if all was right with her world, and never mind Michael's honey-infused voice at her back growling, "You ever try eating a turkey sandwich when what you really want is a pizza? When you finish the sandwich, you're still craving that pizza."

Of course she didn't reply.

"In case that went over your head, I'm the pizza."

Oh, she'd gotten it, all right. And she still didn't reply.

"Damn it, Charlie," Michael said, planting himself in front of her. Narrowing her eyes at him, she veered around him. Walking through him was possible, as she'd just proven, but the truth was it was something she didn't like to do.

"Hey." Tony stood up as she reached the table. "This was dinner," he said, smiling at her, and she remembered that they'd agreed to dinner as a first step in their take-it-slow pact. "Want to try for a dance before we go up?"

There was a cleared area on the far side of the patio, over by another ruffle of potted palms that almost hid the solid brick wall behind it. Couples were dancing there, eight or nine, ranging in age from young professionals to grandmas and grandpas. Nothing fancy, no *Dancing with the Stars* glitz, simply all of them holding each other close as they swayed and turned and circled the floor to the music.

"You don't want to do this," Michael said.

"I'd love to," Charlie told Tony with determination, and when he smiled at her and took her hand she followed him onto the dance floor and turned into his arms.

She had danced with him before, but only as part of working on a case. It had been a careful and formal dance, under the watchful eyes of Kaminsky and Buzz and a camera. This dance was different. This was her plastered right up against Tony, with his arm tight around her waist and his body hard and unmistakably masculine against hers. It was personal. It was romantic. It was *real*.

"You look good," Tony told her, his mouth close to her ear. "You smell good, too."

"Thank you," Charlie said. She tipped her head back to smile at him. The moonlight made his eyes seem very dark as he met her glance, and highlighted the lean hard bones of his face. He looked good. He *felt* good. He *was* good. Really, what was not to fall in love with?

"You actually think you can have a relationship with him? You can't even tell him about the things you see," Michael spoke in her ear. "You're afraid to tell him that you've got a voodoo priestess friend who's saying you're in danger. He has no idea that you're looking at a ghost over there in the corner who's got half his head blown away. And we both know you're sure as hell never going to tell him about me."

Of course Michael was going to be a pain in the ass. So what else was new? Yes, she did see the spirit in the corner, a young man standing over an upscale-looking sixtyish couple talking earnestly over dinner, who clearly had no idea he was there. But so what? She saw ghosts all the time, and this particular one was keeping his distance, and that meant he was none of her business. Just like what she told or didn't tell Tony was none of Michael's business.

As a movement of the dance turned her around, she glared at Michael over Tony's shoulder. And mouthed, *"Go away."*

"So tell me how you came to be an FBI agent," she said to Tony. Manhunting 101: get the guy to talk about himself. It had been a while, but she remembered the drill. Anyway, he knew all (well, almost all) about her from the damned background check he'd run on her. If she was going to start a real relationship with him, it would probably be a good idea to learn a little more about what made him tick.

"It was either be an FBI agent or a lawyer," Tony said. "What would you do?"

She laughed. "FBI, definitely."

His arm tightened around her waist. They were swaying together, turning a little, basic box step stuff. His cheek—she thought it was his cheek, but it could have been his lips—brushed her hair.

"There you go," he said. "They lured me in with the great government salary. And the hours. Then they clenched the deal when they told me that occasionally people might shoot at me with a gun."

She laughed again. She *liked* him. And she felt safe with him. Those were two sturdy pillars on which to begin to build a relationship. *I can do this,* she told herself, as the prospect of the normal life she had always wanted but been afraid to reach for shimmered tantalizingly in her mind's eye. All she had to do was keep her mouth shut about the woo-woo stuff in her life, pretend it (most especially Michael) didn't exist, and she could build her own future just the way she wanted it.

"So did you pick your own team, or were Buzz and Kaminsky assigned to you?" Charlie asked. Tony's hand slid down below her waist, not quite to her butt but getting there. He wasn't quite as tall as—he was tall enough so that they weren't crotch to crotch, but she could still feel what was going on below his waist, and registered it with an interested tingle.

"Didn't your mama ever tell you that classy women don't let men feel them up on the dance floor?" Michael's drawl had an edge to it. He was behind Tony again, so all she had to do was look over Tony's shoulder to see all six-foot-three infuriating inches of him.

She turned her head instead to admire the clean line of Tony's jaw.

"Crane was assigned to me," Tony told her. "Kaminsky was a cop when Crane recommended we use her for a case because she speaks fluent Bulgarian, which we needed. She did an amazing job, not only with the language but with everything. So I told her that if she joined the Bureau, I'd hire her. She did and I did."

Those were definitely Tony's lips brushing her ear, Charlie thought, and then nuzzling the hollow below it. The sensation was pleasant, and as she closed her eyes to enjoy it she could feel herself warming up inside. Sliding her hand along the width of his shoulder, she enjoyed that sensation, too. Beneath the smoothness of his shirt, his shoulder felt muscular and firm to the touch, just like the body she was pressed against felt muscular and firm. She moved a little, wriggling experimentally, and as her breasts pushed harder into his chest she felt a pleasurable little throb.

"Babe, you shouldn't ought to have to work that hard to get turned on. Why don't you give up and admit that Dudley ain't lighting your fire tonight?"

Charlie's eyes shot open. Michael was behind Tony, watching her like a hawk hunting for rodents. His tone was mocking, but the skin over his cheekbones was hard and tight as he focused on her face.

She glared at him. Then she turned her face into Tony's neck and pressed her lips to the smooth warm skin there. It felt good. She was *definitely* getting turned on.

"Charlie," Tony whispered huskily, and she lifted her head and he kissed her mouth. Not a full-out kiss, because they were, after all, on a dance floor, but more of a tasting.

She liked it.

Crash.

The noise was so unexpected that Charlie jumped. So did every-one else, including Tony, whose arms dropped away from her as his hand shot behind his back toward where, she imagined, he had stashed his gun, probably in his waistband. Looking through all the moving shadows that played across the patio, she saw that one of the hurricane lanterns had fallen from its stand to shatter into a million ruby red shards on the stone at the edge of the dance floor.

She saw, too, that Michael was standing next to the stand where, seconds before, the lantern had flickered. Her eyes widened. Was it possible that he had . . . ? As she remembered the remote he'd learned to work, and the computer he'd managed to operate, and the two or three occasions when he'd actually manifested for a few seconds in solid form, her blood pressure skyrocketed. Yes, she grimly answered her own question, it was possible. In fact, knocking that hurricane lantern from its stand was exactly what he had done.

"Yo, babe." Seeing her eyes on him, Michael gave her an insolent little wave.

With Tony able to see her, there was no possible response she could make.

"Whoa," Tony said. His hand had never actually reached his gun, and now it slid around her waist again. "I didn't realize the wind was that strong."

"Me either." Charlie registered that her tone was acerbic only after the words had left her mouth. By then, there was nothing she could do.

The music, which was piped in rather than live, hadn't stopped, and as a server ran off, presumably for a broom, everybody started dancing again. Tony pulled her back into his arms, and Charlie nes-tled there, determined to re-establish the sensual buildup exactly where she'd left off.

Tony seemed to be on the same page. "You've got the softest skin," he murmured, dropping a kiss on her shoulder.

Crash.

Charlie didn't even jump this time. She'd been expecting it. But Tony did, at least enough to let her go and look around at the second hurricane lantern to crash to the ground.

The dancing stopped as everyone around them once again stared at the broken glass.

"I can do this all night long," Michael called to her.

Every muscle in Charlie's body hummed with tension. She caught herself glaring at him, and instantly forced the anger from her face.

Two can play at that game, was the thought she sent winging Michael's way.

"It *is* getting windy. Why don't we go on up?" she said sweetly to Tony. And took his hand.

The flaring of Tony's eyes was the ocular equivalent of a *hell, yes* fist pump: as Michael had so maddeningly put it, Tony thought he was about to get lucky. It was only there for the briefest of instants, but Charlie saw it and was conscious of feeling slightly nettled. She knew masculine sex-on-the-brain when she saw it, and Tony was exhibiting classic symptoms.

Which, she told herself, was exactly what she wanted.

"Good idea," was what Tony said, his voice perfectly bland, his eyes now no more than warmly encouraging.

Men, she thought savagely, and smiled at him as they walked hand in hand to the elevators.

"Something the matter?" Michael was with them. Smirking.

Of course the minute the elevator doors closed Tony pulled her into his arms and kissed her. A deep kiss. Hungry. Promising.

Wrapping her arms around his neck, Charlie shot a one-fingered salute at the devil watching her and kissed Tony back.

The shrilling of the emergency alarm made Tony jump like he'd been goosed.

Having been expecting—not precisely that, but *something*—Charlie didn't jump. Finding herself dropped, she took advantage of her sudden freedom to turn her back to Tony and shoot her nemesis a look that would have killed him if he hadn't already been dead.

"What the hell?" Tony said over the shrilling of the alarm, turning to examine the control panel in obvious hopes of shutting the damned thing off.

Leaning back against the wall, folding his arms over his chest, Michael gave Charlie a malicious grin. "I got to say, this is the most fun I've had since I died."

Charlie was still working on rearranging her features into a rea-sonably pleasant expression for Tony's benefit when the elevator, alarm still trilling wildly, reached their floor and stopped. She walked out first. Catching up with her, Tony slid a hand around her arm.

It took an effort, but she smiled at him.

Michael said, "Watch out, babe, you're shooting poison darts out of those big blue eyes."

She kept the smile, and tried not to clench her teeth.

The guard Tony had scared up to stand sentinel in the hall was nowhere in sight. Had Tony arranged for him to be elsewhere until he was summoned? Because he was astute enough to realize that she would find it embarrassing to invite him into her room under the eyes of an audience?

Charlie didn't know. She didn't really care. Glancing down, thrusting a hand into her purse, she pulled out her room key.

Tony saw it, and his hand tightened possessively on her arm.

"Think I could get the sprinkler above your bed to go off?" Mi-chael asked in a tone that, if Charlie hadn't known better, would have indicated he was just idly wondering. "Well, guess we won't know till I try."

Charlie shot him an evil look. The three of them had reached the door to her room by that time. Turning her back on Satan's spawn, she paused with her key card in her hand to look up into Tony's now subtly gleaming brown eyes.

CHAPTER TWENTY

"So, am I coming in?" Tony asked her with the smallest of crooked smiles.

Charlie's hand tightened on the key card. She looked up into the lean, dark face of the absolutely-perfect-for-the-life-she-wanted man standing so close to her. She did not so much as glance in the direction of the tawny-haired curse with which she was afflicted.

The sad, infuriating truth was, she had no choice.

"We're taking it slow, remember?" Smiling apologetically at Tony—the apology at least was genuine—she slid her key into the lock. And tried to keep a lid on the fury she felt welling up inside her as Michael—not that she was looking at him—responded to that with a wide grin.

Only for a second did Tony's face reveal his disappointment.

"Slow," he said. Then he smiled a little wryly at her. "I got it. Slow."

Then he cupped her face with both hands and gave her a long, lingering kiss good-night.

Gripping his wrists, Charlie responded. Lots of tongue. But, damn it, thanks to the looming presence of the ghost from hell, not so much heat.

When at last Tony let her go, she smiled at him, sweetly apologetic still, then walked into her room and shut the door in Michael's face. She took three strides, turned, and waited.

He strolled through the door just as she'd known he would and grinned mockingly at her.

"Dudley get you turned on yet?"

Charlie felt her whole body quiver with anger. She felt the burning heat of it rising through her veins like red-hot lava. She could feel her face flush with it. She could feel her eyes blaze with it.

"You do not get to ruin my life," she said through her teeth, advancing on him with a pointed finger aimed at the center of his wide chest. She stopped short before she reached him, but once again she made the mistake of coming too close: she had to tilt her head back to glare into his face. His eyes still mocked her. The slight curve of his mouth was—sexy as hell. "I want normal. I want easy. I want happy. I want to do my work in peace, and find a man I can fall in love with, and maybe even get married to and have kids with. If you interfere with that one more time, I'll find a way to send you back on your way to hell, I swear."

His eyes narrowed at her. "You know what I want? I want to be able to eat a nice steak dinner like you had tonight. I want to drink a couple of cold beers. I want to feel the sun on my face when I'm outside. I want to sleep. I want my damned life back. And I want to fuck the hell out of you."

By the time he finished, his eyes were a hard, glittering blue. Charlie glared into them with true fury, but even as she did she could feel the electricity arcing between them, feel the air around them turning to steam. Her heartbeat sped up. Her pulse started to pound. Deep inside, her body quickened. Her nipples suddenly felt all hot and prickly as they pushed against her dress' built-in bra, which inexplicably seemed to have gotten a couple of sizes too tight. Inside the silken scrap of her panties, she felt dampness, and heat.

As he watched her face, his pupils dilated until his eyes were almost black.

"Pay attention, babe: that's what being turned on feels like," he said softly.

Charlie looked into those hot-for-her eyes. She took in the hard, impossibly handsome face—the strong jaw, the sensuous curve of his mouth, the Sun God hair; and then, lower, the veritable mountain of sleek, powerful muscle that was pure sex-on-a-stick. And she felt a fresh burst of anger at him, at herself, at the damned universe, along with another wave of infuriating, overpowering, all-but-irresistible desire.

He hadn't even touched her, and she was melting inside. She wanted to start ripping off her clothes.

And he could tell. She saw it in his eyes.

"I didn't ask to get saddled with you," she threw at him, clenching her fists as she turned sharply away. "I want you out of my life."

"I didn't ask to get saddled with you, either," he growled. "But you're mine now, Doc."

To Charlie's astonishment, before she could take more than a single step, hard hands gripped her waist, and she was spun around and lifted off her feet like she weighed nothing at all until he—Michael!—set her down with her back against the door.

She gaped at him. Eyes flaming, he loomed over her, his hands so solid on her waist that she felt the size and strength of them clear through her dress.

"You're—" Anger forgotten, she started to tell him that he was solid, that he'd somehow crossed the barrier and was in her world now, but she never got the chance.

He pushed up against her, letting her feel every powerful inch of him as he crowded her back against the door. His big hand curved around the vulnerable nape of her neck. His fingers burrowed into her hair. Then he dropped his head and took her mouth.

This was no gentle kiss.

His lips were hard and hot and hungry. And angry. And incredibly, mind-blowingly arousing. As his tongue took bold possession of her mouth, Charlie made a helpless little mewling sound deep in her throat and slid her arms around his waist and her hands up under his shirt and kissed him back with a burning intensity that, until she had met him, she would have said was utterly foreign to her nature. His skin felt warm and satiny to the touch. The flexing muscles beneath were firm and smooth. He was far bigger than she was, far stronger than she was, and he was letting her know it. She couldn't have gotten away from him if she'd tried, which she didn't. Instead she plastered herself against him, arching her body to fit the powerful length of his. Pathetically primitive creature that she apparently was, she felt a rush of mindless pleasure, a blast of torrid heat. Her heart seemed to go haywire. Her blood sizzled. Kissing him with reckless abandon, she slid her palms up over his shoulder blades, reveling in their breadth and strength. She could feel every inch of him: the muscular wall of his chest, the bump of his belt buckle, the unmistakable hardness below. She could feel the brush of his jeans against her bare calves. Her toes touched the tip of his boots. If this was a war, he had already won hands down. The warm, wet invasion of her mouth made her shiver. It made her quake and melt inside. He was kissing her so hot and deep that she was dizzy.

I want you.

If he hadn't been kissing her like he was, she would have said it aloud. But she couldn't talk, could barely think or breathe.

His hand was on her breast, flattened on top of it, rubbing her, caressing her through the thin fabric of her dress. Her body's searing response caught her by surprise. Her nipples tightened. Her breast surged into his palm. If her dress had had buttons, she would have been ripping them open for him. If it had had a zipper, she would have been yanking it down. But it didn't. The only way out of the thing was to pull it over her head, which she couldn't do because he was leaning against her, pressing her back into the door with enough force to keep her pinned there, holding her in place with his body.

He weighed a ton; he radiated heat.

Then he solved her dilemma for her by sliding a hand inside the neckline of her dress.

It was big and hot and masculine, and it covered her breast completely. Her nipple instantly puckered into a small hard nub that quivered against his fingers, then jutted into his palm. She made a little sound of abject surrender into his mouth as his thumb brushed back and forth over the sensitive point, and when he did it again her insides turned to jelly and her knees went weak.

He lifted his head, and she opened her eyes to find that he was looking down at her. His eyes were heavy-lidded and burning hot. His lips were parted, and damp from her kisses.

"Charlie," he said, his voice rough with passion. Then his eyes flickered. Then they widened, and his mouth twisted into a pained grimace, and the big, solid body that was holding her in place shivered. He groaned, a harsh, grating sound that seemed to be dragged out of somewhere deep inside him. The next instant he was gone. Vanished.

She was left clutching air.

"Michael," Charlie said blankly, still stupid with desire, still aching and burning and not quite grasping what had happened. Then in a burst of terrible clarity she knew: for a few moments he had managed to materialize, managed to become as real and solid as he had been when he was alive, and now he was paying the price.

The horrible, painful price.

Pushing away from the door, she glanced a little wildly around the room. There was no mistake. He wasn't there.

Her heart pounded like a kettledrum. But this time it was from fear.

"Michael!" Even as she called his name, she knew it was useless.

He wasn't anywhere where he could hear.

Calm down. Try to think.

The last time he had materialized so fully it had been to take a knife in the back for her. After that, he had been gone for four days.

There was no reason why this time should be any different.

All I have to do is wait.

She still felt shaky with the aftermath of passion, and faintly disoriented, and afraid. Her legs were unsteady. Taking the few steps necessary to reach the nearest bed, Charlie sank down on the foot of the mattress.

Michael. There was no point in calling out to him again, though, so she took a deep breath instead, and fought to clear her head. The last lingering effects of passion dissipated. At the thought of where Michael almost certainly was at that moment, she felt cold all over.

From everything he'd told her, and her own brief personal knowledge of it, Spookville was a terrifying place.

What if he can't get back?

That was the thought that made her insides clench.

He was way past the after-death date when most spirits permanently left this plane. The universe already had been on the verge of
taking him away to meet whatever eternity awaited him when she'd
intervened with her candle and glass. It had him now.

This time the question came as almost a shriek inside her head:
What if he can't get back?

Assessing the likelihood of that, Charlie felt stark fear. She'd
known it all along: ghosts can't stay.

She felt as if a giant hand had grabbed her heart and was squeez-
ing it.

*The universe knows what it's doing. He won't get worse than he
deserves. He's tough. He'll endure.*

Charlie realized she was shivering, and wrapped her arms around
herself.

*You'll get your life back. You'll get your chance with Tony, if
that's what you want. You won't have a ghost that you never asked
for chained to you forever.*

Even as she reminded herself of those things, Charlie found herself battling the urge to scream. To the universe, to send him back. To
God, to have mercy.

He had gone so fast.

Her chest was suddenly so tight that she could hardly breathe.

Maybe he'll make it back, she told herself. After all, he did before.

What she needed to do was stay calm. Turn the process over to
whatever part of Divine Providence handled such matters. Trust in
the ultimate rightness of all things.

She sat perfectly still, taking deep, hopefully calming breaths,
searching for her inner Zen.

Then she thought, *To hell with that.*

Her legs still felt unsteady as she pushed to her feet. Snatching up
her purse from the floor where it had fallen when Michael had grabbed
her—she didn't even remember dropping it—Charlie fished inside it
for her phone and called Tam.

"Cherie, I was just getting ready to call you" was how Tam
greeted her. "I have more: in the dark water, there is a gray house.
The danger is inside the gray house."

It sounded screwy. Lots of times, Charlie recalled, Tam's visions sounded screwy, until they worked out exactly the way Tam said they would. But at the moment, she didn't care.

"Tam," she said, and it was a struggle to keep her voice from cracking. "You remember that ghost you told me how to keep here? A few minutes ago, he"— kissed me senseless—"materialized. All the way. As real and solid as if he was alive. Then he groaned, and looked like he was in terrible pain, and disappeared. It was—fast."

"Spirits shouldn't be materializing," Tam said sharply. "It goes against the way things are supposed to be."

"Well, he did. And now he's gone. I think he's been sucked into Spookville—well, that's what he calls it. A place that's all cold, purple twilight."

"The Dark Place." Tam's tone was stark with horror. "The spirit you wanted to keep earthbound is from there?"

"Yes."

"He should not have materialized. He broke the bond." Tam paused. "Which is probably just as well."

"I need to help him get back."

"No and no and no. If I had known before—"

"Tam. Please."

"But, cherie, if he is of the Dark Place, then you need to leave him be. *He—is—not—good.*" Tam said that last forcefully.

"Tam, for God's sake, if there's anything I can do to help him get back here, tell me what it is."

"Really, cherie?" Tam sounded as disapproving as Tam ever sounded, which Charlie realized ordinarily would have made her think twice about what she was asking. That saying about only count-ing the sunny hours? That was Tam. She always chose to embrace the light.

"Yes. Really." Charlie heard the desperation in her own voice, and briefly closed her eyes. *"Please."*

"Hmm." Tam sighed. "All right, well, let me see. You closed the passage to keep the spirit earthbound, if I recall." Charlie made an affirmative noise. "There is no sure method to bring spirits back from the Beyond, much less from the Dark Place, I must tell you. My best suggestion to you would be that you open the passage again. You have a candle?"

"Yes."

"Light it to open the passage, then call the spirit's name. The spirit may hear, and find the passage, and return."

Charlie heard the second possibility in the other woman's voice loud and clear: or he may not.

She tried to control her too-rapid breathing. "Is there anything else I can do?"

"That's all I know, cherie," Tam said.

"Thanks." As Charlie was disconnecting, she heard Tam call to her, "Take the utmost care."

Charlie never traveled without her Miracle-Go kit, to which she had added a small, heavy glass for the closing of spectral passages since she had realized such a thing might become necessary. Now she grabbed a lighter and one of the squat, round jasmine candles from the kit. Then she pulled out a second and a third candle. It hit her that turning on the water might help, too, so she took the candles into the bathroom, set them on the counter, and lit them. As the scent of jasmine started to fill the air, she closed the door to keep the aroma in and turned the cold water tap in the sink on full blast.

Then she turned off the bathroom light and looked into the flickering flames and called, "Michael."

Again and again and again.

He didn't come.

The terror she felt for him frightened her.

Minutes ticked past, blurred into hours.

Finally Charlie was sitting on the bathroom floor, still in her dress, with her knees drawn up almost to her chin and her back against the cold hard side of the tub. She was growing hoarse. Her eyelids were heavy as lead.

She gave up on calling his name only because she fell asleep.

At first she thought the creeping tendrils of fog that snaked toward her were smoke from the candles. Then she noticed that they were purple and thick. As they reached her they started slowly swirling around her like multiple lariats. Even as she blinked at them, they rose, enveloping her in a way that the puny smoke from her candles never could. Instead of jasmine, they smelled of—rotting things and damp. Eyes widening, Charlie clambered to her feet. Everywhere she looked—and she got the impression that she was confronting vast distances in all directions—the landscape was overlaid with billowing clouds of purple mist.

She shivered, suddenly cold. Her arms and shoulders and legs were bare, and her feet were, too. It took her a second to realize that she was still wearing her red dress, minus the shoes. It seemed to be twilight—there was no sun, but it wasn't quite dark, either. The ground beneath her feet—she couldn't really see it because of the fog—seemed to be composed mostly of solid sheets of rock, with a few patches of what looked like slimy moss.

Where am I?

But even as the question popped into her mind, she knew.

Spookville.

Michael.

Oh, my God, how did I get here? An instant later the more pertinent question brought a thrill of fear with it: *How do I get back?*

In the distance, a bloodcurdling scream tore through the mist. Charlie jumped and looked fearfully all around as a sense of utter dread filled her. Closer at hand, she heard a kind of shuffling, lumbering sound as if something huge was moving toward her at a fast pace. That rhythmic wheezing gasp was its breathing, she realized with horror a split second after she became aware of it.

She caught a glimpse of a huge dark *thing* shrouded by the mist as it rushed past her.

Now the screams were so close that they sent icy ripples of fright coursing through the center of her being. It sounded like a creature was being torn to shreds not more than a stone's throw away, and Charlie thought that the nightmarish shrieks came from something the thing had caught. She barely managed to swallow her own answering scream.

Then she saw another horror in the mist: what looked like two unblinking yellow eyes luminescent enough to glow through the swirling fog, turning in her direction.

She knew, instinctively, that she was in terrible danger.

Swallowing another scream, she ran.

Not far to her left, there was a scrabble of feet, a barely seen leap through the mist as if something pounced, another deathly scream.

Fear washed over her in waves.

Michael. She dared not cry his name out loud, not with whatever these things were so near. He was there somewhere, she was sure. Instinct—a sixth sense, an insistent psychic pull—told her so. It sent her fleeing in a certain direction, but whether it was right or not she had no way of knowing. If she was wrong—the thought made her shake. Creatures bounded past her. Horrific screams pierced the air. Feet bruising on the rocky ground, she fled past stands of what seemed to be shaggy, misshapen trees, past boulders bigger than she was, past a fissure in the ground spewing a sulfurous gray steam.

An orange glow, blurred by the mist but still a beacon in the gloom, drew her. As she neared it, gasping for what little air there was, feeling as though her heart would burst from her chest, she saw that she was running headlong toward the dark edge of a cliff and slowed abruptly. The orange glow came from a fire far below, she discovered as she drew cautiously closer, a roaring, raging conflagration from which screaming people fled while flames consumed them.

Charlie recoiled in fear.

At the edge of the cliff overlooking the horror, a man crouched, his back against a boulder the size of a bus.

His face was turned away from her as he looked down into the abyss, but there was no mistaking those broad shoulders or that tawny hair. Limned in orange, his big body was no more than a dark shape against the glow, but she would know him anywhere.

"Michael!" This time, as she flew toward him, she did cry his name aloud.

He looked sharply around, surged to his feet, leaped toward her. "Charlie!"

She threw herself against him, and he caught her. His face was all sharp planes and angles, and his eyes were as black and fathomless as hell's deepest pit. For a moment the intensity of emotion she felt at having found him swamped everything else. He hugged her tight, and she wrapped her arms around him and clung to him as if he was the only hope of salvation she had left.

"Jesus Christ." The stark fear in his voice penetrated a split second before she heard the growl. It was a low, guttural, threatening sound that had to have come from something huge, and it was close behind her. She looked up at Michael: what she saw in his face made her blood run cold. Whatever could make him look like that, she didn't want to see.

CHAPTER TWENTY-ONE

Michael whirled with her so that his back was turned to whatever it was. Curling himself protectively around her, he pressed her head to his chest. Tensing, clinging close, silently reciting every prayer she had ever learned in her life, Charlie cowered in his arms.

"Think of somewhere safe, quick," he told her urgently.

Even as Charlie did, the growl turned into a roar. She felt a rush of air as the creature leaped at them and they passed it while it was in mid-jump.

The mist swirled. She had the sensation of being hurtled forward, and closed her eyes against a rushing wind. She could feel Michael warm and solid against her, and she held on to him for dear life. The very air seemed to writhe, and suck at her skin. Then the cold was gone, along with the smell, and with those things went the clingy dampness of the fog. Entwined together, the two of them tumbled in what felt like a free fall through the infinite blackness of time and space. Clinging to Michael as if he was the only solid thing left in the universe, Charlie felt as if she were being crushed; as if she couldn't breathe. Then, suddenly, everything around them was still. There seemed to be solid ground beneath her bare feet. Carpet, from the texture of it.

Charlie opened her eyes. They were in her hotel room, in the narrow hall between the bathroom and closet, near the spot where he had disappeared. The room was awash in moonlight that spilled inside because the curtains over the big window across the room were open to the night.

Safe. Thank God.

"You okay?" Michael's voice grated. She looked up at him. Her arms were locked around his waist. His were wrapped tight around her shoulders. His face was harsh. His eyes were still black, blacker even than the night outside the window, but some of the horrible soulless glitter left them as he looked down at her.

Charlie took a deep breath, glad to be able to fill her lungs. "Yes." Then as he closed his eyes she took another breath and added, "What about you?"

He didn't answer, and she frowned. He was his usual handsome self, but—not. He seemed bigger than usual, and badder. Savagery radiated from him like rays from the sun. Ruthlessness was there in the set of his jaw, brutality in the curve of his mouth. There was a hardness around his cheekbones and closed eyes. *This is what a man capable of killing looks like,* was the thought that came to her unbidden, and her mind flicked uneasily back to what Tam had said about the Dark Place, to the question of how innocent or guilty of the heinous crimes that had been attributed to him she really believed him to be. She became fully aware of how solid and real he felt in her arms, and faced all the ramifications of what that meant. There was no cosmic shield between them to protect her, no lack of substance on his part to keep her safe.

They were on the same side of the barrier now, and for better or worse she was locked in his arms.

Charlie faced the terrible truth: there was no place else on earth she would rather be.

"Michael." Her hands unclasped from around his waist to gently stroke his back. Whatever the Dark Place had brought out in him, she chose to attribute to the place, not him. She hoped her touch would remind him that they were away from that horrible place and safe. Beneath the softness of his shirt, his back felt warm and firm. Her hands slid beneath it: his skin was hot and faintly damp. She could feel his back heaving beneath her hands. She asked him again: "Are you okay?"

His eyes opened. She was relieved to see that more of the black had retreated now. But there was a hard, predatory glitter in them still that alarmed her as they raked her face.

"You afraid of me, babe?" he asked. "'Cause you're looking at me like you are."

"Of course I'm not afraid of you," she answered firmly, unsure if right at that moment it was strictly the truth. Dark energy rolled off him in waves. The look on his face, coupled with the rasping voice and the steely prison that his arms around her had become, made her heart beat faster. She could feel his strength, feel the power in the big body that held her, and knew that if he didn't want to let her go, she wasn't getting away.

"Maybe you should be." He drew in air through his teeth, and Charlie got the impression that he was fighting for control. "That place—it does things to people. Bad things."

His hold on her tightened until, if she had been afraid of him, she would have struggled. His body was taut with tension, and she could feel the aggression flowing through him. Her hands flattened and stilled on his broad back, but she didn't let go of him. Didn't want to let go of him, even though every instinct she possessed screamed *danger*. But no matter how menacing he might seem, this was Michael, and she was in his arms, and that by itself was enough to make her go weak at the knees. Instead of trying to pull away from him, she pressed closer still, letting him feel her softness, her femininity. Her breasts swelled against the unyielding wall of his chest; she could feel the delicious prickle as her nipples tightened. She settled her hips more intimately against his. As her breath caught and her body quickened at the rock hardness she found there, she felt the long muscles of his back tense beneath her hands. She looked up then, and met the fierceness of his eyes, which were still only sky blue rims around a center of glittering black.

"I'm going to fuck you all night long," he said, still in that harsh voice.

A shiver went through her as all around them the air turned to steam.

She had no chance to reply before his head dropped and he took her mouth, kissing her like he was a marauder and she was his captive, like he owned her, like she had no say. His hands, big and possessive, closed over her bottom, pulling her up on her toes, cradling her so closely against him that she could feel in graphic detail how aroused he was.

As he rocked her against him her body caught fire, just went up in flames.

"Michael." She moaned his name into his mouth, kissing him back as fiercely as he kissed her, molding her lips to his, meeting the hot deep invasion of her mouth with a passion that matched his. She was shivery with lust, lightheaded, eager. As urgently as he needed to take, she needed to give. He kissed her ear, ran his mouth down the side of her neck, and she felt her bones dissolve.

"You're mine, Doc," he growled just as he had earlier, and even though part of her knew she should protest that women in general and she in particular were not something that could be owned, she was too turned on to do anything except cling to his broad shoulders for support as he bent her back across his hard-muscled arm. Then his mouth was on her breast, opening over her nipple so that she could feel the heat and wetness of it even through the cloth of her dress. Toes curling into the carpet, she arched her back and threaded her fingers into his hair. His hand went beneath her dress to stroke its way up over the smoothness of her bare thigh, then moved between her legs and caressed her through her silky panties, making her gasp, making her burn. Then he was kissing her again, his lips hard and hot and hungry, and his fingers slipped inside her panties to push into the hot, wet center of her so that she turned to liquid fire in his hands and moved with helpless pleasure for him.

"God, I've wanted you," he said thickly, letting her go before she was ready, leaving her wanting more as he caught her dress and pulled it up and over her head. She was naked now except for her panties, and the air in the room felt cool on her overheated skin. Following his gaze, looking down at the pale globes of her own breasts with their dark, eager nipples, at the slender indentation of her waist, at her flat stomach and long slim legs, Charlie felt a wave of desire so intense that she trembled. Her head spun; her pulse drummed in her ears. His eyes were all over her, burning in their intensity, and she felt her muscles liquefy beneath their heat.

"I've wanted you, too," she confessed, and knew even as she said it that it was an understatement. She had ached for him. Burned for him. Still did.

She slid her panties down her legs, stepped out of them. Her heart was hitting about a thousand beats a minute. Her legs were unsteady. Deep inside, her body throbbed.

Watching, dark color suffused his face. He made an inarticulate sound. Then he yanked his shirt over his head, and she reached with shaking fingers for his belt buckle. She barely got it unfastened before he pulled her against him, kissing her with a fierceness that made her dizzy.

His hard-muscled arm curled beneath her bottom, and he lifted her off her feet as if she weighed nothing at all, pushing her back against the door to the hall, spreading her thighs and positioning himself between them. Bending his head, he claimed each nipple with quick, succulent tugs of his mouth. Shivery with desire, she clung to him. His skin was hot and damp with sweat, and his broad shoulders were corded with tension. As his mouth found hers again, and she returned the kiss with wild abandon, Charlie felt the cool smooth wood of the door to the hall against her back. A wave of scalding heat washed over her even as she wrapped her legs around his waist. She felt his hand between them, heard the rasp of his zipper, and her pulse went haywire. Then he pushed himself inside her, huge and hot and urgent, making her cling to him, making her cry out.

"You like that," he growled in her ear as he held himself buried deep. It wasn't a question. He knew.

She told him anyway. "Yes. *Yes.*"

Kissing her, he thrust into her again and again with a ferocity that set her on fire. She could feel the door at her back, and the hard strength of his arms around her and his body pounding into her, and the combination made her spiral out of control. What they were doing felt so unbelievably good that she cried out over and over again. Her body burned and clenched and trembled. It was sex at its rawest, most carnal, most intense. The end, when it came, was explosive.

"*Michael!*" Charlie gasped. Then as he thrust inside her one last time and groaned she came so violently that her body convulsed in a quaking wave of heat.

A moment later, he kissed her again, deeply. As she kissed him back, she felt a shiver run through him, and opened her eyes. A subtle transformation in his face told her that whatever had been going on with him before, he was now at least near to something approaching his usual self. As if he could feel her eyes on him, he broke the kiss and lifted his head. His eyes opened, and she was relieved to see that, except for slightly enlarged pupils, they were once again their normal sky blue as he frowned—not glared—down at her.

"Did I scare you?" He sounded faintly penitent.

Charlie shook her head, still not sure whether or not she was telling the truth. Her heart was beating way too fast. "No."

"It's that damned place. It does things to me." He stepped back to let her slide to her feet. "No matter what happens, I don't ever want you following me into Spookville again, understand?"

"If that's your version of pillow talk, you should probably know that it could use some work," she responded tartly, telling herself that she had *not* been hoping for a hearts and flowers kind of speech from him but realizing even as she did so that, obviously, she had. She leaned back against the door, boneless and still a little shaky, watching him with secret, silent pleasure as he pulled up and refastened his jeans.

His mouth curved in the merest suggestion of a smile. His eyes slid over her, and the sudden hot gleam in them reminded her that she was naked. Her dress was somewhere on the floor. There it was, by his feet.

"You're beautiful," he said. "Sexy as hell. Just what I always wanted."

"That's better." She nodded toward her dress. Since he stood between her and it, asking him for it seemed the best option. "Could you please hand me my dress?"

"No." He stepped closer, imprisoning her with his hands braced against the door, on either side of her as his big body rested on top of hers and he kissed her, a slow, hot sampling that made her heart start to pound again and her body quicken. "I meant what I said about Spookville: stay out."

He gave her a hard look, and Charlie tried to concentrate on that, not his mouth, which next slid across her cheek to nuzzle her ear—or his hand, which found her breast. Or the heat of his bare chest against her breasts, or the abrasion of his jeans against her legs, and her stomach, and the most sensitive, responsive part of her.

Oh, God, can he really turn me on again this fast?

Focus on what he said. Before the part about Spookville.

She narrowed her eyes at him. "What do you mean, no?"

"I like you naked."

That made her heart skip a beat. If she'd really wanted her dress, she would have insisted, but the truth was that being naked in the moonlight with him made her go all quivery inside. Her hands, which had been pressed flat against the door, rose to press flat against his chest instead. Not that she was thinking about pushing him away or anything. No way.

She loved how his chest felt under her hands: warm and strong and satiny smooth.

"About Spookville: I didn't mean to go there, believe me. It just happened." She sounded faintly breathless, and that would be because she found his powerfully muscled chest so sexy to touch. Plus, his mouth on the sensitive hollow below her ear was hot and wet. And his hand was big and warm. And arousing, as it cupped and caressed her breast. "Anyway, if I hadn't followed you, that—that *thing*—would have gotten you."

"Nah. I've gotten pretty good at getting away."

He was kissing the side of her neck, his mouth crawling down the sensitive cord. His thumb brushed back and forth across her nipple. Lightning bolts of sensation shivered through her. Her knees went weak. Carrying on a conversation with him under the circumstances was growing increasingly difficult, but she persevered, because this was something she truly wanted to understand.

"I saw two yellow eyes looking at me through the fog," she said. Remembering the horror of it made her shiver. He lifted his head to look at her, and her blood started to steam at the hot, dark gleam in his eyes.

"That was a hunter. They catch us poor unfortunate souls that wind up in there and drag us off to hell."

Charlie's heart gave an odd little hiccup when she thought about that in relation to him. "Really?"

"I don't know. I've never been caught by one. But I think it's a good guess."

"You know"—she was sounding way too breathless, and that would be because of his hand on her breast—"this would probably be a good time for you to tell me why something would want to drag you off to hell."

Because any and all possible reasons that she could come up with made her go cold all over.

Michael shook his head, refusing to answer. He radiated a hard sexual tension, and Charlie shivered and quaked and burned in instinctive response. The truth was that she was weak with longing, hungry for him again, embarrassingly needy. His eyes flamed at her, and she remembered him saying that he could read her like a neon sign. Then he bent his head and kissed her again.

It was intended as a distraction, she knew. Charlie felt the insistent molding of his mouth to hers, felt him parting her lips, felt the hot slide of his tongue, and considered her situation. She thought about the black soullessness she had seen in his eyes, and the crimes he denied having committed, and what it might take to get a man sent to hell. And the conclusion she came to was that it didn't matter: whatever he was or wasn't, whatever he had or hadn't done, she was now so ensnared in the web they had gotten caught in together, there was no breaking free.

She closed her eyes and slid her arms around his neck and kissed him back. His mouth was hot, and unhurried now, and so mind-blowingly expert that it made her wild all over again.

Still kissing her, he picked her up and carried her to bed.

His heavily muscled shoulders and arms looked silvery in the moonlight, she saw as he laid her down on the mattress and she opened her eyes. When he would have straightened away from her, she held him with her arms around his neck, and pressed her open mouth to his wide chest, kissing and licking the firm, warm flesh. He shuddered against her, and she flicked a look up at him.

His eyes were hot and dark. "Let me take off my pants," he said, his voice hoarse.

As he stood up and unfastened his jeans, she moved to the edge of the bed. Then she stood up, too, in front of him, and slid her hands down inside his shorts to close around him.

He was huge, and hot, and velvety soft and hard as steel at the same time.

She wasn't a child; she knew what to do. As her hands tightened on him, did what she knew he'd like, he groaned. But that was all he could do, because he was busy pulling off his boots, and then shoving his jeans down his legs. By the time he got his clothes off, she was on her knees in front of him, her hands on his ass, pleasuring him with her mouth.

Naked, he stood very still, his body rock solid while sexual tension rolled off him in waves. His hands slid into her hair. By this time it was loose, falling around her shoulders, and she could feel the tug at the roots. She knew he was watching her because she could feel the weight of his eyes. She wanted to make him come, and would have done it, too, if in the nick of time he hadn't freed himself and picked her up by the waist and tumbled her back on the bed. He pushed inside her instantly, thrusting deep, and she cried out.

He kept driving into her, hard and fast, and kissing her breasts and then her mouth, while she wrapped her legs around his waist and her arms around his neck and let the delicious waves of dark, hot passion catch her up until at last they broke and he came and she came for him again.

After that, she lay boneless and pleasantly drifting in his arms as they talked about everything and nothing, really. Until he turned her onto her stomach, and brushed her hair aside to kiss the nape of her neck, which made her sigh a little because she liked the way the touch of his lips on her skin made her feel. He followed that kiss with another, and another, until he was trailing kisses down the length of her spine, licking and nibbling, tracing its curving pathway with his mouth all the way to the cleft in her butt. Then he kissed her bottom, too, his mouth crawling over every inch of the soft round curves until he had her squirming against the mattress and digging into it with her nails. Finally he spread her legs and knelt between them, and pulled her up to meet him. He entered her that way, with fierce demanding strokes and his hand between her legs.

She came so hard for him then that she screamed his name.

"Michael! Oh, my God, *Michael*!"

Lucky no one but him could hear.

Afterward, he pulled her against him, and kissed her mouth. She kissed him back, all languid heat now, then settled in with her head on his shoulder and a hand resting in the center of his wide chest, while his arm curved around her, keeping her close. Already she could see, through the open window, the first pink fingers of dawn creeping across the dark sky. It was beautiful, but as she watched it her heart hurt.

A glance at Michael's face told her that he was watching it, too. The chiseled planes and angles were gorgeous as ever, but there was a bleak cast to them that said he was as aware of the passage of time as she was. Then he must have felt her eyes on him because he looked at her, and rose up on an elbow so that his powerfully built torso blocked out most of her view of the window. She had just a second to absorb the fact that his beautiful mouth was hard now and that grimness lurked behind the hot dark gleam in his eyes before his mouth was on hers and he was rolling on top of her and pushing inside her again.

There was a fierceness to their lovemaking, because they both knew that they would have only this one night, and it was drawing to an end.

She came with a hot rippling pleasure that had her gasping and trembling, and, finally, made the night explode like fireworks against her closed lids. He came with his mouth pressed to the tender curve between her shoulder and neck, and a groan that was muffled against her skin.

When the alarm on her phone went off, it wasn't like it was unexpected, so Charlie didn't know why the sound jolted her so. But it did, catapulting her out of the unlikely sanctuary she had found in his arms, jarring her senses, making her heart leap.

"Michael—" Her eyes flew to his face, but even as his eyes widened and his arms tightened around her, the room seemed to fold in on her. Everything went black as she was buffeted by a blast of cold wind. She lost all conception of time and space until she felt a sudden jarring impact. Her heart leaped, she sucked in air, and then her eyes snapped open.

She was in the bathroom, lying curled on the floor in front of the tub, with only the fluffy white bath mat protecting her face from the tile. The bathroom was dark, not black but gloomy, and there was a rushing sound that she couldn't quite place. For a second she blinked at her shoes, which were under the sink directly within her line of vision, and she recalled kicking them off sometime during last night's long vigil. Then she remembered the candles, and pushed herself into a sitting position to check: sure enough, there they were on the counter, flames now out. The wicks were black and burnt, and from the hollowed-out look of the candles they had guttered on melted wax.

The rushing sound came from the water still running in the sink.

She must have made some small noise, because all of a sudden there was Michael barging through the bathroom door then stopping to look down at her as she sat on the floor. From the speed with which he had arrived, she thought he must have rushed to find her there. For a moment she detected a flicker of relief in his eyes— probably he had been worried about where she had gone when she had vanished from beside him—but then he simply looked grim. She guessed that he was wrestling to come to terms with the fact that their idyll was over, just as she was. They were on different sides of the barrier again. Looking at him, she felt an aching sadness, as though she had lost something precious. Their relationship had been impossible from the first, but knowing that there was no future in it was even harder to bear now. Her heart stuttered as she considered that any physical contact between them was quite possibly over forever, unless she learned how to control the astral projection thing, which was clearly what she had done again last night. But before she could decide if trying to become an expert at astral-projection-on-demand was even something that she wanted to do, much less if it was feasible, she realized exactly what she was looking at, and blinked.

Michael was naked.

Michael was gorgeous.

As her eyes slid up his long, muscular legs, paused for a second to register once again how impressively well endowed he was, then moved on to admire his washboard abs and wide chest and heavily muscled arms and shoulders before stopping on his hard, handsome face, she felt her pulse pick up the pace and her body, which had been feeling a little cold from lying on the floor, start to get warm again. After the night they'd just spent, she would have thought she'd be past getting turned on by anyone or anything for a good long while, but she would've been wrong. Simply looking at Michael was enough to do it. And not only because naked—or not naked, for that matter—he was the hottest guy she had just about ever seen. There was something between them—a sizzling chemistry, a potent sexual attraction— that had been there from the beginning, when she had conducted her first interview with the scary, insolent, way-too-gorgeous convict in chains.

Now, merely the sight of him was enough to make her heart go pitter-pat. Charlie would have told him so if some tiny, self-protective part of her hadn't warned against it: no point in taking this debacle in the making any further than she already had. So if she wasn't going to say something on the order of *every time I look at you I get turned on,* she realized as she met his gaze that she was at a loss. Because, really, what do you say to a naked man you have no future with after a night of truly epic sex with him? She had no clue.

He saved her. Having spent much less time looking at her than she had spent looking at him—she guessed that, in her crumpled red dress, which covered her from her armpits to her knees, and with her hair hanging down in a tangle around her face, she wasn't as much to look at as he was at the moment—he had taken in the candles and the running water, too. He knew what they were for; she didn't have to explain.

"Next time I get sucked in to Spookville, you leave it the hell alone," he warned again. His eyes had turned unreadable. His voice was hard. His words made it clear: he expected to wind up in Spookville again at some point. The terrible truth was, she expected that he would wind up there again, too. Just thinking about it made her feel all raw and vulnerable inside, so she dragged her thoughts away. "I can take care of myself. And there's no telling what might happen to you in there."

Okay, so tender words of mutual affection—or even a classic was-it-as-good-for-you-as-it-was-for-me conversation—seemed to be out. Well, for both their sakes, that was probably a good thing.

"You seemed happy enough to see me last night," she retorted, glad to skip any emotional heartburnings in favor of getting their relationship back to what felt more or less like normal. Scrambling to her feet, she turned off the tap. A glance in the mirror confirmed it: she looked a mess. Surprisingly, she didn't feel all that tired. While her spirit was having world-class sex, apparently her body had gotten some rest.

"I wasn't," he said grimly.

"Probably it would help if you did *your* best to stay out of Spookville." The look she gave him was severe. Or, actually, it started out that way, but then the realization that they were having this conversation while he was leaning a broad shoulder against the wall and standing there casually nude affected the quality of her severity a little, so that she had to give herself a tiny mental shake before refocusing. The sad truth was, she could feel herself starting to get turned on *again*. "For one thing, you can't materialize anymore. Tam said it weakens the bond. That must have been why you got pulled in like you did."

"Brought the voodoo priestess into it, did you?" The slow smile he gave her made her heart beat a little faster. "You must have been worried about me."

There was no point in denying that. The evidence was too clear. Besides, he knew.

"I was."

There was a lot she could have said after that. A lot she would have said if she was foolish, like *I was scared to death that I was never going to see you again,* or even, *Yes, okay, you were right, I am crazy about you,* but neither one of those felt smart—in fact, not only did they not feel smart, they felt stupid and even downright dangerous—so she didn't. Instead she contented herself with a monitory, "Don't materialize, okay?" Then, with the brisk air of getting down to necessary business she stepped toward him, and the light switch, which she flipped on. The sudden brightness made her squint a little as she looked at him. "We should probably go ahead and do the whole light-the-candle, close-the-passage thing again. Then I need to take a shower. I'm supposed to be out in the hall at seven." She glanced at his watch, which dangled braceletlike around her wrist. "Which is in forty-three minutes."

For a moment he simply looked at her. Then he said, "Let me put my pants on first," which she got the impression wasn't what he had been going to say at all, but made her think about when he had taken them *off,* until he turned away and she got distracted by the very nice view that she was afforded of his broad back and small, tight butt.

Watching so much flexing muscle and rippling sinew was making her start to feel all soft and squishy inside. Fortunately he disappeared through the door before she got so hot she dissolved into a steamy little puddle on the floor. Opening the door in anticipation of his return, she found him scooping his clothes up from the floor beside the bed.

When Michael returned, he was fully dressed, down to his boots, and she had a glass and a candle ready to light.

"Fuck," he said, eyeing the setup, and she took that to mean that he was ready.

The ritual went much the same as before, although they were both better prepared for his pain. When it was over, she ordered him out.

"I'm going to take a shower. And the bathroom is still off-limits," she reminded him, just in case he had some notion that last night had changed the rule. "Shoo."

The slightest of wicked smiles touched his mouth. "Babe, at this point I've seen it all. And touched it. And licked it. And—"

Charlie gave him a withering look. She should have known he wasn't going to let her simply forget about everything they'd done. "Go, all right?"

Even as she shut the door on him, he grinned at her.

She was in the middle of her shower before she remembered that, once again, she'd forgotten to bring her clothes into the bathroom with her.

When, wrapped in a towel with another towel wound around her head, she walked out into the room, it was to find him standing in front of the dark TV, frowning. That frown changed to an interested look as he spotted her, which changed to a hot gleam as his eyes slid over her. It was just as well that she was in a hurry, she thought, because that meant she didn't have time to respond to the look in his eyes with more than an inner quiver. Which she immediately ordered herself to ignore.

If she was going to get turned on every time she looked at him or he looked at her, this would be bad.

"You know, you *can* get dressed in front of me," he said dryly when she grabbed clean undies from her suitcase then walked to the closet to extract the clothes she had hung there the night before. "It's not like I can do anything but look."

Actually, merely the thought of him looking was all it took to turn that inner quiver into a delicious melting quake, which was alarming. Charlie had a sudden terrible suspicion that last night's sex-a-thon might have conditioned her to respond to him automatically, like Pavlov's dog.

"Yeah. No," she said.

"Your call. I'll still be around when putting your clothes on in the bathroom gets old, though."

Probably true, but like lots of things concerning him she mentally filed it away under "Stuff to worry about later." Clothes in hand, Charlie was heading back into the bathroom when she noticed the disgusted glance he cast at the remote, which lay on the console table beside the TV. Frowning, she paused to ask, "Is something wrong?"

"I can't work it. The remote." Reaching for it, he demonstrated: his hand passed right through, no traction at all. "I'd gotten to where I could. Before last night. Now I can't."

He looked so bothered by his failure that she would have said something comforting, like *Hmm,* if a knock hadn't sounded on the door.

"Charlie?" It was Tony's voice. Michael immediately looked sour. "You up?"

"Yes. I'll be right there," she called back, and rushed into the bathroom to dress. When she emerged, Michael was leaning against the wall beside the door, waiting for her. As he straightened, his eyes skimmed her. Her hair was twisted up in a loose knot, lots of tendrils which made it, she hoped, both cool and elegantly sexy, and she was wearing another purchase from the gift shop, a sleeveless, knee-length yellow linen shirtdress with a skinny belt around her waist, and last night's kicky little sandals. She thought, with pardonable satisfaction, that she was looking pretty good. When his eyes rose to meet hers again, he smiled.

That slow smile was enough to make Charlie's heart skip a beat. *Oh, boy.*

Well, she'd known she was in trouble.

"You look good enough to eat," he said. Then, right as a quick *thank-you* smile was curving her lips, he added, "Just so we're on the same page, you start making out with Dudley again and it's going to royally piss me off."

Here it was. She'd known this was coming. It was tempting—oh, so tempting—to ignore it, to brush it off, to save this cold splash of reality to be dealt with at a later, more convenient time. But she felt she needed to make herself very clear, for her own sake as well as his.

The scary thing was, she was dangerously close to losing her heart to him, and she wasn't about to let that happen.

Her life would be ruined forever.

"You have no right to object to anything I choose to do," she said evenly. "Last night was only a night. We can't be together; you know that. And I have to live my life. So if I want to make out with *Tony*—or anybody else, for that matter—that's what I'm going to do."

Then, before he could erupt—and it was clear from his face that an eruption was imminent—she turned and walked out the door.

CHAPTER TWENTY-TWO

"Are you fucking kidding me?" Michael's furious growl sliced through the conversation as Charlie headed with Tony, Buzz, and Kaminsky for the elevators. "An hour ago I'm fucking you into next week, and now you're throwing this shit at me?"

Tony was laying out the game plan for the day, so Charlie's reply to Michael was minimal: she narrowed her eyes at him. He stalked along beside her, looking all badass and mad, but she wasn't about to back down. For her own self-preservation, she needed to draw a line in the sand with him while she still could.

"I just heard back from Eric Riva. He was in an ATV wreck as a teenager that killed the friend he was riding with," Kaminsky said excitedly. She was checking her e-mail as they stopped to wait for the elevator. Like Charlie, she was wearing one of her gift shop purchases: a short-sleeved orange blouse worn loose over a white tank and skirt. Charlie presumed the blouse hid Kaminsky's gun.

"You want to get it on with Dudley? Is that it?" Michael had planted himself directly in front of her. "What, did I give you a taste for hot sex last night and now that I can't come through you think you'll get him to pinch hit? Here's a heads-up, babe: it don't work like that." His eyes blazed at her.

Entirely unaware of Michael practically oozing menace over the pair of them, Tony, who was standing beside her, smiled at Charlie. "Did you have a good night?"

"Yes," she replied with an answering smile, while Michael snarled, "You want to see him turn tail and run, tell him how good your night really was."

They were in the elevator on the way down by that time, and Tony was close enough so that if she leaned slightly to her left their arms would brush. But she didn't. Right at that moment she didn't feel in the least little bit like doing anything to further her relationship with Tony. She had just wanted to make her position clear to Michael. To leave her options open, so that when the memory of last night's lust-fest had faded enough, she could move ahead with her life. If not with Tony, then with someone else. Some living, breathing man.

Michael said, "Let's see, how many times did I make you come? Three? Four? Hell, I lost count long about the third time you sucked my—"

"Did you find any more possible single murders around Buggs Island Lake?" Charlie asked Kaminsky before Michael could finish, in a deliberate effort to not hear that last word. Because the scorching memory it conjured up was, in the bright light of day, embarrassing. It also turned her on a little, but she wasn't even going to let herself think about that.

"Oh, so you think you can fucking ignore me now?" Michael growled, and slammed a hand down on the elevator alarm. But instead of going off, as it had last night, nothing happened: his hand passed right through it.

Michael looked totally pissed. Charlie almost smiled.

Kaminsky grimaced. "Right now, four of the accidental deaths could possibly be murders. But what's really interesting is that ten kids between the ages of eleven and seventeen have gone missing from around that lake over the ten years before the Gingerbread Man killings started. That I've found so far. I mean, it's a big area with a lot of people, and ten in ten years isn't actually all that many, but—"

"They're important," Charlie told her, her attention effectively refocused, at least temporarily.

"What I thought was interesting is that Buggs Island Lake is no more than a four-hour drive from any of the grab or kill sites," Buzz said. "If the area we're looking at was a wheel, the lake would be almost in the center of it."

"He started there," Charlie said. "I'm almost sure of it."

"Keep looking into those deaths and disappearances around that lake," Tony said to Kaminsky, who nodded. They reached the lobby, and Kaminsky sheared off toward the hotel conference room which she had set up as a kind of ad hoc War Room, with her computers in place. The rest of them headed for the waiting SUV. Tony and Buzz started comparing notes on which of the victims had confirmed having been exposed to a violent death at a young age, and Charlie tried to stay tuned in to what they were saying, but it was hard with Michael practically vibrating with anger beside her.

"Fine, babe," he said as they all stepped out into the wall of sweltering heat that was the day. "You want to give me the cold shoulder, you do that. For now. But I'm not going anywhere, and neither are you."

That sounded so much like a threat that Charlie flicked a look up at him. He was cold-eyed and hard-mouthed, his tall, powerfully built body sending out waves of aggression. If she'd met him as a stranger in a dark alley right now, she thought, she would have shrunk back into the shadows and tried to escape his notice. But he wasn't a stranger, and she wasn't afraid of him.

What she *was* was teetering on the brink of falling hopelessly, madly in love with him, she realized with dismay. Last night she'd gotten a glimpse deep beneath the gorgeous golden surface, into what lurked in the furthest reaches of his soul. What she'd seen there had been dark and violent and dangerous. And the truth was, as far as the way she felt about him was concerned, it hadn't changed a thing.

And that, she thought, was the scariest thought of all.

They grabbed coffee from a McDonald's, parked the SUV, and started walking along Mallory Street, which was on the route of Jenna's 5K run. They went from store to store, interviewing the workers. The heat was oppressive even so early in the day, and a number of the stores weren't yet open. Buzz was marking those down on a map so they could catch them on the way back up the street, and Tony was thanking a voluble restaurant owner for his cooperation, when Charlie noticed the spirit. It was a well-dressed but blood-drenched elderly man who was following an equally well-dressed (living, not blood-drenched) elderly woman along the sidewalk. Nothing special: she saw spirits like him all the time. At a guess, he'd died in some kind of accident, certainly within the last seven days. But a little farther down the block she saw the spirit of a teenage boy with the blue lips of someone who had died from a lack of oxygen following a middle-aged couple going in the same direction as the elderly pair. And behind him came the spirit of a little girl of maybe five, blond with a pink bow in her hair and not a mark on her that Charlie could see, following a woman of about thirty who had tears running down her face and looked so much like the little girl that Charlie assumed she had to be her mother.

Three spirits of the newly, violently dead on the same block, heading in the same direction, was unusual enough to make Charlie frown.

"So, you got a clue what this whole spook parade going on out here is about?" Michael asked in her ear. He hadn't spoken a word to her since his "I'm not going anywhere" comment, and she knew he absolutely wasn't over being mad at her. That meant that what he was seeing was extraordinary enough to compel him to mention it to her. She didn't think the three spirits she could see would constitute a spook parade in his book, so after a glance to assure herself that Tony and Buzz were still preoccupied Charlie did a quick pivot so that she was facing Michael.

"I see three spirits," she told him, mindful of the other people on the crowded sidewalk. "What do you see?"

The look he gave her bristled with barely contained hostility. But then he glanced around and came back to her with, "I count eleven of 'em. All walking down the street in the same direction, following somebody who's alive."

Charlie frowned thoughtfully. Then, as she saw Tony finishing with the restaurateur and Buzz looking in her direction, she quickly said, "Could you ask one of them where they're going?"

He snorted. "You really think I'm going to keep doing your dirty work? News flash, babe: I ain't the damned ghost whisperer's apprentice."

"We're trying to catch a guy who murdered a bunch of kids here," she hissed.

His lips compressed. But as Tony caught up with her and Buzz came trailing behind, Michael left her to apparently walk beside someone she couldn't see.

"You get anything?" Tony asked Buzz as he joined them. Buzz shook his head. Michael, meanwhile, appeared to be engaging in conversation with the unseen spirit.

"Not a thing." Buzz sounded discouraged. "If Jenna, Laura, or Raylene went inside any of these places, nobody remembers seeing them. Maybe we'll see something on the security camera footage from the ATM at the corner. What about you?"

Tony shook his head. "Nothing. You check the security video from Omar's?"

One corner of Buzz's mouth quirked up. "Yeah. Lena—uh, Kaminsky—and I looked at it last night. We got Laura Parker on it, all right. She's competing in a wet T-shirt contest with about twenty other girls." The quirk turned into a full-blown grin. "It was something to see." At the look Tony gave him, Buzz added hastily, "Kaminsky did facial recognition on all the guys caught on tape watching, but there was nobody who jumped out."

Michael was back. The look he gave Charlie as her eyes turned on him questioningly was dark.

"Damn it." Tony glanced around at the surrounding buildings in frustration. "There's got to be something here. I just don't think he chose those three girls at random, and this is the only place that we know they intersect."

"They're following their loved ones to a grief counseling group session," Michael told Charlie, who sucked in a breath as the connection suddenly became crystal clear in her mind. "Apparently there's a meeting on the second floor of that building on the corner."

He pointed, but he didn't have to: Charlie watched the blood-drenched elderly man follow the elderly woman into the building, and grabbed the sleeve of Tony's jacket.

"It's grief counseling." Charlie could feel the excitement coursing through her veins. "*That's* the connection. I'm sure of it. We'll find that all the victims were with someone who suffered a violent death and then went to *grief counseling*."

"What?" Tony said as he and Buzz gave her identical surprised looks.

"They're getting ready to have a session right now on the second floor of that building on the corner." Charlie tugged on Tony's arm. "Come on."

"You're welcome," Michael said sourly, and Charlie forgot herself enough to give him a quick smile even as she was practically frog-marching Tony toward the building. Michael didn't smile back. Watching her with Tony, his eyes had gone all flinty, and his mouth was grim.

Tony frowned at her questioningly. "What made you think of grief counseling? And how do you know there's a session getting ready to start in that building?"

"I can't wait to hear this." Michael's voice was dry. "Go on, buttercup, tell him how you know."

"The universe speaks to me, remember?" she said lightly, throwing Michael an *eat dirt* look. "Plus, somebody walking past was carrying a brochure."

"Yeah, I thought so," Michael said.

The look Tony gave her was searching. Of course, he knew she *was,* ahem, a little bit psychic, even if he didn't know the half of it. One day, Charlie told herself, she might even sit him down and tell him the whole truth. Minus the part about Michael, of course.

She was never going to be able to tell anybody about Michael.

The Grief Connection was the group's name. It was printed on a sign affixed to the open door of a room that was already filling up with people, dead and alive. Rows of molded plastic chairs, a speaker's podium, a table with coffee and pastries, that was it. According to the social worker getting ready to lead that day's session, open meetings were held every weekday from nine to ten a.m. It was run like an AA meeting. People came, shared the source of their grief, and found comfort. No, there were no records of who attended the meetings, and there were certainly no security cameras. But she was able to give them a list of the meeting leaders, and a number they could use to contact the parent organization for more information.

"What are the chances that Jenna, Raylene, and Laura all ended up in one of these sessions together?" Buzz whispered as they stood at the back of the room watching the meeting get under way.

"It's the only thing that fits." Tony's gaze swung to Charlie. "You want to give Jenna a call when we get out of here and see if she can confirm being at one of these meetings the day she was kidnapped? I'd do it, but I think it'd be better coming from you. Crane, when we get back to the hotel, see if you can find out if any of the other victims went in for some kind of grief counseling."

Charlie nodded, and Crane said, "Will do, boss."

As they watched the elderly woman Charlie had observed on the street stand up and start to share her story of loss—her husband of fifty-two years (who she had no idea was right beside her) had been killed in a traffic accident the previous week—Charlie said thought-fully, "The Gingerbread Man almost had to be at that same session. How else would he know that those girls had suffered that kind of loss?"

"Maybe they have regulars, and one of them will remember a weird guy who stared at all the participants, trying to decide who he was going to kidnap and kill." That was Michael, who was standing beside her looking both pissed off (that would be at her) and seriously formidable, which she assumed was his way of making sure that the spirits she couldn't see steered clear.

None of the participants in that morning's meeting looked as if he could remotely fit the bill, Charlie determined with a glance.

After the organized part of the meeting was concluded, when the participants were milling around the refreshments table, Tony asked the social worker about regulars. She pointed them out, and they went to talk to them. They got nothing.

They were just leaving the meeting when Tony got a call from Kaminsky, who'd been kept abreast of the possible grief counseling connection via a text from Buzz. Charlie, who was in the act of phon-ing Jenna, knew instantly from Tony's expression that something was up.

"Kaminsky thinks she's figured out the identity of the next expert the unsub's going to contact," Tony said as he disconnected. "We need to head back to the hotel."

Jenna wasn't answering her phone. As they sped back to the hotel, Charlie left a message asking the girl to please return the call as soon as possible.

The makeshift War Room was a small conference room down a short hall off the lobby. It was windowless, and Kaminsky had set it up with a system that had her facing a half-dozen laptops placed side by side on the long table that, along with the eight chairs around it, was the room's only furniture.

"It's Dr. Steven Pelletier," Kaminsky burst out excitedly as the others walked into the room. She was seated in a padded leather chair, but stood up as they entered. On one of the laptop screens was the frozen face of the esteemed neuropathologist who had made a name for himself studying the effect of brain disease on criminal behavior. From the look of him on the screen, Kaminsky had hit pause in mid–phone call. "He's the only one of the experts on the list you gave me who was involved in a violent death when he was young. His eighteen months' older sister was killed in a house fire when he was seven. Apparently the two of them were found unconscious at the bottom of some stairs by firefighters. Dr. Pelletier was able to be revived; the sister was not."

"Sounds like you got it," Tony said, nodding at Kaminsky to resume the call. "No way can that be a coincidence."

Kaminsky hit a button, said, "Sorry to put you on hold, Dr. Pelletier. Here's our team leader, Special Agent Anthony Bartoli."

"Dr. Pelletier." Tony slid into the seat beside Kaminsky. "I'm sure Special Agent Kaminsky has filled you in on what's going on."

Pelletier nodded. Charlie had never met him, but she was familiar with his work. In his late thirties, with a round, jovial face and short, reddish hair, he looked like anything but the distinguished researcher he was.

"Everything's been fine," Pelletier said in reply to Tony's question about whether he'd noticed anything out of the ordinary over the last few days.

Tony nodded. "We're going to be putting surveillance on you. I'll have people in place within the hour. Around your home, office, you personally. They'll stay out of sight, but they'll be there."

Pelletier looked a little startled. "You really think a serial killer's going to be contacting *me*?"

"Yes," Tony said uncompromisingly. "And right now you're our best hope of catching this guy, so we'd appreciate your cooperation."

"Sure," Pelletier agreed, and they ended the conversation with him looking alarmed but game. No sooner had he hung up than Jenna called Charlie back: she hadn't attended the Grief Connection counseling session the morning of the run, she said, which caused Charlie momentary consternation. Then Jenna added that she had stopped by the session briefly to drop off flyers about the run, and had stopped to talk to a couple of people near the door about the tragedy in her own life. It was possible that she could have been overheard, she said, although she didn't remember anyone who seemed particularly interested in her. She also didn't remember seeing Laura, or Raylene, although they could have been there. She hadn't been paying much attention, and she hadn't stayed long.

"That's got to be it," Charlie said as she recounted the conversation to the others, who agreed.

"All we can do is look at any security video we can find from the surrounding streets that morning," Tony said. As it had already been collected and was in the process of being reviewed, that base was pretty well covered.

"Look who I've talked to this morning," Kaminsky said as Tony, after refusing Kaminsky's offer to contact the deputy director of the Bureau on Skype, went out to make the call to set up the arrangements for what needed to happen with Pelletier.

Kaminsky punched a button, and immediately faces appeared on all of the screens.

Charlie recognized four of them at a glance. The other two she had no clue about.

"I left messages for Dr. Underwood and Dr. Myers yesterday"— Kaminsky pointed to two of the screens—"and both called back this morning to confirm that at a young age they were present at the violent death of someone close. Dr. Underwood had a friend hit in the chest with a ball at a baseball game—I know, bizarre—and Dr. Myers' cousin was accidentally shot and killed when they were together." She looked around at Charlie and Buzz. "Which means all four of our experts share that common experience. Include Dr. Pelletier—although he is not technically one of our experts *yet*—and we've got a clean sweep. *Plus,* I've talked to Ariane Spencer"—she pointed to the pretty blond teen on the third screen—"who was, if you recall, the surviving victim from Group Two . . . (that was the snakes)—" Kaminsky broke off to shudder. "—and Andrew Russell, the Group Five . . . trash compactor, remember? . . . survivor"—she pointed to the fourth screen—"and Saul Tunney, the Group Six . . . grain silo . . . survivor"—his was another of the faces Charlie recognized—"and they all confirm that they were present at the violent death of someone close, previous to what happened to them with the Gingerbread Man."

"What about grief counseling?" Buzz asked. "Did they get any?"

"I don't know." Kaminsky sounded faintly aggrieved. "When I was talking to them, grief counseling wasn't part of the picture." She made a face. "Well, I guess I get to call them all back."

"You called Ken Ewell?" Charlie was frowning at one of the faces on the screens. The deputy sheriff from Big Stone Gap seemed like an unlikely contact for Kaminsky to need to make.

"He called me," Kaminsky corrected. "Apparently they have a surveillance video of what looks like a gray van on the road leading into Big Stone Gap on the night of the murders. He's e-mailing it to me."

"Maybe we can get a license plate," Buzz said hopefully.

"Like our luck is ever that good," Kaminsky replied. Then she pointed to the last screen. "This is a parent of—"

She broke off as Tony came back into the room. An envelope was in his hand, and the expression on his face as he looked at Charlie—directly at her, instead of at the three of them in general—was concerned.

"This came for you," Tony said as he handed the envelope to her. "It was delivered this morning. The clerk at the front desk thought it might be urgent, so he gave it to me to give to you."

Charlie accepted the envelope. It was one of the cardboard overnight delivery envelopes from FedEx. The name on the return label was unknown to her, she saw as she ripped it open.

Inside was another envelope, a white business-sized one. On it, in spidery black handwriting, was nothing more than her name: Dr. Charlotte Stone.

The flap was unsealed. Inside that was a single sheet of paper. Even before Charlie unfolded it, her heart started to slam in her chest.

She knew, *knew,* in every cell of her body, who it was from.

CHAPTER TWENTY-THREE

YOU DIDN'T CATCH ME was what the message said.

"The Gingerbread Man," Kaminsky breathed, as Michael, who had been looking over Charlie's shoulder, said, "Fuck," and Charlie looked down with growing horror at the small, stiff square of paper that had been tucked inside the folded sheet.

It was a Polaroid photograph of three young girls lying, apparently unconscious, in a wire cage.

"Oh, my God." Charlie dropped the picture like it stung her fingers. The images of the girls—they looked to be young teens—burned itself into her brain. Someone—Buzz—took the letter from her, while Tony picked up the photo, holding it very carefully by the corner with a tissue he'd acquired from somewhere, and positioned it so they all could see.

"He's escalating again," Charlie said. For the first couple of seconds she'd looked at it, she'd thought—hoped—that what she was seeing was one of the groups of victims he had attacked in the past. But she didn't think so. In fact, she was as sure as it was possible to be that this was a new group of victims.

"Find out who those girls are," Tony ordered, and Kaminsky nodded.

"Since we know Dr. Pelletier is the expert the Gingerbread Man's most likely to contact, we can catch him," Buzz said. "Pelletier's at the Virginia Tech Carilion School of Medicine, right? Isn't that in Roanoke? We can be there in a couple of hours, catch the SOB when he drops off the letter."

"Unless he's smart, and mails it, like he just did to you," Michael said dryly to Charlie.

Charlie repeated that, minus the snark.

Frowning, Tony was looking down at the photograph he still held in his hand. "Even if he drops it off in person, by the time he does, at least two of these girls are going to be dead. And we may be totally wrong about the identity of the expert. Or he may not even contact an expert this time. As the change in timing proves, he's flexible enough to make adjustments to his game plan."

"I think our best bet is to try to identify him, and the place we need to look is where the first Gingerbread Man murders occurred." Charlie was thinking it through as she spoke. "He'll have some kind of roots there. Probably a connection to one of the first group of victims."

"We don't have time to dig into all that." Kaminsky's voice was tight as she looked up from the laptop, where she had been frantically working. "He's already got those girls. That means we have—at most—two more days. Or we might not even have that. He's already changed the timing on us."

"You got anything on the identities?" Tony asked Kaminsky while he passed the photo to Buzz, then said to him, "We need to get that, and the letter, to the lab."

"I'll see to it," Buzz said, while Kaminsky answered, "Nothing yet. I'm checking all the databases, but nothing's instantaneous, you know."

"I have a psychic friend whom I know to be very accurate," Charlie said. With lives at stake, and possessing information she felt might be important, concealing her chats with Tam no longer mattered. "She called a couple of days ago to warn me that I'm in danger near dark water. It seems to me that if I'm in danger near dark water, then any water that can turn dark—like Buggs Island Lake, for example—is where the danger has to be. It's possible she's gloamed on to a different danger, but I don't think so. I think the danger I'm in comes from the Gingerbread Man, and the Gingerbread Man will be found near water that is or can be dark."

For a moment everyone else in the room stared at her silently.

Then Kaminsky said, "Well, that sure clinches it for me."

Michael gave a snort of amusement. Charlie shot Kaminsky an unappreciative look. Tony said, "I'm not willing to discount any psychic help we can get." He looked at Charlie. "You got the grief counseling connection pretty much out of nowhere. How strongly do you feel about tracking the unsub down through the Buggs Island Lake connection?"

Charlie hesitated.

"I've got a hit on the girls." The tension in Kaminsky's voice was palpable as she looked up from her laptop. "Diane Townsend, Kim Oates, and Natalie Garza. All fourteen, all reported missing this morning from Twinbrook, a girls' camp in Rocky Mount, North Carolina, that specializes in—get this—grief counseling. Apparently this week's program caters to survivors of school shootings."

"Looks like our guy was in a hurry," Michael said. "Instead of cherry-picking 'em, this time he went straight for the all-you-can-eat buffet."

"Notify the agents down there that we may have a lead on the girls," Tony told Buzz, who nodded, then asked, "Should I tell them we're on our way?"

Tony grimaced. "As I see it, we've got three ways we can go here. We can head for Roanoke and sit on Pelletier. We can head down to Rocky Mount and join the search there. Or we can take a quick trip to Buggs Island Lake and see what we can dig up."

Buzz said, "Dr. Pelletier's covered. If the unsub shows up there, we'll have him."

"Too late for the girls, though," Kaminsky put in.

Buzz continued as if she hadn't spoken. "I'm guessing that they've got half the Bureau, plus the state police and all available local law enforcement, on the scene in Rocky Mount."

"We'd be the only ones looking at Buggs Island Lake," Tony said.

Kaminsky looked up from her computer. "A friend of a girl who went missing at Buggs Island Lake five years ago reported that in the days leading up to her disappearance a man had been following them. She told police she could describe him, although if she ever did, it didn't make it into this file. The witness still lives in the same house, near the lake."

"We could go interview her, get a description, check out any local police records," Buzz said. "If it doesn't look like anything will pan out down there, we could move on."

Tony made up his mind. "Sounds like a plan. Get packed. I want to be in the air in under an hour."

Buggs Island Lake (as they call it in Virginia), which is also known as Kerr Reservoir (to the folks in the Carolinas), was a fifty-thousand-acre swimmers', boaters', and fishermen's paradise. Long and narrow, it ran along the Virginia/North Carolina border and was one of the most popular summer resort areas in both states. Erin Hill, the friend of the disappeared girl, who lived in the little lakeside community of Clarksville, was indeed able to give them a description: a dark-haired man, maybe in his early thirties, who had followed them around in a gray van. The part about the gray van hadn't made it into the police report, and it sent a shaft of excitement through the team. The lead was promising enough that they turned Erin over to a local police sketch artist.

While they waited for the results, in an empty office off the small squad room, Kaminsky was busy checking out a map of the lake area that hung on the wall. Charlie, who like the others was acutely aware of the swift passage of time, was starting to realize that she hadn't gotten as much rest the previous night as she had supposed. She was sitting in one of the hard metal chairs and chugging stale police coffee as she went over the missing persons reports that Kaminsky had thought might be relevant to the case, which the agent had e-mailed to her. Buzz was combing through the police files on the four supposedly-accidental-but-deemed-by-Kaminsky-to-be-suspicious deaths that she had identified in the area during the time period in question. Having stepped outside because the reception was better, Tony was on the phone, talking to agents at the scene of the kidnappings in Rocky Mount, and then to those assigned to conduct surveillance on Dr. Pelletier. Michael was on his feet staring out the window at the beautiful blue water of the lake. It was early evening by this time, but the sunlight was still strong enough to make the surface sparkle. Charlie could read in Michael's body language his longing to be out there as part of the living world again, but he was still palpably angry at her and for the most part wasn't talking. Under the circumstances, she wasn't, either. What could she say? There was nothing in what she had told him that she would take back. And she badly needed to put him in his proper place in her life, which should probably be, as he had sneeringly described it, the ghost whisperer's apprentice and nothing more. But the sad truth was, just letting her eyes run over him evoked feelings in her that were disturbingly sexual. One look at his broad shoulders and muscular back, at his tight butt and long, powerful legs, and she was back in last night's darkened hotel room with him again.

He makes me hotter than any man I've ever known.

That was the thought that was floating through her mind when Kaminsky glanced around at her and asked, "What did that psychic friend of yours tell you, exactly?" Charlie was caught off guard enough so that she had to think for a moment.

"She said I was in danger near dark water." Which—Charlie had noted, to her relief—Buggs Island Lake was not. At least at that moment, its waters were the approximate shade of Michael's eyes. "She said the danger came from a gray house in the dark water. I'm wondering if maybe we'll find our unsub on a houseboat."

"You know I'm fluent in a number of languages, right?" Kaminsky said. "One of them is Algonquin. About fifteen miles from here on this side of the lake is Pocomoke Village. In Pocomoke Village is Pocomoke Street." Buzz was looking at Kaminsky, too, at this point. "In Algonquin, *pocomoke* means *dark water.*"

At that, Michael also swung around to stare at Kaminsky.

"Oh, my God," Charlie said. At the same time Buzz said, "Wow," and Michael said, "Shit."

"It's probably a coincidence." Kaminsky turned away from the map to head for her laptop, which rested on the desk. "But there it is."

"There's no such thing as coincidence," Michael said, and narrowed his eyes at Charlie. "You don't go anywhere near that place."

As Kaminsky plopped herself behind the desk and Buzz rose to look over her shoulder while she called something up on her laptop,

Charlie gave Michael a hard look that could be roughly translated as, *You're not the boss of me.*

He folded his arms over his chest. "Babe, here's a tip: don't mess with me right now. I ain't real happy with you."

Bite me, was what she silently replied.

"I've got it here on Google Earth. Pocomoke Street is dotted with what looks like little fishing cottages. They're far apart, and the area seems really rural," Kaminsky drew her attention by saying.

"Laura said the van smelled like fish," Charlie said before she thought.

"Who?" Kaminsky frowned at her, while Michael, with a taunting smile, said, "Oops."

"Somebody. It doesn't matter." Charlie covered her misstep hastily, and covered herself even further by refusing to look at Michael again. "The point is, someone said the van used in the kidnappings smelled like fish."

"I think I heard that," Buzz said.

"One of the cottages is painted dark gray." Kaminsky got to the point. "What we have here, then, is a gray house on the equivalent of Dark Water Street."

"There are a lot of gray houses on a lot of streets with Indian names," Tony cautioned when he stepped back into the office after finishing his phone calls and Kaminsky's discovery was explained to him. "Who owns it?"

Kaminsky tapped a few keys on her laptop. "Benjamin Motta." Her tone was portentous.

I can't talk right now, Ben.

That's what Laura said she'd overheard the Gingerbread Man saying to someone on the phone.

"Let's go check it out," Tony said.

"Oh, no," Michael said, pointing a finger at Charlie. "Not you."

But she was already on her way out the door with the rest of them.

"Can you say 'death wish,' Doc?" Michael growled as they all piled into the car, a rental that had been waiting for them at the airport.

Charlie's mouth tightened. She hated to admit it, but he had a point.

"What about Ms. Hill, boss?" Buzz asked from the backseat, where he and Kaminsky now sat as a matter of course. Ms. Hill was the witness who was at that moment working with the sketch artist.

"One of the locals can give her a ride home if we're not back by the time she's finished. We'll pick up the sketch later." From the little side street they'd been on, Tony pulled onto the main drag that ran along the lakefront even as he glanced at Kaminsky in the mirror and added, "Kaminsky."

"Taking care of it." Kaminsky pulled her phone out.

"You're not really stupid enough to go to a gray house on dark water, are you?" Michael snarled at Charlie from the backseat, where he was sandwiched between Buzz and Kaminsky, his invisible presence making them both crowd toward their respective doors, which still left him with not near enough room. "Hell, I know you're not."

Actually, much as she might feel like annoying Michael, now that she had a chance to think about it, Charlie wasn't. Reluctantly she said to Tony, "You know, I think I'm going to have to sit this one out. If you could drop me at a restaurant or something . . ."

"Smartest thing you've said all day," Michael said.

"Don't worry, I wasn't going to take you anyway," Tony told her reassuringly. "Even aside from the dark water thing, you're a civilian, and if this pans out it could get ugly. In fact, I think we're going to want the local police with us as backup. If we should need to go in, if there should be some indication that the missing girls might be at this location, we're going to want to have a perimeter set up and plenty of firepower available. Kaminsky, check your Google map or whatever it is you check and find us a place where you and Charlie can hole up while this thing gets done."

"I hate to say this, but I'm actually kind of liking Dudley right now," Michael said.

"What?" Kaminsky screeched, then immediately moderated her voice to add, "I'm not sitting this out."

"No, you're not. You're doing your job, which is to protect our expert." Tony gave her a cool look through the mirror. "Get on it, Kaminsky."

Charlie felt the sizzle of Kaminsky's glare on the back of her head.

"The Bluefly Inn is a small hotel located right outside Pocomoke

Village. They have a good, down-home-style supper buffet Tuesday through Sunday, clean, well-appointed rooms and two conference rooms available for family reunions or any larger groups." Kaminsky sounded like she was reading the words off a virtual brochure. There was no missing the bitterness in her tone.

"Sounds good," Tony said, then got on his phone to make arrangements with the local cops for what he needed.

The Bluefly Inn looked exactly like what it was: an old-fashioned hunting and fishing lodge. Built of dark, unpeeled logs with a green-shingled roof and a covered porch complete with rocking chairs that ran the length of the front of the building, it was set well back from the street in a gravel parking lot. There were a number of cars in the lot, and Charlie realized with a glance at the dashboard clock—it was almost 8:30, she saw with a sense of shock—that this was probably the tail end of the dinner rush.

She also realized two completely disparate things: she was hungry, and the girls they were hoping to save were running out of time.

In the end, she felt like coming here was on her shoulders. The gray house on the dark water owned by Ben Motta was a good lead, but was it right?

There was no way to know. Only, if it wasn't, those girls might very well die tonight.

Charlie sent a wordless prayer for their safety winging skyward.

"This is complete sexist crap." Kaminsky glared at Charlie across the table as they both sat down to eat. Tony and Buzz had been gone maybe ten minutes, and Charlie and Kaminsky had elected to make the best use of their time by having a meal while they reviewed files that had just been updated by the support staff at Quantico on their respective laptops. ("Let 'em starve," was Kaminsky's reaction to Charlie's suggestion that perhaps they should wait for the men to return before they ate.) Located at one end of the lodge, the dining room was dark, log walls, a long steam table set up down one side. The deepening twilight seen through the partially closed blinds covering the two large windows and the glass tops of the front and back doors didn't help the gloom. The smell of fried chicken and fried fish, the main dish staples, was more than enough to make up for it: it was so appetizing that Charlie's stomach growled. Their table was a small four-top pushed against the wall. The only illumination was provided by the steam table, a tiny candle in a small, brown glass globe on each table, and the red glimmer of two signs that labeled the ladies' and men's rooms, which were down a short hall that opened up behind Kaminsky and which Charlie could see faintly sputtering as if their bulbs were about to go out.

There was also the light from their open laptops: the pale glow from Kaminsky's made her look like something out of *The Walking Dead*. Not that Charlie meant to tell her so, and not that she had any hope that the glow from hers made her look any better. Anyway, except for Michael and the waitress who brought their drinks, no one was paying the least attention to either her or Kaminsky.

Maybe a dozen diners remained.

"I agree." Charlie took a bite of fried catfish, and almost closed her eyes at the delicate cornbread flavor of the crispy crust. Even Michael's wry expression as he watched her eat couldn't dim her appreciation.

Kaminsky bit into the catfish, too, but seemed to be in no mood to appreciate it. "He assigns me to you because we're both *women*."

"I'd rather have Buzz," Charlie assured her. "I'll be glad to tell Tony so."

Even the coleslaw was superior, Charlie decided as her gaze drifted down to the file she had been perusing: a detailed background check on Jeff Underwood. Reading it felt like an invasion of privacy, but with the lives of those girls on the line they couldn't afford to overlook any possible clue. She was going over the experts' files, and Kaminsky was reading through the victims' files, and then they were going to switch, because fresh eyes were always a good thing. They were looking for anything, *anything*, that might lead them to the killer.

"Like Bartoli'd listen." Kaminsky gave her a hostile look. "Anyway, that makes me sound like I'm being difficult. Like I'm not a team player."

Charlie didn't say anything. Despite her ire, Kaminsky was eating in a way that made Charlie think she was enjoying her food, too.

"I'd file a complaint, except I like Bartoli. I like our team." Another hostile look that Charlie translated to mean, *Especially when you're not on it.*

Charlie shrugged. "If I were you, I'd just shut up and sit tight. After all, I'm not a permanent fixture."

Her eyes returned to Underwood's file. Reaching the end of it, she clicked onto the next one: David Myers'. At the idea that she might come across details of her own youthful involvement with him inside the next few pages, she barely managed not to grimace.

"Bartoli would like you to be," Kaminsky shot at her. "He thinks you're a real *asset.*"

Michael snorted. "He wants to bang your brains out," he corrected with a sneer.

Charlie ignored that.

"I am," she told Kaminsky serenely, and kept her smile to herself as the other woman almost choked on her food.

"We were doing fine without you," Kaminsky retorted as soon as she finished swallowing a restorative sip of water, but by then Charlie wasn't listening: her attention was riveted on the file in front of her.

"I think I may have found something." Charlie's pulse pounded in her ears as she looked at Kaminsky. She felt a weird, almost light-headed sensation, like her blood was draining toward her toes. "I've always felt that the first Gingerbread Man murders were the most significant. His victims were boys between the ages of twelve and fourteen, remember? It's been my theory that our unsub's original exposure to violent death occurred at that same age. I've also felt that he would have roots, or a connection, to this location, because the first murders occurred near here."

Kaminsky scowled at her. "So you want to cut to the chase?"

Charlie did: "According to this file, David Myers was thirteen years old when he shot his cousin in Granville, which is about twenty miles from here."

Kaminsky's eyes widened. "Are you saying you think *Dr. Myers* might be the Gingerbread Man?"

As hard as it was for her to process, Charlie gave a jerky nod. "I think it's possible."

"Holy shit," Michael said. "That little worm?"

Charlie already had her phone out and was pushing the button that dialed Tony's number.

"You telling Bartoli?" Kaminsky asked with a glance at the phone.

Charlie nodded. But Tony didn't pick up.

"He's not answering," Charlie said tensely.

As Charlie left Tony a message, Kaminsky snatched up her phone, saying, "I'll try Crane."

"Thank God," Kaminsky said as Buzz answered. From where Charlie was sitting, she could hear his end of the conversation as well as Kaminsky's. The other woman's voice was quiet and urgent as she spoke into the phone. "Listen up: Dr. Stone thinks the Gingerbread Man might be Dr. Myers."

"*What?*" Buzz sounded shocked. "How? Why?"

"We'll explain later." Kaminsky broke into his sputtering impatiently. "Just tell Bartoli. Dr. Stone tried to call him, but he's not answering his phone."

"He's got it turned off," Buzz said. "You caught me right as I was turning mine off, too. *Hey, boss!*" It was a loud whisper. "Damn it, he can't hear me. You slowed me down: he's already up there by the garage." From the sound of Buzz's voice, he was now on the move. "We're at the house. The local police have a perimeter set up, and Bartoli and I and a couple of detectives are getting ready to go in. Doesn't look like it's going to amount to much, though. The house is dark and looks deserted. We don't even have to break in. One of the detectives has a universal garage door opener and he's using it to open up the—"

BOOM.

The explosion came out of nowhere. It was loud enough to hurt Charlie's ears, to make the room shake, to rattle dishes and cutlery, to bring everyone in the room, including Charlie, leaping to their feet. Outside one of the big windows, Charlie could see a not-too-distant geyser of black smoke and scarlet flames shooting upward over a jagged skyline of trees.

She gaped at it in shock.

"What the hell?" Michael's eyes were riveted on the mushroom-

ing fire. Everyone rushed toward one of the two doors, clearly meaning to pour out into the parking lot to get a better look at what was
going on.

"Crane! Buzz!" Kaminsky cried into the phone. She gave Charlie
a stricken look. "I could hear the explosion over the phone. I think—
either it knocked out reception or—*Buzz! Buzz!* My God, was it
them?" She started toward the nearest of the doors at a run, her eyes
wild. "Let me see if the reception's better outside. You stay here."
The last part of that, which she threw over her shoulder at Charlie,
was fierce.

Charlie nodded, but Kaminsky, already thrusting through the
door, didn't see. Heart thumping, cold with dread, Charlie felt like
she'd been rooted to the spot. She'd heard it clearly, too: the sound of
the explosion had come through the phone. Which meant that Buzz,
and Tony, had been on the scene.

Oh, my God.

"This ain't good." Michael had moved over to the nearest window, and was staring out at the billowing cloud of smoke and fire as
it reached for the sky.

Out of the corner of her eye, Charlie saw that the last remaining
diner, a man who'd popped out of the restroom at the sound of the
explosion only to drop his briefcase at the sight that greeted him
through the windows, was on one knee hastily gathering up his papers.

Please let Tony and Buzz be fine.

Probably the reception had been knocked out.

Taking a breath, getting a grip, Charlie moved to help him. Giving in to the panic that was surging through her body did no one any
good. Crouching, she scooped up a handful of papers, which looked
like pages of a manuscript. The title page was one of a number in her
hands, and as she glanced at it the title leaped out at her. In large,
bold type it read, *Causative Factors: A Treatise on the Nature of
Evil.*

Charlie blinked at it, then glanced up at the man crouched on the
other side of the briefcase. He was holding a handful of papers, too,
and as their eyes met he looked as astonished as she felt.

Her heart gave a great leap. Every tiny hair on the back of her neck shot upright.

"David," she breathed.

That was all she said, because his name had no sooner left her mouth than he punched her in the face as hard as he could.

Charlie felt an explosion of pain, and everything went black.

CHAPTER TWENTY-FOUR

"Charlie!"

The voice yelling her name was loud enough so that she would've winced if she could have. Michael's voice: she would recognize it anywhere.

Opening her eyes, Charlie nearly blacked out at the pain, and let her lids drop.

My face hurts.

"Michael?" she whispered.

"You need to wake up, babe. Right now."

The urgency of it made her try to open her eyes again. This time, since she was prepared for the pain, it wasn't quite so debilitating. But for whatever reason, her eyes wouldn't quite open all the way, and so she peeped out through narrow slits.

Michael leaned over her. His face was the first thing she saw. It was hard, fierce even. She smiled anyway, or at least made a pathetic attempt at it. That hurt, too, so she stopped.

He didn't smile back. She could feel tension rolling off him in waves.

"Hey," he said. "You with me?"

"Mmm." At least, she was trying. Then she remembered. "You're mad at me."

"No," he said. "Not now."

Relieved, she tried smiling again. It still hurt.

Michael said, "I know you're hurting. But you got to snap out of it."

He moved away from her, out of her line of vision. She tried to track him but failed because it hurt when she moved her head. Wherever she was, it was dark. Not pitch dark: she could see shadows, and flashes of light that seemed to come out of nowhere. The lights ran across the walls—curved metal walls—only to vanish. It took her a second to realize that what she was seeing were the headlights of passing vehicles slicing through the one she was in. She *was* in a vehicle: she knew that for sure because of the movement and the sounds. She was lying down on her side, on a hard, uncomfortable surface, in a moving vehicle. Something warm pressed close against her back. Her face—her nose and cheekbones and eye sockets—ached and throbbed. The skin over them felt swollen, a little tingly, mostly numb.

Charlie realized that she would have been afraid if Michael hadn't been there.

"Michael?"

"Shh." From the sound of his voice, he wasn't very far away. "Keep your voice down. I'm right here."

"What . . . happened?" Whispering, she moved a little, trying to locate him. A quiver of pain shot like an arrow behind her eyes, and her head swam, but she persevered. Breathing through her nose, she discovered, was hard. Clearly she'd been in some kind of accident.

She tried to think, to remember, but the effort made her head pound so she gave up.

"I missed part of it—I was looking out the damned window—but best I can tell you ran into that bastard Myers, and he punched you in the face and knocked you cold." Michael's voice was grim. "You remember any of that?"

"No." Charlie saw Michael now, as a big solid shape in the darkness, through a grid of metal bars mere inches from her poor damaged nose. He was crouched about three feet away, and appeared to be examining the tall metal grid that inexplicably seemed to stand between them. She tried to make sense of what Michael had just said. "David?"

"He's the Gingerbread Man."

"What?" Woozy, she was unable to think clearly. As long as she kept her head relatively still, moving her arms and hands didn't cause her pain, Charlie discovered as she reached out to curl her fingers around the metal wires, each of which was approximately as thick as her pinkie finger. The whole grid felt as sturdy as if it was made of solid steel. "What . . . is this?"

"It's a cage. You're in a damned cage."

That still didn't make sense. Nothing made any sense. She forced out an inarticulate questioning sound.

Michael glanced her way. "Okay, here's the situation as it stands: you're in the back of that gray van you've been looking for, locked in a cage. That bastard Myers is driving. The cage takes up nearly the whole back of the van, it's bolted to the floor, it's got a padlock on the door, and right at the moment I'm not seeing any way to get you out of it. Those three missing girls are in the cage, too, lying next to you. They're out for the count. There's a tank—I think it's empty, thank Jesus—out here, with a hose going into the cage. I'm guessing from its presence that the girls were gassed. Oh, and Sugar Buns is in there with you, too. She got zapped with a stun gun when she went outside hunting for you. From the look of her, she'll be coming around any minute."

Charlie began to frown. Frowning hurt. She stopped. A hard knot of fear formed in her chest. She could feel her heart starting to beat a little faster. Her brain was still missing some of its spark, but at least it was starting to function, bathed by an icy infusion of adrenaline.

"David," she said with horror, as the truth hit her like a slap in the face: David was the Gingerbread Man; David had kidnapped her; David had her locked in the back of his van—

"Charlie, is that you?" A familiar, almost jovial voice from the front seat responded, and she realized that she had forgotten to whisper.

Fear made her blink. Blinking hurt.

"Son of a bitch," Michael said.

"David?" Charlie's gaze slanted in the direction of the voice. Even

as she said his name again the memory of looking up over the manuscript pages in her hand to see David staring back at her surfaced. A
split second later, had he slammed his fist into her face? Yes, Charlie
concluded as anger joined the fear that was turning her icy cold inside, he had. She moved a little, careful to shift her whole body rather
than only her eyes, and strained to see him. The dark shape of his
head was just visible on the other side of what appeared to be the
curved edges of a sliding plastic door similar in type to that which
separates the back of a limo from the chauffeur. At the moment, it
was open. He could talk to her, and obviously to some extent hear
what was going on in the back of the van. He was driving, and past
him, through the windshield, she got a slight glimpse of inky sky. Indignation filled her voice. "You hit me!"

It was such a stupid thing to say. Clearly, since he had locked her
in a cage in the back of a van that smelled (she was a little relieved to
realize she could still smell) of fish, with, according to Michael, the
three kidnapped girls and Kaminsky unconscious beside her, the fact
that David had punched her in the face was a small thing. But it felt
like such a violation of the relationship they'd had that, yes, she was
angry.

"Don't worry, babe. I'll kill him for you later." Michael's tone
was so even that for a moment she almost missed the deadly promise
that ran beneath it. Glancing at him, registering his tall, powerful
body, she knew he meant it, and knew, too, that he could break David
in half with no trouble whatsoever. Then she remembered that he was
dead, and there was, actually, nothing he could do, which he was apparently forgetting, too, and she felt cold sweat start to prickle to life
around her hairline.

"You saw me," David said. "It was the only thing I could think
of to do. I could see in your face that you knew. I stopped at the Inn
to grab a quick dinner before I hit the road, and I went to the restroom, and when I came out there you were. If I'd had any idea you
were around—but I didn't. And then after I put you in the van, when
I was going back for my briefcase, your cop friend saw me, too."

By cop friend, Charlie knew he was referring to Kaminsky.

Charlie caught her breath, sucked in air.

"You're the Gingerbread Man." Again, it was stupid. She even said it with a touch of incredulity, because, she supposed, she was still hoping that this was all some huge mistake, and he would deny it. But then reality set in, and she knew that however unthinkable, however terrible it seemed, it was true.

As she faced the reality of that, her mouth went sour with fear.

"Have bad taste in boyfriends much?" Michael asked grimly from the other side of the cage, which he was slowly circling like a predator trying to get in. Under other circumstances, the sight would have made her smile. She didn't.

In this case, it wasn't that he couldn't get in. It was that he couldn't get any of them out.

The knowledge was terrifying. It settled like a rock in her stomach. She was already battling back a creeping tide of panic. *Tony and Buzz. The explosion.* Oh, God, she remembered everything. Had they been hurt? Were they even alive? *Please let them be okay.* But she had to be careful: the last thing she wanted to do was let David think she and Kaminsky were now alone.

"David, *why*?" she asked when he didn't say anything. Talking felt funny, but it didn't really hurt, and her nose had, thankfully, gone numb. What hurt was blinking, or trying to move her eyes.

"Because I wanted to find out what makes people into killers," David replied as if it was the most natural thing in the world. Charlie saw that he was watching her through the rearview mirror, and goose bumps raced over her skin. What would it take to provoke him to kill? Because hard as it was to get her mind around it, that was clearly what he intended: to kill her. And Kaminsky, and the three girls as well.

The certainty made her shiver. The question was, how much time did they have?

I have to try to get out of here.

She made an abortive movement to sit up, lifting her head, pushing down against the uneven metal floor beneath her with an elbow.

Pain shafted through her head. It hurt too much. She stopped, sank back, rested her eyes.

Michael's voice was tight as he said, "Babe, you want to stay kind of still, and when Sugar Buns wakes up you want to tell her to stay still, too. He's got the ability to incapacitate you, either with that stun gun of his or more of whatever he used to knock out these girls, and you don't want to give him cause to do it."

Charlie felt her blood turn to ice at Michael's words. She could tell from his tone that he was trying not to scare her, but that he was expecting something bad to go down soon. And if they were all incapacitated, none of them would stand a chance.

She tried to think, tried to concentrate, tried to come up with a plan. But all she could focus on was the relentless pounding of her pulse in her ears.

"There's a reason people become killers," David continued, and she opened her eyes and forced herself to pay attention. Maybe, if she listened, she could latch on to something that she'd be able to use to talk him out of killing them. He sounded perfectly normal, perfectly rational. Hearing the familiar voice under such circumstances was surreal. Charlie's stomach turned inside out. Her mouth went dry. "There's always a reason for everything. I wanted to find out what it is. It's the same reason you do your research."

Pull yourself together. Use what you know.

"*Causative Factors: A Treatise on the Nature of Evil,*" Charlie enunciated each word precisely. The title, she had discovered, was branded on her brain. Easing onto her back so that she could get a more complete view of her surroundings, feeling the wire grid beneath her digging into her shoulder blades and butt through the thin linen of her dress, she was able to see all three of the girls. They were right beside her, sprawled across one another as though they had been huddling together when they'd collapsed, limp as fresh corpses now, although Charlie could see—and hear—that they still breathed. Little girls, really, two with blond ponytails, one with long, loose dark hair. Shorts and tees and tennis shoes. Children. Innocents. What were their names? Oh, yes: Natalie and Diane and Kim. Beyond them, on the far side of the cage, lay Kaminsky. Her breathing had changed; she was moving a little.

"I wish you could read it." David sounded enthused suddenly, and proud as well. Charlie realized that in his mind he had been doing serious work. "My working theory is, there's something inborn in some people that makes them more able to kill than others. I could never tell who in each group the killer was going to be, though."

Searching for some way to reach him, working hard to keep the fear that was making her feel all shaky inside at a manageable level, Charlie remembered the violent death they'd uncovered in his past. Could she use it to try to throw him off balance? The last thing she wanted him to do was get into his groove, his serial killer mode. They all had them: every serial killer she had studied had presented as perfectly normal until something triggered the monster within.

"Did you kill your cousin on purpose, David?"

She could see his eyes on her in the mirror.

He said, "I was never sure. Tommy—that was his name—was my best friend as well as my cousin, you know. I stayed at his house near the lake here every summer when I was a kid, and we hung out together. One day when we were thirteen, we found his dad's—my uncle's—pistol in a drawer. We were looking at it, and I pointed it at him and pulled the trigger. It was loaded. It killed him. Everybody thought it was an accident, but to this day I'm not sure." He paused. "All I know is I liked watching him die."

There was the serial killer talking. Charlie felt as if an icy hand had just closed around her heart.

"So you killed again." It wasn't a question: Charlie knew the answer too well from her own work. They were called serial killers for a reason: they killed serially. Insatiably, one victim after another, again and again and again.

"I did, once I started coming back to the lake in the summers. For a number of years after Tommy's death, though, I didn't. My uncle and aunt sold the house Tommy died in, everything changed, and I didn't really have the urge. But then, when I was in college, I got a summer job working for one of the marinas here. And it suddenly came back to me: Tommy's death, and how it had felt to watch him die. I kind of considered myself like a shark: I'd had a taste of blood, and I needed more."

"Who did you kill next?" Charlie asked. As long as she didn't move her head too quickly, she could do what she needed to do, she decided. The pain behind her eyes had subsided into no more than a dull throb. The middle of her face felt swollen, but the good news was it was also numb.

Shifting positions a little, she was able to see Michael. He was on his feet, back bent to accommodate his height to the van's ceiling as he feverishly examined every inch of the cage's door. From his strained expression the result wasn't pleasing him.

"A girl. A stranger. She was swimming. I drowned her. Everybody thought that was an accident, too. No one knew I was involved." He drew in an audible breath. It was a sound of excitement, and she realized that he was taking pleasure in remembering. Her heart gave an odd little kick. Her life's work was studying serial killers. She knew the signs: David was getting worked up for the kill. "After that, I just kept killing. One or two a year. If I couldn't make it look like an accident, I'd hide the bodies. But as I got older and began teaching and doing research, and people started looking up to me, I realized I had a lot to lose, and I tried to stop. But I couldn't. I simply had this compulsion to kill. I can't give you a reason for it. Except—I like watching people die."

Charlie's heart was pounding, as if her body had finally processed and recognized the extent of the danger she was in. Kaminsky stirred again, and her breathing was lighter and faster. Charlie hoped it wouldn't be long before she regained consciousness: a highly trained FBI agent was a valuable ally. Was it possible that Kaminsky still had her gun? Charlie thought about what she knew of David, and answered herself: no, it was not.

He was intelligent, methodical. A highly organized killer. He would never be that careless.

Keep him talking. Keep him remembering who he's talking to.

"So you decided to conduct some experiments to learn why you felt the need to behave as you did," Charlie said. She actually could understand that: she'd run experiments on subjects (serial killers) herself to understand why they behaved the way they did. Only her tools involved things like inkblots, not murder.

The van jolted, and Charlie felt something jab hard into her left shoulder. She was, she saw as she cautiously shifted position again, lying on one of the bolts that fastened the cage to the floor. That was the least of her concerns: the quality of the ride had changed. It was now rough and bouncy, and Charlie could hear the rattle of gravel beneath the tires.

"Hell, he's turned off the road." The savage note in Michael's voice scared her to death. She knew he sounded like that because of her. Because he was afraid for her.

"Yes, I did," David responded, pleased that she understood. "My first theory was that it was purely genetic, so I took my nephew—he was the closest I could come to someone who shared my genes who was of an appropriate size and weight to work with easily—and two other boys, and locked them in an abandoned tractor-trailer with an abundance of weapons but without any water, and told them that if one of them killed the other two, I would let that one live. I was hoping that stress would cause my nephew's relevant genes to surface. But it didn't. They all just—died." He sounded disgusted. "So then I started wondering if environmental factors played a role."

"You thought that killing your cousin might have been the trigger that caused you to kill others," Charlie said.

"That's right." His tone was that of a teacher pleased with the performance of a star pupil. Charlie remembered him sounding exactly the same when she'd been in his class. "So I started looking for subjects with a similar trigger. But it was difficult to find young, malleable people who had actually killed someone else, so I settled for suitable subjects who had firsthand exposure to sudden, violent death."

"You found them at grief counseling sessions." It wasn't a question. Charlie knew the answer. Beside her, one of the girls gave a sudden little gasp, and moved her arm.

"Keep 'em quiet," Michael warned, even as Charlie felt a rush of fear. If David thought he needed to, he would knock them all out again, she was sure. Her worst fear was that he had more of the oblivion producing gas, because if he used it to knock them all out it would be game over.

David said, "My parents made me go to a lot of grief counseling sessions after Tommy died. People spill their guts at those things. All I had to do was go to one and sit and listen. Hearing what they had to say—they talked about nightmares they had, terrible experiences, everything—gave me some ideas for certain modes of death to threaten them with that played on their deepest fears. I hoped that might act as a trigger as well. I even followed the survivors of my experiments, like Saul Tunney, to see if the trauma of being forced to kill might turn them into killers afterward. It didn't. Not one." He shook his head. "That's the fascinating thing. What I found is, you never can tell. Some people just have it in them to kill, and others don't."

Kaminsky's eyes were open now. Charlie watched them widen in sudden alarm as Kaminsky started to take in her surroundings. With a quick glance at the rearview mirror to make sure David wasn't watching, Charlie waved a hand to get her attention. As Kaminsky looked her way, Charlie shook her head at her.

"Stay down. Don't move," Charlie mouthed. Kaminsky blinked and frowned.

Then she nodded.

Thank God.

"You kept records," Charlie said to David, thinking of the manuscript. "You wrote it all down."

"It's the greatest research project I've ever done," David agreed happily. "I wanted to bring other researchers in on it, but it took me a long time to figure out how. Then I read the newspaper articles by that reporter—Eric Riva. I was impressed with some of his conclusions. So I thought I'd get him to contribute some more of his thoughts by inviting him to try to catch me. That worked so well I decided to invite the researchers I most respected to contribute to the project as well." Charlie could see him looking at her in the rearview mirror again. Feeling his eyes on her made her skin crawl. How had she missed the fact that he was insane? The only excuse she could come up with for herself was that she had known him years ago, before she'd gone to medical school, before she'd become a psychiatrist and started studying serial killers. "You've come the closest to catching me. I should have expected it. You were my most brilliant student, Charlie."

"Thank you," she said, doing her best to keep the irony out of her voice. Charlie reached past the pain in her head and the dread that was making her feel shaky all over and forced herself to concentrate. Wherever David was taking them, when he got there he was going to turn into the monster he was at his core. If she had any chance of talking him out of killing them, she was going to have to do it soon. "You know, I could help you with your research, David. We could continue it together. It takes my work and expands on it in a way that is truly groundbreaking. I feel you are on the verge of some major break-throughs. I could help you get there."

To her dismay, David laughed. "You can't pull that one on me, Charlie. I know you through and through. I watched you when you were my student, when you were my intern. I knew you had that encounter with the serial killer who murdered your friend in your past. I thought maybe you were like me. But by the end, I knew you weren't. Then, when I started to think about including you in my project, I started watching you again. You know how many nights I spent outside your house looking in? A lot. That night I sent that girl running down to you I hung around to observe how you'd handle it. I thought maybe you had developed more—let's call it ruthlessness—over time. But you took care of her, stayed with her until the ambulance people took her away. I was right there, looking in the back window at first, standing by your front door later, watching as you put yourself at risk for her."

He paused to shake his head, and Charlie thought, *Raylene*. He'd been outside her door when Raylene had appeared, and Raylene had been attached to him. If Charlie had gone out her front door, if she had seen him then, she would have known.

"But you're still not what I hoped you'd become," David concluded almost sadly. "You're one of those people who doesn't have it in them to kill."

There was a change in his voice that made Charlie fear he was starting to get jazzed by the prospect of killing her. Beside her, one of the girls gave a little gasp and turned her head. Charlie didn't know whether to hope they woke up or not. It all depended on what was going to happen.

Talking past the tightness in her throat, she tried a new tactic. "David, I can help you if you'll let me. You know my friend and I aren't here alone. Special Agent Bartoli and Special Agent Crane are here, too." Charlie prayed once again that they were all right. She didn't know what had blown up, but it had been big and the men had been close. Thankfully, David wasn't aware of that, and she wanted to keep it that way. "They already know you're the man they're looking for. You've been using Ben Motta's house as a staging area, haven't you? There will be all kinds of evidence there: DNA, fingerprints, the works. They have other evidence, too, that points to you. Irrefutable evidence. What I'm telling you is, you can't get away with this. You're going to get caught no matter what happens to me, to us. I'm a psychiatrist. I can testify on your behalf. I can help you avoid the death penalty, help you stay out of prison. I know you. I can be your friend, and your doctor, and your advocate. And I will."

David looked at her in the mirror again. "You're trying to talk me out of killing you, I know. And I don't want to. I never meant to. But now I have no choice. I knew yesterday, when your friend back there called me to ask about Tommy's death, that the FBI was on to the connection with traumatic deaths at a young age in the researchers' pasts. I knew they only would have started looking into that if they'd found out about the link to violent deaths in the victims' pasts. I knew they would find Dr. Pelletier, whom I intended to be the next researcher I invited to join the study, and the study site I had set up for the next set of subjects. I was afraid if I didn't take steps, they might keep digging until they found me. So I've decided to quit for a while, and let things die down. The plan was to keep them—you—busy by taking these three girls so everyone would be frantically searching for them, while I cleaned up a few odds and ends around here. You almost spoiled things for me."

Charlie could hear it in his tone: time was growing short. The objectification, the coldness, the distancing—he'd lumped her in with "them"—necessary for him to kill her was coalescing.

Kaminsky's eyes were wide open. Charlie could hear the controlled quality of her breathing. One of the girls made a sound, a whimper. She glanced that way: the girl's eyelids were moving. She was one of the blondes, the second one down. If she woke up, what would David do? If the girl got agitated, started moving around, maybe cried or screamed, that might be all the trigger he needed. Kaminsky was looking at the girl, too: Charlie's eyes met Kaminsky's, held. "Keep her quiet," she mouthed. Kaminsky nodded. The other woman was frightened, she could see, but had herself in hand. Charlie's gaze was drawn to Michael, who was cursing a blue streak as he tried, and failed, to grab hold of the padlock.

Another of the girls stirred.

The sense that the situation was getting ready to spiral out of control was strong.

Dread wrapped around Charlie like a pall. Putting a hand on the arm of the moving girl in hopes of keeping her down and calm if she should awaken, Charlie did the only thing she could think of to do: she talked.

"David, you're overlooking something." She kept her tone very even, very sure. "Special Agent Bartoli and Special Agent Crane *know your identity.* And they'll be looking for Special Agent Kaminsky and me. Every law enforcement agent in the state will be looking for us. If you harm us, every law enforcement agent in the country will be looking for you. You can't possibly get away."

David laughed. "Oh, Charlie. Do you think I didn't consider the possibility that this day might come? I have a second identity, a second life that I can go to. David Myers is going to disappear tonight." He laughed again. "Trust me, I've thought of everything. No one will find me."

"Bartoli and Crane already will have missed us." Charlie fought to keep her growing desperation out of her voice. "They probably have every police officer in the area looking for us right now. They'll put up roadblocks. They'll send up helicopters. They'll watch the airports. They *are* going to catch you. Your only chance is to let me help you."

"Your FBI special agents aren't doing anything right now." David sounded almost gleeful. "I heard your friend back there screaming about them being in an explosion into her phone right before I zapped her. That explosion was my house going up. I disconnected the hose from the gas stove, and as I was leaving, gas was already filling the house. All it took was a spark to set it off. I knew it would happen soon, although I have to say I didn't expect it to happen *that* soon. I was thinking pilot light from the water heater, but I doubt it was that." He paused a second. "I'm guessing your special agents set it off. Yes, I bet that's what happened. In that case, they're most likely already dead. So I don't have to worry about them."

The garage door opener. Horror widened Charlie's eyes. An indrawn breath from Kaminsky told Charlie she was thinking the same thing.

Please let Tony and Buzz still be alive.

"If that's the case, I really did clean up after myself." David sounded highly pleased.

"Oh." One of the girls was definitely waking up. It was the brunette: she rolled free of the others and, before either Charlie or Kaminsky could do anything to prevent her, sat up. She was plump, with a snub nose.

"Oh," she said again, looking around. Then she began to scream like her fingernails were being pulled out.

The hair stood up on the back of Charlie's neck.

"Holy shit, shut her up," Michael barked. "He's got another can of gas back here."

"No, it's all right," Charlie cried to the girl at the same time as, moving almost simultaneously and with Charlie resolutely ignoring the shooting pain in her head, she and Kaminsky scrambled to crouch beside her.

"Hush, hush, you're all right," Charlie babbled at the girl, grabbing one arm, while Kaminsky grabbed the other, shook it, and snapped, "Shut up, you little idiot."

When the girl didn't, Kaminsky hauled off and slapped her across the face.

Charlie felt as shocked as the girl looked, but at least the screaming stopped. Eyes wide and tear-filled, her breath coming in gasping sobs, the girl stared at Kaminsky. Charlie slid an arm around her, and the girl collapsed against her shoulder and, more quietly this time, wept.

Across her shaking shoulders, Charlie and Kaminsky exchanged speaking looks.

"That didn't suit me, that didn't suit me at all," David said. "I think I'm going to have to give you ladies another little dose of gas." Charlie could feel him looking at her, and she glanced up to meet his eyes in the mirror. "It'll make things easier for you," he told her comfortingly. "I won't wake you up."

Charlie's blood ran cold. Then, when he reached behind him to slide the plastic door closed, her heart shot into her throat.

"What's he doing?" The girl jerked upright in Charlie's arms. Her voice shook with fear. Her head swiveled so that she was looking at Charlie. "I want to go home! I want my mom!"

"*Shut up,*" Kaminsky and Michael roared at the same time, and when the girl did, burying her face in Charlie's shoulder and shaking silently in her arms, Charlie could hear the soft, sibilant hiss of gas.

"It's coming through the vents." Michael was making valiant attempts to close them, but Charlie could see his hands passing right through the black plastic slots. She could feel his frustration, his terror for her. Realizing that he was helpless to help her, helpless to save her, Charlie felt cold sweat wash over her in a wave. "Babe, you've got to get out of that cage. It's weakest in the corners. You and Sugar Buns are going to have to try to kick your way through. Try the one on the back left, near the door."

An instant vision of her kitten-heeled sandals and Kaminsky's towering pumps flashed through Charlie's mind, along with the conclusion, *At least it's better than bare feet.* Charlie looked at Kaminsky. "We've got to try to kick through one of the corners of the cage." She pointed at the one Michael had indicated. "That one there."

Kaminsky scrambled toward it. Charlie said, "It's going to be okay" to the girl, released her—she crumpled into a sobbing ball— and scrambled after Kaminsky. The other woman was already slamming her foot in its high stiletto heel against the wire when Charlie reached her.

"We need to do it together," Charlie cried, and Kaminsky nodded. "One, two, *three.*"

They were just slamming their feet against the wire strut in unison when, so loud it made them jump, they heard the wail of a police siren. Revolving red lights flashed through the van.

"Thank God," Kaminsky breathed, and she and Charlie stopped kicking the cage and looked at each other.

"Thank God," Charlie echoed. She was already starting to feel a little dizzy from the gas.

"Did I ever say I don't believe in miracles? I take it back. Two cop cars are right behind us." Michael, jubilant, came to crouch in front of them. "It's going to be okay, babe."

With a screech of tires, the van sped up as if it had been shot from a gun. Charlie was thrown back onto her butt. Kaminsky was spared the same fate only because she grabbed hold of the wire grid. The van rocketed down the road; Charlie could hear the spray of gravel hitting the sides.

"He's making a run for it," Michael groaned as the wail of the sirens seemed to fall behind. He rushed toward the cab, for what purpose Charlie didn't know. The gas was starting to make itself felt: everything Charlie could see was starting to spin. Kaminsky coughed; the girl whimpered, a high, keening sound that grated on Charlie's nerves.

"It's a bridge." Michael was back, roaring. "He's driving us off a fucking bridge into the lake! *Hold on!*"

Even as he said it, there was a tremendous jolt, and the van seemed to jump forward.

For a moment, Charlie got the terrifying impression that they were suspended in space. Then the front of the van tilted down, and with a tremendous splash and enough force to send all of them flying, it plunged into the lake.

CHAPTER TWENTY-FIVE

Charlie tumbled head over heels, crashing into bodies, bouncing off the sides of the cage, which had broken loose from its moorings and was tumbling around, too. When the violent motion stopped, water was already pouring inside the van. It was gushing in through the cab, and from the angle she realized they were going into the water front end first. Unsecured now, the cage lay snugly against the plastic doors that divided the driver's compartment from the cargo area. A glimpse of night sky at the rear told her that one of the cargo doors had flown open on impact. The strip of starry sky she could see provided the only illumination.

What had become of David she had no idea. She, Kaminsky, and the girls were tangled together in a barely moving heap on what was now the bottom of the cage.

We're still locked in the cage.

As Charlie realized that, panic sent a rush of adrenaline shooting through her veins.

Cop cars had been close behind them. Rescue had to be on its way.

Charlie felt cold water gushing over her ankles, and knew they dare not wait.

"Get up! You got to get out! *Now!*" Michael bent over them, yelling, and Charlie, dazed and hurting as she was, still knew he was right. Water was already rising around her, rising around all of them as it filled the cargo area from front to back. It was cold, fishy-smelling, and shiny black as oil.

Dark water. Her heart lurched.

Even as Charlie had the thought, she was scrambling upright, grabbing at the wire grid. She couldn't see much, only the pale shapes that were Kaminsky and the girls. Pain stabbed her behind her eyes; her head swam. She ignored all of it. The van was sinking into the water; if they didn't get out, they would die.

"Help! Help!" One of the girls shrieked as she struggled to her feet. "Somebody, help us!"

"What's happening?" another cried. "Diane, where are you?"

Two of them were on their feet now, screaming and clutching each other as they tried to keep their balance in the rising water. As water edged up around her knees, Charlie ignored them, frantically rattling the grid, seeking an area of weakness. There just wasn't any give—

"Charlie, do you see any way out?" The cry came from Kaminsky, who was sloshing around to her left. Charlie saw that she was hauling the third girl's head clear of the water, and thrusting her into the arms of one of her friends with the admonition, *"Hang on to her."*

"Babe, there's a hole in the wire where the bottom of the cage was fastened to the floor of the van. Right here."

With the water swirling around her thighs now, Charlie followed Michael to the hole. It was small, with jagged edges, but she thought they could fit through it.

"Here," she called to Kaminsky, holding on to the grid as the van tilted forward a little more and water rose almost to her waist. "Give me one of the girls."

An instant later, a small cold hand clutched hers.

"This is Kim," Kaminsky said. "Get her out of here."

"Oh, my God! Oh, my God!" Kim—she was one of the blondes—gasped over and over again as Charlie helped her wiggle through the hole.

"Go out the door back there and swim," Charlie ordered when Kim was free. She watched the girl scramble on all fours up the slippery floor toward the open cargo door, and realized that the van was tilting more.

"Come on, Diane," Kim cried, stopping to look back as she teetered at the edge of the open door.

"Jump!" Charlie yelled at her. With one last look over her shoulder at the girl Kaminsky was thrusting toward Charlie, Kim did. The sound of the splash told Charlie that the rear of the van was still a good distance above the water.

The problem was, it was sinking fast.

"Hurry," Michael said urgently.

"*Hurry,*" Charlie repeated to Kaminsky as she thrust the second girl—the brunette, who had regained consciousness first—through the hole.

"I'm not a very good swimmer," the girl—Diane?—cried, looking back.

"Go! We'll be up there to help you soon," Kaminsky yelled. She was struggling with the third girl, a delicately built blonde, who, although her eyes were open and she seemed responsive, was still clearly under the influence of the gas.

"You go through and I'll hand her up to you," Charlie said, ignoring her pounding heart in favor of holding on to the girl as the water swirled ever higher around them. The angle of the van was increasingly precarious, and keeping her footing was growing ever more difficult.

Nodding, Kaminsky pulled herself through the hole, then reached down for the girl.

"Hold your hands up," Charlie ordered, then when the girl looked at her blankly she snapped, "Natalie! You're Natalie, right?" The girl nodded. *"Hold up your hands!"*

Natalie did. Kaminsky grabbed them—"I've got her!"—and despite the girl's apparent inability to help much, with Charlie pushing from beneath they managed to get her through.

"Take her on out." Charlie was already working her way through the hole. "I can manage."

Kaminsky nodded and started half-helping, half-pushing Natalie toward the door, where Diane, poised in the opening like a swimmer on the block, hesitated, looking back at them.

"Jump!" Kaminsky yelled at her.

Diane did. Seconds later, Kaminsky and Natalie reached the door.

"I'm out," Charlie called to Kaminsky as, having made it through the hole, she knelt on top of the cage preparatory to standing up. "Go!"

With a glance back to make sure Charlie really was through, Kaminsky locked a hand in the back of Natalie's shirt and they both disappeared. A splash an instant later told Charlie they were in the lake.

"Goddamn it, babe, move your ass," Michael snarled at her.

With a terrifying slurping sound, water reached the top of the cage as Charlie scrambled to her feet. Her heart thudded when the van tilted, and she almost lost her balance.

"Go," Michael roared, and Charlie pushed off from the top of the cage, meaning to follow the others to the door and jump into the lake.

But something cold and hard latched on to her ankle, snatched her back. A hand! David! Circumstances—like, say, a short in the electrical system caused by the water which prevented him from operating the doors or windows—must have left him with no choice but to exit the cab through the plastic doors, and force his way into the cage, which he had to pass through to reach the open cargo door. Charlie looked down to see the pale circle of his face glaring up at her through the water as he pushed his way through the hole after her, and her heart gave a great leap.

"Let go!" she cried, kicking at his imprisoning hand. The water rose around her ankles even as David's head burst through the hole. He only had one arm through. His shoulders, she saw, were too big to fit. "Michael, help!"

David's head cleared the surface of the water, and Michael saw what was happening. "Fuck!"

Even as Charlie fought to yank her ankle free, Michael was at her side, throwing punches, stomping at David's head, but David never felt a thing. Realizing that Michael really, truly couldn't materialize, Charlie felt her stomach drop clear to her toes. Her heart pounded. Her pulse raced.

"Help me get out of here," David groaned. His eyes were wild as they fixed on her, and Charlie fought the urge to scream. She was afraid that if she did, it would incite him, push him into the kind of frenzy that serial killers were typically capable of. Already he was horrifying to look at: his expression made his face a grotesque parody of his usual good looks. His hair was plastered to his skull. Water streamed down his face, running dark on one side, and Charlie realized that his head was bleeding: he must have been injured in the crash. But his hand gripping her ankle felt stronger than it had any right to be, and she remembered that serial killers, when in the zone, often had far greater than normal strength.

"Let me go and I'll help you!" she promised, tamping down on the hysteria that bubbled into her throat, fighting to stay calm in the face of burgeoning terror, but he laughed. The van swayed, and as he struggled to force himself through the hole the water rose to lap at his chin.

"You better get me out of here! If I go down, you're going with me," he threatened her, and she could tell he meant every word. His fingers dug into her flesh, hurting her. Water inched up her calves, the van rocked, and panic surged in an icy tide through her veins. Talking him into letting her go might work, given enough time. But time was what she didn't have. If she didn't get free, soon, she was going to drown. To hell with inciting him into a frenzy: she screamed—please God, let Kaminsky hear and come to her aid—and kicked at his face.

Yanking her ankle hard, he knocked her off her feet. Charlie landed on her back with a splash. Surprise widened her eyes, made her suck in air. The water slurped around her. The van swayed.

"No!" Charlie screamed as David started pulling her toward him, and she realized that he meant to drag her back down through the hole. Holding on to the grid for dear life, kicking and struggling with every ounce of strength she possessed, she fought to get free even as he inexorably dragged her closer, inch by desperate inch.

"Babe! Behind you!" Michael yelled. Charlie glanced frantically around to see moonlight glinting on a metal canister the size of an oxygen tank that had floated—with Michael's help?—within her reach. "Grab it and bash him in the head! Now! Quick!"

To do it she had to let go of the grid. She did, snatching the canister up with both hands. It was heavy, solid.

"Got you!" David screeched, jerking her toward him. The lubrication of the water beneath her caused her slide to be terrifyingly fast.

"Hit him!" Michael yelled.

Screaming, Charlie smashed the canister into David's head with all her might. The thud was sickening. The look in his eyes was worse. They went wide and black. His fingers slackened on her ankle. Shaky with terror, she jerked her leg free, and scrambled out of his reach.

The van slid another few inches into the water.

David just had time to gasp out, "Charlie!" before the water covered his mouth, and then his nose—

"Get the hell out of here!" Michael screamed.

Blocking the horrible sounds of David's frenzied flailing from her mind, Charlie pushed off from the top of the cage and scrambled toward the strip of night sky she could see through the open cargo door.

Even as she struggled to climb the now nearly vertical floor, the water gave a great gurgle. Her heart jackhammered. She clawed frantically for the door as the van sank, taking her with it as it plunged with terrifying speed toward the depths of the lake. Quick as a blink, the water closed over her, swallowing her, rushing up her nose, blinding her.

Holding her breath, she tried frantically to swim up through the sudden fierce suction that pulled at her from below.

Lungs burning, heart pounding, pulse racing, she fought valiantly as she was dragged down and down and down into the dark, swirling water. Soon her lungs felt as if they would explode and she opened her mouth to suck in air because she couldn't resist the urgent need any longer, only there was no air anywhere and what she sucked in was water.

Lost in blackness, dizzy and weak, struggling until she couldn't any longer, Charlie saw beautiful shimmery stars pinwheeling through the darkness in front of her eyes and felt the cold water rushing past her turn warm and comforting, like a lover's arms.

She could hear Michael screaming, "No, no, no," in her ears as she died.

CHAPTER TWENTY-SIX

Seen from the green, grassy shore, the lake at night was beautiful. Its smooth dark surface rippled in the moonlight, reflecting the icy white sickle of the moon itself, and the glitter of thousands of stars. The breeze blowing in off the water was warm and smelled of flowers.

Charlie felt happy. She felt at peace.

Even so, there was a tremendous amount of commotion around her. The red flashing lights of police cars ringed an area not far away. She could hear voices, cries, weeping. She looked closer. Although she was not physically near, she recognized the three young girls huddled together, the woman and two men kneeling around a second woman lying supine in the grass.

She even remembered their names: the girls were Natalie and Diane and Kim; the kneeling woman was Lena, and the men were Tony and Buzz.

The supine woman in the soaked yellow dress, with the heavy man's watch glinting silver on her slender, motionless wrist, pulled at her. Charlie felt a drift of gentle sadness as she realized: that woman, drenched and drowned, lying unmoving and pale in the moonlight, was her.

Dr. Charlotte Stone.

She drew closer.

"I thought she was right behind me." Lena sounded as if the words were being ripped out of her throat. She was wet and shivering despite the warmth of the night. Moonlight gleamed on what looked like a tear sliding down her cheek.

Buzz slid an arm around Lena. His clothes were dirty, ripped. A grayish powder—ash, she remembered there had been an explosion—dusted his hair. "It's not your fault. We should have come back faster. By the time we got to the Inn, saw your laptops still on the table, and figured out what had happened, Myers was long gone."

"If one of the waitresses hadn't remembered seeing a gray van tearing out of the parking lot and been able to tell us which way it went, we never would have found you." Tony's voice was hoarse. His white shirt was torn and smeared with grime, and he had a cut on his cheek. Like Buzz, his black hair was full of ash. His face was white with shock, twisted with grief. "I can't believe we got to you too late. *Charlie*. Dear God in heaven, how could I have let this happen?"

The raw pain in his voice made Charlie want to reassure him. But Buzz and Lena already were, and then more people joined them, police officers and others, official types. She heard one of them say, "We've got divers down there trying to extract Myers' body. It's still trapped in the van," and then because she didn't want to hear anything more about that, she moved away.

"Charlie!" From out of the shadows Michael appeared, tawny hair washed silver by the moonlight, tall body powerful as ever, handsome face solemn and unsmiling as he walked across the grass toward her.

She knew him instantly, as she knew she would always know him in any realm, in any universe, in any dimension, in any time.

"Michael," she said, and smiled at him as the slight uneasiness Tony's pain had caused her gave way to pure joy.

He opened his arms to her. She walked into them. They closed around her, hugging her close. She could feel every hard, muscular inch of him. She lifted her face to him, and he kissed her, his lips hot and slow. Sliding her arms around his neck, she kissed him back.

She could feel every thrilling nuance of that kiss.

She never wanted it to end.

They were on the same side of the barrier now, and he was hers, just like she was his. Nothing to separate them any longer.

Ghosts couldn't stay. But what she hadn't realized was, she could go. With him.

"I'm dead?" It was both a question and a statement, asked when he stopped kissing her at last.

"Charlie." His honeyed voice was husky, low. She was in his arms still, with her cheek resting against his wide chest, knowing there was no place else in heaven or hell where she would rather be. When he hesitated, when he said nothing more beyond her name, she tilted her face up so that she could see his eyes. They gleamed down at her, their usual sky blue veiled by moonlight.

A faint tinkling of chimes blew in on the breeze. Charlie turned her head to listen.

Not too far away, in a clearing in the middle of a copse of tall trees, a sprinkle of falling moonbeams turned into a column of solid light.

Her mouth fell open as she looked at it. The light was beautiful, celestial, divine.

She knew what it was. The gateway. The passage.

The light mesmerized her. Drew her. It was everything she could do to tear her eyes away to look up at him, to draw his attention to it. All of a sudden it occurred to her that maybe she could take him with her into it, that maybe its power would hold his weight as well as her own, that maybe there could be an eternity for them together, after all.

"Michael." Pulling out of his arms, she caught his hand instead, tugging him with her toward it. "There's the light. Come with me into the light."

"Charlie." He resisted. He was too big, she couldn't budge him against his will. "No."

"You see it, don't you?" she asked in sudden consternation, because she remembered then that he'd never been able to see it before.

"I see it."

"You can walk into it with me. It's strong enough for both of us. I can feel it. I'm"—*almost*—"sure it will take us both."

"Maybe." His tone was grim. "Whether it will or not, babe, you don't want to go."

Charlie frowned at him. "What? Yes, I do."

He shook his head. "No, you don't. Being dead sucks. You want to stay here. You want your life."

She answered almost piteously: "No."

"Yes." He was inexorable. "They're over there giving you CPR again. You can still go back."

"No." But then she thought of her house, and her work, and her mother, who would grieve. So, it seemed, would Tony, and Buzz and Lena, too. And—others. Her colleagues. Her friends. Then there was Michael. What if he couldn't walk into the light with her? What if he was torn away from her, and she never saw him again?

Until that moment, she hadn't really noticed that the breeze had turned into a gentle suction, wafting her toward that poor drowned body in the grass.

She looked up at him, undecided, and he pulled her into his arms and kissed her. Kissed her as if he was promising her forever, as if he had found eternity in her arms. Clinging, she kissed him back, and was still kissing him when—*swoosh*—he was no longer there.

A moment later, she was lying in the grass coughing and sputtering and spewing out lake water like a fountain.

———————

Michael stood where she had left him.

The feel of her was still in his arms. The taste of her was still on his lips. She was back in her body. He could see her moving over there in the grass. She would be fine, he knew. She would live, and have her life.

He wished with every glimmer of his being that he could say the same.

The light was still there. The white light that she'd been talking about for so long. It had come for her. Not for him.

But he could feel it pulling at him. He walked toward it, curious. It waited for him, beautiful and shimmering. He could feel the hope of it, the promise of it. Looking at it, he was tempted. Just to try.

For a long moment he stood there, resisting the pull, deep in thought. Then he turned his back on the light and walked away.

There was a woman he wasn't yet ready to leave.

ABOUT THE AUTHOR

KAREN ROBARDS is the *New York Times* and *USA Today* bestselling author of over forty books and one novella. The mother of three boys, she lives in her hometown of Louisville, Kentucky.

In the best books, the ending often comes as a shock.
Not just because of that one last twist in the tale,
but because you have been so absorbed in their world,
that coming back to the harsh light of reality is a jolt.

If that describes you now, then perhaps you should track down
some new leads, and find new suspense in other worlds.

Join us at www.hodder.co.uk, or follow us on
Twitter @hodderbooks, and you can tap in to a
community of fellow thrill-seekers.

Whether you want to find out more about this book,
or a particular author, watch trailers and interviews, have
the chance to win early limited editions, or simply browse
our expert readers' selection of the very best books,
we think you'll find what you're looking for.

And if you don't, that's the place to tell us what's missing.

We love what we do, and we'd love you to be part of it.

www.hodder.co.uk

 @hodderbooks

HodderBooks

 HodderBooks